The Lincoln Secret

John A. McKinsey

Martin Pearl Publishing
http//:www.martinpearl.com

Published by
Martin Pearl Publishing
P.O. Box 1441 Dixon, CA 95620

First Edition: November 2008

ISBN: 9780981482200
Library of Congress Control Number: 2008906211

PRINTED IN THE UNITED STATES OF AMERICA

10 9 8 7 6 5 4 3 2 1

Acknowledgements

This book is dedicated to my lovely wife, Angie. Were it not for her commitment, sacrifice and belief in me, this book would never have made it into print. Her drive is amazing.

I also wish to acknowledge and thank my editors and readers, Corie Barloggi, Bill West, Gena Gallegos, Stephen Zinatto, Lisa Case, Jean Schettler, Sue Harrison, Erin Case, Kelly Thistle, and James Christensen. Your efforts, criticism and ideas helped me shape this story and present a clean, crisp manuscript. Thank You!

Prologue

June, 2003
Los Angeles, California.

William McGee heard nothing. He was so terrified, so shocked, so confused that his mind was on overload. The man was speaking in front of him, but his ears registered nothing.

It's the gun that must be doing it, he thought. *I can't think of any-thing but that gun. It's big and very deadly looking.* William never had been so close to a handgun, and he now understood how easily just seeing one pointed at you could create terror that paralyzed.

Watching the intruder's finger shift ever so slightly on the trigger, William trembled. With each tiny movement, each twitch, William felt a new surge of terror. *He could so easily put just a little too much pressure on it and the gun would explode in my face.* And that was exactly where the gun was aimed, right at William's face. *I'd be dead.*

The gunner had an amazingly pleasing demeanor, passive and calm despite the violent intentions the rest of his body conveyed. His deep brown eyes were centered on a heavy pug-nosed face shadowed with some black beard stubble. *He needs to shave,* William uselessly thought. The man's brown hair was cropped short, like an IBM salesperson, and his clothes were pressed and neat. He appeared very strong and potent, which gave his calm look a dangerous and explosive edge.

As William stared at the intruder, he wondered if this was the end. Shot for no clear reason. He tried to shake the fear. *Get a grip Bill, get a grip! This guy doesn't have to kill you. Be smart! Pay attention and do what he says.* William tried to focus on the words the man was repeating, and finally the sound made it through to his brain.

"Mr. McGee, can you hear me? Can you hear me?" The man spoke as simply and passively as he acted. His tone was not one of concern or interest. His inquiry was presented like a detached, professional obligation.

William glanced past the intruder to a clock located on the wall above a small book shelf. *What kind of lunatic breaks into a house at nine in the morning? Thank God Phyllis is gone and won't be back for a couple of hours.* But then, yet another rush of panic set in as Phyllis' face flashed before his eyes. *What if he waits for her to come home? I've got to do something!* Desperately, he searched for the courage to speak.

"Wha, wha, what do you want?" he stammered.

The man smiled, as if he knew that William would do whatever was required of him. "That's better, Mr. McGee. Now take a deep breath and calm yourself down. I need to ask you some questions."

"Are you going to kill me? Don't kill me!" William did not want to add the plea, but it flew out of his mouth uncontrollably.

"No, Mr. McGee, I'm not going to kill you…if you cooperate. You understand that, right?" The man was nodding his head and William found himself furiously nodding back in unison. He knew, though, that he was fooling himself. He was in horrible danger.

"Good, then let's talk about your genealogy research. What is your interest in Abraham Enloe?"

William's eyes bulged out with a sense of bewilderment. *Why does he care about my research on the Enloes?* Before he could answer his own question, a sudden searing pain erupted on his face, and he felt his head being snapped violently back to one side. He flew from his chair, slamming hard into the floor. The man had struck him with the gun.

"Mr. McGee, when I ask you a question, don't pause or think. Answer quickly and completely. No hesitation."

William pushed his hands under his shoulders and struggled getting up. He was weak, but managed to rise up, clutching the desk and pulling himself into the chair. He touched the side of his face feeling warm blood oozing between his fingers.

"I don't understand," William said meekly. "Why do you care about…"

"It does not matter why, Mr. McGee," the man interrupted. "Only that you answer my questions. ANSWER MY QUESTION!"

The man barked his final order and William did not need to be told again. "Abraham Enloe was an ancestor on my mother's side. I was researching him for my family tree."

"What do you know about him?" the man rifled back.

"I know he was born in South Carolina, that he moved to North Carolina, where he lived and died." As William spoke, he looked down, afraid to make eye contact. Deep inside, he worried that the man would kill him regardless of what answers he gave. That was something William did not want to consider. So, it was easier to speak if he looked down.

"He was a tobacco farmer near the Great Smokey Mountains. I think he had three brothers."

Before William could continue, the intruder interrupted him once again. "Why are you interested in his connection to Abraham Lincoln?"

William, still feeling the throbbing pain and the blood trickling on the side of his face, answered quickly this time, despite the further bewilderment he felt at the man's questions. "Mr. Enloe is said to be Abraham Lincoln's real father."

William paused and forced himself to glance at the man, just to make sure he was actually interested in what William had to say. The man was watching him closely, so William looked down and quickly continued explaining.

"I found a story about that and wanted to learn more about it. It was fascinating to think that I might be related to Abraham Lincoln, but I have not found much more. It's like the story was forgotten." With that, William looked up again at the man, looking into his eyes to see if the man was going to kill him or not. The man smiled back at him, which felt more chilling than when he was looking angry.

"Very good, Mr. McGee. Now show me your files about this Abraham Enloe."

"They're here in my genealogy file and in my computer." William pointed at a box of files on a table against the wall and at the computer behind him.

The stranger gestured with his gun towards the computer. "Show me," he said.

William swiveled, grabbing his computer mouse with his trembling hand. He began showing the man his computer files, clinging to the hope that he would live through the day.

.....

About an hour later, a man exited the McGee house through the front door carrying a briefcase. He was dressed in gray slacks and a blue sport coat. Quickly walking to the sidewalk of the suburban neighborhood, he turned right, and continued down the street. Phyllis would come home several hours later, alerting her neighbors with her screams. Sirens soon wailed. Her neighbors, however, would not recall seeing or hearing anything out of the ordinary and William's death would ultimately be considered another interrupted robbery that Los Angeles suffered far too many.

Part One

Secrets

Chapter One

Friday, April 17, 2004
Kansas City

The words stunned her, seemingly jumping from the page she held, hitting her in the face:

Our real family name is Thomas, not Poole.

Feeling confused and angry, Kim read it again. *Getting mad at my dead father should be difficult,* she thought. *Especially when he doted on me most of my life. But here's a letter from him, essentially from the grave, that he must have known would horribly upset me. Thomas, not Poole? How can that be? Why did he wait to tell me this way?*

Kimberly Poole was sitting at the kitchen table in the early morning. She was alone in her house, her daughter, Abigail, having left for school early. The night before, Kim had started to go through a box of notes and documents that her father had left for her. This morning, she was continuing to go through them before she had to leave to open her store. Her father's death from cancer was more than four months ago and it had taken her this long to finally start attacking the leftover pieces of his life.

She had just found an envelope in the box with her name inscribed on it in large red letters 'Kimberly Jacob Poole.' She opened it to find a letter from her father and a very old handwritten note.

Now, stunned, she sat there holding the letter in disbelief. It was short and simple, very much to the point, like her father always had been. She read it again, trying to make some sense of what her father was telling her.

> *My Daughter,*
>
> *If you are reading this it can only mean one thing: I have left you. I apologize for what I must now tell you and I only hope you will understand my reasons for what I did.*
>
> *Our real family name is Thomas, not Poole. It is a secret that I have carried with me since my father's death and he since his father's death. It began with your great, great grandfather Jacob. He too told his son our true family name on his deathbed. He also warned him to do nothing with that information because it was too dangerous. He was serious about that. He handed his son, your great grandfather Abraham, this very note that I have enclosed. This note has been handed down from generation to generation. It says to take action when the Enloes come forth. Read it carefully.*
>
> *I have long thought, certainly by now, that enough time had passed. I never told anyone though, and so now I leave this information in your hands. Please be careful. Jacob must have had very good reasons for his actions and his caution.*
>
> *It pained me to watch you passionately pursuing our family history, knowing that, as far as the Pooles went, you were very much off course. But I could never bring myself to tell you or do something with our family secret. Please know that having and raising you always has been my proudest achievement. I rest knowing our secret is in the best hands it could be.*
>
> *Love always,*
> *Dad*

A very yellowed, creased piece of paper, the edges of it thin and tattered from being stored and handled over the generations, was sitting on the table next to Kim's shaking and clammy hands. It read:

> *Wait until the Enloes come forth and then tell our secret of President Lincoln and the War. Look then, and only then, at my*

words and discover their other meaning. You will know then what to do. Be careful.

The handwriting in the note was broad and flourishing, much grander than the kind of handwriting Kim was used to reading. It was clearly the note penned by her great, great grandfather Jacob. But the message confused her. *What secret?* she thought. *And what words?*

Thomas, not Poole. Kim was having the hardest time accepting this simple concept. After ten years of researching her family genealogy, she finally had found out why she was completely unable to get past Jacob Poole on her fathers' side. *He didn't exist! I was researching the wrong person. I should have searched for Jacob Thomas, not Jacob Poole.* This revelation gave her no comfort.

Her mind now racing, she continued trying to comprehend the letter. *President Lincoln and the War? What's that all about? A secret so dangerous that he changed his name? What secret?*

Kim read her father's letter and the enclosed note again. *The Enloes. Who were they? What did they have to do with us?* Many questions were surfacing in her thoughts, too numerous to process at once. She glanced up at the kitchen clock on the wall. It was already 9:45, and she had to open the shop today. She folded the letter along with the fragile, aged note and carefully put them back in their envelope. She put the envelope in a fairly rigid file in her canvas bag, mindful of the fragility of the note.

Kim stood up from the round wooden kitchen table, feeling unready to go to work, but knowing she had too. She shoved her lunch into her canvas bag, and reluctantly walked out the door into the garage. She backed her SUV out the garage door a little too far to the left, but somehow managed to make it onto the street without incident.

Kim lived in the south end of Kansas City, in Lenexa, Kansas. She owned a garden and kitchen shop, "Garden World," at the Country Club Plaza in Kansas City. The district was thriving and a great place for owning nearly any business. Her shop was one of four businesses in a remodeled older building that fronted Broadway, the heart of the shopping and dining area.

Her drive to work was usually pretty painless and today was no exception. She arrived a little after 10:30. After parking the SUV in its usual spot in the garage beneath her building, she headed up the stairs to the shop level, reached the store, quickly unlocked its doors, slipped in, and then locked them behind her. Shortly, the register was set up, the doors unlocked and the OPEN sign put in place. Another business day had begun.

However, her heart and her head were not in it. Normally, her slim frame and brown wavy hair were animated and constantly moving. Kim had always had a passionate energy in everything she did. She was in a fog that first hour, though, as she answered the phone, helped customers, and made sales. Her father's letter, and the questions aroused with it, continued to race around in her head.

At noon, her afternoon employee, Bridget Caloway, entered through the front door of the store. Bridget was in her mid-sixties, a retired office secretary who worked in Kim's shop mostly for the fun of it. Bridget was in her second year at the shop and had become an incredibly reliable employee. She immediately sensed Kim's distracted condition and quickly began taking over the routine shop tasks. Later, the store traffic thinned, and only a couple of "just looking" shoppers remained. It was then that Bridget urged Kim to take a break.

"You've got something on your mind. Why don't you let me handle things up here?" Bridget suggested.

Bridget's horn rimmed glasses, combined with her white hair, gave her a very grandmotherly appearance. She was about the same height and build as Kim, and many customers often thought she was Kim's mother. She also was assertive enough to make customers think it was her shop, not Kim's. As far as Kim was concerned, those were all star qualities.

Kim accepted her employee's offer. "I think I will. Call me if you get too busy." Kim quickly surrendered the front of her shop and retreated to a small office in the back, part of the stockroom. At first she worked on paperwork, but her father's letter stuck in her mind, calling to her. Reluctantly, Kim let herself return to her father's envelope and its contents. She opened her lunch, a steak salad made up from leftovers of last night's dinner, and then pulled out the envelope. She opened it and read the letter and note again.

Enloe? Thomas? Those two names were at the core of the questions circulating in her mind, so Kim decided to do some web-based genealogy research on them. Settling in at her keyboard, she logged into her genealogy service and started searching those names. Thomas, was, as she had suspected, a very common name. She found many people named Jacob Thomas. Enloe was not so common; there were only a few entries. Her ancestor's note mentioned no given name, only the surname "Enloe." Searching for answers to questions she didn't really understand was frustrating. Based on the cryptic note, she felt like she needed to search for an Enloe who not only knew Lincoln, but was also related to Jacob Thomas. The mystery was too confusing and too shocking to fathom.

Kim glanced up at the clock and was startled that it already was past three. Bridget had not bothered her at all for a good two hours. She decided to finish her efforts by posting inquiries at a couple of websites. She had learned from experience that others using the online genealogy sites would leave electronic requests to be informed any time someone else inquired about the same names they were interested in. The end result would be that she could quickly learn from others the information she needed to know and, at the same time, get a better feel for the intricacies of the family names she was researching. On a couple of Thomas boards, she posted requests for information about any Jacob Thomas that would have come to Denver after the Civil War. She left a request on an Enloe website for information about Enloes that would have existed at the time of or after the Civil War. After considering the warnings from her great, great grandfather Jacob, she decided, in what she felt was sure to be wasted caution, not to add the name of Abraham Lincoln to the mix yet. Though she did hold back from including Lincoln, she found it almost silly, thinking, *"What could Abraham Lincoln have to do with my family?"*

Having finished her online posts, she arose and headed back up front. Although she had learned nothing, she did feel that a good start had been made at making sense of the bizarre letter she had found early that morning. Now, waiting for replies online, she would be able to focus on the store tasks. Her head felt cleared, as if she would be able to handle what she was sure would be a busy weekend in the store.

Monday, April 20, 2004
Seattle, Washington

Sean knew Jesus was in trouble. His cry was sharp, short and pained. They were pinned down against the dirt, all of them, by several shooters above them and across from the creek. Because they were on an uphill slope with their assailants above them, it was virtually impossible to move without exposing themselves to gunfire. Worse, they were on their own, as they had been since this mission had begun. There was no support to call in for help. Jesus was right in front of him, but he might as well have been 50 yards away. It did not matter. Sean had a boulder and a tree for cover. Jesus had a rocky ledge, barely high enough to cover his prone body. Sean couldn't move without attracting fire. *Shit. It's not supposed to be this way*, Sean fumed to himself. *Clearly someone knew we were coming. But how is that possible? Hardly anyone even knows we're in this damned country.* They had been traversing a creek, working their way upslope to observe a site in a valley over the top of the ridge. Then, suddenly, shots had come out of the dark above them. They had scrambled, and Jesus, their point man, had been hit in his stomach by at least one bullet.

"I need cover now! I'm bleeding man. I'm hit!" Jesus gasped this time, sounding even more panicked.

"Johnson, can you provide cover?" Will's voice hissed from somewhere behind and below Sean's left shoulder. Sean, the next highest up the slope, was the nearest person to Jesus.

"Negative," Sean answered quietly.

As if their words had helped their assailants locate them, several muzzle flashes signaled another barrage of fire. Sean heard a burst of shots around him—or felt them—he was not sure he could tell the difference anymore. Automatic weapons splayed bullets rapidly at them, too many to count. The lead slugs not only hit the earth near him, but also skipped off the rock he was behind as they whistled and whined in the hot night air above him. He cowered down lower than he thought possible, the pine needles prickling his cheek next to his night vision goggle strap.

And then it was quiet. He could smell the forest floor. The normally pleasant aroma went unappreciated as Sean's mind raced though his options. *I have to get up. I have to give cover fire or Jesus will bleed to death just six feet from me. Shit, shit, shit!* He expected his hands to squeeze his rifle in response to the activity surrounding him, but they were numb. Once he popped up from his hiding place, he knew, the men behind him would act also. But he lay frozen, his mind fixated on an imaginary bullet on the other side of the creek with his name on it. If he exposed himself, the bullet would emerge from a barrel in the dark and head straight for him, looming large as it hit his face. His numbness spread like a television fading to blackness, and he knew he was leaving Jesus to die. *No, I won't leave this time,* Sean pleaded with himself. *Not this time.*

Sean's eyes blinked open. Above him was darkness. He thrashed as he rolled to his side. The pine needles and dirt were gone. Sweaty sheets now took their place. As his hands felt the fabric, he moaned and let his body press back into the bed. *Back in your own home, Sean old boy. You're nowhere near that damned, cursed place.* He sighed, feeling a little relieved

"I hate that dream," Sean muttered into his pillow. He relaxed his hands, which had grabbed clumps of his sheets in tightly clenched fists. He tried to close his eyes, but knew it was too late. Reliving that night had brought back with it all the adrenalin, sweat, and pounding pulse that he had experienced. There would be no going back to sleep for a while. Slowly, he lifted his head to see the red numbers on the alarm clock. *Three o'clock in the morning.* Moaning, he tried for a few more moments to pretend he was going to fall back asleep, even though he knew it was a total waste of time. After less than a minute, he gave up and shoved his feet out of the sweaty sheets and down onto the cold wooden floor. Sitting there, he could still feel the tension in his body. The sweat-drenched sheet stuck to his naked back. He reached behind himself, pulling it away from him. Rubbing his eyes, he got up and headed to the bathroom clad only in his briefs.

In a few minutes he was downstairs in the kitchen, wearing a blue tee-shirt and gray flannel sweat pants. The coffee maker was soon gurgling away. Sean gazed out the window at the lights of the city below him. *Seattle always looks so peaceful this time of night.* His house was perched on a hill north of the downtown area with the Space Needle climbing up to his eye level right in front of him. Past it, a dark space marked the bay that was about 15 miles wide. On the other side of the bay, he could make out tiny, faint lights marking the homes and businesses of the Bremerton region. Not many lights at this time of night, though, he realized.

Sean was in great shape for a mid-thirties journalist. His short brown hair, matching brown eyes and tanned face topped his lean and muscled body. He was not the typical journalist, he knew. On the contrary, he had a deep passion for extreme exercise, physical challenges and adventure. That was the reason the Navy had attracted him. Being a Seal seemed to him the ultimate challenge. He faced that challenge, though, and conquered it. Now his adventure was mostly about finding obscure people and convincing them to tell their stories. To his surprise, he turned out to be good at this as well.

Just to hear a voice, he said aloud, "Not a lot of people are dumb enough to be up at this hour." After a pause, where nobody spoke to him, he declared, "I better make some good use of this time since it's so damn early."

Sean pulled the still gurgling coffee pot out of its receptor, filled his coffee mug and then slipped the container back under the spring-loaded mechanism. He pulled a Danish muffin from an already opened bag that was sitting on a bowl of fruit. He inspected it lightly. Satisfied it was still edible, he turned and headed down the hall and out of the kitchen, his socks padding quietly on the wood floor. His tall frame moved more gracefully than most people might have expected, given someone of his height. Sean's office and writing room was located upstairs in the corner of his two-story home. He quickly climbed the stairs and turned left down a short hallway into the corner room. A window looked out on the same view as the kitchen. Using the elbow of the arm that held his coffee mug, he flipped the light switch on, fully illuminating a room stuffed with book-filled shelves. Sean settled into a leather office chair at his computer desk, set the Danish down on the deep cherry-colored wood, and reached down to turn on the computer. Pushing the start button in, he could hear the computer's fan come whirling to life. Yawning, he leaned back in his chair, sipped the hot coffee and stared out the window at the city lights again.

His mind revisited his dream and he thought of Jesus. *That has to rank as the worst day of my life,* he remembered. *Probably not just for me either, but for most of my squad.* They really had come close to never returning, being "lost" as the Agency would no doubt have called it. But they returned, albeit with Jesus in a body bag. Jesus was "lost." For some reason, though, Jesus' memory somehow failed to realize its lost status and continued to visit Sean. *Hell, it's been more then ten years and here I am reliving that mission yet again.* He gritted his teeth, gave Jesus one last faithful thought, and then forced himself to turn away from the cityscape, away from the window, and toward the now illuminated computer screen. *Jesus and I will be together forever, I guess, at least in my dreams.* Smiling, he finished his thought: *Kind of like having my own personal ghost.*

The blinking cursor beckoned. Sean typed in his name "Sean Johnson" and his password "Padre2B," selected in honor of his father, who had left him this house six years ago. In fact, this house had belonged to his grandparents as well, thus Sean was a third generation Johnson roaming the house.

"I doubt my dad roamed this house at three in the morning though," Sean said aloud as his computer completed starting up. Sean felt a shiver creep through his bones and an eerie sense of foreboding came over him. The bad dream had probably planted the seed. Being all alone in the middle of the night in his office was eerie enough; except for the computer, the dead silence and the old age of his house only added to the feeling. Sean had no reason to be afraid of his ghosts, though. Now, as a writer instead of a soldier, he wrote about, rather than chased, paranormal things. Both careers were really very similar: they required he shed any fears of the unknown and simply attack the task at hand.

With a stretch of his lengthy arms and another drag on his now lukewarm coffee, he settled in and started his work. Checking his email, he saw that his article on homeless teenagers had come back from the editor. He opened the article and began going through the comments, accepting, rejecting, and occasionally making other changes. Fifteen minutes later he returned the completed article to the editor.

"Send that check quickly now," Sean said, talking to the computer. "We starving writers have to eat."

Having completed that task, Sean checked his email again, noticed nothing other than junk mail, and deleted the contents of his inbox. Then he pulled a yellow pad from a slim shelf to the right of his desk. It was his idea list. He had another story to write, about a supposedly haunted gold mine being brought back into operation, but first he felt like getting another article started. As he sipped his coffee, which had gone from too hot to lukewarm and was now too cold, he looked through his article idea list. There were many ideas. A feel-good story on a retiring school teacher who had devoted her life to helping her former students reach and graduate from college. An investigation of a chemical dump in the Los Angeles area. Nothing really caught Sean's interest though, and he sat back feeling uninspired. He had skipped over one story on the list, mostly because it was really his editor's idea and not his. He kept telling himself and Paul, his editor, that he did not like the story. But Paul insisted he think about it and kept reminding him of it. It was a story investigating the truth of Abraham Lincoln's parentage. Paul had somehow stumbled across a website that claimed that Thomas Lincoln was not really Abraham Lincoln's father. Sean thought for a few moments and decided the only way he would ever get Paul to quit nagging him about it would be to take a stab at the story.

He pulled a blank manila file folder from a stack and scribbled "Lincoln" on its tab. He grabbed a pad of paper, turned to the computer and started in on the task of researching the story.

An hour or so later and with one trip downstairs for a coffee refill, Sean had scribbled out the basic theory. The story was that some fellow named Abraham Enloe had gotten a servant girl pregnant at his farm in western North Carolina. This servant girl had the same name as Abraham Lincoln's mother, Nancy Hanks, who bore her famous son around the same time. According to the "alternative history theory," these ladies were one and the same. The theory held that Nancy had been sent back north to Kentucky, returning to her family in disgrace. There she met and married Thomas Lincoln, who accepted the child as his own, concealing his true origin. Nancy Hanks died early in Abraham's childhood and Thomas Lincoln remarried, helping to keep the secret hidden. For the alternative history theory to be true, Thomas Lincoln and Nancy Hanks must have concealed the origins of Abraham Lincoln and Thomas must have married Nancy Hanks while she was pregnant, accepting the child as his own. Therefore, Abraham Lincoln was actually Abraham Enloe. Some believed the truth had been covered up, that a conspiracy was involved.

It certainly sounded plausible to Sean, though he had questions about the timing and the provability of the alternative theory. Rising above those questions, though, were fundamental questions about whether it was worthy of writing about. *Why write the story at all? And from what angle?*

Sean continued searching the web for information. He began looking for modern day Enloe descendants. There were plenty, he quickly found, almost too many. Then he caught one that really stood out, a history professor named James Enloe who had published quite a bit about Abraham Lincoln. *Too good to be true.* Better yet, he taught at the University of Tennessee in Knoxville, not far from the supposed place of conception of young Abe. Sean looked up the professor's website. This James Enloe taught a President Lincoln class at the University.

Well, if I had to write the story, that would be the angle.

Sean added James' contact information to his own electronic contact base and then composed a short email to Professor Enloe explaining who he was, what he did for a living, and asking if the esteemed professor knew anything about the Lincoln-Enloe story. He decided against using the word "conspiracy," sensing that, at least at this point, it would be too provocative, too sensationalistic. Experience had taught Sean to be patient and learn his subjects' cares and desires before asking for too much.

A few minutes later, the mail was sent and his notes shoved into the manila folder on the corner of his desk. He planned to run the idea by Paul, and then, if Paul continued to insist on it, he would interview the professor and write the story. He looked out the window and realized the world was beginning to wake up. Several hours had passed since he had settled down to work at his computer. Sean pushed his chair back from the desk, spun around and stood up. He ran his hand through his closely cut hair and felt the stiffness in his muscles that were a result of sitting too long. He was becoming more aware of the physical limitations middle age imposed. He certainly did not have the same body that had ran, swum, and jumped out of airplanes a decade ago. *All the better reason to go for a run,* Sean thought as he headed across the floor toward his bedroom on the other side of the house.

.....

Sean was in a third-floor office of the Seattle Press Daily, the newspaper he wrote for. He had just finished a meeting with his editor, Paul Clovis, and had been given the go-ahead on the haunted mine story. As he stood up from Paul's desk he paused, then explained his quick preliminary research on the Lincoln-Enloe story.

"So if you insist, I'll call up the professor, interview him, and write a nice story for you," Sean finished.

Paul looked at him for a few moments. "Let me get this straight. You want to write a piece that says that Lincoln was the bastard-son of a tobacco farmer who screwed his mom while she worked as a servant girl at his plantation? And you want to do all of this with an hour of research and a quick phone call?"

"Hey, wait a minute! This was all your idea in the first place! I'm more than happy to drop the idea."

Paul smiled slyly, and Sean knew he was trapped.

"No, no, I think the idea is good. You've just got to take it more seriously. I think you'll need to go visit some of these places. Maybe meet this professor in person."

"Doesn't that seem like overkill?" Sean responded. "It's just a story on an alternate history theory."

Paul looked Sean over through the thick, black-framed eyeglasses that complimented his twinkling black eyes. "You want to attack the person who many consider to be the greatest president we have ever had by calling him a bastard? You want to cast shadows on the 'Great Emancipator'? And you want to do it with a quick, unprofessional story?"

"No," Sean sighed. "I don't want to do the story at all. It's your idea."

Paul spoke carefully. "Listen Sean, I admit that I'm pushing this story on you, but it should be very interesting to most Americans. Abraham Lincoln is not just a man. He is a myth, a legend, a hero, and a very admired man for what he did and what he stood for in history. He is also probably still hated by frozen-in-time rebel families in the South that have never forgotten what the Civil War did to them. He was assassinated at the peak of his achievements, thus becoming either martyr or villain, preserved in that state for all eternity. Writing this story will take great care and require that you deal with all of these complexities. You might find yourself in deeper than you expected."

Sean started to reply, but Paul cut him off. "No, don't say anything else. Just think about what I have said."

Paul then looked down and began scrutinizing his agenda on the desk in front of him. Sean knew that meant Paul was done talking and was dismissing him. Paul ran a tight ship, not always the fuzziest or warmest. But he was usually right. Sean turned and left Paul's office, heading out of the building.

Now, walking down the steep streets that flowed towards the waterfront, Sean pondered the story and the editor's advice. He considered dropping the whole story right then and tossing the files in the trash. He doubted that Paul would let it go, though. Sean also felt a bit of a challenge in the story. So, despite his misgivings, he decided to move ahead.

Chapter Two

Mary Fester was settling into what had become the favorite part of her day. After rising and "turning on the house," as she called it, she would go outside like clockwork and water the plants on her front porch. Her husband, Phillip, and she would then have coffee with fruit and toast in the kitchen. Afterwards, he would head out to play tennis with his buddies and she would head into her home office.

Mary was one of many retirees living in Phoenix. She and Phillip moved from Cincinnati five years ago after they both retired. Mary had been a clerk in a tool supply business and Phillip had been a manager at an auto parts production facility. They considered themselves lucky, retiring from jobs they had worked at their entire lives into solid retirements that allowed comfortable living in a golf course development in sunny Phoenix. Of course, "sunny" was just a nice way to avoid saying "hot." Phillip had adjusted to the heat easily, playing golf on the hottest days of their first summer. But even after five years, Mary had never truly gotten used to the heat. Starting in June or so, she still limited her outdoor summertime activities to early mornings.

Phillip played tennis nearly every morning and golf two or three days during the week. She played golf two or three days a week with a group of ladies and usually joined Phillip for a round each Saturday. Phillip's tennis time, however, was her family-history time. At least two days a week, and sometimes three or four, she would settle down next to her computer and continue filling out her family tree. It was a passion of hers, bordering on an obsession. Since beginning her genealogy quest, she had "met" more family members online than she ever could keep track of, let alone meet. Her passion and dedication to keeping a handle on the growing world of her known family gave her life an ongoing fulfillment in retirement. Phillip was completely comfortable living a retired life of sports and reading. Mary, though, had always needed a challenging task to be happy. Genealogy replaced her job, filling the void of retirement. She truly enjoyed herself while busy exploring her family tree.

At 69 years of age, Mary was still quite healthy. Her greying hair was thinning a bit in some areas, especially at the top. She permed it, but so far had refused to dye it. *Better to accept the changes that age brings*, she thought. Golf and light gardening kept her body toned so she was not as frail as her age might otherwise indicate.

The home office she settled into was simply decorated. A computer desk dominated the window wall. Several filing cabinets and book-shelves occupied the wall to the right of the desk and some favorite photos and paintings rounded out the room. The first impression coming into the room was of a tidy, bright and well-organized home office.

Mary turned on the computer and waited for it to "boot up" and link to the internet. She still found it amusing how dramatically life had changed in the computer age. Most young people had no grasp of how much technology had simplified the tasks of communicating, study-ing, learning, and writing. *Sure they think they do,* she thought, *but they really have nothing to compare it with. I remember typewriters. I remember envelopes, stamps, and paper. I remember crafting a letter, sending it, and then forgetting about it for a few weeks. Then, when a return letter arrived, it was so pleasantly surprising. Today's youth have no patience, and certainly don't appreciate how much commu-nication has evolved. Now everything is more casual, even reckless. Everything!*

Mary usually began her time on the computer, like most people, she suspected, by checking her email. Afterwards, she typically moved onto the genealogy bulletin boards. She liked checking them regularly. Some days the bulletin boards would lead her on impossible tasks she never completed, like trying to find a birth record that didn't exist. One task could distract her for the remainder of that day on the computer. Other days, she would tire of the bulletin boards and move into her planned family researching.

Today, her email was fairly sparse. Just a few messages from friends mixed among the usual junk mail. After replying to friends and deleting the junk mail, she launched her internet browser and began visiting her bookmarked family history websites. Her favorite, of course, was the Enloe website, as that was her maiden name. Many of her Enloe cousins were members of this page and constantly posted information or documents they had found on the web or in some archive or library somewhere for members to find and read.

Today was no different. One member had posted information about a John Enloe, who had purchased a piece of land in South Carolina in 1799. The record was from an office of documents neither indexed nor online. Apparently some genealogist had visited a county records office and quickly scribbled down the basic data of about 200 property deeds—information such as the buyer and seller's names and the date of the transaction. An Enloe cousin had come across this genealogist's posting while searching the web, and had then posted the specifics of John Enloe's deed on the Enloe webpage. *Somebody needs to go down there and copy all of that information, digitize it, and get it online,* she thought. *But there are a million things like that to do.*

Mary then noticed an inquiry posted by a non-member. It was from a lady living in Kansas City named Kim Poole. The post read:
Hi,

I am interested in learning more about any Enloes that were living in the Denver area during or after the Civil War. In particular I am looking for information about Jacob Thomas. He was most likely born around 1845 and is somehow related to an Enloe. I might be searching for a man named Jacob Enloe. Is this the only Enloe website? Please respond directly to me.

Thanks,
Kim Poole

Mary checked her records. There were a few Enloes in Colorado, but none mentioned in the 1860's or earlier. She searched for Jacob Enloes, but none of them matched the year Kim had mentioned. Mary then noticed that the woman had used the term "around" when describing the birth year. Mary searched for any Jacob Enloe born between 1835 through 1855. Again she found nothing. On a hunch she ran a search for "J" Enloes and found a few. After looking at each, she noticed one was listed as being born between the birth dates of two sisters who were born in 1855 and 1859. That would place this J. Enloe as being born between those years, she mused.

But then she realized she was getting way off track. *This woman is really looking for Jacob Thomas.* Mary ran a search for Thomases in the Enloe family tree she was building. She found two hits, but they were both very recent ones. Puzzled, she read the post again, then decided to reply.

Dear Kim,

I am an Enloe historian, but I don't show a Jacob Thomas or Jacob Enloe in the timeframe mentioned in your posted message. Can you explain more about who you are inquiring about? Sometimes the context helps unravel mysteries.

Very truly yours,

Mary

Mary read through her email, spell-checking it before she even considered sending it off. Unlike most modern youngsters, Mary treated emails just as she would a formal, handwritten letter, checking grammar and spelling and correctly formatting them with all the necessary salutations and closings. Satisfied with the email, she clicked on send. As the "compose email" screen disappeared, Mary returned to her routine of checking favorite bulletin boards. Finding nothing else of much interest, she began researching one of her family tree branch projects. Then she glanced at the time.

It was after noon, and she had a one o'clock tee time with her lady friends! Mary shut down her computer and then pulled herself out of her chair, hurrying to keep her date. As she stretched her now stiff limbs, she muttered to herself about getting old too fast. She then headed to the bedroom to get ready.

Seattle

Paul had gently muttered, "It's only a suggestion," but Sean knew better. Paul was telling him to dig further into the Lincoln-Enloe story and find an angle. Sean was back in Paul's office on the hill above the bay. He came by after Paul left a voicemail asking how soon he could have an outline ready. Sean pondered how to best respond to his editor, but deep inside he knew how it would turn out.

"Isn't there someone else who would be gung-ho to take on this story?" he asked.

"No, there's not," Paul shot back. He was sitting upright in his chair with his arms on the desk. It was a look that conveyed confidence. "What's more, there is no one else better for this story than you. Oh sure, you're complaining now, but you'll like it. You don't have to crucify Lincoln. Hell, this will be great for the Lincoln legend."

Paul paused, leaning a bit closer towards Sean. "I'm choosing you because you have the best sense of history and of our country's rich political depth. I trust you to strike the right balance."

"You cannot 'choose' me for a story I am not volunteering for," Sean protested. "I am a free lance journalist, not your hack."

"Yeah, yeah, sure." Paul waved his arm around his office. "How do you think I got here? Turning down stories? Just do it, okay."

Sean sat quietly for a moment. *If I say no to Paul, he'll be mad and not give me as many opportunities. But I don't like this story!*

Sean thought his way through his options, and quickly realized he really had no choice.

"Okay, I'll do it, but you've got to cover my costs."

Paul smiled broadly. "Deal, but nothing too wild on the costs. Your usual."

Sean smiled politely back, thinking to himself how little he understood the man smiling at him from across the desk.

.....

Sean stepped back into his house. The walk downhill from the Seattle Press Daily, then uphill to his house had been refreshing, even if a bit chilly and wet. On the way home from his meeting with Paul, he stopped at a bookstore and purchased a Lincoln biography that seemed thorough, at least based on its thickness. On entering the foyer of his house, he dropped the bag containing the book on a small table by the inner door, then discarded his raincoat and wet shoes. Following this ritual, Sean entered his house. After depositing his package on the kitchen counter, he trotted upstairs in his socks to check for messages on his answering machine. Finding none, he came back down and set about making an early dinner, a grilled cheese sandwich with an apple and a glass of low fat milk.

Once his dinner was ready, he carried it upstairs to his office and sat down. While eating a little and pondering the Lincoln-Enloe story he decided to call the professor in Tennessee. He found the phone number in his notes and dialed it with one hand while taking a big gulp of milk to wash down a mouthful of sandwich. Sean completed dialing the number and waited patiently for the electronic signals to bounce through the ethereal phone networks and landlines in Knoxville, Tennessee. It was four in the afternoon in Seattle, so it was seven in the evening at the University of Tennessee campus. Thus, he did not expect to get the professor in person.

"I'll leave him a friendly message, asking him to call," Sean said outloud. He realized, as he had been noticing more often, that he was talking to himself. *The life of a lonely investigative reporter,* he mused. He wasn't fooling himself. He loved his job, his life of chasing down stories and rounding them out. But it was a bit nomadic.

The phone was ringing now. Sean found himself trying to imagine the professor. A taciturn, portly old man? A handsome middle-aged talker? Based on what he had dug up on the professor, Sean guessed he was middle-aged and probably spent too much time hunched over books or his computer. *That will be me in ten years if I don't watch out.* Surprisingly, the phone was answered by what sounded to be a real voice and not a recording.

"Hello?" The voice was deep, resonant, confident. Sean was startled enough that he hesitated for a moment, expecting the voice to continue speaking to him, asking him to leave a message. But the line remained silent.

"Professor Enloe?" Sean inquired in his best professional and friendly voice.

"That's me last time I checked. James Enloe." The hearty voice seemed to be chuckling as it spoke. "And to whom do I have the pleasure? If you're selling me something, better just hang up now, I won't buy."

"No, no, Professor Enloe, I'm not selling anything." Sean tried to chuckle in return as he spoke. "Sean Johnson speaking. Journalist in Seattle, Washington. All I have to sell is cloudy wet weather. Interested?"

"We get enough of that around here, Mr. Johnson. Care for some sleet, snow and an occasional tornado?" the hearty voice fired right back.

He has a good sense of humor. That's good. This should be easy. Sean let himself shift into professional journalist mode. "Journalist" was a much less threatening term than "investigative reporter." Truth be told, Sean had no idea what the difference really was between the two.

"Professor Enloe, I'm calling you in your capacity as a Lincoln expert. I'm trying to learn more information about a story from Lincoln's early life."

"Ah, I see you are truly a professional, feeding my ego by calling me an expert. I have written a few books and a few articles, I'll give you that, but that hardly makes me an expert."

"You look like one to me professor, and very well suited for my line of inquiry."

"Okay, well, I won't complain about being called an expert," the chuckle returned to the professor's voice. "What is your inquiry?"

Sean hesitated a bit. *This seems absurd, and might actually irritate him.* Sean decided to approach it delicately.

"Are you familiar with Lincoln's childhood?"

"Well yes, I should be," the tone of his voice had shifted a bit.

Better get to the point without too much delay. "I am tracking down a story about Abraham Lincoln's parentage."

"Yes, well I can probably give you some direction, if you tell me what your question is." Sean detected some emphasis on the word "if" and realized he needed to come out and ask directly.

"In this case Professor, I am trying to learn more about an alternate theory about his parenthood." Sean paused, only to hear silence. He continued. "It has to do with whether Lincoln's father was really Thomas Lincoln."

Christ Sean, just ask the damned question, you wimp!

Silence was still his only response. Sean jumped in with more.

"I have found references to the president's mother, Nancy Hanks, working for a family in North Carolina and being impregnated by the master of that home." Sean paused again. "They were ah, Enloes." Sean winced on how poorly he had gotten to his point.

This time the silence was not too long.

"Oh, I see. You figured that with me being not only a Lincoln 'expert', but also an Enloe, I would be the perfect person to get juicy quotes from so you could write up a story of a nutty professor in Kentucky claiming to be related to the president. Is that your true angle Mr. Johnson?" The professor's enunciation of "expert" had been dripping with sarcasm.

Well, you've ticked him off, alienated him, and brought out strong hostility. Great job, Sean. You're really a professional.

"Professor, I am not trying to do a story on you, or to humiliate you, or to demean Lincoln." Sean tried to sound as honest and sincere as he possibly could. "This story attracted me because I had never heard it before. And because it could illustrate how uncertain our concrete history really is. Mostly, I thought it was amazing that a person dead for more than a century could even generate interest in such stories. Even if that person is our most famous and greatest president."

"I chose you as a starting point, because you came up as an authority on Lincoln and because your name was Enloe. I figured if there was any truth to this story you had to know it, and that you might at least know exactly where this story originated."

Sean stopped speaking and waited patiently for the professor to respond. After a short pause he did.

"Okay, Mr. Johnson, I will accept your explanation as being truthful, even if it might not be." The professor seemed to be shifting into a very professorial voice. "And yes, I know all about this silly story regarding the Enloes. It would be very hard to be a Lincoln historian with the last name Enloe without having come across it."

The professor paused, and Sean could almost imagine him shaking an accusing finger at him as he continued.

"Understand, Mr. Johnson, this is not a line of investigation that gets any attention by any Lincoln historian. It is not credible, not provable and would only cast shadows on the greatness of our finest president. Thus, historians, including myself, do not wish to propagate it at all."

Sean interrupted before the professor could continue.

"Professor, I ask you only as a source of guidance as to where to look. I will not cite you or quote you, and will even treat what I learn in this conversation as being from a non-disclosed source. If this story is unfounded and without support, shouldn't you want to at least explain that to me?"

"You make a good point, Mr. Johnson." The chuckling tone had returned to his voice.

That's good. You're through the worst of it. He'll be candid now. Before Sean could start focusing the conversation, though, the professor began again.

"But understand, it is a sensitive topic for me. I found myself fascinated with Lincoln at a young age and became a history professor with a focus on Lincoln long before I uncovered this story about the Enloes. The story irritates me deeply, because it can create a very false impression that I am a Lincoln historian because of it."

"I understand that completely, Professor. "If I could..."

"No, I doubt you really understand completely, but I appreciate your willingness to try," the professor interrupted him. "So why don't you ask me your questions. I will answer them the best that I can."

I was trying to, Professor, before you interrupted me. This really is a sensitive topic for you. Sean decided to jump quickly into the heart of the matter, while he still had some level of cooperation.

"Okay, well my first question is, where does this story come from? Is it a modern fabrication or does it have historical support?"

The professor sighed before he spoke. "I would like to tell you that it is a modern fabrication, but it is not. I consider it a historical fabrication. I say that because there is no documentary evidence that I know of that directly supports it, but we have written evidence that the story was being told at the time of Lincoln's death. The written evidence suggests that people spoke about it while he was president."

"So there is written evidence?"

"Yes and no. The written evidence comes from contemporaneous 'journalists' writing about what people were saying." Sean did not miss the hint of sarcasm that the professor used when speaking of journalists.

"There is not, for instance, a letter written by somebody claiming to have first-hand knowledge," the professor continued.

"But Lincoln was born in a time when there was little writing, isn't that true?"

"February 18, 1809," the professor answered. "Yes, in 1809 most of the country was a wilderness of illiterate farmers trying to scratch out a homestead. There was little time for luxuries such as reading or writing. Indians, disease, weather, and the sheer difficulty of feeding oneself were all anyone had time to handle. When a person crossed over the Appalachians, they were in a wild and harsh country. It was in this type of setting that Lincoln was born."

"Was it in this setting that this alternate version of history might have occurred?"

"Yes, that's right. Nobody disagrees with who Lincoln's mother was. She was Nancy Hanks. For that matter, nobody disagrees with who Lincoln's father was either. He was Thomas Lincoln. This story, however, says that Nancy Hanks was impregnated while working as a servant girl in North Carolina a year or so earlier."

"North Carolina?" Sean interrupted. "I thought that Lincoln was born in Kentucky."

"That's right, also. You just raised one of the flaws in the story. Nancy Hanks supposedly was sent back home to Kentucky after she got pregnant in North Carolina. Out of sight, out of mind, if you will. Upon arriving at home she discreetly had the child. The theory goes that Thomas Lincoln married her to give the child a father, that they moved from place to place, and had a second child, all the while pretending, for young Abraham's sake, that Nancy's first child was really a 'Lincoln' as well."

"Is this story unreasonable?"

"Not at all, Mr. Johnson." The professor had a habit of using a very academic, confident voice when he started speaking and then shifting gradually towards a more understanding, softer voice. "This was wilderness, but the moral and religious standards of the day did not allow pre-marital sex. I am most certain these activities happened much of the time anyway, but everyone pretended otherwise. It is certainly reasonable that a young servant girl could have been impregnated by the master of a home and then sent away. It is certainly reasonable to think this same mother could have the child and merge it into a not-so-later marriage without anyone realizing that the child was from a different father."

"Life expectancies were short back then. Many children died early. Mothers died early, often while giving birth. Families moved about, trying to find a place where they could survive. There were no birth certificates, and often no doctor or midwife was available to help with the birth of a child." The professor seemed to be slowing down, as if he was bored with the conversation.

"So if it's so possible, why don't you believe the story, Professor?" Sean tried to fire the professor up a bit.

"I don't believe something just because it could be true, Mr. Johnson," the professor intoned. "I believe something because it is proven to be at least probable. This is definitely not the case here. The evidence is only suggestive at best. To be honest, we know very little of Nancy Hank's family. Historians have spent large amounts of time trying to trace her origins. But this was a poor and wild country and there are not many records available. When Nancy died, she took most of that information with her. She died having no idea that her child would grow up to be President of the United States, and that he would lead our country in a most noble way through a terrible conflict and challenge."

"But, just because we know so little does not mean that we can guess at the circumstances of the birth of her first child." The professor now sounded completely bored.

"Let me ask you just a few more questions, Professor," Sean began. "Can you point me toward the best authority about the accepted dogma of Lincoln's childhood? Can you also point me toward the best authority on this alternate history? If you'll do that for me, I'll get them and read them. I won't bother you unless I need more help understanding the details. Is that acceptable to you?"

"Certainly, Mr. Johnson. Don't get me wrong. I am a historian. I know as well as anyone that recorded history is often wrong. Yet it's accepted by modern persons as if it were personally witnessed by them. It is a fault of the way we teach history. Too much politics involved." Professor Enloe paused to collect his thoughts.

"There are many books covering Lincoln's childhood. Several are written by historians that directly observed the written evidence. I suggest you consider the Angston book. It is a well-documented and respected tome on Lincoln." The professor paused again.

"Meanwhile, there are only two books I know of that discuss the alternate history. Both are very old and long out of print. You can often find them with antique book sellers. If you like, I can send you the necessary information about them. Do you have my email address?"

"Yes I do, Professor," Sean replied. "I'll send you an email. Let me finish by thanking you for your time. I truly appreciate your help."

"Not at all, Mr. Johnson, but I'm afraid you are wasting your time here. I doubt anyone today is really going to be very interested in an unsupported story that might have happened almost two hundred years ago, even if it is about President Lincoln. Still, I wish you luck."

"Thank you Professor. Good evening."

"Goodbye."

Sean hung up the phone and finished his notes from the call. He then pushed back from his desk, stretched, and turned to look out the window at Puget Sound, barely visible through the drizzle now hounding Seattle. *You say that nobody would be interested, Professor Enloe,* he mused. *But you yourself got very heated and are, or at least were at one point or another, very interested. I think this story does have something to prove.*

Sean thought about the conversation a bit more and then turned back to his computer to send the professor an email.

.....

A little while later, Sean was ensconced in his favorite living room recliner. He was looking to his right out the bay window. The drizzle prevented him from clearly making out the dock area, but he identified the gray shapes of buildings that he would otherwise see clearly when the weather was nicer. As he nibbled on the remainder of his now-cold grilled cheese sandwich, he began thumbing through the Lincoln biography he had picked up downtown.

Two hours later he put the book down and turned to stare out into the mist. He ran through Lincoln's childhood in his head. The book had corroborated the stories he had known from grade school of Abraham Lincoln living in a one-room, dirt floor log cabin, reading by the light from the fireplace. While all of that was true, there were other events he had not been aware of.

Lincoln had lived a very nomadic life in his early years. He lived in his first home, on Nolin Creek near Hodgenville, Kentucky, for only two years. Thomas Lincoln soon gave up trying to survive in Hodgenville and moved to Knob Creek in 1811. That lasted only five years, and at age seven, young Lincoln and his family moved once again, this time to Little Pigeon Creek in Indiana. There, Abraham grew to young adulthood. It was also there, in 1818, when Abe was only nine years old, that his mother, the former Nancy Hanks, died.

Of Nancy Hanks, little was known. She was reported to be from Virginia, and that was apparently based on oral statements made by Abraham, who must have been told that by his mother or father, Thomas Lincoln. Nancy's birthdate was not clear, nor exactly where she had spent her early years, nor how she had come to be in Kentucky. This was all fascinating to Sean, and he began comparing the notes from his internet research, and from his call with the Professor, to the verifiable facts he could glean from the biography.

In the midst of this pondering, the sudden ringing of the phone startled him. He rose from his chair and grabbed the nearby cordless in the kitchen.

"Hello."

"Sean, buddy, how's it goin?" Sean recognized the cheerful voice of his childhood friend Allan.

"Great, Allan, and you?"

"Same ol, same ol. Hey listen, pal, I'm feeling a bit bored and could use a round of beers with an old friend. You got plans for tonight?"

Sean was used to Allan's tendency to use different nicknames for his friends even within the same sentence. Everyone knew that Allan spoke every one of them from the heart.

"I had no plans until now. But from the machinery sounds in the background, I find it hard believing you're really bored."

"Naw, but from one bachelor to another, I need a night out. Murphy's sound good? Say. Seven?"

"That'll work. See you then."

Sean hung up to the sound of Allan's long "Okayyyy." He glanced over at the clock and saw that it was already well past six o'clock. He moved to straighten out his stuff in the living room before getting ready to go.

Chapter Three

Kansas City

The low light of the early evening was descending on Kansas City's rolling hills as Kim arrived home. She gladly had left the store in the hands of her weekday evening manager for closing up. As her car approached and entered her cul-de-sac, the visible lights in the house told Kim that Abby was home, probably at the kitchen table doing homework. She hit the remote button clipped onto the visor of her SUV and then pulled into the garage. *It's a plain home*, Kim thought, *in a nice neighborhood with a great school*. That was important to her, that Abby have a good place to grow up. After moving up here after their divorce, Kim realized she needed a solid place to raise Abby on her own. That had been five years ago and Abby had made it to fifteen without too much going wrong. There was the usual teenage anger and rebellion, but she continued to earn good grades, and so far, *knock on wood,* she thought, *no big trouble worth worrying about*. After parking her vehicle in the garage, Kim reached up again and pressed the remote button.

Kim got out of the car as the garage door slid silently closed. *Abby probably got the mail. Maybe she made dinner,* she wondered. *Yeah, right!* Kim grabbed her bag from the seat behind her, closed the car door and walked to the door leading into the house. As she opened the door, sounds of music and television descended upon her. Abby was, as expected, sitting at the kitchen table, working on math by the looks of it. *How can she study with that racket in the background?*

As if Abby was reading her thoughts, she looked up at her mom, smiled and grabbed for the stereo remote. She hit the mute button and the music disappeared, allowing the television sound to resonate more clearly.

"Hi Mom," Abby said as she turned her eyes back down to the homework in front of her.

That's all I get from a long day's work, Kim thought, *a muted stereo and a 'Hi mom?' Still, I guess it's better than a frown or being ignored. And way better than her not being here at all.*

"Hi sweetheart. How was your day?"

"Fine," Abby replied without looking up.

"That's great honey."

Kim deposited her bag on the table and looked into the kitchen. *Nothing happening in there,* she thought.

"I'm going to change and freshen up and then I'll start dinner, okay?"

This time Abby did briefly look up, "Sure, Mom."

Kim studied her daughter for a moment. She looked more like her ex-husband, and was, in fact, already as tall as her. Abby's hair was brown, but wavy like her dad's. She had lighter brown eyes and some of her mannerisms were reminiscent of her ex as well. *Like how much she ignores me,* she thought. Abby dressed nicely, at least in typical blouses and pants or skirts. So far, she was not pushing the envelope in that direction. Kim surrendered her study of Abby, turned, and headed to her bedroom.

A little while later, Kim was chopping some vegetables for their salad. Dinner was cooking, and Kim even succeeded in getting the TV volume turned down. As she cooked, she broached the topic that had been on her mind for several days.

"Abby, the other day I was going through some of grandpa's things and came across an amazing note." Kim said this half-looking towards Abigail, who was no longer studying but instead splitting her attention between Kim and the TV.

Abby looked at her mom. "Yeah?"

"He left me a letter he intended me to read after he passed away. In it he told me that our family name is not really Poole at all."

Kim had used "our" in front of "family name" but knew that Abby was probably thinking "your" since she carried the last name of her father, Jason Wilcox. Kim often suspected that Abby was more bothered by her decision to adopt her maiden name than she was by anything else, perhaps even the divorce itself. That topic had been the source of many arguments between them, though not recently. Indeed, Abby looked up, and Kim thought she saw a flash of anger briefly pass over her. Abby responded more disinterested than anything, though.

"So, that's it?"

"Yes, but that's a very big deal. My...our...family has apparently been running around with a false name for more than a hundred years."

"Chill, it's just a name mom, that's all."

Now Kim felt the anger flash over her. *Just a goddamn name!,* she thought. *How dare you say that after all the grief you gave me over going back to my maiden name.* Kim suppressed the anger though, and tried to speak calmly.

"It's more than a name, honey. It tells us where we come from and who we are. It connects us to our past. I'm surprised you can say that after the talks we had about me returning to 'Poole' as my last name."

Abby looked defensive. "That was different mom. You were changing your name away from mine, and Dad's. You had a choice, and there was someone living. Me mom! I cared! I doubt any one cares whether some long dead ancestor decided to change his name. Except maybe you."

"Okay, okay, but it is different. Poole was, or at least I thought it was, my last name. Oh, never mind, silly me for thinking you might be interested."

Abby thought for a moment.

"Okay, I am interested… some." She grinned. "Sorry Mom, it's just that you take all this family history stuff so seriously."

"Well, I guess I do." Kim had finished chopping the tomatoes, carrots, and olives and dumped them into the salad bowl on top of the lettuce. "But, it is fascinating to know all the people that had to meet, to survive, to make you. And where they lived...and what they went through."

Kim glanced over at Abby. *Hey, I seem to have her attention a bit!*

"Grandpa left a letter explaining that my two-times great, your three-times great-grandfather, changed his last name from Thomas to Poole. He also explained it was for dangerous reasons that had to do with the Civil War and Abraham Lincoln."

Abby laughed. "You're making that up."

"No, I'm not! That is the honest to goodness truth."

"Can I see the letter?"

Kim paused at this point. Suddenly, she remembered the undertone of the letter and of the aged note. She decided to stop at this point for now.

"Maybe later. I'm still unraveling this story some," Kim explained. "There may be more to it, and I want you to hear it correctly the first time. I just wanted you to know about this okay?"

Abby paused, mumbled her "okay" and shifted her focus fully to the weight-loss reality show on the TV.

.....

About an hour later, after dinner was over and she and Abby had cleaned up, Kim found herself at her computer, relaxed with a glass of deep red merlot in her hand. Kim was tired, it had been an exhausting day at work. Like the days before, she felt distracted. For her, the mystery that had been dumped in her lap still felt deeply disturbing. Her father had essentially lied to her nearly all of his life, until he had written that letter. Then, and only then, had he been honest. *Our real family name is Thomas, not Poole. But he is not here to talk to!*

Kim reached into her bag and retrieved the thick manila envelope in which she had placed the letter and note. She had made a few copies of each and now she pulled out a set. She preferred to handle copies rather than originals, as if somehow it made it easier to pretend that she was removed from this, like a historian. She glanced at them, then read them through for what seemed like the fiftieth time.

Finally, Kim turned her attention to her computer. She sipped at her wine while launching her email program. Glancing through her messages, she immediately noted two emails containing the word "Enloe" in the subject header. She opened the first one only to quickly find that it was just an automated response from one website on which she had posted a message. Turning her attention to the second email, she noticed it was addressed by an actual person with the handle of "Maryhistnut." The subject line read "Your inquiry about Enloe and Thomas." Anxiously, she opened the email to find the short note from Mary Fester. After reading it, Kim sat back.

She pondered the caution embedded in both the ancient note from her ancestor and in the letter from her father. *Please be careful. Jacob must have had very good reasons for his actions and his caution.*

But what were those reasons? How cautious am I supposed to be? Do I spill the beans to someone I have never met? As Kim thought about this, she thought again of her daughter, Abby, a few rooms away from her. *I do need to be careful. But, even caution has its limits. I've started unraveling this mystery. I'm not going to stop now.*

Having made up her mind, she clicked on "reply" and composed an email to Mary Fester. She began by asking Mary not to forward the information, at least not yet. She then gave Mary a slightly better explanation of what her inquiry was about, still keeping key parts of it reserved for a later time.

> *Mary,*
>
> *I ask because I have obtained information that suggests that my father's real last name was Thomas, not Poole. The name change occurred years ago and somehow, the Enloes may have been involved. Don't ask me more than that yet, because I am still sorting it out. The most I can say right now is this all happened back around the Civil War. Does any of this make any sense to you? Are the Enloes and Thomases intertwined at some point? Are you also a Thomas? Sorry for all these questions.*
>
> *Kim*

Kim hit the send button and stared at the screen for a minute, then she pulled herself out of her reverie and continued to go through her email. Once it was cleaned out, she went into her genealogy program and started running Thomas searches.

One empty wine glass and an hour later, Kim gave up. There were too many Thomases out there, even when she limited her search to Jacob. *And besides, I don't even know if Jacob was his first name.* When she limited her search to Colorado, she failed to find a Jacob Thomas at all. Feeling frustrated, she tried to find the energy to dig into another branch of her family, but soon tired of that also. Her mind was still fixed on her newly found family name, Thomas. Shutting down her computer, she readied herself for bed.

North of Atlanta, Georgia

The estate home, essentially a mansion, stood on top of a hill looking out on the property it governed. Located outside of Atlanta proper, the mansion was headquarters for the Sheriden family. Its white plaster finish, tall columns, and tiled roofs gave it a grandeur that connected with the manicured grounds surrounding it. Hedges, flower beds, lawns and ponds merged towards the mansion on three sides. A slightly weaving, cut stone driveway worked its way towards the mansion from the front, always offering stunning views as the mansion grew in size. On one flank, slightly below and separate, stood a single story sprawling building that appeared to serve as a garage and support staff area. Behind the house, at the foot of the hill, sat a modest and beautiful lake. Except for the manicured area behind the mansion, the forest crept right to the lake's edge. Guests coming up the driveway had no idea of the presence of the lake. Instead, they learned of it after reaching a room near the back of the mansion. Not that they needed to know of the lake to be impressed, for the property was stunning from every view. The lake, the forest and the grounds were all part of the estate, totaling about 150 acres of the most desirable forested real estate north of Atlanta.

Sheriden "family" probably is not quite the right word. Sheriden "empire" connotes a better description. Rising into prominence in the waste and tension of the post-Civil War south, the Sheridens owned a large security and technology company, Sheriden Corporation, providing military and security services. The company quietly maintained itself and its services, staying behind the scenes of most of the events it was involved in. It accomplished this in part by doing business using many different subsidiaries with a variety of names. When Sheriden occasionally acquired a company, it often left the company's names and operations largely intact, making only certain specific adjustments to its missions, services and reporting path.

On this cool spring evening, light flowed from large windows at the rear of the second floor of the mansion. Inside, two men were sitting across from each other, separated by a long low table, each comfortably ensconced in deep leather chairs. A light wind blew off the lake and pushed up against the windows, trying to find a way inside. But the home was well built and maintained; only soft light found its way out, while sounds and the breeze remained stuck in the outside world.

The oak table was deeply stained to a mahogany color. Its rectangular shape placed the two men at a slight distance from each other. They appeared very comfortable talking to one another, suggesting that close quarters were not necessary for them to discuss the most personal of matters. The room was large, with photographs and art sprinkled around the darkly wood paneled walls. The high ceiling contained two chandeliers creating a brightness that seemed to clash with the walls, the furniture, and the burgundy carpeting. There was a wet bar contained within a wall of cabinets and shelves and a large globe sitting in a stand in the room.

At one end of the table sat a well-built, light-skinned man, with carefully cut and prepared brown hair. His blue eyes, rounding out the face of a fifty-something man, moved carefully as he observed the other man. He wore a light business suit, but its jacket was hanging on a rack near a doorway, allowing his crisp white dress shirt and red silk tie to stand out. He looked as if he had just dressed, which seemed out of kilter with the lateness of this meeting.

"Tell me Terry," he was saying to his younger brother. "What brings you out of your usual world of keeping an eye on all of our activities?" The speaker was Michael Sheriden, currently a Georgia State Senator. Before he had won the election to this position, Michael had been Chairman and CEO of Sheriden Corporation. Upon election, and as promised, he had stepped down from that position, allowing his brother, Terry, to assume responsibility of their vast empire.

Terry looked back at his older brother. Terry was shorter and a bit stockier than his brother, and while also having brown hair, but with brown eyes as well, his appearance had a much more evasive and shrewd look. Michael was the politician, Terry was the spy, the general, the commander. They were different, but shared a bond that evolved from their shared, luxurious childhood. Their largest contrast was in their wardrobe. Terry wore a polo shirt and jeans which clashed with Michael's suit. But somehow, Terry looked as if he fit in, as if he belonged in this elegant room. Which he did.

Terry studied his brother for a few more moments before making a short and simple statement. "The name has surfaced." He said it with emphasis and kept his eyes on Michael's face watching, his brother's reaction.

Michael, for his part, did not blink. He did pause though, managing only a fairly weak surprise.

"Really? THE name?"

At that moment, Terry knew that Michael had probably hoped, if not expected, that the name would never surface, or at least not in their lifetimes. That, in and of itself, surprised Terry. And he did not surprise easily.

"Yes, yesterday, on the internet. Our automated search engines picked it up."

Michael got better control over his thinking. "What makes you think it is THE name. There could be others."

Terry smiled, "Its context. The name appeared in the right context. That makes this appearance very, very interesting."

Michael did not smile. Instead, he frowned and sat quietly for a minute. Then he stood and walked over to the bar. Terry remained sitting in the leather chair silently watching him as he poured a scotch over a single ice cube. After one glance over at Terry, he began preparing a bourbon on the rocks, Terry's usual drink. He picked up the two drinks, walked over to Terry, and placed the bourbon on the table in front of Terry as he passed by. Terry turned and watched his brother approach the large globe set in a marble stand. With his free hand casually turning the sphere, Michael sipped his scotch, and enjoyed the fine, soft peat flavor wafting down his throat.

Finally Michael spoke, "Well, that is remarkable, except we were told to expect, or at least to be prepared for that. With the passage of time, I had come to expect it to never happen. I had assumed it was lost in time."

"Did you forget my last mission brother?" Terry gently inquired. "The internet is causing all sorts of things that had been lost in the fog of history and the dust of storage rooms, to resurface."

"Yes, you are right." Michael paused. "The timing is bad. Can we let this be for awhile?"

"I don't think so," Terry answered. "A woman posted a message on a website in a way that practically begs immediate attention from us. Still, I will be discreet. She may know nothing at all. But the use of the other name, makes me suspect otherwise."

Michael turned away from the globe, leaving it lightly spinning in the air. He returned to his original seat at the table.

"We have to be extremely cautious, but you are right. The secret must stay lost." Michael paused and grinned. "Or at least, part of the secret needs to stay lost. There is one part that would, if it was revealed to us, be ideal."

Michael frowned again. "But in the end, it would be better that all of it stays lost, rather than have any part of it exposed."

Terry watched his older brother for a moment. Then he spoke, this time with a cruel smile.

"Brother, you are the soft one. I always have, and always will do whatever is necessary, without reservation, to take care of us. While you grow in public circles, I act in private ones. I can handle this."

Terry paused to think inwardly for a moment. He continued.

"Though, I think caution requires that we minimize the involvement of others to the maximum extent possible. Less threads to keep track of. This could require some help from you."

Michael looked back at his brother and smiled.

"And you are presumptuous. I am as hard as I need to be. I can also do what is necessary." Michael now took on a very hard look.

"I am the driven one, Terry. My drive and my determination have fueled our success and it will continue." Michael paused and finished his oratory with a simple statement, almost shrugging his shoulders as he spoke. "I will be there as needed."

Terry looked at his brother and grunted. Then he leaned forward, reaching even farther with his glass. Michael in turn did likewise and their glasses barely met in the middle for a toast.

"To the family," they intoned together.

After gulping his bourbon, Terry leaned back and considered what his next action would be.

Seattle

Sean made his way up the hill to his house late at night. The drizzle that had seemed stuck over Seattle all day had left the area while Allan and Sean had been inside Murphy's. The pavement was wet and the air cool. As Sean worked his way to his house, he continued to reflect on Abraham Lincoln. Earlier, Allan and Sean had discussed old Abe, and Allan had sounded much like his editor, Paul, the day before.

"Look, Abraham Lincoln is our greatest president, hands down. He saved our country, stood up against slavery and was struck down at the height of his success. There isn't a more admired person in our history. If I understand this correctly, you want to write a story suggesting that he was not really a Lincoln? That he was a bastard named Enloe?"

"First, it's my editor that wants me to do the story," Sean had fired back. "I'm starting to like the story, but I might never write it. If I do though, I might write that the story is not supported, not provable. I might do nothing more than help illustrate what life was like back when Lincoln was born. But, even IF, and that is a big IF, I do conclude that it is possible that Lincoln was a bastard, that doesn't weaken him or insult him. It makes him even greater, because he overcomes even more."

Sean had paused and took a gulp from his beer. "What is so bad about telling the story about a possible history? If it's true, it's true."

Allan had shook his head. "You're missing my point. Regardless of what you write, your story will be attacked and misunderstood."

Sean and Allan had then debated the merits and problems of Sean's storyline while drinking a few beers and enjoying some excellent seafood. Now approaching his home, Sean realized that no matter how it was received, his story would be a hot one. He paused on his steps letting the silence of the evening set in. Then he went up the steps, unlocked the door and entered his home.

Once inside, Sean quickly found himself at his computer again. Upon checking his email, he found a reply from Professor Enloe. In it, the professor said he had enjoyed their conversation. He also identified two books both printed in the late 1800's and focused on the Lincoln-Enloe theory. The professor said both books were hard to find. Sean noted the names and began searching for them online. At first he failed to find any trace of either of them. But then, on a website that specialized in out-of-print books he found a copy of one of them. It was a whopping $250! Sean grimaced, but bought the book anyway. He requested immediate delivery. Given that it was already fairly late, he knew it wouldn't ship until the next day at the earliest.

Next, Sean sat back and pondered his next move. There was a lull in any other obligations or storylines to explore and he thought about taking a trip to some of the "Lincoln country" he was continuing to read about. Most of Lincoln's life was spent in three core states, Kentucky, Indiana and Illinois. Kentucky, though of keen interest to Sean, was only a part of the first six years of Lincoln's life. He pulled out a map and plotted some of the key places: Hodgenville, Kentucky; Knob Creek, Kentucky; Little Pigeon Creek, Indiana; and, of course, Springfield, Illinois which appeared to be the Lincoln Mecca. Still, Sean realized his focus needed to be on Lincoln's early childhood. He noted that Professor Enloe's campus in Knoxville, Tennessee was not that far from the Kentucky locations, so he decided to start his trip at the Lincoln sites in Kentucky and then head to Knoxville for an eye-to-eye meeting with the professor.

Having made up his mind, Sean quickly booked his flights, a rental car and his first hotel online. He would begin by flying to Louisville, Kentucky. He then would head west over to the Lincoln birth site in Hodgenville, Kentucky. He would make the drive to Knoxville, Tennessee to see the professor.

With the reservations confirmed, he continued exploring on the internet. He did some more searches for Enloe related sites. At first he found sites that maintained data on a variety of persons named Enloe.

Eventually, he found the Enloe website operated by Mary Fester. After paying to become a member of the genealogical service that hosted the Enloe site among its many sites, he entered it. Inside the webpage he found various documents posted about Enloe heritage. He tried searching for "Lincoln" but had zero hits. He then began surfing the internet.

"There are enough of you Enloes to leave me completely confused about who lived where and when," Sean said aloud as he clicked away.

Finishing his search through the site, he posted a message on the general bulletin board asking if anyone had information about the Enloes and President Lincoln. He had seen, but not really paid any attention to, the short post by Kim asking about Jacob Thomas.

Chapter Four

Wednesday, April 22
Knoxville, Tennessee

As Professor James Enloe peered down at the computer screen in front of him, scanning his lecture slides for final changes or updates, he pondered how things had changed in teaching. At age 58 he was proud to be thoroughly "modernized." When he had begun teaching, back in the dark ages of the 1970's, he used paper notes and a chalkboard. As technology evolved, he had evolved with it. Today, most of his students took notes on laptops, downloaded his lectures, and generally used paper and pen only for things like note cards. Hell, he was even doing his exams electronically now, over the internet of all things. He was not complaining though. Truthfully, the electronic age was reducing the amount of work involved in teaching classes. Preparation time was shorter, he was able to prepare, administer and grade exams much easier, and complete student grading faster. All of that meant more time for research, which he loved. But, he also was discovering that it led to less student interaction. Increasingly, his students emailed him instead of calling or, better, actually visiting. All in all, what he missed the most was face-to-face conversation.

James's thoughts returned to the lecture slides he was reviewing. Progressively, he worked his way through them. He was a big man, with big fingers and hands, yet he was fairly nimble on the keyboard. His short blonde hair, which he knew was becoming thin gray hair, was in its usual mussed condition that came from reaching up and running a hand though it subconsciously as he worked. The door to his office was open and occasionally he could hear a person walking by in the hallway. He finally reached the last slide and completed his review. "Looks good," he muttered as he closed the document.

Glancing at the clock perched on a shelf above the monitor, he verified that there still was some time before his midmorning class on U.S. History. He leaned back in his desk chair feeling the spring provide steady reciprocal pressure. He lifted his arms, hands clenched into fists and stretched his upper torso satisfyingly. The cuffs of his white dress shirt pulled down along his arms a few inches revealing a simple leather banded watch with large numbers and hands. As his head leaned back, he noticed the watch. It struck him how odd it was that he had so many ways to tell time that his watch was essentially nothing more than jewelry. His computer screen showed the time. His cell phone, of course, also knew what time it was. Even the LCD display on his office phone displayed not only the time, but the date as well.

So why carry a watch? he mused. *They're really an archaic relic of a different era. But we keep buying them, wearing them, even vainly showing them.*

As he was lowering his now happily stretched arms back down, a knocking on the doorjamb pulled him out of his reverie.

"Yes?" he called out before he even completed turning his chair enough to see who was at the door. His greeting was deep and loud, much as he sounded while lecturing. Completing his turn, his eyes locked on a student, dressed in jeans, a pullover shirt and a Tennessee orange ball cap with the traditional "T" embroidered on it. The student was tall with long curly hair that pushed out around the edge of the ball cap. Professor Enloe recognized the face, but no name came to mind.

"Uh, hi Professor," the student began. "Do you have a moment?"

James's face lit up. *A real student*, he thought. *Actually visiting me!*

"Certainly, come on in." As he spoke, James waved his hand in a gesture that drew the student towards a chair inside the room in front of a cluttered bookshelf that reached all the way to the ceiling. "Have a seat, please."

The student entered the office, swung a backpack off his shoulder onto the floor and sat down. He glanced around the office taking in the walls of books towering over a paper-covered desk. Located behind the professor was the computer that he had just finished working on. Behind that was a window that looked out from the second floor of the building into the hickory and poplar trees that surrounded the building. The tree branches were already covered with leaves, a sign of an early spring.

Professor Enloe regarded the student for a minute and then started the conversation.

"Forgive me, please, for not knowing you by name. I recognize you though. You're in my afternoon section I believe. And your name is?..." He let his voice linger in a question mode prompting the student to answer.

"Mark. Mark Ellis."

"Okay Mark, what brings you to my office today?" Professor Enloe queried.

"Well, Professor, I was confused about my grade on the last exam and hoped to talk to you," the student said a bit awkwardly. "I studied really hard. I thought I was ready. I even thought I did really well, but my grade was awful."

And there it is, the professor thought, *the usual 'I studied really hard but still failed' routine.* Still James did not mind. It was better than no student at all. *And besides,* he thought, *at least this student is not coming to me at the last possible minute in the course, crying because of failing.*

"Well, let's talk about how you studied," the professor led off. With that, Professor James Enloe eased into his standard routine for helping such students. After about twenty minutes of discussing study habits, test taking strategies and the fairness of his tests, the professor could tell that he had made about all the progress he was going to make. The conversation ended with the student promising to study better and more often. He picked up his backpack and trotted out into the hallway appearing somewhat perked up and motivated.

Professor Enloe was under no illusions about the long-term effect of his counseling, but it was satisfying having a chance to interact with a live student by giving him some guidance. As the student disappeared from view, James realized the student's name was already forgotten. *That's a shame,* the professor thought, *a student visits me and I don't even remember his name.* He was left with this fleeting feeling that he had missed an opportunity to enrich his teaching experience. *Every year, it feels like I know my students less,* he concluded.

Glancing again at one of his variety of clocks, he noted he still had some time before needing to depart towards his lecture room. Looking down at his notes, he noticed his scribbling from the call with the newspaper reporter about the Lincoln-Enloe legend. As he stared at the notes, it occurred to him that his sister would be ecstatic to learn of the inquiry.

She loves that story, he mused. *Different from me.*

On an impulse, he decided to give his sister a quick call. He pulled the phone closer to him, grabbed the handset and shoved it up against his ear, listening for a dial tone. He visually scrolled down a list of phone numbers on a piece of paper taped to his desk and punched in her number. As the phone rang, he swiveled in his chair to look out the window at the tree branches nearly scraping on the glass. He noticed the remaining buds on the tips of the branches, ready to push out of the wood with their leaves. *Down in Phoenix where Mary lives they probably don't notice spring,* he thought. *It's probably just a little warmer than it was during the winter. What a dull life.* He was brought out of his reverie by the sound of his sister's voice answering the phone.

"Hello?" Mary's voice greeted him.

"Hi sis, it's James." He had long ago stopped expecting to hear her screech with joy or something like that.

"James?" The excitement in Mary's voice was rising as she spoke. "What a wonderful surprise to get a call from my brother who NEVER calls me. This must be a special occasion."

"Ah Mary, I'm not that bad." James paused, thinking that yes, he probably was that bad. "Didn't we just talk…."

"Before Christmas, months ago?" Mary teased him. "Oh yes, I recall that occasion with some clarity, even though it was MONNTHS ago." Mary emphasized the word 'months' by dragging it out in the middle sound, a habit James had been used to since they were little kids growing up together in Kentucky.

"Okay, okay, but I'm calling you today aren't I?"

"Oh yes, and that makes me so happy. How's my professor of a brother doing?"

"Just fine." James responded. "Spring is in the air here and the campus is thriving as usual. I assume you must have some trees that actually drop their leaves in the winter down there in Phoenix? That is, if you have winter?" James felt himself warming up to their usual bantering and ribbing conversation.

"Of course, just the other day I saw a leaf on the ground," Mary fired back. "It was the most amazing thing." She paused.

"You know James, you would actually love it here, if you could ever get over your stereotype of Arizona desert living. We really do have winters. They're mild, but we have them. The summers are the harder part, but I would take this dry heat over humid Tennessee any day."

"Maybe so sis," James responded. "But your 'dry' heat is really a dry inferno. I would wither up in no time there I suspect. I'll stick with my beautiful Appalachian seasons, thank you. Besides, the real reason you live there is to golf. And we both remember what happened the one and only time I ventured onto a golf course."

"Fine, but promise to come visit me some day, please?" Mary sounded sincere now, not teasing.

"I will sis, I will." James paused to gather his thoughts. "Listen, I actually called you to share an interesting call I had from a reporter earlier. You're going to love it. This reporter actually wants to write about the crackpot Enloe legend. He called me after doing Lincoln research and noting my name."

"Really?" Mary's surprised tone revealed her immediate interest. "It is not a crackpot theory James. It's just as provable as the accepted version of Lincoln's heritage. It's all just history, the usual half-true, incomplete type of history we accept as the truth every day. You just don't like it because it would complicate your teaching."

James felt a surge of irritation. He began wondering why he even bothered to call Mary about the reporter. *She's always slamming my rejection of the theory. And she's always expanding it to an insult on my profession.*

"Look Mary," James tried to keep his tone down. "I should have known you would jump all over me on this, but at least I'm calling you to tell you about the inquiry. Why, I have no idea!"

"Sorry James, it's just that you never can mention the legend without adding one of your adjectives like today's 'crackpot' comment. Why can't you simply accept that there is an alternate theory that competes with the accepted dogma?"

"I can't do that because there would be no limit to the number of 'alternate theories' I would then have to accept. As a historian, I do try to have an open mind. But I also have to be discerning. Something you never seem to be able to do."

As soon as James said his last line, he wished he could take it back. He always did this, he reflected. *Something about my sister just goads me,* he thought.

There was a long silent pause before Mary responded.

"Can I just pretend you actually called me to brighten up my day?" she asked heavy with sarcasm. "Or do I have to accept that my only brother just delights in calling me out of the blue and then insulting me?"

"Mary, I'm sorry," James responded. "Sometimes I feel like we are as bad as cats and dogs. I certainly didn't mean everything I said. It just came out. I truly did call you to brighten up your day. I thought you would be excited to hear that a reporter is actually contemplating a story on the Enloe legend."

There was another brief pause, but Mary came out of it with her sarcasm gone, replaced by her more merry optimism.

"Thanks, I am actually interested. Sometimes I feel like the last librarian in a library about to close. As if the legend will be lost for all time when I die."

"Sis, for all my hostility towards the theory, I don't really belittle you for believing it. It is just something of which I don't believe."

"Well, we've certainly disagreed on enough in our lives that one more thing doesn't really matter does it?" Mary inquired.

"No, not at all," James answered. "Tell you what, if this story goes further, perhaps I'll refer this reporter to you."

"That would be sweet, James."

As Mary spoke, James glanced at the time on his computer and realized he was going to be late for his class if he didn't leave right away. He looked at his watch confirming the time and then quickly told Mary.

"Look sis, I'm late for a class, so I have to go. I will keep you informed," James promised.

Mary sighed, "Okay, I understand, but next time call me when you have more time to talk. Okay?"

"Will do sis. Love you. Bye."

James hung up the phone and quickly began collecting his teaching materials. As he hustled out the door, he looked up at the clock on the wall and realized that having multiple ways to tell time everywhere did serve a purpose.

"Keeps you on schedule," he mused.

Phoenix

Mary heard her brother's phone click indicating he had hung up. For a minute she stared at a picture of James and herself with arms over each other's shoulders. She tried to remember where and when the photo had been taken, but the memory was elusive. Her thoughts turned to the main topic of his call, the Enloe story. She could remember when she first heard the story. It was her grandmother talking to her and James while they were visiting at their grandparent's house in Louisville. She still remembered her grandmother's soft drawl as she declared, "You know we're really related to Abraham Lincoln, though they try to hide it."

For grandma, "they" meant the government, some secret conspirators somewhere in a poorly lit room. But as young children, she and James had listened with rapt attention.

"Your grandfather's great, grand uncle was the real father of Abraham Lincoln, the greatest president that ever lived, God bless his soul."

Mary remembered being very confused with all the "greats" and "grands" mixed together with the word "uncle." Her grandmother had tried to explain this concept, but then moved on to explain the story. Mary always had assumed that the Enloe story, as told to her by her grandmother, was probably exaggerated or had fictitious parts. But at the core, her grandmother seemed very convincing that Abraham Lincoln had been fathered by an Enloe. Her grandmother had also been very certain that, after Lincoln's assassination, the story had been intentionally swept under the carpet. The story had made a deep impression on Mary and she always held out hope that her genealogy work would uncover evidence that would make even her insolent brother, James, have to admit that their grandmother had been right all along.

Mary shook herself out of her daydream, and turned her attention to her computer. When James had called she was settling in to attack her email and continue her genealogy research. She promptly found the email from Kim Poole, opened it, and read Kim's story explaining that her family's name had changed from Thomas to Poole.

Well Kim, I don't see how that relates to the Enloes. Nor do I see how I can help you. Mary thought a little more and then began crafting a reply email.

Dear Kim,

I don't have any records linking Thomases and Enloes in that era. I am also somewhat perplexed. You indicate that your family changed its name from Thomas to Poole. But how does this relate to the Enloes? In any case, I do not show any Enloes in the Denver area during the post-Civil War era. That does not mean that there were not any, of course. We certainly do not have records for every Enloe that lived back then. In fact, I know that there are some Enloes from that era that we cannot account for. They quite well could have wound up working in Colorado and never left a paper trial for us modern-day folks to follow. I would like to better understand how this relates to the Enloes.

Very truly yours,
Mary

As always, Mary ran a spell check and reviewed her email before sending it. She turned to her other email and, once she had polished that off, began to dig into genealogy. She looked at her research checklist of what assignments she had given herself. They were a mixture of searches for particular names, research to do on possible databases that might be lurking somewhere, and some records to go through looking for related names. When Mary searched, she used both general internet searches as well as research in genealogy websites and databases. She had learned that the internet was acquiring information faster than genealogists could pull it out and put it into family trees and other online genealogy documents. She had also learned to carefully craft her searches. There was so much information out there that you could skip right by the one piece of information you truly wanted while wasting valuable time chasing red herrings and minor pieces of information.

After looking at her list, nothing really jumped out at her. *Probably the effect my brother has on me,* she thought. So, instead of tackling any particular task, she decided to visit her regular genealogy bulletin boards. After signing in to several, she reached the Enloe bulletin board where she had seen Kim's post. Today, a few of her "regular" Enloe cousins had posted a few comments and started a dialogue about them. She joined one dialogue for a few minutes, adding her own comments and insights. Once she felt like she had adequately added to the flurry of comments, she went through some of the posts made by strangers and persons new to the board.

In the midst of those posts, she found Sean's message about Enloe and Lincoln. *Wow, two times in one day!* Mary thought. *First my brother and now a posted message.* The post read:

> *Hello, I am looking for information about any relation between an Enloe and Abraham Lincoln. Please reply or email me directly if you have any such information.*
>
> *Thanks, Sean*

Mary noted the email address associated with the post and decided to reply directly to him via email. She switched over to her email program and began typing a reply:

> *Dear Sean,*
>
> *I am an Enloe, and a genealogist-hobbyist. I have information about the story of Abraham Lincoln being fathered by Abraham*

Enloe. Please feel free to contact me with any questions you have.
Very truly yours,
Mary

After her faithful spell check, she sent the email. She thought about forwarding a copy to her brother with a snide remark, but decided against it. She smiled to herself as she clicked back to the Enloe bulletin board. The dialogue there was heating up about whether Paul Enloe who had lived in Florida was the same Paul Enloe born 40 years earlier in Philadelphia. Mary eagerly jumped into the "conversation" with a post of her own.

Seattle

Sean slammed his car door shut and then pulled up on the handle to make sure it locked. It was an early model car and lacked the modern remote key chain locking device. But he was fine with that. He turned away from his car and began rolling his luggage to the shuttle station. He felt embarrassed with a roller bag. *Quite unmanly.* After a recent trip that led him to lugging his large duffle style bag for what seemed like miles, though, he decided to break down and bring a rolling bag.

I have to admit, he thought, *the rolling thing feels easier. Bet it will get stuck on cobblestones though.* In his mind he saw himself bouncing his way down a French or Italian street and cursing his roller bag. *Maybe I'll leave it behind for my next trip to Europe,* he thought.

He reached the shuttle stop and paused, noticing how nicely the roller bag sat upright with his smaller backpack perched on top. He glanced at his watch and then looked around at the colorful sea of cars, all left behind by departing passengers. Now, his car had joined the herd. He had time and the shuttle was nowhere in sight, so he decided to call the professor. He reached into a jacket pocket and pulled out his cell phone. He scrolled to Professor Enloe's office number and selected it. Holding it up to his ear, he heard the ringing followed by the professor's recorded greeting.

"Hello, this is Professor James Enloe. You have reached my voicemail so please leave me a brief message. If you are a student in one of my classes, please indicate which class. Thanks."

His greeting was followed by the familiar beep. Sean spoke.

"Hi Professor. This is Sean Johnson, the journalist from Seattle. Listen, I am making a trip to the Kentucky Lincoln sites. I then would like to drop by Knoxville to meet and perhaps interview you further. I expect that visiting the sites will help me gain more concrete knowledge. Interviewing you afterwards should really help draw it all together. You can reach me on my cell to confirm or tell me to leave you alone. I will understand either choice. I know you're not very keen on the Enloe side of this story, but you are still a great source for understanding Lincoln's childhood and how it shaped him as an adult and as the president. So, for that reason, alone, I hope you will meet with me. I'll be in Knoxville the twenty-fifth and twenty-sixth. Thanks."

Sean ended his call by leaving his cell number for the professor and then hung up. As he pushed his phone back into the deep inner pocket of his black windbreaker, he saw the shuttle approaching.

…..

A little while later, Sean reached the inner gate area of the Seattle airport. Security was light and fairly painless. The airport had completed a substantial renovation and now featured a huge glass wall that stretched at least 100 feet in the air and provided a panoramic view of the runways and planes parked or moving about. Sean got himself a cup of coffee and began walking to his gate, his earpiece hanging out of his ear so he could talk hands free on his cell as he "rolled" along. He dialed up Paul's desk number and initiated the call. He then began walking towards his gate, coffee in one hand and roller bag following behind him, pulled with the other hand. He was really hoping the editor was not at his desk, which would allow him to leave a voicemail. His hope was not awarded though, as he heard Paul's voice in his ear.

"Sean, how are you?" Paul's cheerful voice asked him.

"Fine, just fine," Sean answered back.

"That's great, Sean. How's that Lincoln story?"

"You'll be happy to hear that I'm on my way this very instant to a one room cabin in Hodgenville, Kentucky."

"Great. I'm confident you'll do a great job." Sean was not sure whether Paul was smirking or his eyes were twinkling on the other end of the line, but he was certain it was one or the other.

"Honestly Paul, I'm more enamored with the story now. Everyone I talk to has a very strong opinion one way or the other and I get a sense of evasiveness in the academic community."

"I suspected as much," Paul replied confidently.

"Yes you did," Sean admitted. "Most people don't believe it. Or perhaps better said, don't want to believe it. But they're all interested, if not passionate. That's exactly what will make this story hot. Even better, I have picked up on another element to the story."

Sean hesitated, forcing Paul to have to ask, which he did.

"What other element?"

"Genealogy, Paul. Genealogy. There's a whole army of Americans out there researching their family trees. The web has turned them into amateur genealogists. They maintain websites, spend all their free time digging for facts, sharing information and building files in family tree software. It's a big movement Paul, and the Lincoln-Enloe story cuts right into the heart of genealogy. The idea that the greatest president could be an illegitimate child is the ultimate example of the kinds of skeletons that family history researchers might unearth."

Sean stopped to catch his breath, realizing that he himself was beginning to sound a bit passionate. "So, my story hits two veins of culture, and really weaves them together."

Paul laughed. "Okay, okay. I don't think I ever have heard you so passionate before. Is this all you called me for? To tell me I was right?"

"That, and I wanted to keep you updated on my whereabouts."

"Thanks," Paul replied. "Now be careful and make sure you don't decide to stay in Kentucky. I'm told the rolling meadows, white-fenced horse corrals, and especially the women, can be quite enticing."

Sean laughed, "No worries, Paul. How could I ever move so far away from my favorite editor."

"That is exactly what I was thinking, Sean, exactly what I was thinking."

Atlanta

Terry Sheriden looked at his computer monitor as he scrolled through the search engine results. He had done a basic name search on the internet for Kim Poole. The results were a little too numerous though, so he had entered her city name, Kansas City, to see if that gave him better results. It had. There was only one Kim Poole in Kansas City. Better, he had found her home address, as well as her business name.

It's too easy, Terry thought. *With the internet, anybody can do what my security company used to do as a specialized data service.*

Still, there were things that his company could do that the internet could not. Like abortion records, credit reports, phone records, and all sorts of other more personal and useful information. Still, internet search engines had become the starting point for most investigations. This search was no exception.

As Terry was reviewing Kim's data, his mind flashed back to his conversation with his brother. Mike was, as usual, concerned but less willing to do what was necessary to solve the problem. He, Terry, on the other hand was less worried, but willing to do whatever was necessary. That always had been the defining difference between he and his brother. That, and Mike's public ambition. Born into the Sheriden fortune, their father had quickly taught them of ruthlessness, preservation of the fortune, and of course, family history.

Mike had shown a desire to be greater than his predecessors. If their father and grandfather had been powerful and successful, then Mike had to be more so. Mike had, Terry reflected, shown signs early on in childhood of the need for public acclaim. In their private grade school, Mike had been insatiable in his quest to lead his classmates.

Not that Terry had a problem with any of his brother's ambitions. Terry's passion was secret power. Being in charge of the Sheriden security company brought him that. He had grown both the company and the power he wielded, but so much had to be kept so secret. Especially in this day and age where government, though as corrupt as ever, was also more capable of detecting behavior it declared illegal. Mike was willing to do what was necessary, but not stupidly so. Where bribery or threats failed, elimination often succeeded. But eliminating threats was getting more dangerous. Every murder brought him closer to being caught, and he knew it. Terry also loved the challenge, though, the sheer raw power of the ultimate weapon in his arsenal of power.

Terry's eyes had glossed over in his reverie; then he realized the information he was collecting was being ignored. He pushed away from his laptop on the desk in his study and stood up to stretch. His eyes darted across the woolen carpeting and luxuriously furnished interior out the window of the Sheriden mansion. He preferred this half submerged room where the window was at ground level. As a child, he had played in this room, considered a basement by his parents. The view from the window was framed by spring flowers and beyond those he could see the evergreen forest across the meadow. It was late in the afternoon and the sun was on the opposite side of the house. He knew his brother was gone for the day. The servants would be in their various assigned rooms cleaning, or getting ready to go home.

Terry cared little for "help," preferring, instead, to work alone. On occasion, he relied on certain security specialists he had weaned and recruited over the years. In some ways they were his private army; most were former military. They did his bidding well, though he was smart enough to never task them with the real tough jobs, or the ones personal to the family. Those were his alone.

Sitting back down in the desk chair, Terry returned to the laptop and continued reviewing Kim's story. Single mom. Child enrolled in public school. Ex-husband in Dallas, a lawyer. Not satisfied with the information the basic internet search had offered, he entered his company portal and ordered up more confidential information. First, he found her social security number from some loan files and then ordered her credit report. While waiting for that to download, he began noting down details of her life in a small notebook. The credit report arrived, telling him that her business was not all that healthy.

"Must really need the alimony from your ex, Kim." Terry muttered as he made more notes.

Satisfied that he now knew enough specifics about where Kim lived, worked, the hours of her business, the make of her car and all the other helpful data he might need, he decided to check the searches that had spotted her inquiry and alerted him in the first place. Nothing new had appeared from the target of his inquiry. Nothing new mentioning Jacob Thomas either. And nothing connecting Enloe to Thomas. He pondered the original post.

Denver? Is that where the young Thomas had disappeared to so many years ago?

It made sense, he realized. At the end of the Civil War, the transcontinental railroad led the way into a great western expansion that many young men could join, find new identities and live out their lives.

Terry leaned back and stared up towards the ceiling. His eyes lost their focus again as his face developed a hard expression.

I think I need to pay you a visit, Ms. Poole, he thought. *See what you know and what caused you to head down this path.*

Satisfied that he had chosen a course of action, Terry's gaze flipped back down from the ceiling. He turned his laptop off, closed and shoved it into his ever present travel bag along with his notebook and usual desk items. Then he grabbed the bag and pulled it over his shoulder, grabbing his cell phone with his other hand. As he headed out of his office to go up to his bedroom in the mansion, he pulled up his brother's cell number and dialed it.

A few rings later his brother answered. "Hello, what's up?"

Terry smiled, eager for his next task. "I'm heading west to visit the subject of our interest. Not sure what the right course will be, but this person appears to have started this inquiry out of the blue. She may have stumbled onto something that gave her a clue."

He listened for his brother's voice to respond. It took a few moments though as Mike digested Terry's words.

"Okay. Be careful," Mike began. "Don't leave any traces of your presence. I realize you hear this from me every time, but my campaign is heating up and there will be little room for adverse news, even if it's only loosely connected to us or the company."

Mike paused again.

"Keep it clean brother," he finally warned. "I know you are capable of anything, but think before you act."

"Don't I always, my brother, don't I always?" Terry hung up without letting Mike respond. Mike, he was sure, could handle that. He always did. While they were talking, Terry had reached his bedroom and headed in to grab a few clothes.

Chapter Five

Thursday, April 23
Kansas City

Kim managed to arrive early at her store, leaving Abby to make her own breakfast and then go to school. It was a rainy, thunderstorm threatening, and windy day and she expected a very slow day in the store. Nevertheless, she had awoken early and found herself restless and feeling a need to tackle business-related tasks. Her windshield wipers had been busy all the way to work, pushing some large rain pellets off the windshield faster than nature could dump them on. Mostly, it had been a tie, she thought, with a constant smearing of water on the windshield deterring her view the whole early morning drive to her business. Now in her store, hours before opening, she had time to get some paperwork done, as well as do some digging into her new passion and quest.

Kim was tucked back in her office, a hot coffee in one hand as her computer started up. Around her, plenty of undone paperwork was calling for her attention. Payroll needed attention. Receipts and daily summaries needed organizing and filing. Inventory and supplies needed ordering. Returns and defectives needed processing. Running a business always left her feeling behind schedule and out-of-control. She had ostensibly come into work early to attack that feeling.

But right now she could not get her mind off one thing. *Who was Jacob Thomas?* She considered her father's message and felt the anger rising. *How could he never tell me this? Half of my family tree has been a waste of time!* As she reviewed the events of the last few days, she tried to sum it up, tried to make sense of it. But it just did not make sense. She could accept the probability that it was true that her ancestor had really been a Thomas, not a Poole, but nothing made sense about Lincoln, the Civil War and the Enloes. *Was Jacob really an Enloe and not a Thomas? Was that what he was trying to say? Was being a Thomas a lie behind a lie to hide a truth? But why hide anything?* she thought. *What could be so damaging and so dangerous to go to such lengths?*

Finding no answers amongst all those questions, she decided to turn back to the internet. Logging on, she first checked her email. She immediately saw the email from Mary and opened it. After reading Mary's explanation and seeing her questions, Kim contemplated whether to tell Mary more of what she knew.

I would like to better understand how this relates to the Enloes, Mary had wrote.

Kim thought about this. *I'm getting nowhere and Mary seems as straight as they come. She also seems to know more about the Enloes than anybody else I have found.* Her father's repeated warning, coming originally from her great, great grandfather, also came to her mind. *"He also warned him to do nothing with that information because it was too dangerous."* She was told to *"Wait until the Enloes come forward."* Kim weighed those cautions against her need to find answers.

Hell, the Enloes have already come forward. I'm exchanging emails with one right now. This is silly, how can information about Enloes, Thomases and Pooles, all from 150 years ago, be so dangerous today?

Kim made up her mind and began composing a reply to Mary.

Mary

　　I am going to tell you some things that I ask you to not make public, at least not now. I have been told by my family that my great, great grandfather Jacob Poole was really Jacob Thomas and that he changed his name. So, I am not really looking for a Jacob Enloe, though I might be.

Kim paused and thought, *This is so damned confusing, I don't actu-*

ally know who I am looking for. She continued her email to Mary.

> *What I mean is that I am not certain what the truth is. The information I received tells me that somehow Enloes are involved. I have been warned to do nothing with the information, but to wait until the Enloes come forward. I am not sure what that means. Since you are an Enloe, maybe this means something to you. Finally, I was told that the Enloes would tell a secret regarding Abraham Lincoln and the war.*
>
> *Does any of this make sense to you at all? I am still trying to grapple with the idea that I am not really a Poole descendant, but instead a Thomas descendant. So, maybe what I need to find is a Jacob Thomas from Denver, not a Jacob Poole.*
>
> *In any case, I will be very appreciative of any information you have.*
>
> *Thanks,*
>
> *Kim*

Kim finished her email and clicked "send." She watched the email blink away. Curious, she clicked on her "sent emails" folder and opened the email she had just sent to Mary, just to reread it. She read it and stared for a few minutes, the questions and thoughts swirling once more in her head. Finally, she shook herself, turned her attention away from her computer towards the stacks of paper scattered around her desk and began focusing on her business. She started in on her paperwork, the real reason she had come in early. Outside, she could hear the sound of a heavy downpour picking up once again.

Hodgenville, Kentucky

Sean looked up from his map at the highway signs approaching on the right. The Kentucky countryside was mostly gentle rolling hills with sporadic clumps of trees and shrubs occasionally mixed with homes and roadside businesses. Sean had landed in Louisville late yesterday after changing planes in Kansas City. He had picked up his rental car and headed west in the night, staying at a hotel just outside of Louisville. This morning, he rose, checked out early, grabbed a bite to eat at a chain restaurant and began studying his maps.

His plan was to drive farther west, visiting the Abraham Lincoln birthplace park. He found himself already starting to say "supposed" to himself after referring to Lincoln's birth location, birthdate and even when noting Lincoln's "supposed" father, Thomas Lincoln. Not that he necessarily believed the story, but just that he felt the alternative history deserved some respect. Earlier, Sean had read that, once at the birthplace, he would find a replica of the famous "one room" cabin that Lincoln had been reared in. Actually, Sean already had come to understand that even this information was somewhat misleading.

In reality, Abraham Lincoln's family had been somewhat nomadic and the child Abraham not only moved around within Kentucky, but also between Kentucky and Indiana. So, this birthplace was Lincoln's home for only a few years, and old Abe probably remembered nothing of it. If the Lincoln-Enloe story was true, Sean figured that Abraham had either been born before they got to the Hodgenville location or the whole timeline itself was messed up. So far, Sean had learned that a lot of the "true" Lincoln history was based upon things written down after-the-fact and "remembered history." Some of those conclusions were made significantly after-the-fact, which was one more reason Sean felt a need to give the alternative Lincoln-Enloe story some respect. He still had some books coming, more learning to do, and was not ready to decide whether or not he believed the Lincoln-Enloe story. For now, he was willing to give it respect.

Still, accurate or not, the established Lincoln story began at the Abraham Lincoln birthplace and that was Sean's first destination on this trip. Right now, he was stopped at the side of the road, just before a turn-off, trying to decide whether to take it or not. He was near Hodegenville, but not in it. Looking at his map, he decided to continue going straight. He looked back to make sure no cars were coming and pulled back onto the road. By his calculations, he should be a mile or so away. The road was a two lane country highway replete with dusty, gravely sides and driveways with mailboxes perched on posts. It did not look particularly rich, in fact it appeared typical of the rural Kentucky he had seen since leaving Louisville. Nothing super rich or super busy. Just a kind of quiet and remote world separated from the denser, more urban way of life Sean lived within. He had never been to Kentucky, or even Tennessee. He had visited North Carolina once before, but not the western Appalachian end he was heading for on this trip.

A mile and a half down the road he was rewarded with a sign informing him that the Abraham Lincoln Birthplace National Monument entrance was approaching. He came upon it and turned in. He noticed a sleepy motel and store along the entrance drive where guests could walk into the park. The park itself appeared to consist of a tree covered parking lot sloping down from the highway to a park-like building with an area to the rear that must house the cabin. Sean pulled into the mostly empty parking lot and parked his car. *I guess I'm out of season on a late April weekday,* he thought. *Still, the parking lot is not entirely empty.* He could see a few stereotypical vacation RV's and campers, as well as some large cars scattered around the parking lot.

Sean got out of his economy rental car, feeling the warmer midday air and hearing the buzz of happy bugs in the air. *Need to find out what kind of bugs those are,* he noted to himself. He grabbed his camera and notebook from the seat behind him, closed the car up and headed toward the building.

Once inside, he found himself amidst brochures, welcome signs and various photos on the wall. A friendly ranger, a young, blonde-haired lady, was sitting on a stool behind a counter. "Welcome. How can I help you?" she asked.

"I'd like to see the sites. Is there a fee?" Sean already knew there was a five-dollar fee, but he was trying to open the conversation and be friendly.

"It's five dollars to enter the park itself, which includes the cabin and birthplace, as well as a show that starts in..." the ranger paused glancing at a clock on the wall, "six minutes."

"That's a deal." Sean smiled and reached into his pocket for the money. After Sean paid her, the ranger handed him a brochure gesturing toward a room to one side.

"Right that way. The theatre is at the rear of the exhibits. Go through that door for access to the cabin area." Sean thanked her and headed into the exhibit room.

He spent little time browsing the exhibits. Nothing new or surprising stood out. It was as expected: how the family had come to be here, how long they lived here, how hard life was and so on. Sean looked for, but was not surprised to find no mention of any ambiguity or alternative history about Lincoln's birth. *After all, this is a park dedicated to being his birthplace,* he thought. He did see confirmation that this had been a very rural, very un-conquered wilderness in the early 1800's. In Sean's mind, that was a very relevant point. It showed that records would be less frequent and less reliable. It allowed for things to happen differently than they were recorded or remembered.

"The show will be starting now." Sean looked up from the exhibit he was reading to see the ranger herding him and two families toward the theatre door. For a moment, Sean felt his old dislike of lines and crowds surfacing, leftover from his military days. He suppressed the feeling to "rebel" and allowed himself to be shepherded into the room. Once inside, he settled into a comfortable chair and waited for the film to begin.

About thirty minutes later, Sean emerged from the building, walking towards the cabin area. The movie had been much like the exhibits, except that the music and alternating images had done a much better job of creating a sense of the drama of Lincoln's life and how it had all begun at this location. It also reminded Sean of a less relevant but interesting fact that he had read. Thomas Lincoln, perhaps capable of being a good farmer, had failed at it here and in later locations, mostly because of poor choice of location. Sean had read and been told that the soil here was of miserable quality for farming. Looking about as he walked to the cabin, he could see why. The ground felt sunken, dry and tired. He found himself wondering if there had been a rich forest here when Abraham Lincoln's family had arrived, for he could not imagine a reason to stop here and raise a family.

He walked over a slight ridge and the cabin came into view. Actually, what came into view was a Jefferson-like building that looked more at home in Washington D.C. than in the rural setting in which it stood. Sean knew that inside this building would be a replica of the one room cabin. As he approached it, he noticed a few plaques conveying various stories about life for the Lincolns. He entered the building and found himself staring at and into a simple, small cabin. Again, he learned nothing new. Still, he felt that seeing this replica of Lincoln's cabin, in this location where the Lincolns had lived and where Abraham had supposedly been born, gave him a sense of finally nearing the beginning of his story.

Once satisfied that he had seen everything, Sean returned to the main building. As he passed through, he stopped and bought a few souvenirs. As he paid the ranger, he could not resist the temptation to ask her a few questions.

"I wonder if you could answer a question for me?" Sean began. The ranger looked at him with a sense of trained readiness, as if she was ready to hand back the usual standard answers to the usual standard questions.

"What do you know about the story that Abraham Lincoln was actually not fathered by Thomas Lincoln, and that he might not have been born here at all?"

The ranger's expression froze for a moment, and then shifted to a mixture of confusion and, what seemed to Sean, also to be pity. *She thinks I'm a nut,* Sean thought. He now definitely regretted asking her. He was certain she would know nothing of the Lincoln-Enloe story.

"I have never heard of such a story sir," the ranger replied. "Abraham Lincoln was born here at this location on February 12, 1809. His father was Thomas Lincoln…"

"I know, I know, I'm sorry to have asked you that question," Sean interrupted her. "I am a journalist researching an alternative history for a story I'm doing and I really just wanted to get a sense of whether you had even heard of it."

The ranger paused again, studying Sean. "A real story?" She now sounded confused.

"Yes, well as real as anything from almost two hundred years ago can be. So far, it seems possible but I am not done with all my research."

"But we know that Lincoln was born here to Thomas and Nancy Lincoln?" The ranger's voice was quizzical, a slight improvement from confused.

"Do we really?" Sean asked. "I am not so sure exactly what we know. I know there is no birth certificate from a hospital certifying where he was born. I also know that lots of children are born to fathers that are never acknowledged because the mother was married to someone else. Look, I don't mean to try and convince you of this story. It's odd and surprising to you. It is for me, too. But I can tell you that there are a few books about it from the late 1800's all telling of a spoken history about Abraham Lincoln's mother. I have also been learning that we really know little about Nancy Hanks, his mother, and where she was before marrying Thomas Lincoln."

Sean paused after noticing a slightly condescending look come over the ranger's face as if to say, "*Yep he's a nut alright, but I have to be polite and listen to him.*"

"I'm sorry I bothered you ma'am." He muttered and turned to leave as quickly as he could. A family was entering, giving him perfect cover to exit by letting her attention turn to someone else.

Phoenix

Mary was thunderstruck. *Lincoln? Enloe? The War? I just had this conversation with my brother!* Kim's email to her was on the screen. She read it again. *A secret?* Mary sat back. It was clear that Kim was not telling her everything. It also seemed obvious that Kim was sincere. *Why would there need to be caution?* That part was the most confusing to Mary. There was nothing dangerous about history. *Well, nothing dangerous about this old history,* she corrected herself. *Certainly the need to cover up history always had led to dangers. So maybe there was something dangerous a long time ago? But now?*

Mary's routine had been off today. She had gone golfing with Phillip in the morning and was now, at midday, reading her email. Phillip was puttering in the garage, tinkering with who knew what. Soon after they returned, Mary settled into her office where she encountered Kim's cryptic email.

She leaned back and thought. *So, if I am not looking for a Jacob Enloe, then what?* Instead, she realized she was being given a clue about a Lincoln-Enloe angle. *But, then, who is Jacob Thomas and what does*

he have to do with the Enloes? Or Lincoln? Considering this some
more, Mary realized she needed to know more about Kim's source of
information. She leaned towards the computer and began a reply.

> *Dear Kim,*
>   *Your email is confusing, but also surprising. You ask about
> Lincoln and the Enloes. There is a story that Abraham Lincoln's
> real father was an Enloe. The story goes that Nancy Hanks was
> impregnated by Abraham Enloe while working as a servant girl at
> Abraham's household. She was sent back to her home community
> immediately, and the truth was covered over by her marriage to
> Thomas Lincoln who accepted the child as his own. My own grand-
> mother swore that this was the truth. My brother, who is a Lincoln
> historian, does not believe the story, but I do. Still, I am not sure
> how this relates to your inquiry. If you are really looking for Jacob
> Thomas, then why did you ask about Jacob Enloe? And what does
> your inquiry then have to do with Abraham Enloe or Abraham Lin-
> coln? And what is this about the war and about being cautious? I
> am not sure I understand how information from almost 200 years
> ago would have anything to do with the present. It certainly may be
> of interest to historians, particularly Enloe family historians like
> me. I would like to know more about your information, where you
> got it and what it is. Please share.*
>   *Very truly yours,*
>   *Mary*

Mary was excited enough that she clicked send without even spell-
checking the email. She realized this afterwards.

"Mary, you're worse than a teenager sending a text message," she
said aloud. She then began going through the rest of her email. Once
done, Mary returned to Kim's email. Deciding it was worthy of going
into a paper file, she printed a copy. She printed the other emails as
well and then read through them all. It occurred to her that Kim had
mentioned Denver in her earlier correspondence. Curious, she ran a
check for Enloes in Denver. In the 19th Century. She found a few related cousins, but no one coming from the North Carolina community of

Abraham Enloe. Frustrated, she turned to the internet and began doing some searches, trying to connect lines between Lincoln, the Enloes, Jacob Thomas, and Denver, Colorado.

After half an hour of getting nowhere, she gave up. She realized she could do no more until Kim gave her more information. She got up from her desk chair to go make some iced tea and stretch her weary muscles. Golf all morning and computer all afternoon was hard for her to keep up with, she realized as she rubbed her neck.

Atlanta

Michael Sheriden moved gracefully through the rooms and their clumps of people. Not far from his elbow, and always available in a few moments, was his campaign and personal manager, Jessica Ronnels. At five foot, seven inches her medium build, light complexion and brown hair and eyes did not stand out in a crowd. But that was fine, because one of her jobs was ensuring that Michael always stood out. She always dressed in business suits with colors blending her into the crowd. She also always wore a remote earpiece/microphone for her cell phone.

This night, she was fielding inquiries from Michael, meeting and greeting people, and providing them information. This was an important fundraiser for her candidate and so far it was going smoothly. Not that Michael really needed to fundraise, at least not at this political level. If needed, he could personally fund any campaign at the state office level. Later would come a time when he would need fundraising skills. But fundraisers served all sorts of other purposes. They helped build networks of supporters, helped establish positions on issues, and helped set up alliances and deals that would lead to yet more supporters.

The evening began with a briefing before guests arrived. Jessica went over who was attending, explained what interests they represented, and how important or unimportant they were. They also reviewed their strategies and plans for the evening. Now it was mingling and talking-time and Jessica was keeping one eye on Michael and one eye out for targets of interest. When needed, she could step in to steer him somewhere else, whisper information in his ear, or speak to supporters about donations or follow-up meetings. Michael was doing well, she thought, showing signs of mastering politics and running for office. She mused that, assuming everything went as planned in the fall, it was going to be time for Michael to move up a step, either to Governor or Congress. She would be there to do all that was necessary, including fixing problems, facilitating deals, and channeling the energy of his teams to victory.

She watched as a recognizable, but unwelcome, large man in a blue suit approached Michael. Inside she seethed, though no one would know by looking at her. *This guy should not even be here. I bet the Cooks brought him as a guest.* The Cooks, of course, were also not really desired, but since this fundraiser was focused on the timber industry, and since Brian Cook's district was heavy with timber companies they had to invite Brian and his wife Laura. But Brian Cook was the chief reason Michael had decided not to run for Congress several years ago. Brian had some dirt on Michael and it had taken Jessica too long to silence it with some dirt of her own. Brian, everyone knew, had run and lost the race for Congress and was forced to settle back in his state seat. The man in the blue suit, Frank Stone, was a political consultant in the capital and, everyone knew, a strong ally of Brian Cook. To see him here, and even worse, walking right up to Michael, was infuriating to Jessica. She moved to intervene, but Michael beat her to it.

"Ah, Frank. So nice to see you," Michael opened with a smile. "Let me introduce you to the Cavitts. You don't know them, I bet, but you should."

Jessica stopped moving in and watched as Frank actually appeared confused. *Priceless*, she thought.

"You should know them because you lobbied for that successful bill that rescinded all development incentives for forest preservation. The Cavitts were about to conduct a large scale restoration project when YOUR bill killed that. Jeff and Mary Cavitt, may I introduce Frank Stone?"

Michael gestured politely with a sweeping motion that was all grandeur, but of course, was more like a dagger being stuck into Frank's back.

Jessica was so pleased, she was certain her smile was real for a change.

Just as smoothly, Michael stepped out of the conversation leaving Frank seething while quickly trying to gain his composure and develop a strategy for escaping the Cavitts.

Michael moved close to Jessica and hissed with a smile, "See that he gets out of here fast, and tell me later how he got in here."

Jessica, still pleased with how well her boss had swept Frank aside, only managed a quick retort "Well, he was obviously very un-briefed and unprepared. Unlike you, who handled that perfectly."

Michael looked at her for a moment and then let his own smile shift from forced to real. "You're right of course, good job."

Michael then turned and began moving towards another group while Jessica made a quick call on her voice activated cell phone earpiece summoning one of her "bouncers." She hated having to use the goons in a public setting like this, but Frank was probably ready to leave at this point anyway.

Kansas City

Terry stepped down from the Sheriden jet and stepped onto the tarmac at the Kansas City airport. He carried his own bags over his shoulder, holding a disdain for rolling suitcases. Mostly, he was not mobile enough with rigid square bags that had to be rolled or carried by handles. More than once, he had needed to sprint where he was going. For that reason, he also dressed in sporty light clothing and had dress shoes with gripping rubber soles. While not a hit man, in the strict sense of the word, he certainly was nearly always on missions that could turn violent very quickly. So he had learned. Some of the learning was at the hands of Sheriden security teams when he was a younger man, though he had since greatly expanded even that team's skills and abilities from the days when his father managed it. The rest was self taught or by instructors he had sought out.

Looking about his surroundings he spotted the exit gate. Walking briskly, he exited the tarmac into an aviation building. At a desk, a woman in a white polo shirt with a logo on it called out, "Mr. Sheriden?"

"That's me." Terry nodded while walking over to her. She handed him a rental contract and a set of car keys. Taking them from her, he turned towards the door leading outside.

"You will find it alongside the building about five cars down," the woman called to him.

Terry nodded over his shoulder and exited the building. Once outside, he clicked on the remote key chain, watching for the telltale blinking lights. He spotted them instantly, exactly where the woman had predicted the car would be. He approached it as he pushed down on the trunk-opening button on the key chain. The car was a silver, sporty, two-door sedan. Tossing his larger bag in the trunk, he shut it and got into the car. Placing his small bag on the passenger seat he unzipped it and pulled a cord out of the bag. He quickly plugged in his cell phone, activated his earpiece and checked his phone.

Finally, Terry reached into his bag, pulled his notebook out and began reviewing his notes and maps briefly to re-commit them to memory. He had been to Kansas City before, but not the areas he was headed to now. Satisfied he was ready, he started the car and began his trek to Kim's house.

.....

At the same time Terry was pulling out of the parking lot, Kim was at home reviewing her email. She left work right after turning over closing duties to Cara and arrived home to find to her surprise that Abby had made dinner. Never mind that it was just salad and some from-the-box noodle dish, Kim was still happily surprised. Much of the time living with a child was a burden and responsibility. But sometimes it was a pleasure, an unexpected bonus. Having dinner waiting was one such time. Of course, sadly, it also made her mildly suspicious, as if there was something Abby wanted, or worse, had done. But she was long past the era when she brought such suspicions out in the open. Now, she was satisfied to let her suspicion linger for a while and if something came of it fine, but if not then that was even better. Another way she justified this approach was simply believing that "whatever will be, will be."

In any case, teenage daughter suspicions or not, Kim was now at her home computer and had found Mary's reply. It made her think about just how serious she should take the caution that she had mentioned to Mary. Something was still lurking in the back of her mind. It was as if her father was whispering in her ear to "be careful." Still, she also felt like she needed desperately to talk with someone about her father's letter. About her family's past. *If not Mary, then who?* she asked herself.

Mary's reply, replete with all its questions back to her, prompted a few new thoughts. She wondered how the story of Lincoln being fathered by an Enloe could connect to her own family history. She thought again, if perhaps her great, great grandfather, Jacob Poole-Thomas was really an Enloe and for some reason was so afraid that he hid this behind a double secret, purposely revealing only the first one. Except, then, she thought, what is the Lincoln connection? *Jacob had been born long after Lincoln's birth, right?* She realized that she did not know exactly when Lincoln was born and quickly went online to look it up. She found his date of birth quickly: February 12, 1809. *Okay, so that makes no sense. Jacob comes along at the closest, twenty years later. Thirty-ish years later, if the date I have for Jacob Poole's birth is accurate.* Kim pondered this some more, considering whether to tell Mary more information.

In the end caution still won out, but not entirely.

Dear Mary,

I really expected most of your questions. Please understand that I have told you most all, but not everything. It is all I can explain to you now, at least in writing. I am surprised to learn of the connection between Lincoln and the Enloes. Is that the only connection you know of? I ask because Lincoln's birth is so much earlier than any reasonable date for when Jacob was around that it seems very unlikely that my Jacob Thomas-to-Jacob Poole story is related to Abraham Lincoln's birth. Still, I have information somehow linking Jacob Thomas, Abraham Lincoln and the Enloes. Can I suggest we talk tomorrow about this? Below, I have listed my work number where you can call me. Before 11 AM central time is ideal.

Kim

Kim then typed her work phone number, adding her home number as well. She sent the email and then thought about the questions some more. She was left with a feeling that she was missing something obvious, something that could connect the dots, explaining this mess. But nothing came to her.

Had Kim gone outside, she might have seen the car parked under a tree, shadowed from the street light. She might have been able to make out a man in the driver's seat. She might even have sensed that the danger she was supposed to be cautious about was sitting one hundred feet away. But she did not go outside, choosing instead to shut her computer off, going to sleep for the night.

Chapter Six

Kim awoke still feeling troubled. A shower and a fresh cup of coffee did little to lift her mood. It was Friday, a week since she had found the troubling letters. She felt more confused now then when the week started. *The shock has worn off, replaced by confusion,* she reflected. *I am going to solve this or go nuts.* She refilled her coffee mug, grabbed her things, and headed toward the garage door. Opening the door to the garage, she called out.

"Abby, I'm leaving. Eat some cereal or a bagel before you go to school, okay?"

Kim heard the usual reply, "Okay Mom" with a hint of annoyance coming through in the pronunciation of the word "mom." She closed the garage door behind her, walked around the front of her SUV and got in, tossing her bag on the passenger seat and sticking her coffee mug in the center console. The mug fit perfectly, though it had taken her a while to find a cup that properly fit. She tapped the button on the visor that activated her garage door opener. As the garage door was opening, she started up the SUV. Once the garage door was open, she quickly backed out, turned into the cul-de-sac and drove away.

She noticed the clouds were gone and that it was looking like a much nicer day than yesterday. Perhaps because her attention was on the sky, she barely noticed the car parked ahead under the tree. In her

peripheral vision she failed to see anyone in it. Had she looked carefully in her rear view mirror after passing, she could have seen a head
peaking up, looking back at her from the driver's rear view mirror. But
again, she did not see the person in the car because she did not look.

.....

Terry watched as Kim left, noting there was only one person in
the vehicle, the mother. Knowing the daughter was probably still in
the house, he settled in to wait. He was not disappointed, as about 20
minutes later a brown-haired teenage girl in pants and a sweater came
out of the house. Terry panicked for a minute, realizing she would be
walking right by the car on the other side of the street. As he pondered
his options, he was relieved to see her pull a cell phone from her purse
and press it to her ear, the ear closest to him. Knowing this would
naturally shift her vision away from him, he slid back down in the car
seat. He could hear her begin to talk as she walked by on the other side
of the street. *Thank God for cell phones*, he thought. *She has no idea
how very thankful she should be.*

After the girl's voice disappeared, Terry glanced at his watch. Still
early. A neighbor might still have to head out. He had seen three cars
leaving from two of the three other houses on the cul-de-sac. Four
adults, two kids. Realizing that he needed to give a bit more time for
the neighborhood to clear out and settle down, he decided to go have
a cup of coffee and come back in an hour.

.....

Arriving at work, Kim parked in her reserved parking spot. She
went up to the rear entrance of her store. After entering a code to turn
off the alarm, she entered, putting her bag down in the office and proceeded to the front, coffee mug still in hand. After tidying the front end
for a while, she retired to the rear area. The phone rang out just as she
was reaching the door to her office. She quickly slid into her office,
switching on the light, and snatched up the phone.

"Hello, Garden World," the practiced words flowed from her
mouth.

"Hello, I'm calling for Kim Poole. Is she available?" Kim heard the
pleasant voice of a woman and knew in an instant it was Mary Enloe.

"This is Kim. I bet this is Mary Enloe."

"It is," Mary replied. "How did you know it was me?"

"Oh, I don't get that many calls in the morning before I open. Besides, your voice sounded just as I had imagined."

"Well, so does yours, honey. Did I call at a good time?"

"Yes this is great, I don't open for another hour and I have finished my work in the front."

"You have a store then?"

"Yep, a lot of work for a little money. But I truly love being my own boss and having a chance to manage something that is all mine." Kim was used to having to explain her "small business" to people.

"Well," Mary began with a subtle change in tone suggesting she was getting down to business. "Your email yesterday certainly surprised me. I am still trying to understand how to go about trying to answer this. Is there more you can tell me?"

Kim thought for a moment. It was now or never, she realized.

"Okay, but you should understand, first, that this week has been shocking. After years of researching my family tree I was up against a dead end on my father's side, at least on the Poole name. Once I reached my great, great grandfather Jacob Poole, there was nothing. No records at all. My father was always evasive the few times I asked him about it." Kim paused, as she realized suddenly why her dad had somehow avoided ever answering her questions directly. *He didn't want to lie to me!*

"I have hit similar snags like that with other people and I'm sure you have."

"Oh yes," Mary affirmed. "Road blocks happen all the time for me."

"So, a week ago today I read that Jacob Poole was actually Jacob Thomas. It was in a letter my dad had written for me as he was dying of cancer. It was a letter intended for me to find after he had died." Kim paused, feeling a bit overwhelmed.

"I'm sorry about your father Kim. When did he pass?"

"December, just before Christmas. I'm doing better these days when I think about him, but sometimes…" Kim let her voice dwindle off. Mary stepped in right away.

"That's okay, it's good to remember and cry sometimes. It brings out the memories of the things we loved about them."

Kim sniffled and then cleared her throat. "Well, my dad left me quite the message." Kim smiled. "It has actually allowed me to replace some of my sadness with anger. About that, he is laughing, I'm sure."

Mary laughed and Kim laughed with her. This seemed to make Kim feel more relaxed. "I'm very glad you called. How long have you been researching the Enloes."

"Oh, for at least thirty years. I inherited my grandmother's records and never really put them down. But with the internet, my efforts have intensified. I have accomplished so much more. About ten years ago, I began seriously trying to complete an Enloe family tree for all my Enloe cousins. It has been wonderful. I meet new cousins all the time, some via email, some via phone, and occasionally some in person. That's my favorite. Nothing is quite like staring at a cousin in the face for the first time and thinking of the two different routes and the time that it took for our branches of the family to connect once again."

"Well, I haven't had that kind of success. Of course, if all my information is as good as Jacob Poole-Thomas then I probably won't get anywhere."

Mary took the chance to bring the conversation back on topic. "So the letter from your father told you more than just the name change?"

"Yes, my father's letter was both cryptic and straightforward." Kim paused and instinctively decided to tell Mary all of the instructions. "He told me, uhh, hold on. Let me pull the letter out."

Kim reached into the file she brought from home. She grabbed the originals rather than the copies, hoping there would be something on them she had missed.

"He tells me that Jacob spoke to his son, my great grandfather, while on his deathbed. That he warned him to be careful. He warned him to act only when the time was right. He gave him a letter which was passed down from generation to generation. It was enclosed with my father's letter. It reads 'Wait until the Enloes come forth and then tell our secret of President Lincoln and the War. Look then, and only then, at my words and discover their other meaning'." Kim finished reading and paused. "That's it, that's all I have to go on."

"Wow, that is truly amazing." Kim could tell that Mary was excited. "It's a real mystery. And it involves Abraham Lincoln."

"Well, it claims to." Kim felt the skeptic role coming on. "I mean, it could all be a farce."

"Oh no, Kim, nobody does something like that on their deathbed. At least nobody sane." Mary paused. "Any history of mental illness in your family?"

"None that I know of, except for maybe me, now. I have been questioning whether this is all a dream."

Mary and Kim both laughed again. After the merriment, it was Mary who first turned serious. "Look. I think this is real, and it's very fascinating, especially the warning. That adds a whole other element to your story. Whatever the secret was, it was something that could endanger your great, great grandfather. That makes it a hell of a secret. And one that has presumably stayed secret."

Mary thought out loud. "Let's see, Lincoln, the War, Enloes, and a man changing his name. Why does a man change his name? Jacob Thomas not only warned his family, he even changed his name presumably to keep safe."

Kim could tell that Mary was getting more excited. "Okay, but I am still stuck at the beginning. I cannot get beyond Jacob. Beyond these clues. The only thing I have found is what you told me, that there is a story that an Enloe was the real father of Lincoln."

"Tell me everything you know about Jacob," Mary jumped in. "Where he lived, who his children were, what he did for a living. Everything!"

Kim did, pulling mostly from memory, but also from a few documents she had thrown into the file. She ended by explaining that she had never heard any mention of his parents or where he was born. She had always assumed he was from Denver.

"Okay, that is all real good," Mary said, sounding a bit distracted. Kim suspected Mary's mind was now churning through the information she had provided. "I am going to ponder this. I'll do some more research and then see what I can come up with. Give me a day or so."

"Take as long as you need. I really appreciate your help."

"Okay then, I'd better get to work. It was very nice talking with you Kim. I hope we can meet in person someday."

" Me too, Mary."

They said good-bye and Kim hung up the phone. Her ear had become numb from the length of the phone call. She glanced at the clock above her desk. *Eleven o'clock, time to open up the store.* She grabbed her keys and headed to the front.

.....

At the same time, Terry was just about done with Kim's house. He had returned at 9:30. He simply walked up to the front door and quickly jimmied the lock. Entering, he then closed the door behind him after a quick glance around to verify that he had not been noticed. He then repeated his look out the front and side windows. Satisfied that all was calm, he next turned to the task at hand. The task, of course, was to scour the house for information about why Kim Poole was searching for Jacob Thomas and the Enloes. He followed his usual routine. First, a walk through every room taking inventory. Then a methodical check in order of priority from most likely source to lowest likelihood. He had put the daughter's room at the bottom of the list and that was the space he had just finished an hour and a half after entering. He had struck gold mostly on the computer. It had been unprotected so he had full access to all the computer's files, including her emails. He quickly found the emails to Mary Enloe and read them through. That was the goldmine. For the next hour he searched the house very carefully for the documents or whatever the source of Kim's information had been.

It had been an effort in futility. Terry had found nothing. Standing now in front of Kim's computer, he realized that she had probably taken her records with her. Because he had found Kim's genealogy files, it made sense that he would have found the source of Kim's information, had it been here. Satisfied there was nothing left to find in the house, Terry mentally checked off his actions in the house. Doors were in their original condition. He had kept gloves on the whole time. Computer was off. His notebook, tools and camera were back in his bag. Convinced he was ready to leave, he looked out the front and side windows again. All appeared quiet. He locked the front door from the inside and exited the house through the garage where it was easiest to leave the door locked behind him. After peering over the side fence, he went through the gate, walked down to the sidewalk and turned to leave the cul-de-sac. One more glance around showed nothing and he continued walking out of the cul-de-sac and down the next street to the right, where his car was waiting. Terry got in, started the car and drove off.

He went only a few blocks, pulling into a shopping center parking lot where he parked the car. He reclined his seat and began thinking things over. He had not found the source of information that Kim Poole-Thomas was working from, but he had learned that Mary Enloe might already know more than she should. His choices were to stay or leave. He could stay in town until the evening, when Kim would be home. She would most likely bring the records home with her, but there was a chance she would not. Then he would be forced to make her take him to the store. There was also the complication of the daughter. It sounded too messy. Returning to the same house in the same day was also something he did not want to do. At least not before changing cars, and probably even his appearance.

No, Terry concluded, better to go follow up on the Mary woman. She was too experienced to not figure things out further. *Just like the old man in Los Angeles,* he thought. *It would be a shame, but that might be what is necessary.* Satisfied with his new course of action, he started the car and drove toward his hotel. On the way he called the airport, scheduling the next leg of his journey. With a quick shower, checkout and meal, he would be on his way to Phoenix. Tonight, he could completely research the lady.

Terry's last task was to call his brother to update him. He tapped his ear piece and said aloud, "Call Michael." Shortly, he heard the phone ring and then Michael answered.

"Hi bro, I have some news," Terry started off.

"Tell me."

"The lady in Kansas City definitely has something. It sounds like she is a descendant of Jacob Thomas, and if I was a gambling man, I bet she has found some family document that points her towards things that do not tell the whole story."

"You are a gambling man, Terry," Michael explained patiently. "And a very good one. So chances are, you are right."

"My sense is that it's not a very good idea to grab the documents, and besides, maybe we could let her try to chase down the secret some. But keep her isolated."

"I'm not so sure brother," Michael objected. "The longer we wait the higher the risk that she might copy and share the documents."

"Yes, but as a descendant of Jacob Thomas, she is perhaps much better equipped to find the truth than we are."

"Yes, but we don't need the truth exposed," Mike continued his objection. "We should be fine suppressing this recent activity."

"I think that this woman is on the cusp of solving the mystery of what happened to Jacob Thomas. This is more than a genealogist digging around the Lincoln-Enloe connection." Terry paused to collect his thoughts and then continued.

"Meanwhile, she has managed to drag an Enloe family historian into the mix. A lady in Phoenix. They were planning to talk this morning. I am more nervous of her figuring things out too publicly." Terry let his voice drift off. He preferred to never expressly state some things.

Mike read his mind, however. "I understand. So you're headed to Phoenix?"

"Yep, I'll call again tomorrow."

"Okay you do that. Enjoy the weather while you're there. Play a little golf." But Terry had hung up before Michael had finished speaking.

Knoxville

Sean had arrived at the café a little early for his date with the professor. After driving most of yesterday he spent the night in a highway motel on the outskirts of Knoxville. His evening was spent devouring a Lincoln book over beer and pizza. The story was fleshed out enough, he realized. *Just get a bit more color and you'll be ready to write it Sean.* Which was good, because he was getting second thoughts. Nobody liked the story, even though many were intrigued by it.

But, it was a story that should stay alive. It was a viable historical theory. For that reason, the professor's rejection, his dismissal, really bothered Sean. If he, a lowly journalist felt the ethical need to tell this story, perhaps at the risk of his career, then why didn't the professor, a true historian, feel the obligation to ensure that the story was told?

That was the lingering question bothering Sean. As he sat in the café waiting for the professor to arrive, he mulled this question over.

Around him, lots of students, alone and in groups, were studying and talking. He was on the edge of the University of Tennessee campus, in a small café on the ground floor. He liked the pulse, the feel of this town and this school. It was bustling with students. Some seemed serious and others quite celebratory.

His own mind, however, was wrapped around Abraham Lincoln's birth. After meeting with the professor, he was going to head southeast over the Great Smokey Mountains to visit the land of Abraham Enloe in North Carolina. It was tempting to stay here for the night and head over there tomorrow. Deep inside, though, he knew it was the same reluctance he was feeling about the story. The burning question remained whether telling the story would be good or bad for Lincoln.

As Sean sat thinking, his eyes stayed alert, a part of his old training. He noticed those who came and left, what they carried, and how they acted. Thus, he noticed the professor the moment he entered the café. He was tall, in his mid-fifties and dressed in a brown sports coat with tan slacks. The classic professor look, Sean thought. His hair was short, thinning and going gray. Sean stood and waved with a small hand gesture. Probably, the professor had already spotted him. *He and I are the oldest persons in this place.*

"Professor Enloe?" Sean began while reaching out with his hand.

"Yes. Good to meet you, Mr. Johnson." The professor extended his own hand and they shook with firm grips. Sean noticed how large the professor's hands were.

"Can I get you something to drink?" Sean dropped the title of professor, but was going to have a hard time calling him "James" which meant in turn he was going to suffer being called "Mr. Johnson" during the whole interview.

"No, no, I've had more than enough tea and coffee already today."

Sean now could see the smile he "heard" throughout his phone interview. *The professor is truly jovial. Now, I just need to keep him smiling.*

"Okay. Well, let me say that I was up in Hodgenville yesterday, paying my respects to the official birthplace. It was like I was visiting a shrine. I have always admired President Lincoln, and it feels like the more I study his life, his accomplishments, the higher I elevate him. What he took our country through..."

"You're right of course. That is the Lincoln mystique. He seems superhuman for what he endured, how he acted, how firmly he stood and how he led our nation through its worst time. Those were dark days, especially for the southern states." The professor had a great lecture style voice that Sean felt himself falling for. It was too easy to sit back and let him talk.

"It was his origin, his path through life that made him so capable of enduring the stresses he suffered. I think that we could not have elected a better person to serve as president for those times. It is a shining example of a time when our politics did something correct for a change. In this day and age, I think we have given up on there ever being a 'Lincoln President' again."

"And his death, right when the war was ending, elevated him further, as if that were possible. He became a martyr, a hero beyond mere human heroes. We made giant statues of him. We've named streets, buildings and towns after him. Today, we even have cars, pennies, you name it. His name is synonymous with feeling good about yourself."

"I guess that is where my story comes in right?"

"Or does it, Mr. Johnson? Perhaps Abraham Lincoln's life is a reason not to tell a story about his birth that serves no purpose."

"I don't think telling the story serves no purpose. It could be the truth. And history is nothing if we don't strive to tell the whole history, whether we like it or not."

While speaking, Sean watched the professor and could see he was getting to him. He hammered home an important point. "I also have thought about the orphaned children, the bastards, the unwanted kids of our world. Sure, we certainly accept such circumstances more than we did in those days, but those kids still carry a burden. Why can't the greatest president our country ever had also be one of them, an inspiration to lift them?"

A smile came over Professor Enloe's face. "Very good, Mr. Johnson. Well said. You're right of course. For all those reasons."

The professor looked away for a minute and then focused back on

Sean. "I think that for me, it is very hard to tell the story, or to endorse it. Yes, I am a Lincoln historian, but I am also an Enloe. I will be perceived as a nut, or at least as being biased, if I promote a story that says I am related to Lincoln, illegitimately or otherwise. So, I think I suppress the story to protect myself."

Professor Enloe, pausing again, looked about before continuing. "I had a conversation about this topic with my sister two days ago. I was hard on her. It came up because of you." He pointed a finger at Sean, but with a twinkle in his eye.

"I told her about you calling me. The conversation went downhill from there. She truly believes the story." He sighed. "She reminded me of our grandmother, who told us the story many times. She believed it and she was not even an Enloe, just married to one. But her family came from the country where Abraham Enloe had lived and it was a strong oral history. I think the nation was just not ready to hear it. Not right after their president was assassinated. Not right after he had given his life to keep the nation whole. Not right after so many people had died or been gravely harmed. No, the nation wanted a simpler story and there was no room for a story about Lincoln not being a Lincoln."

"Look, I should tell you this. I don't know whether the story is true or not. I can tell you it seems possible. But beyond that, the story died with the people that populated western North Carolina in the early 1800's. We have little to go on. Even the use of DNA could probably never answer the question. So many of the people of that era were buried in small cemeteries that have long since faded off the face of the earth. But even if it could, I don't think finding the answer would be a good idea. Better to let the story live as it will live."

Sean waited for the professor to finish talking. He had gotten a sad and tired look on his face as he continued. Sean decided to bring him back to a more factual discussion. He had been scribbling notes furiously, an act that seemed almost sacrilege to the professor's heartfelt words. But it did not seem to bother the professor at all.

"So, I think I understand the story itself pretty well. I bought a copy of one of the books from back then that you suggested. It was published around 1890 and recites a version of the story." Sean tried to go on, but the professor held up his hand to pause him, then reached into his sport coat pulling out a small red book.

"This one?" he asked. Seeing Sean's head nod in acknowledgement, he continued. "There were two titles published near the turn of the century. This one is really the only one you can find anywhere. They are mostly in private collections." On a look from Sean, he laughed.

"Yes, I do own the book. I just don't talk about this story. As I said, you are right, history does obligate us to examine all evidence and not paint the story the way we want it to be told, but rather to recite all evidence as much as possible."

Sean examined the book briefly and recognized the title. It was the book he had bought. Seeing how small it was made him grimace at what he had paid for it.

"Yes, this is the book waiting for me at home. Or at least it better be." Sean smiled at his own joke. "So, give me the best evidence supporting the Lincoln-Enloe story."

"Well, it is the presence of a strong oral history of the story and our lack of knowing much about Nancy Hanks. She died long before she was anybody, before Abraham Lincoln was anybody. I think there are possibly three scraps of paper recording something about her. None of them tell us how she came to be with Thomas Lincoln or even where she grew up, or who her parents were. I recall that we do know she was an illegitimate child and that she saw firsthand what that kind of life was like. So she had good reason to cover the story up, to convince Thomas Lincoln to accept the child as his own."

"And the best evidence against it?"

"I think the best evidence is that Abraham would have had to have been older than his sister, unless her birth date was also changed. Under the alternate theory, Abraham Lincoln would likely have been born around 1806, making him three years older than he was treated as being. Instead of being born two years after his sister, he would have been born a year before. Sure, it's possible and families had good reasons to go to great lengths to hide illegitimacy then, but it seems like we would have had some clues that something was wrong. Abe being too tall for his age for instance. Given how tall he was, you would think his height would have stood out compared to his sister."

"We really have no direct evidence informing us when Lincoln was born. So, it's an oral history on the accepted side as well. Also, we can presume, if Abe was illegitimate, that the oral history would have been distorted, manipulated, or covered up to hide that."

The professor paused and looked at his hands. "When you read your copy of that book, you will note one other thing. The author notes that Abraham Lincoln was abnormally tall, with really big hands. Those characteristics did not match his father or others that we know of in his family. Interestingly, the Enloes of western North Carolina were also abnormally tall."

The professor held out his hands and smiled. "I suspect that is where I get my hands from, and my build. Now don't get me wrong. That could cut both ways. The story could have been fabricated because of the height similarity."

"I sometimes think that the most likely explanation is that there was an improper pregnancy in the Abraham Enloe household, that it did involve a woman named Nancy, and that after Lincoln's rise to the presidency, folks in that region, noting the similar build between the Enloes and Abraham, fed the story with rumors. It then took on a life of its own."

"Now note that my 'most likely' version does not exclude Nancy indeed being Abe's mother, but it does not prove that, even if she was, that Abraham was the product of that coupling."

Professor Enloe finished and smiled, "Any more questions?"

Sean looked up from his note scribbling and smiled back. "One more thing. Tomorrow I am heading over to North Carolina to visit Abraham Enloe's old home, or at least the area. I have a few maps, and I know generally where the area is, but I don't know exactly where to go. I figured just seeing the area would be enough to visualize the setting. Any pointers or directions?"

"Sure, head to the area now called Cherokee, south of the Great Smokey Mountains. There is an Indian Casino that dominates the valley's business these days. Back then, the area north of Cherokee was known as the Ocona Lufta valley. It was named after the Ocona Lufta River that flows out of the Smokies. The river is named the "Oconaluftee" now. Abraham Enloe's home was on the river, just inside what is today the Great Smokey Mountain National Park. Let me sketch you a map."

Sean handed over his notebook and pen and watched as the professor drew a map. Once completed, the professor walked him though the directions. Sean took the notebook back and looked at the little red book one more time.

"I did notice the mention of Ocona Lufta in here."

"Yes, I think that name was around until the twenties. I think it and the current name, Oconaluftee, were Cherokee Indian names for the river." The professor peered at Sean. "Anything else?"

"Just one more thing. Is it okay if I contact your sister? Same rules. I just think it may help me to get a different perspective on the story."

Professor Enloe looked at Sean closely for a moment and then nodded. "Yes, that is fine with me. She will probably be thrilled to talk to you. Let me give you her phone number." He grinned. "She thinks I don't know her number, based on how infrequently I call her, but I know it by heart. Don't tell her." With that, the professor reached out for the notebook and pen and jotted Mary's phone number down on the same page as the map.

"Okay, now, is there anything else?"

"Nope, this has been really useful and I truly appreciate your time." He handed the red book back. "Thanks a lot Professor. I'll be in touch if I need more."

They stood up and shook hands again. The professor smiled at Sean and then turned and headed out of the café. Sean sat down and went through his notes, cleaning them up and adding pieces that he had not jotted down on paper the first go around. After some time, he was finished and stood. He gathered his notebook, cell phone and pen and shoved them in his bag which he then slung over his shoulder and headed out. His mind shifted to his next destination, the western end of North Carolina, the old home of Abraham Enloe.

Chapter Seven

Mary was excited. It was Saturday morning and she awoke filled with anticipation. Yesterday, she spent several hours using the internet to search sources. She had focused on Jacob Thomas, knowing that name was the wild card that might make sense of everything. Mary believed that the Poole letters were the key. She had actually begun thinking of the letters as the "Thomas letters" since she concluded that Jacob had been a Thomas. She reached this conclusion after considering whether or not Jacob would have been likely to lie in his deathbed letter. She was convinced his letter was accurate, albeit very mysterious.

For quite a while she had gotten nowhere. Her husband, Phillip, had long since given up on her going anywhere Friday afternoon and she stayed in her office working away, but then, as she kept trying ideas and thinking her way through the clues from Kim's family, she thought of a direction not yet explored. All this required even more time, but finally, she made a connection, by finding a tidbit of information that loomed as the best clue she had found yet. Following up on it had confirmed that she may have found the link between the various themes and people involved.

The first clue she found made one connection for her, but did not completely link everyone. But then, some more searching had told her where to go next: an archive of old documents related to Lincoln's presidency. There was a microfiche version of the documents in the reserved room at the University of Arizona just down the road from her home.

About a decade ago, the university had received a large collection of documents on Lincoln along with a big cash donation to create a western Lincoln archive. They had obtained or copied, in paper, film and digital format, tons of additional Lincoln records and now provided one of the best Lincoln document sources in the west. Mary had been searching on the internet and kept finding references to documents there. Late last night, she went to the University of Arizona website and found they had a complete archive of what she wanted.

This morning, as soon as the opening hour of the library rolled around, she called and arranged an appointment to inspect certain documents in the archive. The librarian first claimed that the archives were not available on weekends, but Mary had worked her way past that hurdle through gentle pleading and local influence.

Shortly, she was heading to the University of Arizona campus library. Phillip was not all that happy to hear that she was cancelling their golf date, but she knew he would get over it. After seeing her husband off, she straightened the kitchen before heading into her office. She decided to send Kim an email briefly outlining what she had found so far.

Dear Kim,

I may have found some useful clues that will unravel this mystery. I am inspecting some documents today that may prove my theory. If I am correct, then most of this will make sense. Actually, it feels more like I am wrapping it up into a package than unraveling it. I do not want to say more until I am completely convinced that I am right. Let's just say I may have found your Jacob Thomas.

Very truly yours,
Mary

After sending her email, and signing off, she packed her bag and headed to her car in the garage. *This is kind of exciting*, she thought. *Secrets about the President of the United States*. She was also feeling a bit giddy about heading off to a college campus with a bookbag. *It's like I'm eighteen all over again*. Cheerfully, she loaded her bag into the car, got in, and prepared to drive to campus.

Atlanta

Mike watched the rain falling across the valley from his home office window. Unlike his brother, Mike's office was on the top floor of the family mansion and offered a beautiful view across the grassy fields to the tree covered hills. But today, with the rain descending on the Atlanta region, he could not see that far. Mostly, he was staring at the smear of raindrops hitting the glass, then running downward. It was midday Saturday and Michael had retired to his study to do some work. He was scheduled to be at a fundraiser in the evening and knew he would probably stay in Atlanta until Monday when he would need to be there anyway. So, this was his one good opportunity to be alone for some quiet, focused time. His study was mostly off-limits to the staff. He allowed them in to clean his room only when he was present and they were invited, but for the most part he kept them out.

My study. That's a joke. This was my father's study and I've hardly touched a thing since I took it over.

He looked around at the old furniture in the expansive room. Fine mahogany shelves and tables with their deep red hues highlighted a mixture of old books and new files. His desk was the same desk his great grandfather had put in this room, if his father's story was accurate. It was a comfortable room with two doors. One led into his living area and the other into the central hallway that ran through the upper floor of the home. Both doors had advanced locks his brother had installed when their security company had entered the digital age. He could open it with his right index finger or a code. That was it. He could remember Terry warning him to not lose both his finger and his memory or the door would practically have to be destroyed to get inside.

Thinking of his brother made him think of where he was now, on another mission related to their family's past. He had been on these before, but mostly they had been protection missions. This time it appeared different. For the first time, there seemed to be some potential for a chance to put an end to the risk to their family. *Someone has come forward asking all the right questions!*

Michael pushed back from his desk and walked over to the window being pelted by the downpour. He could imagine his father and grandfather looking out this same window. Perhaps even his great grandfather. The words of his father came back to him clearly.

"We have a secret Michael that we must always guard against being exposed," his father had warned him. "A long time ago, when our family rose from the ashes of the Civil War, there were others that wanted us to fail. You must not allow that to happen in your generation."

My generation, Michael mused. *I don't even have any children yet. If I get married right now, it is likely to be more for political reasons than for love. But either reason could produce an heir.*

Michael knew that Terry would never have children. Or if he did, they would never surface in his life. So, it would be left up to him. But for now, his focus, his ambition, was not on furthering his family's future, just his. That meant winning this next campaign as well as taking care of business. In other words, Terry had to be both careful and complete in his efforts.

"No mistakes brother," he said out loud.

He continued in his recollection of his father's warning. His father had explained to Terry and his brother that their family had been highly placed in the Union Army, both at the War Department in the Capital and in Sherman's army marching across the south. Their ancestors had taken on an obligation to invest in and develop in the south following the war. But there were people that disagreed with their tactics and reported their efforts to President Lincoln. The president had penned a letter about the Sheriden effort that was dispatched with another letter. Their family, informed of the letters, had tried to intercept them but their agent disappeared along with the letters. Their father had told them that the family had to be forever on the alert for those letters to surface. Then their father had added another twist, one that changed everything. Something else had been disclosed in the letter that was unexpected. Michael realized he needed to restudy exactly what they knew and did not know about those mysteries.

Turning away from the window, Michael approached a file cabinet built into a wall. It was surrounded by a large bookcase. Reaching out, he grasped the combination lock and spun the dial through its numbers. Once complete, he grasped the locking handle of the cabinet and squeezed. He could hear the satisfying metallic sound that told him the locking mechanism had been released. He pulled the drawer open and quickly spotted the file he needed. He pulled it out, noting the yellowed pages peeking through the edges of the file folder. He took it back to his desk, sat down and flipped it open. There, within the folder, was the guidance left behind by his great grandfather. He had not read it in quite a while. But it was time to go revisit its contents again. He pulled the top sheet of paper closer and began reading.

Oconaluftee River, North Carolina (Cherokee area)

It was a cloudy day in the high country of North Carolina. Still, Sean could make out the ridges of the Great Smokey Mountains located to the north. They were slightly opaque behind a light mist of clouds that were hanging low over the valley. He had driven over the mountains yesterday, mostly in the dark. But even in the night, he could sense their mystique and grandeur. Today, having driven from Bryson to a gently rolling area closer to the foot of the mountains, he could feel their presence looming nearby. His car was in the parking lot of a country store and gas station just south of the Great Smokey Mountain National Park. There was a house nearby, and then fields. And old fences. A little farther down the road he could make out a corral with horses. The country looked poor. *No, that's not it Sean*, he thought to himself. *The buildings are well tended. The people here look more like they have no need to be rich. Like their lives are rich enough just living here.* It made him think of a television show but he could not put his finger on it. Something about the farm life. The show was more of a mockery. *A city person could not comprehend the attraction that a life in the country might offer. If he did, he wouldn't live in the City.*

Sean let his eyes drift downwards from their survey of the land, focusing on the map in his hand. Unfolding it, he spread the map across the hood of the car and bent over studying it. He was north of Cherokee. According to all his research, he was close to the original home of Abraham Enloe. He had asked in Bryson, and in Cherokee, but the mention of "Enloe" brought only blank stares. Clearly, the name was long forgotten. He looked up from the map turning it slightly for a new orientation. Then he continued studying it again. Satisfied where to go next, he folded it up and shoved it into the deep inner pocket of the jacket he was wearing.

Visiting the store seemed like a good idea. Walking across the pavement, he noticed its crumbled condition. Clearly, business was slow. He approached a glass door and pulled it open. It swung easily and he entered. Inside, he was greeted with the standard crowded—*No make that overflowing,* he thought—presentation of merchandise and packaged food. *I could be anywhere in America right now.* In a way, the store felt comforting. To the left, a counter was guarded by a middle aged, heavy set woman studying him.

"Did you figure out where you are?" she asked him in a country-like drawl. It was a pretty voice. Sean realized that she had watched him since he pulled in the parking lot. *You're getting so sloppy. A few years ago, you never would have been surprised to discover you were being watched. It's your soft life.*

"I think so, but where I'm going is not so clear." He smiled and walked over to her. The counter was, of course, carpeted with all sorts of impulse items. His eyes wandered briefly from cigarette lighters shaped like an American Flag to sunglass clips for visors. Looking up at her, he noticed that she was closely watching him. *She's more alert than you Sean,* he teased himself.

Seeing her puzzled expression, he continued.

"You see, I am looking for a very old homestead. It is probably long gone. It was still standing a hundred years ago, but has probably long since been erased. It was the home of Abraham Enloe."

Again, Sean immediately recognized the same blank stare he had seen earlier. *Clearly the Enloes are long gone from these parts.*

"He lived along the Oconaluftee River." This time Sean spoke with a slight questioning sound to his voice, hoping to prompt her to speak. He saw a similar empty expression but still he could see she was considering what he had to say.

"Well there is, or was, an old homestead down the road and up to the left towards the mountains a bit." Now, the clerk's face showed she was considering his inquiry pretty hard. Her forehead was wrinkled up in thought. "There is a creek up there that my brother fished a lot. It feeds into the Oconaluftee. About a mile down the way, you'll see an old dirt road on the left leading up to it."

The clerk paused again and looked at Sean as if deciding whether he could handle more complicated directions. Apparently he passed her inspection.

"As you are going up that road you'll see a clump of trees on the left. There's some old garbage around there and some old wood. I don't know if that is your old homestead, but it's probably as good as any around here." She smiled at him. "Your car should be able to handle it."

Sean smiled back. "Thanks, you've been a big help. I'll get a soda and one of these lighters." He picked up one of the American flag lighters and gave it to her.

"Is there much farming around here anymore?" he asked her as she was tapping on the register keyboard.

Without looking up she answered him. "Nah, I don't think it pays. My husband works at a shop down by the main highway and my brother works at the Indian casino. My parents, they left here a few years back to be closer to Ashville."

She giggled. "Kind of funny really. Parents leave, but us kids are still here."

"Yeah, pretty funny," Sean replied back. "It usually works the other way around."

Sean paid her and grabbed a can of soda from the reach in cooler by the door on his way out. He trotted across the pavement to his car and got inside.

.....

A few minutes later he spotted the dirt road on the left. Or at least he thought it was the one she was talking about. He turned into it, grimacing as the car scratched and bounced on its rutty surface. Along the way were mostly weeds. Everything was green, and Sean wondered why the dirt path was not grown over. He concluded that people had to drive this pretty regularly.

Soon, Sean came upon a clump of trees in a flat area and knew instinctively that he had come upon what had to have been a homestead at one time. The view, the position, even the terrain, all told him that any homesteader would have gone no farther to find a place to set up shop. Parking the car, he got out. He could see some rusty metal and various clumps of paper and other garbage. Weeds and trees were springing up right through the middle of the stuff. Still he could see some very old trees that seemed to create an outline of what had to have been a homestead. Little was left, beyond that.

Sean walked around the site and noticed a few pieces of what looked to be old lumber. But even then, he really had no sense of whether it was from twenty years ago or two hundred. He sat down on the trunk of an old tree that fell down a long time ago.

Sean felt unsatisfied. He was sitting in a place that might have been the Enloe residence. *Might have been. And so what? Even if it was, what good is it to be here? Nobody here knows anything about the Enloes.*

Sean looked about his surroundings. He could see hints that the land around him had been farmed. Clear flat areas with no trees. He tried to imagine life at this location almost two hundred years ago. *When Nancy Hanks might have been here. What a hard life. The land was very untamed back then. There is a reason a town here is named Cherokee.* Then his thoughts turned to Nancy Hank's journey. *Did she come here from Kentucky? Over the Appalachians? A long trip for sure. Did she go back while being pregnant?*

As Sean tapped his legs against the log he sat on, he thought through the story of Nancy Hanks being in the Abraham Enloe household. Looking towards the Great Smokey Mountains he realized that they were passable, not like the Rockies or Sierra Nevada Mountains out west. *But, still, a journey down from and back up to Kentucky would have been long and harrowing.* Sean knew that he probably had a copy of the red book the professor had showed him waiting for him back at his home. It supposedly told a story of how Nancy Hanks made the trip. With that thought, Sean lifted himself up from the log and decided it was time to head home. He realized coming to the Oconaluftee valley had not been extremely educational, but it still helped him gain perspective. Once he had a chance to interview the professor's sister, Mary, he should be able to write his story.

Now in the car and back on the even paved road, he flipped his cell phone open. Looking at his notes on the seat next to him, he read Mary's phone number written on one of the pages and entered it into the phone with one hand while steering with the other. Immediately after dialing, he placed the phone up to his ear. After a pause, he could hear the ringing. After several rings, he heard the predictable "click" followed by a woman's voice.

"Hi, we cannot come to the phone right now. Please leave a message and we'll call you back when we can." *Sounds like an energetic elderly woman*, he thought.

"Hi. This is Sean Johnson calling for Mary Fester. I'm a journalist based in Seattle. I'm doing research for a story on the Lincoln-Enloe theory and have interviewed and met your brother, James. He said it would be fine to talk with you and that you'd probably have some useful insights to offer. You can reach me on Sunday or Monday at this number, my cell." Sean provided his phone number and then decided to add a bit more to his message to intrigue her some. "It is midday Saturday and I have just finished visiting what I think was the homestead of Abraham Enloe. I'll be in route home the rest of the weekend. So perhaps we can talk on Monday. Thanks."

Sean pulled the phone away from his face and pressed the call-end button with his finger. He then dropped the phone on top of his notes and shifted his full attention to finding his way back to Knoxville.

Knoxville

James was sitting in his study at home. He was reading his way through a new article about Lincoln's life as a lawyer in Springfield, Illinois and what hints it gave about his character while president. His thoughts invariably drifted to Sean Johnson and his recent discussions with him about the Lincoln-Enloe connection. For what felt like the umpteenth time, he considered whether he made the right decision to ignore the theory in his professional life as a historian and Lincoln scholar. It was the right thing to do, given that he was personally connected to the story. Promoting it would raise credibility questions about his research and work. This topic was also very sketchy anyway. But, the reporter's questions also rung true in his heart. Historians were supposed to be open and unbiased, he knew. Who would have been better to research and tell the story than himself? He also knew it would have made Mary very happy if he had even acknowledged it in the slightest.

Now curious, James realized that there were pieces to the story he could not remember that well. Getting up from his comfortable leather chair he walked over to the small table at the entrance of his study. There, where he placed it the day before, was the small red book he had shown the reporter. He took the book and returned to his chair.

James settled back into his chair and stared at the book for a moment before opening it. *Such a simple thing, a book. Yet by writing it and seeing it published, the author has probably done more to preserve this version of history than any professional historian.* Feeling the guilt grow from those thoughts, James flipped the book open. *Written by a man with no connections to the Enloes.* He remembered determining that much a long time ago. The book was published in 1898, a time when Lincoln's image was being reworked and lifted up higher as an inspiration for Americans. The Civil War had been over for a couple of generations and the United States was thriving. *Proof that President Lincoln really had saved the nation.* Right after the war, James knew, the elation of the war's end was quickly overcome by the reality of the terrible toll the war had taken on the whole country. The country turned to the west with a vengeance and probably tried to suppress thinking about the war. But, veterans had been everywhere, many maimed.

Forty years later though, the nation had mostly healed, though the South probably never fully recovered. *Here in Appalachia, a region quite divided in its loyalties, many people went west. Others stayed. Many were bitter about the war and all of its leaders.* James knew that Lincoln would not have been nearly as admired and worshiped then or now if he had not been assassinated just as the war was ending. But John Wilkes Booth, in trying to destroy Lincoln, had actually given him a new life, one at a level far greater than the mere mortal taken away by the assassin's bullet. A martyr. A man who did not live on for his imperfections to really show themselves to the world. But instead, a man who died in the moment of his greatest achievement, the security of the nation.

In the period afterwards, there was little need for, or tolerance of, a story of Lincoln being a bastard child of an Enloe. Why dare to strike out at the hero who had died saving a great nation for all? Of course, in the South, feelings were most likely very different for some. But in the decade after the war, the South was essentially an occupied country, suppressed more by the exhaustion of its people from the war than a show of might by the North. But occupied it was. Those in the south, James knew, could little afford the attention they would garner by expressing happiness about throwing mud at the martyred president's reputation. They all saw the quick death of nearly all those involved in the plot to kill Lincoln. Of course, that plot reached deep into the South, a fact only recently being openly stated by historians.

So no, James thought, *nobody was ready or willing to cast a dark light on anything Lincoln then.* But forty years later, an author was willing to do just that and did. As James flipped through the book he noted the quotes from the writer who had taken the time to visit the area and also to interview some Enloes scattered around the county. In fact, James noted, the book provided some excellent material about Enloe ancestors, wholly apart from its documentation of the Lincoln-Enloe story. But as James finished scanning through it, his thoughts came back to the question of whether he, an Enloe and a Lincoln historian, should have, or should now tackle the Lincoln-Enloe story.

James could not find a satisfactory answer and put the book down with a decision to wait until the reporter's story got into circulation.

.....

Several miles outside of Knoxville, Sean had just pulled into a coffee shop along the highway that looked promising as a place to camp for a while so he could go online. He grabbed his work bag from the seat behind him and gathered up his notes and files from the seat next to him and climbed out of his car. Putting his bag down on the blacktop, he leaned forward, arching his back with his arms pushing on his hips. *God, that feels good!* He could feel his back and legs loosening up as he finished stretching out his body. He then picked up his bag and headed into a decidedly non-chain looking coffee shop. *One of the laments of modern America*, he thought for not the first time, *is the endless stream of chain stores all selling the same stuff.* This trip had been no different. Well, slightly different. There was a dissimilar pattern of restaurants in this area than he had seen in most other areas. *Give it a few years, then they'll all be the same.*

A few minutes later, Sean was working on his laptop, mocha and pastry on his left and his notebook and calendar on his right. The coffee shop was not very busy at this late afternoon time. There was one couple sharing coffee gazing at each other from across a table on the other side of the shop, but no other patrons were in sight. Sean had gone online via the local wireless network offered in the coffee shop, and first tackled his email. Lots of the usual stuff, he noted. He found a delivery confirmation for the little red book. He recognized the name of the person who had signed for it. It was the elderly lady next door.

It was sad that he had few friends. His closest friends had probably been his special forces buddies, but after getting out he had little contact with them. They had all scattered in the wind and were now separated by distance, as well as the different lives they were struggling with. He could not blame them. The life they led in the service was so different. He himself had gone from being a trained killer to a journalist.

Sean recalled a history professor he had in college who had spent the better part of an hour lecturing that the most important characteristic of a nation in completing a war, was not whether it won or lost, but how well its army put down their swords and picked up their plows. If they did not, then revolution, civil war or another battle were all likely. Sean reflected, *The professor should be happy about how well his special forces colleagues had indeed separated and moved on with their lives. In fact, that was the essential characteristic of the United States so far. After every war, the military forces energetically went back to being citizens again.*

Sean's thoughts shifted to his quest. He had seen Lincoln's birth-place and the alterative history location where Lincoln could have been conceived. Neither place was very noble or impressive. Just the reverse. It was most interesting to think a great future president of the United States could have had his origins in either one of these locations. Sean began trying to outline the article as he perused his notes. As his eyes reached Mary's name on the notepad, he paused and thought. *Her name actually looks familiar. I've seen it before.* He thought deeply about where he had seen her name. Then it clicked. *An Enloe website! Of course!* He had not connected this Mary with the professor's sister Mary because their last names were different.

Sean launched his web browser and selected the bookmark for the Enloe family genealogy website. A log in screen popped up and Sean had to flip back to some of his early notes to find the name and password he had selected for the site. He found them and entered the required data and was soon back into the genealogy section. He searched for "Mary Fester" and quickly came across many posts made by her. He read a few of them and then clicked on her address to send her an email.

Hi Mary,

My name is Sean Johnson. I left you a voicemail earlier today. I am a freelance journalist doing a story on the Lincoln-Enloe link. I have interviewed your brother James extensively and he suggested I interview you as well. I have traveled the Kentucky, Tennessee and North Carolina circuit for the past few days and would love to get your thoughts and comments on this story before I sit down to write it.

Please give me a call or send me an email with a time to contact you.

Sean

Sean clicked "send" and watched as the email disappeared from view. He then continued reading some of Mary's posts for a few minutes and finally exited the site. Upon reflection, Sean decided to hang around Knoxville for a couple of days to see if he could inter-view the professor face-to-face one more time, especially after he had a chance to talk with his sister. Once he had made up his mind to change his plans, he realized he needed to update Paul and the lady next door of his whereabouts and new schedule. He picked up his cell phone and began making the calls.

Chapter Eight

Sunday, April 26
Phoenix

Mary was buzzing with excitement, but she hardly had any time before she and Phillip would be headed out the door to play golf and visit with some friends afterwards. After skipping out on doing anything with him for two days, she could detect that his frustration had risen enough to merit her devoting some time to him. *Men,* she thought, *tough as nails on the outside, but teddy bears on the inside. Just break through that rough exterior and you'll have yourself a puppy dog. At least privately.* Publicly, Phillip was like any other husband: carefree, nonchalant and independent.

Mary knew there was no cancelling today, or else Phillip would be sulking for a week. That left her little time to update Kim on her research. Her work yesterday at University of Arizona had been very productive and she was excited to share her news. She had found the paper confirmation of what she had been looking for and thought she had also found a clue as to what connected the Enloes to Kim's questions about her family, the Thomases. But, it had taken her hours of going through the microfiche, and she had been extremely exhausted when she returned home. So, she gave some attention to Phillip and then went to sleep, dreaming of Abraham Lincoln's White House amidst the Civil War.

Mary got up early and, after setting out breakfast for her husband, hustled into her office to check her emails. She was distracted by an email from an old friend and fired off a reply. Then she opened Sean's email about calling for an interview. *Funny, I don't remember a phone message,* she thought. Then, she realized that Phillip would have gotten it and had probably forgotten to tell her it was on the machine. *Typical,* she thought, *another man trait.*

Mary thought for a minute. A reporter doing a story on the Lincoln-Enloe connection. *What timing!* She thought about whether she should tell the reporter about Kim's family mystery. After thinking it through she decided Kim should be fine with her explaining only the broad topic with no specific names. So she clicked on reply and crafted an email to Sean.

Dear Sean,

Thank you so much for your email and phone message. I am certainly interested and willing to be interviewed by you. Your inquiry and research comes at a very interesting (and exciting!) time. A lady in Kansas City asked some questions about her family and the Enloes. Her questions have also led towards Lincoln. I have been researching and believe I have found some answers for her, but there still remains some work to be completed. Monday would be a great day to talk.

Very truly yours,

Mary

Mary read through her email, spell checked it, and then sent it. Next, she began a short email to Kim to explain that she had made progress. It occurred to her that Sean might find that Kim had an interesting story to tell as well. So, she wrote a short email to Kim promising to update her on her findings. Finally, she prepared an email to both of them.

Dear Sean and Kim,

Sean is a reporter doing a story on the Lincoln-Enloe connection. Kim is trying to track down information on an ancestor

*of hers and his possible link to the Enloes and Abraham Lincoln.
I think that you, Sean, should contact Kim and see if she will
share her story with you. So now you both have each other's
email addresses.*

> *Very truly yours,*
> *Mary*

Mary checked her email with a little twinkle in her eye. *Kim is probably going to be furious when she sees I've shared a bit of her story with a reporter!* Mary finished her spell check, sent the email and then signed off. *Time for Phillip to get some well deserved attention.*

Knoxville

Sunday began beautifully. Yesterday's clouds were gone and the day looked to be a classic spring day. Sean rose early at his downtown hotel and went running through the University of Tennessee campus. It was early, so he had nearly the whole campus to himself. The staid brick architecture had contrasted perfectly, with the spring foliage and the awakening birds, to put him in a great mood. *The endorphins probably didn't hurt either*, he thought.

Sean was now back at the same café where he had met Professor Enloe two days earlier, but this time he had no appointments. Instead, he was planning on sitting a while, working on outlining the Lincoln story and then turning towards some new story ideas. The day was a distraction though, and he felt a strong urge to take his work to a lawn somewhere where he would find students reading or dozing. They were walking by in front of the café constantly, some stopping briefly to buy a drink. It made Sean feel old to realize that these kids could be his own kids if he had ever had any. Ultimately though, he simply enjoyed having such youthful exuberance around him.

It was Sunday and most students appeared to have little to do. Or perhaps, like him, the students felt the call of nature on this spring day, but unlike him, had completely succumbed to it. As the morning wore on, more and more students passed by the coffee shop with more coming in and staying. Soon, there was a buzz of optimism and energy all around him. That energy and the effects of his early morning run left him happily and energetically working away.

Sean saw Mary's email the moment she sent it. Then, as he was reading it and thinking about it, her second email, sent to him and the Kim Poole person, arrived. He read that one too. He was somewhat confused, but certainly intrigued. *Is Kim another Enloe or is there somehow another family story lurking in the Lincoln-Enloe one?* He read the emails and noted that Mary had said "her family and the Enloes" which certainly implied that Kim's family was different from the Enloes. Leaning back from his laptop he placed his hand on his forehead and studied his notes for a minute. He found nothing suggesting any other connections. *Maybe another family from the Ocona Lufta Valley?* In any case, it seemed clear to him that he should try and talk with Kim, as well as Mary. In some ways, he found this a bit annoying. He had just began feeling like he had his hands around the story and, with a few more questions, would be ready to write it. This Kim woman was a bit of a wrench in the works. However, the reporter in him knew instinctively never to miss a chance to explore the complexity of a story, even if the complexity might be too much, in the end, to include.

Sean crafted a quick reply to Mary, thanking her and indicating he would love to talk with her on Monday. After sending that email he thought about how to approach Kim Poole. She had probably not yet even seen the email introducing them to each other, so Sean sensed he needed to build some credibility quickly if he was going to interview her in time for his story. He also sensed a bit of holding back by Mary, as if Kim might not approve of Mary drawing another person in to her research. After thinking it through, he crafted an email to Kim.

Hi Kim,

I am Sean Johnson. As Mary noted, I am a journalist/reporter researching a story about how Abraham Enloe might be the father of Abraham Lincoln. I am currently in Knoxville, Tennessee where I have interviewed Mary's brother, James Enloe, a history professor and Lincoln scholar.

Sean went on to describe the professor's personality and his reticence to openly endorse or really speak about the Lincoln-Enloe theory. He then explained his story's focus and even candidly admitted his own reservations about insulting or sullying the reputation of the revered Abraham Lincoln.

So, my goal is to write the story with reverence for Abraham Lincoln, with delicacy about the idea that he might be a bastard. But I also want to use the story as an example of how all history is only a rough guess at what actually happened, colored by the biases and preferences of those who wrote it.

I am interviewing Mary Fester tomorrow and would like to interview you as well. However, my time is short and I need to finish this story. So, I am hoping to interview you soon as well. Please let me know if you might have an opportunity on Monday to talk with me.

In the offhand chance that you might not read this email in time, I am going to see if I can find your phone number and call you directly. Please feel free to contact me on my cell any time today (Sunday) or tomorrow.

Thanks,
Sean

Sean sent the email, next turning to the internet to search for a Kim Poole in Kansas City. He quickly found a number for "Kimberly Poole" and placed a call. After a few rings, a young woman answered the phone.

"Hello?"

"Hi, is Kim Poole home?"

"Nope, you'll have to call back later." Sean detected a strong shift in tone and attitude that immediately told him two things. *Teenager and she thinks I'm a solicitor.*

"No wait, please, I'm not a salesperson," Sean said quickly, trying to stop the girl from hanging up.

"Oh really? So you're not going to ask for any money at all? After ten minutes of surveys you're not going ask my mother to join some organization or something?" The girl's voice was half suspicious and half sarcastic. *So this is the daughter,* Sean thought, happy that he had correctly predicted a teenager from the girl's opening remarks. He laughed.

"No, I swear to you, I'm not selling. If I was, believe me you would have driven me away already. I'm a reporter and a lady that has been communicating with your mother, has suggested that your mom would probably like to speak to me." Sean knew he was overstating his knowledge of her mother's interest, but also knew it was very unlikely that the girl would communicate these details to her mom. *I'll be lucky if I can get her to write a message down on paper.*

"My name is Sean Johnson, I'm a reporter and journalist from Seattle, though at the moment I am in Knoxville, Tennessee."

"Knoxville?" the girl said. "What's in Knoxville? Isn't that the country music capital of the world?"

"I think you mean Nashville. Knoxville is the home of the University of Tennessee and aluminum, or at least so far that is what I've learned," Sean explained. "I'm here for a story I'm writing."

"Story? And you want to interview my mom?" Now Sean could detect the girl gaining some interest. "What's it about?"

"I really can't tell you at this point. I have to respect the privacy of others, even if one of the others is your mom. But, I can tell you that my story will probably run in papers all over the country."

"Wow…" Sean could tell the girl's interest was waning. "So you want me to tell her?"

"Well kind of," Sean began. "Listen, what's your name?"

"Abby."

"Okay Abby, what I would really love is if you could grab a pen and paper and jot down a message and a number for me. Okay?" Sean used his most charming voice. It apparently worked.

"No prob. Hold on a minute." There was a thud from the phone being set down. He heard rustling of paper and then Abby returned.

"Okay, shoot."

"My name is Sean Johnson. Tell your mom that I sent her an email too. It's urgent I speak with her if I'm going to include her in my story." He then provided his phone number. "She can call me anytime today."

"Okay." There was a slight pause and then she spoke.

"Well listen, my mom won't be back for a while, so don't expect a call today. Okay?"

"I won't Abby, but you'll see she gets that message?"

"Yep, sure will!"

Sean tried to say good bye, but Abby hung up before he could even start. *Teenagers,* he thought as he hung up as well. *They're the same everywhere.* Still, he was satisfied that Kim's daughter, Abby, would get her mom the message.

Sean turned his focus back to his laptop and decided to research some more, including searches for any Pooles connected to the Enloes or the Lincolns.

Phoenix

Terry patiently sat in his car. He had been sitting in this location for quite a while though and was beginning to sense it was time to leave and come back later. He was parked about 100 yards from Mary's house. He had not seen signs of anyone for two hours and had already moved his car from the other end of the street. It was not the time he had been here that was making him nervous, though, it was the quiet environs of the street. *Apparently,* he reflected, *folks in this retirement community either stay in their homes all day on Sundays or they all leave in the early morning to do things and never come back.* Out of about twenty houses in his zone of observation, he had seen only two cars leave with people in them and not a single walker. That was in three hours. He was concerned that he stood out too much as a single man parked on such a quiet street.

Another reason for both the lack of activity and his lack of comfort was the steady increase in temperature. He had cracked all four windows, but even then he had to start the car every twenty-five minutes or so to cool it down. The sweat dripping down the back of his neck could serve as an indicator for when the car needed cooling. He could simply wait until the stream of moisture trickled all the way down his neck and reached his back. Starting his car like this also bothered him. It could make him stand out too much.

In reality, Terry thought, *my patience has become impatience.* He knew, professionally, that impatience was dangerous and a strong indicator it was time to depart. Without thinking it through further, he started the car, pulled away from the curb and drove down the street, past his target, and out of the neighborhood. His drive took him to a road paralleling a golf course fairway. Out on the course, clumps of golfers, each with two carts, were spread around sporadically as far as he could see. It looked random, but he knew that there was a steady string of golfers following the numbered holes. From the looks of it, most were standing around or leaning on golf clubs or the side of carts and were growing more impatient than he had been.

That's why I don't golf. You can't do it at your preferred speed.

Seeing the backed up golfers made him feel better.

"Perhaps, that's where everyone is," he chuckled to himself. "All out golfing and not enjoying it." His car reached a security gate which opened automatically for him in the exit direction. On the way into the community he had simply tailgated another car. He had been relieved that this development did not have attended security gates, but he also knew that it meant it would be hard to get in during the wee hours of the morning.

Terry decided to return to his hotel and perhaps take a nap. As he drove back, he considered his options. He did not like the feel of the place on Sundays and the more he thought about it, coming back on Monday seemed much better. He also did not want to get stuck outside the golf course community waiting for a car to enter that he could follow to gain access. In the early hours of the morning, he reflected, tailgating in would stand out far too much. So, coming back the next morning, mid-morning, seemed best. He then considered whether he should stake out the place at all. Perhaps it would be better to simply enter the house. If someone were home, so be it. He would cut the phone line first, so there could be no calling out on it. Worse, someone could be talking on the phone just as he approached them.

Terry thought his way through these things as he drove to his hotel near the airport. Traffic was thick, especially for a Sunday. Once he reached his hotel, he parked in the underground garage and took the elevator up to his room. After freshening up, he pulled his laptop out of his bag and set it up. His computer used an encrypted wireless card that found its signal in cellular phone networks and worked over most of the country. Once his computer was up and online he signed into his Sheriden portal and began investigating more about Mary Fester and her life in Phoenix.

Kansas City

It had been a busy Sunday at the shop. Despite any fatigue Kim might have felt from having been on her feet the whole day, the knowledge that her business had benefited from good sales always lifted her spirit. Bridget and a teen that Kim used part-time on the weekends were both on for the Sunday evening closing, so Kim was on her way home early. Traffic was light, and she quickly reached her destination. After parking in the garage, she headed into the house.

Kim could hear the television as soon as she opened the door from the garage. As usual, it was louder than she would have liked, but it was not as loud as Abby often had it. What struck Kim next, though, was far better. The delicious smell of dinner cooking. Her daughter was certainly showing a better side these days, one that Kim certainly felt she could enjoy. She pushed the door fully open and saw Abby at the stove stirring something.

"Hi Mom," Abby called out without taking any attention away from the stove. "You're earlier than I expected. Dinner is close to being ready." Abby turned her head briefly to look over her shoulder at Kim before turning it back.

"I hope you feel like spaghetti with salad, homemade bread and a surprise dessert," she announced happily.

Kim stood still for a moment taking in the sight. Her daughter was acting like the most responsible and considerate teenager in Kansas City. *For the second time in a week no less! It's more than any mom could hope for*, she thought. But, as before, her mind also immediately descended briefly into a mode of suspicion. *What does she want? She must want something!* She repressed that thought as quickly as it had emerged though, and focused back on the pleasure of seeing her daughter enjoying pleasing others.

"You are an absolute delight. You are most certainly my daughter,"

Kim proclaimed as she started moving again. She dropped her bag on the counter by the door to the garage and walked towards Abby. "You have no idea how wonderful it is to see my own daughter busy in the kitchen after my long, busy day in the fields."

Kim reached Abby and extended her arm out to caress the side of Abby's neck and then leaned in and kissed her on the back of her head.

"Oh Mom," Abby squirmed a bit. "Don't get too mushy on me. I'm still that daughter capable of all sorts of insensitive remarks and acts, as you would say. Just remember this the next time I do something to make you angry."

Kim laughed. "Okay, but I still love it!" She dropped her hand, walked past Abby and then turned to look down at the vegetables that Abby was sautéing. "A little less heat, or you'll burn them before they're ready."

"Okay, but that's it," Abby replied, half in irritation and half in humor. "Now out of the kitchen until I call you for dinner!"

"Okay, okay," Kim replied back laughing. She turned to head to her bedroom to change into something more comfortable. As she was leaving the kitchen, Abby called her back.

"Oh, Mom," she called. "There's a message for you by the phone. A reporter wants to talk to you about something that sounds mysterious to me." She paused. "And, he sounds cute."

Kim stopped and turned to the small table with the phone by the wall. *A reporter? That's odd.* Then, Abby's final remark registered with her. "Cute?" she uttered incredulously. "Is this my daughter talking about a man for her mother?"

Abby stopped her stirring at the stove and turned to her mom. A much more serious expression came over her face. "Mom, I love dad and part of me always thinks it would be wonderful to have the two of you back together again. But another part of me knows that will never happen. Sometimes I am acting from the hope. But in the end, I want to see you happy one way or another."

Abby's serious tone stopped Kim in her tracks. *Decidedly more mature than she has ever been,* she thought. She watched as Abby's look mischievously shifted.

"Mom, he really did sound cute," she said, now in a cute girly conspiracy voice.

Abby arched her eyebrows at Kim and they erupted in a short laugh together. Kim turned back to the table. *My daughter is becoming an adult,* she thought, *and very manipulative too. I have to keep an eye on her. Still, it's incredibly pleasant to see Abby acting so balanced, so easy to be around. I could grow to like this version.*

Kim's focus had reached the table and she spotted a handwritten note on a pile of junk mail and letters. She picked it up and read it.

"An email also? What's it all about?"

"Yeah, he said he had also emailed you. He wouldn't tell me what he was calling about. Some story he's writing. Said a lady told him to call you." Abby was back at the stove. "Oh, and he said it was urgent and that you could call him anytime at that number."

"Hmm," Kim pondered out loud. "Okay, thanks."

Finally, Kim turned and headed to her bedroom. *A reporter? A story? He also emailed me? A lady?* Kim thought of Mary when Abby had said "lady." *Why would Mary be talking with a reporter?* Kim decided to check her email.

A few minutes later, after freshening up, Kim was at the computer in her office that occupied the third bedroom of the house. The computer had already been on and online when she had gotten there, having been left in that state by Abby. Kim was quickly into her email inbox and spotted several emails from Mary. She opened them and read Mary's elusive updates on her research, as well as her introduction to Sean Johnson, a reporter. Kim first found the fact that Mary had discussed the Lincoln-Enloe story with a reporter a bit annoying, but as she scrutinized the email she realized that Mary did not actually say much about what Kim had to offer.

What do I have to offer? she thought. *I don't really know anything. All I really have is a sentence or two mentioning 'Enloe' and 'Lincoln.' And a reporter? I was told to be careful!*

As Kim was thinking this through, she spotted the email from Sean, recognizing "sjohnson" in the email address. She double clicked on the email and read it. It was a long email, she noted and fairly descriptive of the reporter's purpose. *He's interviewing Mary?* She found herself wondering what, if anything, Mary had already told him. Again, she felt irritated that Mary had shared the story with the reporter. But then, Kim realized, she herself had not really told Mary everything, nor had she extracted a promise of secrecy. She also told herself, for the umpteenth time, that the need for secrecy and being cautious seemed tremendously overblown. In the back of her mind though, Kim felt she could still hear her dad telling her to be careful.

Kim glanced at the time on the computer screen. It was only 6:30 in the evening. She decided to call the reporter and cautiously find out what exactly he knew. She picked up the cordless phone and dialed the cell number Sean had provided. After a few rings a male voice answered.

"Hello," the voice answered. "This must be Kimberly Poole."

Kim liked the voice, it sounded strong and friendly. She mostly felt suspicious and defensive though, and suppressed the urges to respond to his friendly tone.

"Sean Johnson?"

"Yep that's me," Sean replied. "I really appreciate you returning my call."

Kim replied, keeping a strong tone. "You're welcome. I have to tell you that I am not certain how or why Mary invited you to call me. I had shared some information, in confidence, with her and had expected her to keep it confidential. So, I would like to know what Mary has told you." Kim stopped her speech in a demanding tone, to make it clear she meant business."

"Okay, okay," Sean replied still speaking with a friendly voice, but now he adopted a serious tone. "I can completely understand how you feel. Let me first tell you that Mary told me very little about your interest. In fact, I think I detected her being cautious and respectful of your reservations. Privacy and confidentiality are two things I take very seriously."

Sean paused and then continued, "All Mary told me was that you had asked some questions about your family, Lincoln, and the Enloes, and that I would probably benefit by talking with you. She was decidedly vague."

"I see," Kim said, still sounding quite firm. "What led you to Mary? What's your story about?"

"Let me give you some background," Sean began. "I am a free-lance journalist from Seattle. I mostly write stories for newspapers and magazines and I do a lot with a local paper there."

Sean went on to explain his story and how he had gotten on to it. He finished with a summary of his interviews and conversations with Mary's brother, James. "So the Professor suggested I interview his sister Mary and Mary suggested I include you. I have not yet actually spoken with Mary."

Kim listened patiently to his story. Listening to Sean, fairly openly describe his research and travels and what he had learned from them had relieved her and put her more at ease. Sean also seemed logical in his thinking.

"So, what would be your purpose in including me in your story, Mr. Johnson?"

"Please, call me Sean. I had a hard enough time getting the professor to call me Sean. For that matter, do you know how hard it is to call a professor anything but "professor?""

Kim laughed. "I had that problem in college. Professors always seemed so hard to refer to or speak to without using the title of professor at the beginning."

"Well Professor Enloe has been like that for me," Sean laughed back. "But anyway, I am not sure exactly what your role might be in the story. I really don't know anything about your connection to the Lincoln-Enloe theory."

"Oh yes, that's right." Kim paused and thought about whether to tell some or all of her story. It took her a moment or two and she noticed that Sean was very patient, not saying a thing. She made up her mind to talk to him briefly.

"Okay," Kim began. "I'll tell you some of my connection. But, for reasons I don't want to entirely explain, I may not tell you everything. I have found out that my family name was changed, a long time ago, and that somehow it has to do with President Lincoln and the Enloes." Kim pronounced her last four words as if she was quoting something, even though she knew what she was describing was not actually the way her ancestors had explained things. Before she could continue though, Sean interrupted her.

"Okay, Kim. Hold on. What you've just told me is something very interesting and very different than anything I have come across before." Sean then paused, clearly thinking of how to proceed.

"Listen, I think I want to interview you more formally. I will agree now not to mention you or your story with specifics, unless you give me further permission to do so after our interview." Sean paused again, thinking and then continued. "And I think I would like to meet you and interview you in person. I can come to Kansas City tomorrow, stopping on my way home to Seattle. Does this sound okay with you?"

Kim thought, trying to be rational, but found herself making a quick decision.

"Okay. Yes. If you think it's worth your time. I don't really know much more about the Enloes and this Lincoln story than you have just recited. What makes you think it's worth your time?"

"My sense is that you have a story to tell, Kim," Sean said, back in his friendly voice. "Candidly, I think if we can meet, you'll get more comfortable telling me more of what you know."

At this moment, Abby called to Kim from the Kitchen. "Mom, dinner's ready."

Kim glanced at the time again. It was nearly seven. *Wow, I've been talking to this guy for almost half an hour.*

"Okay, I'm willing to be interviewed. But for now, full confidentiality. Right?"

"You bet," Sean replied. "I've got to change my travel plans. How about if I call you tomorrow, once I get to Kansas City, to set a time and place?"

"That will work. I own a shop, so maybe we could meet there or even nearby. You want to call me on my cell?"

"That sounds good."

Kim gave Sean her cell phone number and then said good-bye.

"I've enjoyed talking with you, Sean. I'm looking forward to meeting you."

"Likewise, Kim."

Kim hung up and thought for a second, not sure why she had so quickly opened up to Sean. *I must intuitively trust him, or I'm just a desperate single mother.* She thought about Abby's comment about

Sean seeming cute. *Well, she's right, he does.*

With that thought, Kim realized that she was keeping Abby waiting and got up to head to the kitchen. She definitely did not want to deter her daughter from cooking dinner more often.

Chapter Nine

In the early morning, Sean was already on the freeway, heading to the airport to fly to Kansas City once he returned his rental car. He was not entirely sure why he was going to Kansas City. It was his instinct, he knew, but he still wanted to understand it. *She's a nice sounding woman, but she barely told you her story, Sean,* he thought. *And here you are running across the country to meet her.* But, he knew it was more than that. She could introduce an entirely different angle for him to inject into his story. Some mystery. Some mystique. *She's not an Enloe, but her ancestor had changed his name because of the Enloes and Lincoln?* It was also a bit confusing. That was where Sean's instinct had kicked in.

Kim's not telling me everything and I think she's onto something good. I think Mary was trying to tell me that. Kim might be afraid of being embarrassed. Or is she just plain afraid? Sean ran these ideas around in his head as he sped south toward the airport. The sky was not overcast, but the television weather forecast predicted rain, a conflict Sean found amusing. It was supposed to be clear in Kansas City, he recalled. *I guess I should expect it to be cloudy.* Sean had booked a mid-morning flight and was staying overnight at a downtown hotel in Kansas City. He had not yet booked his next flight as he was uncertain where he would be going. His choices were to go back to Knoxville, to go to Phoenix to meet Mary, or to head home to Seattle. *In an ideal world, I'd head home.* But after feeling on the cusp of being ready to write the story, he now felt he had a few more stones to overturn.

In some ways, Sean was certain he was going beyond normal efforts for a short story about President Lincoln's lineage. The trip had brought him closer to Abraham Lincoln, the person, rather than Abraham Lincoln, the President. School taught him lots of the details about the president. It had, of course, also taught him details about Lincoln, the person, as well. But seeing Lincoln's birthplace—"supposed" birthplace he reminded himself—and visiting the countryside of the president's youth had given him insights into the president. New interest and energy as well. In fact, Sean was simply enjoying this trip. *Besides, this trip is on Paul's dime, not mine.* Sean knew, though, that his spending was not unlimited and that if he went too far, Paul would balk at reimbursing him fully.

Sean was approaching the highway exit for the small Knoxville airport when he realized he should update the professor about his plans. He pulled his cell phone out and quickly selected and dialed the professor's office number. After a few rings, he heard the professor's recorded response telling him to leave a message.

"Professor, this is Sean Johnson. We were going to possibly meet today, Monday, for a final interview, but I have somewhat changed my plans. I am headed to Kansas City to interview a woman your sister, Mary, suggested I meet. I am also going to interview Mary via the phone today as well. Afterwards, I'll have a better sense of whether I need to return to Knoxville to interview you in person or perhaps call you tomorrow to finish off. I'll call later today or send an email with an update to my plans. You have been a huge help, and I really appreciate that. I also have to tell you that I have thoroughly enjoyed my time in Knoxville, and all over this area. It's hard to leave. Thanks again."

Sean hung up and put the phone down. He saw the signs for his rental car company and turned towards it.

Kansas City

The webpage opened and Kim scanned it. This morning, she was in the back office of her shop before her store opened. As in a previous morning, she had found herself drawn to her computer after ensuring herself the storefront was ready to open. This time, though, it was the reporter that had drawn her to her office.

After hanging up from her call with Sean the night before, she went into the kitchen for dinner only to find herself being grilled by Abby. Her daughter had teased her and, Kim admitted to herself, Sean had added a new element to her newfound quest to unravel the mystery of her father's letter. So, this morning, after tidying up the front end and readying the cash register, she had retired to the back office and went online. She had started by searching for information about Sean Johnson, the reporter. She was now looking at an article he had written about a bridge scheduled to be torn down and the people that cared about it.

Kim read the article, using her mouse to scroll through it. Once done, she acknowledged that it seemed well written and very sensitive to the people that were committed to saving the bridge. *They were probably pretty nutty people*, Kim thought, *but he managed to present them in a very reasonable manner.* They were people that Kim could identify with. *And*, Kim reflected, *I would probably be perceived as pretty nutty if I went out and started explaining that I had found a letter from my dead father telling me my family harbored an important secret about Lincoln. They'd lock me up!*

But maybe not. After all, Kim had the letter along with the very old note. *But,* Kim thought, *they would say the letters were forgeries.* After all the whole thing was so melodramatic. Kim knew it was the truth, though. She knew, anyway, that the letters were real, that her family name was really changed, and that her father had really warned her. But, then she was struck with the thought that maybe her father was duped, that her whole family had been led on over the years by a ruse started by Jacob. *Maybe Jacob had meant it all as a joke, but some other letter that he intended to be found as the punch line to the joke has been lost.* This new line of thought was disturbing to Kim, but again, as she thought it through, she realized that she knew and believed the letters and the story were factual.

As Kim thought some more, it seemed very clear that the only connection between President Lincoln and the Enloes was the Abraham Enloe parentage theory. So, that would have to be what Jacob was referring to. But, that seemed so strange. *What could have been so terrifying or dangerous about the fact that Abraham Lincoln might have been a bastard child?* It was that question that kept making Kim re-check her logic. It seemed so illogical that she kept trying to go back and rework the facts to find a different direction. But each time, she kept returning to the same idea: Jacob Thomas changed his name because of something about Abraham Enloe being the real father of Abraham Lincoln.

Kim's thoughts returned to the article in front of her and to Sean Johnson. He was conveniently researching a story on the Enloes and Lincoln. It seemed too convenient to Kim that a reporter had surfaced at just this time. But then, seeing that Sean was really a reporter, she found herself questioning her own logic again. *You're going nuts! And you're paranoid. Whatever it was that Jacob had been afraid of must be long since passed.* She had been paranoid with Mary and now she was being paranoid with this reporter. Kim clicked the "back" button on her internet browser and noted that there were several more articles she could read if she wanted to. Clearly, Sean Johnson was legitimately a reporter. *And, clearly, I'm way too paranoid about this whole thing. I have no reason not to share the story with him. Maybe he can help solve it.*

Kim decided to tell Sean all about her discovery of the letter, assuming Sean really did call her back and arrange a meeting later in the day. Having decided how to handle the newcomer to her family name issue, her thoughts returned to the topic of the Lincoln-Enloe story and how that could possibly relate to her ancestor Jacob Thomas-Poole. To her, it just seemed too weird. She did not have the letters with her, but she could recall the words very well. She said them out loud.

"Wait until the Enloes come forth and then tell our secret of President Lincoln and the War."

'Come forth' implies that the Enloes were hiding as well, she

thought. *But why? If they were hiding, does that mean that maybe Jacob was an Enloe or perhaps related to an Enloe?*

Leaning back, Kim sighed. Something just did not make sense. She rubbed her hand on her face. *Clearly, the Lincoln-Enloe theory has to be part of this, it's the only connection between Abraham Lincoln and the Enloes.* Then it struck her that maybe there was some other connection between an Enloe and President Lincoln; a connection that was lost. *The only event that would seem to carry this kind of gravity that would make a man change his name, was, of course, Lincoln's assassination by John Wilkes Booth. And if that is what this is about, then maybe an Enloe or a Thomas knew something about the assassination!*

Kim decided to search for Lincoln conspiracy theories. She selected her bookmarked search engine and watched as the page came up on the screen. After typing in "Lincoln" and "conspiracy" in the search engine window, she clicked on the search button. Within moments, she was overwhelmed by a flurry of results. There was a movie, tons of websites and many books. Worse, there were clearly many theories of conspiracy, since many websites referred to Lincoln conspiracy "theories" not "theory." Sighing again, Kim realized in many ways she was out of her depth. Her focus was on her ancestor and his place of origin, who his parents were and other good genealogical information, but the letter from her dad and the letter from Jacob really had stood her on end and spun her around, so that now she was trying to become an expert on Lincoln.

Kim's thoughts were broken by the jingle of the shop's front door opening. She had left it locked so she took the jingle to be Bridget coming in to work. *That's what I need to do. Focus on my store and see if this reporter calls me.* Kim got up and headed out of her office and towards the store front to greet Bridget.

Phoenix

Mary stood up from her computer and walked into the kitchen to make some hot tea. She had been clicking, scrolling and reading most of the morning without many results and needed a break. Her day had begun as usual with Phillip up and out early for golf with his buddies. After cleaning up the kitchen, she headed for her office computer to begin searching for clues to the last piece of the puzzle she was solving. After more than an hour though, she felt no success. *That's not completely true*, she thought, *because several possibly good sources of information have been eliminated.* But she knew that was not the same as actually getting anywhere.

Mary reached the kitchen, began heating water and getting her tea supplies out of the cupboard. It was probably time for her to simply explain to Kim what she had found and discuss with her what to do next. It was hard for her to let go of control over her new discovery, because what she was finding suggested there might be some great new information about the Enloes and their role in history. But, she was beginning to sense that she could not get any farther in working solely from her home in Phoenix, maybe not even from anywhere.

The water reached its boiling point and the whistling of the hot water kettle snapped her out of her reverie. She had not readied the teapot, so she turned down the heat on the stove and went about preparing the tea. Once she had poured the hot water in, she put the teapot and her mug on a tray and carried it back into her office. She set the tray down on one side of her desk and sat down. Knowing that the tea was not quite ready, she decided to check her email. After logging in, she found no useful or interesting emails and turned the program back off before she let herself get distracted by it. Sensing her tea should be ready, she turned her attention to that.

Once Mary had a nice cup of tea in her hands, she thought about what her next step would be. She now was very certain she knew who Jacob Thomas was and had a pretty good idea why he appeared in Denver under a new name a few years after the Civil War. She was also pretty certain she now could connect him to Abraham Lincoln. Of course, she knew what the ostensible link between the Enloes and Abraham Lincoln was, but what was missing was how Jacob connected to the Enloes. The answer, she was certain, lay in determining exactly why Jacob disappeared as a Thomas and re-appeared as a Poole. Mary knew she needed to identify enough of the possible reasons that she could thoroughly explore them, and hopefully spot a Thomas-Enloe connection.

But first, Mary acknowledged, it was time to bring Kim up to speed. She deserved that. And perhaps, she thought, *it's time to try and walk my brother through this as well. James would be much better equipped to conduct this next round of research.* She shifted her attention back to her computer and again launched her email program. But then, as she was waiting for her email to appear, she heard a noise behind her and turned around to see that a man had walked up to her office door-way. He was not an overly large man, dressed in a nice sport coat over a collared shirt. Then, her brain registered the sight of the gun he was pointing straight at her. It was black and he held it low, so it seemed to point straight out of the dark sport coat, almost camouflaged. She froze in horror and disbelief. She could not speak or even breathe. She was petrified.

"Don't do anything stupid! I'm here for a reason and if you cooper-ate, you'll be fine."

The intruder spoke softly and carefully. To Mary, the voice seemed like it was coming from a psychiatrist. But the gun clashed terribly with that thought and made his calmness more like a mocking satire of a psychiatrist. She found her voice, but she felt like she dare not make the slightest move with her hands or body for fear that he might pull the trigger on the black gun in his hand.

"What do you want?"

"First, I want you to do nothing. Second, I want you to answer some questions for me, okay?" He had answered very promptly and again seemed icily calm. Mary knew that this man was very dangerous and that he was lying to her. She managed to slowly nod her head without taking her eyes off his. Her heart was pounding.

"Good." He continued. "Is your husband or anybody else home?" His question flowed just as quickly and made him seem very prepared.

She gently shook her head and uttered a soft, "No."

"When will your husband return?" was his next question, again equally smooth and fast.

"This afternoon at some point, he's golfing." Mary had thought out a better response, but his questions were coming at her fast and she was behind in trying to get a grip on herself fast enough to get ahead of him mentally.

This time he studied her for a moment, his eyes squinting a bit. *He is trying to decide whether I'm lying or not,* she thought. Apparently, he believed her because his face relaxed just a bit and he moved into the room some and glanced around at her computer, the shelves and the desk.

"You know a lot about your family history, don't you Mary."

The simple question hit Mary very hard. *This is no thief. He knows who I am! What is going on?* She felt bewildered. Still, she managed to nod. The man continued his questioning.

"What I want to know is where all your notes and files about Abraham Lincoln and Jacob Thomas are. Everything about your recent research." The man paused and his eyes darted about, now showing more energy and alertness. They briefly locked on the computer screen. Then his eyes shifted to her desk where a stack of notes and folders were sitting. Then they came back to her. That took about ten seconds as Mary had been frozen speechless in a growing state of fear and bewilderment. The man made no sense. Why would he be robbing her of her notes?

The man thrust the gun into his sport coat, briefly flashing a leather holster across his side. It was now that Mary noticed he had black gloves on both hands. He moved towards her, grasping her wrists and squeezing them against the arms of the chair. He had moved very quickly and slightly to the side so she could not kick at anything, even if she had the courage. She felt pain from stark fear.

"Mary, you need to answer me completely, it's your only hope!"

His voice was now menacing, having lost all trace of its earlier kindness. Mary nodded her head quickly, afraid that he would strike her at any moment. *This makes no sense. I need to calm down. There is some mistake.* She took a deep breath.

"I understand!" Mary blurted. "You don't need to hurt me. I can tell you whatever you need to know."

"Good then. Why don't you tell me something even more important. What made you search for Jacob Thomas?"

"I, uh," Mary stammered. " I was told of a belief that he was related to the Enloes." Mary was adlibbing now and thinking furiously. *The warning in the letter to Kim! Could this be part of it? If so..."* Her sensibilities were returning.

Mary's thoughts were cut off as the man's gloved right hand released from her wrist and swung quickly across the left side of her face. She actually barely saw it move, but she felt a screaming pain across the side of her face as her head was wrenched sideways. Something in her neck pulled and also sent out stabs of pain down her spine. The man then shoved the chair violently against the desk throwing her backwards against the computer. The back of her head painfully struck the monitor.

"Mary," the man hissed. "You just lied to me. And you were thinking about how to lie more. No more. Tell me. WHY WERE YOU SEARCHING FOR JACOB THOMAS?" He screamed the last words at her and Mary felt utter despair overwhelming her. *He is going to kill me. And Kim is in danger!* Mary reached this last thought and then knew she needed to say nothing and do nothing. But, it was as if he had read her thoughts.

"You cannot protect Kim Poole, if that is what you're thinking," he warned. "Actually, your best chance to protect her is to tell me everything. I might not need to bother her. Tell me Mary, what made Kim search for Jacob Thomas? Who is he to her or even to you?"

Mary now thought of Kim's words *"My father left me a letter..."* Mary knew that Kim had not told her everything. Mary knew she must reveal nothing, but that even then, Kim was probably in danger. With her brain racing, she tried thinking of something she could do. She thought about email and then realized that her email program was open on the screen behind her. Her mind sped through the history of her communications, trying to think of what she and Kim had shared in writing. *Did we mention the letter in email? Did I write it down anywhere.* But, there was no time for thinking clearly.

Mary's thoughts were violently interrupted. The man grabbed her throat with both hands and began squeezing down hard.

"Mary, you're not listening to me. Talk now, tell me what you know, or it's going to get worse!" He shook her briefly and again the back of her head bounced against the monitor screen. Her neck was screaming in pain. She shut her eyes and tried to will herself the courage to endure whatever she had to. And to reveal nothing.

The man seemed to grow infuriated and again shook her by the throat. Mary reached her hands up to try and grab his head, or to get a finger into an eye. He was faster than her though, and quickly released his hands and flung her hands away. As her arms flailed to the side, his hands grabbed her head. Mary's last sensation was of his hands grasping her skull through her hair and beginning a wrenching turn to the left.

Terry released his hands from the head attached to the now-limp body and let it drop back against the monitor. He sighed, realizing that the best source of information about exactly what the woman in Kansas City knew was eliminated. He looked at Mary's dull eyes and felt a tinge of irritation with himself. But then, he thought of her stubbornness. He had seen it in her eyes. She was smart and was calculating, even in the face of his best efforts to immobilize her through fear.

"You would not have told me anything anyway," he said out loud, breaking the silence.

Terry pulled back the glove on his left hand and glanced at his watch, observing the time. He then looked about the office taking inventory of its contents and calculating the time it would take him to process them. After a brief focus on that task, he turned and walked back to the door where he had entered the house. He picked up a brief-case he had left on the floor by the door and carried it to the kitchen table. He set it down and opened it. He pulled out a CD-Rom and a small, portable hard drive with a cable dangling from it. Terry carried these items back to the office and pushed the chair with the sprawling body of Mary aside with his foot. He set the small rectangular hard drive down by the computer and plugged its cable into the USB port on the front of the computer case. Next, he pressed the button to open the CD-Rom tray and slid his CD-Rom into the drawer. He then initiated a download of the computer's hard drive onto his portable hard-drive. Terry then turned his attention to the rest of the office. His eyes already had noted the convenient stack of files on the desk. Now, he observed all the other possible sources of documents in the office. Then he set to work.

About half an hour later, Terry had completed his search of the office and other likely areas for files and documents related to Mary's research on the Enloes and Jacob Thomas. He stuffed the files he found into a small light nylon shoulder bag. He also removed his CD-Rom, unplugged the portable hard drive from Mary's computer and put them back in his briefcase. Terry also added the woman's purse and a folder with US Savings Bonds he had found in a filing cabinet to the nylon shoulder bag. He finished his work by dragging Mary's body into the kitchen where he lifted her onto a chair at the kitchen table. He pushed her forward so her head fell against the table with a dull thudding sound.

For a moment, Terry looked at the inert body It was still fascinating how easy it was to convert a living, thriving human being into an empty shell. *This Mary Fester probably was a very nice woman and certainly had not expected such an end to her life.* That thought gave Terry a small rush of power and control that he enjoyed for only a moment. He slipped out the side door into the backyard, carrying his nylon bag and briefcase. After closing and locking it behind him, he spun quickly and kicked the door, just next to the door knob, causing it to fly open, tearing the wooded door jamb. He then turned and walked around the garage, down the driveway and up the sidewalk to his car which was parked two houses away.

Though Terry ensured his body conveyed the slow and tired look of a salesman walking to his car, his eyes, ears and senses were on full alert. Just as he was reaching the car, to his dismay, an SUV turned the corner and began driving down the street towards him. He raced through a quick mental checklist and satisfied himself that he presented the most unnoticeable presence he could. Still, Terry decided to walk past his car at first. The car drove up to and passed him before he reached his own car. Out of the corner of his eyes he could see an older man briefly glance at him as the SUV went past. Terry walked past his car about twenty steps listening carefully for the sound of the vehicle that had passed him. It continued on at the same speed, so he casually turned around and began walking back towards his car. He could now see the white SUV that had passed him and was happy to see it was at least sixty yards down the street and continuing away from him. He also was pleased the driver did not appear to be looking back. He quickly walked out onto the street and around the front of his car, opened the door and slid inside, tossing his briefcase and bag onto the passenger seat. Now, looking in his rear view mirror as he started the car, he could see the SUV turning into a driveway. Terry inconspicuously drove away with a mental note that his exit might have been observed.

Chapter Ten

Kansas City

"Thank you very much," Kim said smiling and handing the customer her purchases.

The customer, a young woman in jeans and a light colored sweater, smiled back, took the bag and exited the store. Kim glanced at her watch. It was 2:30. Bridget was back from her lunch break and Sean Johnson should be arriving any moment. Looking around the store, she saw Bridget talking to an older man by a display of wind chimes. They were chit-chatting comfortably as Kim noted the similarities in their ages. The customer might be a bit older than Bridget, but not by much.

So far, it had been a typical spring business day. Warming temperatures naturally started people working more outdoors and Kim's garden sales would grow steadily out of the post-Christmas slow period. *This year is shaping up just like the last,* she thought. *At least in the store. But, this year my father is gone and I'm trying to solve a mystery he left behind. That's different.*

Kim was looking forward to meeting the reporter, and in fact, she admitted to herself, it helped that he was of the opposite sex. She was lonely. Watching Bridget flirt with a customer her age was reminding Kim that she too was single. After divorcing her husband and winning a tough custody battle for her daughter, Kim and Abby had moved up to Kansas City, where her father lived. He helped her start this business four years ago and then came down with cancer. Now it was just her and Abby, and she realized that being around her father had allowed her to ignore men and dating. Not that she felt like dating at all. That seemed too forced and structured. Occasionally men in the store would flirt with her. Often they were married, which was bad enough, but sometimes, to her revulsion, their wives were with them! Other times they were too young, or not her type or whatever excuse came to mind. The truth was, she admitted, she was just not ready. Between her father, her painful divorce, raising her daughter and starting a store, she had no further capacity to focus, neither mentally, nor emotionally.

But Sean had intrigued Kim. He seemed intelligent and friendly on the phone. He certainly looked handsome in the photo she had found on the internet. Plus, no signs of a wife or a partner. As she worked her way through those thoughts, her more logical and professional side took over. *He probably has a girlfriend, you idiot. And even if he doesn't, it's a professional meeting for professional reasons. So, focus on the reason you are meeting him. He can help you solve the mystery of Jacob, your great, great grandfather.*

Kim sighed quietly, shifting her thoughts to the meeting. Sean had called her from his rental car earlier and they set a time of three o'clock to meet. She had given him directions to the store. They talked a bit more and then hung up. Kim and Bridget discussed the meeting and they modified their lunch schedules to accommodate it. But the change was slight, as Kim's normal Monday afternoon routine, once the lunch rush was over, was to leave Bridget alone in the front while she retreated to the office and worked on ordering, inventory and accounting.

Another man walked in the store, but she knew it was not Sean. Kim left her thoughts about Sean behind as she approached him. A little while later, after shifting from the customer to helping an elderly lady pick out a hummingbird feeder, Kim suddenly noticed a tall gentleman near the entrance looking at the lawn ornaments on display. He was wearing brown slacks and a light blue windbreaker. He was facing away, but she knew intuitively that it was Sean. She did not see him come in the store, which she found puzzling. Usually, she was very observant. *He must move quietly,* she mused.

Kim approached him.

"Hi, can I help you?" she inquired.

The man turned around and smiled. Kim noticed his eyes first. They were deep and appeared to twinkle. His tanned face had a look of the outdoors. He held himself upright. As he turned around, she saw his hands clasping a leather notebook. He lowered his left hand to his side with the notebook in it, and extended the other forward.

"Kimberly Poole?" he inquired, as he offered his hand.

"Yep, that's me. You must be Sean Johnson."

They shook hands. She felt his firm grip. *Not too hard, but not wimpy either.*

"Please call me Kim. Did you find your way here okay?"

Sean nodded, "Yes, your directions worked perfectly." They released their handshake and he swept his hand across the store. "Nice shop and a great selection of merchandise. It's also very bright and cheerful."

"Thanks, I try to please."

Kim felt the presence of Bridget at her side and, after glancing at Bridget, she introduced them to each other. "Sean, this is my trusted employee, Bridget. Bridget, this is Sean, the reporter I told you about."

Kim shifted her voice to a mellow tone. "Bridget is the real reason this store looks so nice and the reason I am able to run it without losing my sanity."

Bridget chuckled. "That is not true at all, Sean. Kim runs this place and I am a mere employee that does her bidding."

Kim could see that Bridget had warmed up to Sean immediately. Sean apparently warmed as well.

"I am sure Kim's description of your worth is far more accurate than your own," he said to Bridget. "It's very nice to meet you."

Kim turned to Bridget. "We're going to run over to the coffee shop for a while. Things seem pretty mellow. I'll have my cell, so call if it gets too busy."

"Nonsense," Bridget replied. "I'll take care of everything, so take all the time you need." She smiled at Kim with a slight twinkle in her eye. Kim knew that her look meant, *He's a very handsome man, you should get to know him better.*

Kim gave Bridget a very brief frown in return. "Thanks Bridget. I'm sure we won't be too long." She then turned to Sean.

"Let me get my purse and the file. I'll be right back."

"Okay, that sounds good. I'll be right here," Sean replied.

Kim turned and retreated to the office for her things. She noticed that Bridget almost immediately engaged Sean in conversation. *I better hurry or she'll be telling him all sorts of things about me that I'll regret later.* While walking, she reviewed their introduction. *He seems very polite, and he's tall and fairly handsome,* she thought. *He's also observant.* She also found him very friendly and engaging.

Kim reached her office, picked up her purse, as well as the file folder containing her notes. She originally was going to tell him everything, but was still uneasy about that. So she now planned on taking the interview slow and easy. While thinking, she returned to the front. *Sure enough,* she thought, *Bridget already has him dialed in.* As she approached, they turned toward her while breaking their conversation, and looking at her with conspiratorial smiles. *Christ, Bridget only had thirty seconds, tops.* She smiled back.

"Okay I'm ready. Bridget, the store is all yours!"

Bridget nodded and shook hands with Sean. "It was very nice meeting you, Sean."

Kim noted the emphasis that Bridget had placed on "very." Kim turned to Sean. "Shall we?"

Sean affirmed and they walked out of the store together.

.....

Sean was impressed by Kim. He could tell she was assertive, sharp, and careful. *How could you not be, in her business?* he thought. She had no ring, he noted. Since she had a daughter, he concluded she was likely divorced. *Probably not too long ago. But not recent either.* As they walked along the street, passing shops, he noticed their reflection in store windows. He was taller than Kim, but she walked with more energy, which seemed to make up for the height difference.

"So your employee, Bridget, is quite the matchmaker isn't she?" he said breaking the silence.

Kim laughed, looking at him. "Yes, she thinks I need a man and probably thinks you're a good one, but don't let that go to your head. She thinks that about a lot of men."

"I won't, don't worry," Sean said back. "Besides, I really am here to interview you and learn more about your story. Not that it bothers me to interview a beautiful, organized and confident woman such as yourself." Sean added the compliment, but felt it came out awkwardly.

Kim laughed, and as they were glancing at each other, he saw a slight blush appear on her face. *Well it worked I guess. She must not be all business.*

"Sorry I didn't mean to say...oh, forget it," Sean muttered.

"Nothing to apologize for, I'll take any compliment I can get," Kim told him. "Besides, I'm also here to be interviewed and to learn what I can from you that will help me in my efforts."

They reached the coffee shop. Sean noticed her gesture towards it. He opened the door and let her pass him inside. He followed.

.....

They settled down at a table beside a window. A few feet away, on the other side of the glass, shoppers were strolling. Behind the strollers, the street beckoned with only a few cars driving by each minute. The glass was thick though, and they could only hear the cars when someone entered or left the coffee shop. But, that was not often, as it was a slow afternoon for the place. Kim and Sean were the only couple in there. A girl working behind the counter made their lattes while an apparent college student was studying at a table along a side wall wearing headphones. His head rocked slowly to whatever music was playing in his ears. The coffee shop had a concrete floor sealed and buffed to a dull shine. The ceiling was open to the roof, and thick, old, dark wood trusses spanned the overhead.

One effect of the architecture was to heighten sound reflection and Kim and Sean found themselves talking quietly over their lattes. They were seated opposite each other, but the table was small enough so they could easily hear each other's quiet voices.

"Okay Kim, let me begin by giving you a brief summary of the story as I have formulated it," Sean began. "Will that work?"

Kim nodded and Sean launched into a summary or recap of his research.

"I started this with a basic understanding of there being a supposed real father of Abraham Lincoln, a man named Abraham Enloe. The main theory goes like this: somewhere around 1806, a young girl named Nancy Hanks is sent south, probably through the Cumberland Gap, from wherever her family lived, to western North Carolina at the foot of the Smokies to work in the household of Abraham Enloe."

"There she works until she gets pregnant from a straying Abraham Enloe. The wife returns, is upset and demands Abraham send Nancy Hanks home. She is escorted home, perhaps to eastern Kentucky."

"Nancy is secretly taken in and gives birth to her child who she names Abraham. Back then, both she and the child would have been ostracized for their illegitimacy, so it's reasonable to think she could have left the child with someone else to help protect him from such scorn!"

"The official story of Lincoln's origin has his mother, Nancy Hanks, moving in with what might have been a cousin. She soon thereafter meets and marries Thomas Lincoln. They move to Sinking Springs Farm and have children."

"The Lincoln-Enloe theory holds that the person named Nancy Hanks that is sent home from the Enloe residence is the same Nancy Hanks that appears in eastern Kentucky and marries Thomas Lincoln. The problem with the story involves the timing of Abraham Lincoln's birth. Several competing ideas address this problem."

"One idea is that she gave birth to Abraham Lincoln secretly, then moved in with her cousin, and then met Thomas Lincoln. They then moved to the Sinking Springs Farm, picking up her illegitimate child along the way. They then hold Abe out as their child."

"There's a problem with that idea though, as the official history has Abraham being the second child, not the first."

"An alternate version to the whole Lincoln-Enloe story has Nancy working at the Enloe household after giving birth to Abe's older sister, Sarah. Nancy returns from Ocona Lufta to her husband, Thomas Lincoln, pregnant and they quickly move to another part of the country, near Hodgenville, where Abraham is born."

Sean paused, sipping his latte. Kim appeared deeply drawn into the story. He continued.

"The official history has Sarah being born shortly after Nancy marries Thomas Lincoln and Abraham being born a few years later. The Enloe theories struggle with this sequence because they mostly suggest that Abraham was born before his sister. That seems unlikely, however, as you would expect Abraham to have memories of his sister being older than him. But, if they had been born close enough together, then perhaps Nancy and Thomas could have fooled others, including their own children into thinking Sarah was the older child. They would have been highly motivated to keep Abraham's real parentage a secret and might have been more than willing to convince their children, but that still seems like a stretch to me."

"Nancy Hanks dies when her children are very young. Thomas remarries. The Lincolns also move several times. Back then, there was little structured government in northern Kentucky and southern Indiana, so records are few and far between. James Enloe, Mary Fester's brother, told me that there is a wedding record of some type. There is no birth certificate or any other contemporaneous record of either of the children's birth, though."

"It's worth mentioning, as well, that we are actually not even sure where Nancy Hanks came from or who her parents were. To me, that adds credibility to the Enloe story."

Sean stopped talking and picked up his latte to take a sip. Kim had been listening attentively and now also sipped. It was quiet for a moment. Then, Sean continued talking.

"Some of what I just described may not completely or accurately describe all of the alternate history. I'm still putting all the pieces together. But I think it's fairly accurate. At this point, I'm not convinced any of the alternate Lincoln-Enloe theories are correct, but I'm not convinced they're false."

Sean stopped speaking again. Kim finally spoke.

"I have learned some of what you describe, but not in so much detail. My issue is that I don't understand how this relates to my family." She stopped for a moment and smiled. "Of course, you're wondering that as well."

"Well, you told me there was some link to your family, but you were uncertain of where it came from or what exactly that link is," Sean prompted.

"Right." Kim took a deep breath. "You may think I'm some loony after hearing this. I've shared this only with Mary, and I did not tell her all of it. It's very mysterious and actually very dramatic, or at least I think it is." Kim was smiling nervously now, as if she was mildly embarrassed. But, she also appeared to be getting somewhat comfortable with Sean.

"So, I think I told you my father died last year."

"Yes, you told me," Sean replied. "You have my sympathy. Both of my parents are dead, my father died just a few years ago."

"Thanks. Yes, I guess we all go through this at some point. My father was very good to me. My mom died when I was young. Recently, my dad has been...uh was...very helpful to me in returning to Kansas City as a recently divorced, single mom of a teenage daughter." Kim paused to get her breath and release a tightness in her chest that she could feel sometimes when she spoke about or thought of her dad.

"Anyway, he died in December, and then a week and a half ago today, I found a letter from him. Not an old letter, mind you, but a letter he had written before his death. He had cancer and we knew for a while that he was going to die. That was not a fun time at all. Bridget, the lady you met back in the store, was a godsend in November and December." Kim could see Sean nodding and trying not to smile.

"Damn, I'm rambling aren't I?"

Sean laughed lightly. "Not at all. It's just that Bridget is quite a character isn't she?"

Kim laughed back. "Yes. So, anyway, the letter from my dad was placed for me to find. It was in a box labeled 'important legal documents.' It was a stunning letter."

Kim paused again and looked at Sean. Sean sat still allowing her to examine him. He apparently passed whatever test Kim was applying since she continued.

"Mary doesn't even know about this letter. I don't think...or in any case, I certainly have not told her much about it. Here's why. The letter warns me to be careful and keep the contents private until I know that some unknown danger has past. Actually, there are two letters, or rather a letter and a note, and I might be mixing their contents a bit. You see, my father also enclosed a note written by my great, great grandfather and it contains information. My dad also repeated what he was told by his father who had been told by his father, etcetera, reaching back to the author of the first note, Jacob Poole my great, great grandfather. He started it all."

Kim's face got serious for a moment. "Wait, let me see if I got that right." She paused and thought. "Yes, that's it. So, this Jacob Poole, my great, great grandfather, is apparently not really Jacob Poole, but Jacob Thomas. He apparently changed his name out of fear of something. This is where it gets weird, as if it hasn't already." Kim smiled at her joke and Sean smiled back.

"So, Jacob Poole gave us a mysterious warning about the Enloes and Lincoln and about not telling whatever it is we are supposed to know until the Enloes come forward and tell something about Lincoln. Everything was quite serious about being extremely careful. It seems clear that Jacob was very afraid of someone out there."

"Now, what's even weirder about all of this is that somehow this fear might be relevant today. Of course, that really does not make sense. Nobody alive today could possibly care about anything from 150 years ago. Right?"

Sean jumped in at the prompt. "Well, I have been taught that you can never be too careful. But yeah, it seems like you shouldn't need to worry about it today."

"At least now, that's what I also think. Last week I was more cautious. I did not tell Mary many of the specifics I just told you."

Kim looked carefully at Sean. "So, do you think this is nuts? What am I supposed to do? Ignore it?"   .

Sean thought for a moment. "Letters written by dying people are rarely false. They're sometimes jokes, but this sounds real to me."

He continued, "So, you've homed in on the Lincoln-Enloe theory as being connected to Jacob Thomas and his name change?"

"Yes. That's the only link to Lincoln we could find or think of. Mary that is, she has been my main source of help here." Kim glanced at her watch. "In fact, Mary was a bit mysterious this weekend and told me she had found something, but wanted to confirm it first. I should call her and see what she knows."

"That's a good idea. I need to call her, too," Sean said. "But let me ask you a few more questions, if I can."

"Sure."

"Okay, so when and where did Jacob Thomas...or Poole...which do you call him now?"

Kim smiled. "Yes, I've been stumbling with that. I call him Jacob Thomas. I think that part is definitely true. I never have been able to find records of Jacob Poole's birth or parents. I think now that is the reason."

"Okay, so where did Jacob Thomas live, here in Kansas City?"

"He lived in Denver in the late 1800's. Post-Civil War, maybe before as well. He was probably born there."

"And this Jacob wrote a note that was given to you?"

"Yes, with my father's letter." Kim reached down for her file and opened it. "Oh damn, I only brought my father's letter with me. I really meant to show you both."

She handed over the letter from her dad. "Here's the letter from my dad."

Sean took the letter and read it. Kim watched him reading while trying a sip from her latte, but it was too cold to enjoy. Sean took a few minutes to read the letter. He seemed to read it several times and even glanced at the back side of each sheet. Then, he put the letter down and leaned back.

"Wow! That is very interesting. You're right, it's very mysterious," Sean said, looking at her. "And serious too, for that matter."

"You think so?" Kim was clearly pleased that Sean was not laughing at her or rejecting the letter's credibility. Sean was staring up at the ceiling area, as if he was studying the old beams of the place.

Kim continued, "I have felt as though I was losing my mind. The events have been very surreal. I was probably nuts initially worrying about it so much. Just sharing the events makes me feel less nutty and more focused."

Sean flipped his head down.

"I don't think you were nuts being careful. Your father tells you to respect the warning and the caution." Sean stroked the side of his face with a finger. "Let's see. When did Jacob die?"

"Uh, about 1900."

"And when was your father born?"

"1939," Kim answered, without hesitation this time.

"Well that is only a thirty-nine year gap. Your father probably knew his grandfather and might have had a sense of the danger that Jacob passed along. Your father's letter appears serious."

Sean started to speak again, but noticed that Kim had acted startled, as if she had just thought of something.

"What? What did I say?"

Kim stared at him for a moment longer.

"I just realized that Jacob named his son, my great grandfather, my dad's grandfather, Abraham. He named him Abraham. Shit, how did I miss that."

"Relax, don't be so hard on yourself." You said you've only had this letter a couple of weeks."

"Okay, okay," Kim said, clearly thinking. "But that has to be a clue, right? I need to look at all my genealogy files again."

Sean laughed. "Well, yes. Listen, can we go through them together? I can stay another day here in Kansas City before I go home. We could meet tomorrow. I'd also like to see the note from your ancestor."

Kim looked at Sean for a moment. "Yes. I mean, you're willing to do that?"

"I am. There is a very good story lurking in here, and I want to help you out."

Kim smiled. "Okay, then let's meet tomorrow morning at my store. I'll look at my files tonight and bring them all in. Does eight o'clock work?"

"Yep. I'll be there." Sean glanced at his watch. "Let me call Mary, I had promised to interview her today, but I think I'll put it off until tomorrow."

Sean pulled his cell phone out of a pocket in his windbreaker and quickly started the call to Mary. It rang a few times and then he got the answering machine. Once the greeting was done and he heard the beep he left her a message.

"Mary, this is Sean. I'm with Kim. I won't get to interview you today, but will try again tomorrow. Meanwhile, Kim has thought of some things on her end so you should also check with her. We are going to meet tomorrow and go through things again."

He hung up the phone.

"Okay. I'd better let you get back to your store. It's been a while."

Kim glanced at her watch. "Oh my God! Bridget is probably ready to quit." She hopped up grabbing her file. "I've got to go. Tomorrow morning, eight sharp?"

"I'll be there." Sean stood reaching out his hand.

Kim extended her own hand. "I've really enjoyed meeting you." She put a little more emphasis on the word "really" than had Bridget.

Sean shook her hand and smiled, "Me, too."

Kim whirled around and quickly walked out of the shop and down the street. Sean paused for a moment, watching her hair blowing as she strode towards her store. Then he smiled turning his attention to his notebook to begin writing down as much as he could recall.

Phoenix

Terry was examining his computer screen in his hotel room. On it, he called up emails and documents, going through Mary's computer contents carefully. The program he had run on her computer was a product of his security division, though it was really part of his investigation group. *In fact,* he thought, *it's really a spy tool. We should be marketing our company to provide spy services for countries overseas.*

The program had simply downloaded the contents of Mary's computer and then erased the hard drive in a way that made it look to a specialist as though it had failed. The hoax would not survive deep scrutiny, but it would work most of the time. He had another program that allowed his laptop to mimic Mary's computer. It overrode or provided ways around any encryption or passwords. He had plugged the portable hard drive in and launched the program. The only barrier his program encountered was getting around her email password, which had added only a few minutes to disable.

He saw the emails between Kim and Mary, as well as emails with a man named "Sean Johnson." That was a new name and the email trail made it seem like he was a reporter. He was surprised to find records of her brother, James, who was a professor of history, with a focus on Lincoln no less. Finally, he already had gone through Mary's paper records. It was pretty obvious to him that she had determined who Jacob Thomas was, but he found no evidence that she had told anyone else. The problem was, he knew, that she could have orally told any number of people including her husband, Kim, this Sean Johnson, or her brother.

Clearly, she had gotten farther than anyone else had to date on finding the trail within the historical record. That fact, combined with the revelation that Kim had uncovered some family information related to Jacob Thomas, put Terry on full alert.

The emails made it clear that Kim probably had a family document, perhaps a document from Jacob Thomas himself, who was apparently her ancestor. Terry's sense was that whatever family document she had, it was not the letter he was interested in. *No, if she had that document or the other letter, she would have described things differently. But, clearly, she is confused and has some type of a mystery on her hands. And, she is hung up on the Lincoln-Enloe theory.* Thus, the facts showed that things were very likely to unravel. Kim might already know enough to home in on the nature of things. She might also have what she needed to actually uncover the missing letters. If that was the case, Terry knew, she was closer than anyone had ever been, by a large margin.

Next, Terry considered James Enloe, Mary's brother. There was not much email traffic between them, and none about this. But, that made him nervous. The email traffic made it clear that her brother had sent the reporter to Mary. Mary had sent the reporter to Kim. That drew them all into a circle The brother, however, was a Lincoln professor. That made him extraordinarily dangerous and very qualified to truly get at the secrets lurking behind all of this. More so than Mary had been, and Mary had gotten very far. For that reason, this James Enloe was now very high on Terry's list of concern.

Then there was this reporter, Sean Johnson. Terry searched on the internet and found him quickly. *He's from Seattle? How does a Seattle reporter get caught up in Tennessee with a Lincoln professor who is also an Enloe?* Terry dug up several documents and found a biography on Sean. As Terry read a statement about Sean's military service, red flags started waving in the back of his head. The sentence describing his military service was vague and also not consistent with any real division that Terry knew of. That smelled of something the reporter was hiding or at least trying to distract people from noting. He did not like that at all.

Terry clicked on a link on his computer that took him into a portal for Sheriden Security Corporation. He quickly used a connection there to call up the company's access to federal military service files. They had the files thanks to a contract they had for a couple of highly classified agencies within the federal government that needed to train and deploy secret force teams. Within a few minutes, Terry had found Sean Johnson's records. Or at least part of them. He immediately noted what he had smelled in the vague description Sean had provided of his service: Sean Johnson had been a U.S. Navy Seal, a commando. *Damn!* Terry thought, *that adds a very messy component to all of this!* Terry launched Sean's service files and then got his second surprise. The files were not there. There was a note in the file that Sean Johnson's service records were classified and removed from the regular files. Terry knew what that meant. Sean had done some extremely classified operations for the CIA or some secret spinoff created for some issue around the country. Sean's age placed him in either South American drug war operations or in the early Mediterranean anti-terrorist raids. In any case, Terry knew, that meant this Sean Johnson was a Seal who had seen some action. That made the situation even worse.

"So why does a Seal become a reporter?" Terry said aloud to his hotel room. "And then, why does this reporter from Seattle get caught up with an Enloe who is a Lincoln professor in Tennessee?"

Terry paused as if he was waiting for a response. Which he wasn't, of course. The more Terry thought, the more he became convinced that he needed to take immediate and more serious action. He had been a little irritated with himself for losing control and killing Mary before he had forced her to tell him more, but he was satisfied that killing her had been a wise move.

Terry also knew that he may have been spotted exiting the scene at Mary's house. That made him very nervous. He reviewed his options and decided to stay in Phoenix for another day. He would do an inspection at one of Sheriden Corporation's accounts in the Phoenix area to create a credible reason for him to have been in the area. Then, late Tuesday or Wednesday, he would head to Knoxville. He would also begin covering his movement behind pseudonyms and using the various covert systems Sheriden maintained.

Satisfied with his new plan, he decided to call his brother. He picked up his cell phone, stood up and walked over to the large window of his room that looked out upon the greater Phoenix area. *It looks like Los Angeles. An endless stream of buildings and roads in a big, hot, flat desert.* He pressed the quick dial key for Michael's cell phone and waited patiently for it to connect, ring and for Michael to answer.

"Brother," Mike greeted him. "How are you?"

"Fine." Terry replied. "I have completed most of my work in Phoenix and have learned quite a bit of new and surprising information. Is this a good time?"

"Kind of. I'm in my senate office. Jessica is here with me."

"Okay, well let me give you a run down then. You don't have to say anything."

"Okay, shoot."

"Things are more advanced and serious than we thought and have ever been. I'm headed to another location and probably another one after that. I'll call you from a Sheriden system phone tomorrow to fully update you."

Terry paused and thought for a moment and then continued. "If this goes right, brother, we may find the missing documents and more."

"Okay." Michael said.

"Okay, talk to you soon." Terry said and hung up. He lowered his cell phone and stared out the window at the twilight across the city.

Atlanta

Michael put his phone down on the desk.

"Where were we?" he asked Jessica.

Jessica smiled coyly. "I was done with my briefing. Was that your brother?"

Michael stared at Jessica. She was dressed in a professional suit complete with a very short skirt.

"Yes it was. Some security company issues have arisen that could be very important. If they get complicated, I may have to brief you on them. But for now, you can be blissfully unaware." He gestured at her to come closer.

Jessica put her files down on the small coffee table next to the armchair she was sitting in. She stood up, walked over to the office door and locked it. She then turned around.

"Do I sense that I am done serving you in my professional role?" she asked in a teasing voice.

"Yes." Michael smiled. *I should really marry this woman*, he thought. It was not love, he knew, but she was the best manager he would every find and their sex was also the best ever. He pondered for a moment whether marriage with Jessica would be valuable publicly and politically. *Maybe*, he acknowledged to himself, *but why mess with a good situation.*

"Come here."

"Oh, but Senator, this is your office. We might get caught." Jessica had found an innocent and mocking voice.

Michael smiled. "All the better, all the better. Now come here."

Jessica walked over to him, reaching up and letting her hair down. She reached him, close enough that their knees almost touched. Reaching out with his hands, he began stroking the backs of her thighs, causing her to twitch. His hands began moving higher and she quickly began losing whatever control she had left. She pressed herself against his chest and began breathing heavily.

Michael smiled.

Part Two

Riddle

Chapter Eleven

The knocking sound prompted Kim to look up from the documents she was studying at the register counter. She was standing there waiting for Sean to show up, concerned that she might not hear him from the back office. As she peered at the store entrance, she saw Sean standing there on the other side of the locked door. He was dressed in jeans with the same windbreaker he had worn the day before. A small bag was slung over his shoulder this time, she noted. Better, he was holding a cardboard drink tray with two drinks inserted in it. Kim recognized the logo on the cups as being from the coffee shop they visited the day before. Smiling at him, she waved briefly before walking over and unlocking the door with the key she had left in the lock.

"Good morning," she greeted Sean, swinging the door open.

"And a good morning to you," Sean replied, walking in the store, drink tray leading the way.

He set the tray of drinks on the register counter as Kim was locking the door again. Turning around she saw him pulling the beverages out of the tray.

"I thought you might enjoy a coffee," Sean said, holding out the cup. "Non-fat latte, right?"

"That's right. Thank you." Kim said appreciatively. She took the drink. "You're impressive. Do you treat all your interview subjects this nicely?"

"Oh no, you're special. It's not everyone that has a 'Lincoln's real father knew my great, great grandpa' story."

"Ha Ha," Kim fired back. "It's great, great grandfather to you."

Sean stood upright. "I stand corrected, ma'am."

Sean relaxed a bit and turned slightly, looking at the papers Kim had left scattered on the register counter. "It appears you brought your entire family history in."

It was Kim's turn to laugh. "Not at all. You should see how much genealogy stuff I have managed to accumulate these past several years. I'm just an amateur. I suspect that the pros out there like Mary have filing cabinets full of files."

She paused, thinking briefly. "By the way, did you make contact with her?"

Sean shook his head. "Nope. She never called back. I never called again either, but I'll call her today."

"Are you flying home today?"

"That's my plan, yes. I'm booked on a flight at 4:30 this afternoon."

They paused and Kim briefly looked down at her drink. Then she looked up and spoke firmly.

"Okay. So let's get to it. I have to open the store in a little over two hours."

She walked past Sean to the other side of the counter.

"There's more space here than anywhere else. This is the letter from my father and the enclosed note from my great, great grandfather."

Sean had turned with her as she walked past him and around the counter. He set his drink down, away from the papers, and picked up the letter from her father. He read it quickly, refreshing his memory from his reading of the letter the day before. Then, he swapped it for the note that was underneath it. It was old paper, he could tell, but not the old parchment style stationary that looked yellow and ready to crack. Instead, it only looked somewhat brittle and yellowed. *That makes sense, this is a note from near the end of Jacob's life, around the turn of the century, not from the Civil War era or earlier.*

"So, this is the note your great, great grandfather wrote?" he asked, glancing up at Kim.

"Yes, that's it," she replied, eagerly studying him. It made her uneasy now that someone else was reading the note, much like she had felt the day before when Sean had read the letter from her father for the first time.

Sean nodded slightly and turned his attention back to the note. He read it through a few times, noting the warning and the mysterious wording of Kim's ancestor. While he studied it, Kim continued her nervous scrutiny of him. He finished reading it and looked up slightly.

"Well, what do you think?" Kim asked him almost immediately.

Sean paused, pursing his lips for a moment.

"It's convincing. Yes, it's weird and yes, it's mysterious. But it's also very believable and serious. This guy, Jacob Thomas, if that was his real name, was definitely scared about something."

Sean paused, glancing at the note again. "Let's see, it's dated 1901. That's about forty years or so after Lincoln's death right?" Sean did not pause or look up, but continued on. "So, he was still scared forty years after the last event in Lincoln's life...his assassination."

Again Sean looked up, but this time right at Kim. "It could be that Jacob knew something about Lincoln's assassination."

Kim smiled grimly. "I've considered that, Mary has too. The assassination is the most controversial event in Lincoln's life. The timing is about right. I did a quick search about Lincoln's murder. Unfortunately, it seems as though there are as many conspiracy theories about Lincoln's assassination as there are about Kennedy's. So, I'm not sure where to begin."

Kim let her voice dwindle down as if prompting Sean to step in and give his direction. Sean failed to provide such clarity though.

"But what does that have to do with the Enloes?" he asked. "That story is about Lincoln's birth, not his death. Those two events, the alternate birth theory and his assassination, are the bookends on Lincoln's life. There has to be something we're missing."

"I know, I know, that's my thought exactly," Kim explained grimly. "There are two questions. First, why would Jacob be afraid so long after whatever the event was. Second, what connection could the Enloes have to Lincoln that would trigger his fear or require his warning. How could it be both Lincoln's birth and death?"

"Well, Jacob does not mention the assassination," Sean responded. "You would think he would've if it was involved. Instead, he just mentions the 'Enloes' and their 'story' of Abraham Lincoln. That clearly would seem to be the Lincoln-Enloe bastard story, wouldn't it?"

"Yes, but then we're back to the question of what could possibly be dangerous about that."

"True, true," Sean mused. Then he lifted Jacob's note, holding it out towards Kim. "The key is in these words from Jacob. We need to decipher his message to you and your family."

Sean pulled the note back to read quotes from it out loud.

"...'wait until the Enloe's emerge' and 'tell our secret of President Lincoln and the war' and 'look at my words and discover their other meaning.' I think that final phrase is the most important. He says, precisely, 'Look then and only then at my words and discover their other meaning.' That's part warning and part a carefully worded instruction."

"Yes," Kim interrupted. "But his words are so simple and short that there is not much else to glean from them."

"True, true," Sean admitted. He stood quietly and then carefully put the note down on top of the letter from Kim's father.

"What do you know about Jacob? You said you don't know when or where he was born, right?"

Kim nodded. "That's kind of right. I have a birth year for him in my records. I think that comes from some record that told our family how old he was when he died." She reached into her stacks of papers on the counter and opened a file labeled "Jacob." She sorted through the documents in it.

"I have his death certificate. Ah, here it is."

She lifted a piece of paper.

"He is buried in a cemetery in Denver. The cemetery's headstones were all recorded and posted in a database somewhere online. This is the printout of the information on his headstone."

She handed the document to Sean. He read it out loud.

"Jacob Poole. Born 1848. Died June 4, 1901. Aged 53 Years." Sean looked up at Kim. "Hmm, that's not much, but it's something."

"Did he live in Denver his whole life?"

"I don't know," Kim admitted. "I just know he lived most of his life in Denver. His first child, Abraham, my great grandfather, was born in Denver in 1883, I think. I'm not sure when he married his wife. She died during the birth of his second child a few years after their first. I learned that from my father."

Sean was pulling on his lower lip slightly. It was a sign that he was thinking very deeply, though Kim did not yet know that. He shifted his eyes from the letter to the various files on the register counter. Suddenly he looked up.

"Do you have any other documents from Jacob? His will? Letters he wrote?"

Kim looked at him, slightly startled. "Well, yes we have a few letters from him to my great grandfather."

She paused and then thought out loud. "Yes of course, 'my words.' That does not have to be that note. It could be anything he wrote. Hold on." She hurriedly grabbed another file.

"They're in Abraham's file," she explained. "Letters, I mean. To Abraham, my great grandfather."

She pulled out a clump of pages.

"If I remember correctly, Abraham went to work in western Colorado at a very young age for a mining company. He came back to Denver a few years later. Abraham and Jacob exchanged letters, but Abraham's letters to Jacob did not survive."

Sean took the letters. It was a thick stack. That was partly because the paper was thick itself, he noted. He glanced through them quickly.

"Looks like four letters," he said. "You've read them?"

"Yes. They are fairly ordinary family letters if I remember. Nothing about mysteries or presidents. But still, I read those a long time ago and certainly not with an eye towards clues."

"Okay, okay, that's one direction we need to pursue," Sean said. "Is there anything else?"

"I don't think so, but I should check through all my files to make sure. I don't think I have his will. I assume his will would be recorded in some file in Denver, though I don't know where. That's assuming he had one."

"Yes, check his files for anything else. Do you have a copier?"

"No, but there's a copy shop down the street."

"Okay, so I think we need to explore Jacob's life and written words very closely," Sean said. "Also, I think I need to talk more with our resident Enloe and Lincoln expert, Professor James Enloe."

He paused and looked at Kim.

"Are you okay sharing this material with him?"

"Yes," Kim replied without hesitation. "I should have done this a while ago. I feel better with two brains wrapped around this mystery."

"Yeah. Mary can probably also help in digging up more on Jacob." Sean smiled. "This is very interesting. Thanks for entrusting me."

"The appreciation is all mine, Sean." She said, smiling right back.

They paused for a moment both staring at the papers on the counter, before Kim broke the silence.

"Do you get this 'into' all of your stories?"

"No," Sean admitted. "This is a very special story and has turned out to be extremely interesting. I do have the reputation of being like a tenacious bulldog, though."

"Well, I'm glad you wandered into my family mystery."

They looked awkwardly at each other for a moment before Sean found the words urging them onward to the copy machine.

Phoenix

Kevin Falls frowned as he surveyed the scene again. From one point of view it looked like a simple break-in and murder. *Old lady is robbed and killed in her home*, he thought. But on the other hand, it looked suspiciously like it was supposed to be interpreted that way. *Instead, the headline should read 'Husband kills wife making it look like home burglary'*.

Such a story did not jive very well with Kevin, however. *This husband seems truly shocked and distraught. Nor does he seem the type. Nor is there a reason for him to kill her. They had a good simple life of retirement.* Or so it seemed, he reminded himself. The next task was to carefully confirm all of the first impressions and facts. Were they really financially okay? Was it really true that he was with friends while she was killed? He knew, from his own experience and all the standard teachings, that the husband clearly had to be the primary suspect. He wondered if the husband had been having an affair. *Or this woman? Maybe she was having an affair*, he thought.

The house had been broken into by a side door leading from the backyard. Kicked in, probably. That had to have made some noise. The intruder then entered the house, killed the woman and searched it for valuables. He had apparently taken her purse, but there was something very wrong her. He intuitively knew it.

Kevin decided he needed to have a much closer inspection of the home. He sighed. Doing that meant keeping the husband out for at least another day. It meant more work for him and the homicide department. *Is it worth it?* he asked himself. It was tempting to terminate the crime scene investigation and simply let the investigation of the outside facts play its course. Something about the contradiction and inconsistency of the basic logic of who really killed the woman truly bothered him, though.

Kevin was a short muscular investigator. He wore jeans and a tight fitting, dark blue, collared polo shirt. It showed off his muscles, something he was proud of. It also demonstrated his commitment to the gym. It showed that he was not becoming fat and lazy after moving from patrol to homicide investigation. He leaned his torso against the door frame and stared into the small home office where the woman, Mary Fester, had apparently spent much of her time recently on some geology project, according to her husband, Phillip. *No that's not right,* he thought. *It's genealogy, not geology.*

Kevin noticed the answering machine located at the corner of the desk. The small blinking red light indicated that there were unheard messages on the machine. He found this quite annoying. Somebody should have observed the phone already and asked him to listen as they played them. He pushed himself off of the door frame and walked over to the desk pressing the "messages" button just below the blinking red light. He then stood there listening. The machine indicated there were two unheard messages. The first one was from somebody named Sean and mentioned a woman named Kim. He found that message very interesting. It was a business-like voice talking importantly, but the subject matter sounded more about family. *Genealogy,* he thought.

The time stamp told him the message was a few hours after the estimated time of death for the woman. The next message was a little while later from her husband, Phillip. It sounded truly innocent, but also curious as to why she did not answer the phone. The husband indicated he was going to stay at the golf club a bit longer.

"Consistent with his story," Kevin said out loud.

"Is it?" a voice said from over his shoulder.

Kevin turned around to see one of the crime scene staff, Jeff, looking at him.

"Yes it is," he said challengingly. "But I still don't trust him. There's something wrong here."

Kevin thought for a moment. "Let's get a full record of all phone calls made or received for the last thirty days. Did you hear the first message?"

Seeing Jeff shake his head, he continued, "It's from a man named Sean saying he's with a woman named Kim. Let's see if there are any Seans or Kims in the phone records."

He turned away from Jeff and pointed at the computer. "I think we need to have our information technology guys get into this. I want to see her email, if she used email, that is."

Kevin turned more away from Jeff, signaling that he was done giving instructions. He heard Jeff mutter a "yes sir" and turn to leave. Kevin focused his attention on the office some more.

There was an open filing cabinet drawer. A file folder was slightly pulled up, sticking out. *Something was disturbed or removed,* he instinctively thought. *Need to talk with the husband some more.*

Kevin left the office, heading back to the kitchen where the woman's body was found. He entered the combined kitchen/dining area and stopped to examine the scene.

The woman is found dead here. No cuts or signs of strangulation. She's in a chair at the kitchen table slumped over. Neck broken? Probably. But why here and why in a chair?

He realized that was one of the inconsistencies that was nagging him. *If she was really killed on the stool, snuck up on from behind, then the killer was a professional. But, if he was a super professional, then what's with the missing purse crap? And if it was a burglary, the*

*woman would have been drug around the place. And probably cut,
strangled or shot. It would have been messy.*

Something was clearly wrong here. Things did not make sense on
all sorts of levels. Kevin sighed again and conceded that he needed to
keep the crime scene preserved for at least another day.

Kansas City

Kim knew Abby was teasing her. *Still, it's kind of nice*, she thought.
"Come on mom," she was saying. "You met with him twice? You
can't tell me you didn't notice what he looked like."

Abby was determined to get Kim to admit that she thought Sean
was cute. *No that's not quite it,* she knew. *She wants me to admit that I
might be attracted to another man. That's closer to the truth.*

Kim had to admit to herself that Sean had been impressive. Besides
being nice looking and intelligent, he was sincere and seemed quite
resourceful. But then, she thought, she had not really learned anything
about him. For all she knew, he might have a girlfriend. But no, she
concluded, that did not ring true. *He's extended his trip several days
and seems truly independent from his home, like there is no one there
for him to call or report to.*

"Mom, hello?" Abby's voice broke through her thoughts. Kim
forced herself to address her daughter.

"Abby," she began using her most exasperated voice. "Sean is a
very nice man and our meetings were entirely professional. I am not
attracted to him. He's a reporter writing a story, and he can help me
unravel a mystery about our family history. A mystery your grandfather left us, I might add."

Abby was just staring at her annoyingly with a huge grin on her
face. It was a grin that said, *Sure Mom, whatever you say, right.* Kim
knew that look all too well.

"I'm serious Abby. In fact, you should be more interested in the
reason why I met with him than what he looked like."

Without really breaking her grin Abby replied, "Of course I am
Mom, but first tell me what he looked like."

"Okay, okay, but only to make you feel better." Kim thought for a moment. "He is tall with short brown hair. He has brown eyes as well. He seems athletic, but he is also sharp with words. This morning he brought me a latte, the same one I ordered at the coffee shop when we met the day before. That tells me he's observant and thoughtful. So frankly I'm not sure he's even a man."

Kim started to laugh at her own joke, but stopped when she noticed that Abby was not laughing with her.

"What? You think most men that you're going to meet are going to get the door for you and bring you coffee? I've got news for you, kiddo."

But then Abby started steering the conversation, as she periodically did, in a different direction.

"Mom, was dad like that to you when you first met?"

Wow that's a loaded question if there ever was one, Kim thought. *If I say he was, then I'm probably implying that he quit doing it. If I say he wasn't like that, then I'm saying he was not a good man to marry in the first place.* Kim thought this over quickly and then answered.

"Abby, I loved your dad when we first met and for quite a while afterwards. Somewhere along the way though, we started growing apart. I wanted to do more with my life and he wanted me to be more of a stay-at-home mom. You know we started fighting a lot." Kim paused and then plunged into her own questions. "So, why are you asking me that? Do you think I am looking for a replacement in my life? In your life? Because I'm not. The love of my life is right here before my eyes. You are all I want and all I need."

Abby just looked blankly at Kim so she continued. "I'm not saying that if the right man came along and things were right, I might not pursue something. I still believe in love, Abby. Don't think I don't. But, the love of another man is just not high on my priority list. You are! And then my business."

Abby smiled and Kim took that as some form of agreement. "And yes, Sean was cute. But I swear, I'm solely interested in him for his help. That's it!"

Kim stood up from the kitchen chair. "Abigail, I know you have lots of homework to do, so get busy."

Abby replied as Kim left the room, "Okay, Mom."

Knoxville

Sean leaned back into the large, soft pillow and closed his eyes. He was back in the same downtown hotel in Knoxville, located next to the University of Tennessee campus. He wondered how he managed tangling himself up in a story that was blossoming into a personal quest. *I'm neglecting my home and my work for that matter. I've been gone for almost a week. I've traveled through Kentucky, Tennessee, North Carolina and Kansas City. And what have I got to show for it? I'm squeezing information from a grouchy professor, helping a single mother find out who her ancestor was, and being ignored by the nicest lady of them all, the grouchy professor's sister.*

Sean's meeting with the professor was set for tomorrow, though not until the evening. If he was going to interview Mary, he figured he better do it by phone, as trying to meet with her in Phoenix would probably keep him away from home until the weekend. But, she had not returned his second call to her. At least not so far.

Kim had added a potentially new aspect to the story, but he was unsure it would fit. It seemed too bizarre to be credible. It was one thing, telling an old story, backing it up in several ways, that Abraham Lincoln might have been fathered by someone other than Thomas Lincoln. It was quite another adding in a mysterious warning from a grave that insinuated existence of a conspiracy theory involving Abraham Lincoln. But, Sean liked Kim. She was assertive and focused, yet she also had a lighter side. He admired her for running a business while raising a teenage daughter. Finally, he had to admit, she was attractive. She had a nice smile and a great face. Perhaps most of all, she had an energy that he really liked.

But, that's not why you can't sleep, Sean old boy. You are bothered by the contradiction in the link between Jacob's fear and the Enloes. Or is there something else?

Sean sighed, trying to relax. It was always a bad sign when he silently talked to himself. It was late and he was tired. The pillow and mattress were soft and quite comfortable. But, for some reason, he felt restless and tense. Something was not quite right and he could not put his finger on it. Still, it was time to sleep. He flipped over onto his side and his eyelids finally began feeling heavy. Drifting into sleep, the words of Jacob went floating in his head, whispering, "*be careful.*"

…..

About that same time, ten miles to the south, Terry Sheriden was stepping into a car that had been waiting for him after landing at the Knoxville airport. He had used his time in Phoenix to establish a false identity connected with a special Sheriden subsidiary registered outside of the United States. He then arranged for the private jet, as well as the car under that identity. Closing the door, he started the car up. He was staying at a highway-side hotel that was only a few miles up the road and just below Knoxville itself. As soon as he was on the road, he touched his phone ear piece with his finger and said, "Call Michael." He had changed phones as well. The phone obliged, and he was soon hearing the ringing of a phone. Michael answered shortly thereafter.

"Hello brother," he greeted Terry.

'Hello to you," Terry responded. "I'm in Knoxville. I'm confident I exited Phoenix without any issues."

"That's good,s" Michael replied. "So, this woman's brother lives there?"

"Yes, and he's the Enloe who is a Lincoln scholar."

"Hmm. Anything more on the reporter?"

"Yes," Terry replied. "He's a former Seal who had been assigned to a CIA-coordinated 'special ops' team. He appears to have left that life completely behind him, though."

"Interesting," Michael mused. "We are going to need to switch over to encrypted phone links if this gets any more complicated. We probably need to already."

"Yes, I agree. I've already requisitioned a set for us. I'll pick them up at the headquarters when I get back. For now, I'm going to see what I can learn about the professor. "

"What else do we know about the woman in Kansas City?" Michael asked.

"Not much. It certainly sounds like the woman in Kansas City, Kimberly Poole, is the offspring of Jacob Thomas and that she just found out about it. She is the reason for this new activity around Jacob Thomas. I think she found a family document. What's strange though, is the reporter, this Sean Johnson. I really don't know how he got tangled up in this. That bothers me. Letting the professor unravel the clues would be okay with me if it wasn't for the reporter. But somehow he got involved."

"Well, we need to proceed carefully, but firmly here."

"Very true brother. I'll call you tomorrow with an update."

"Very well. Good-bye."

They hung up just as Terry was reaching the turn off for his hotel. He took the exit, humming to himself.

Chapter Twelve

Kevin sat in his cubicle, his chair pulled up close to his desk. His cubicle was one of many in a large central room of police headquarters. Staff were walking, talking and working all around him. The result was a gentle buzz, where any single voice mostly blended into the overall background noise. Occasionally, one word or a phrase was timed or spoken loud enough that it could be distinguished above the gentle din. Kevin, however, found the background noise soothing and was lost deep in thought.

He was hunched over, examining several documents spread out on his desk. One was a printout of all calls made or received at the Fester residence over the last thirty days. Amazingly, neither the deceased nor the husband owned a cell phone, so the home phone records were likely to be a complete record of their telephone calls. Another stack of documents contained bank and credit card statements for the last six months that the husband had allowed be taken from the house and evaluated. He also now had the coroner's preliminary report. The last stack contained the reports made by himself and others, recording various interviews or inspections. He had just completed reading the report on the two people that the husband, Phillip, had said he had spent the day with. *The report cleanly and completely backs up his alibi.* The sergeant who had done the questioning of the couple had given his opinion that they were telling the truth. *So, it appears very unlikely the husband committed the murder,* he concluded.

Kevin shifted his thoughts and scrutiny to the coroner's report. No results yet on drugs or substance abuse. Still, the coroner had reported her death was most likely the result of a severed spinal cord between the second and third vertebrae. There was neck bruising, but it was not consistent with such an injury, which, the coroner had noted, suggested that the head had been used like a tool to twist and snap the spinal cord. Kevin knew what that meant: *A very cold, confident, trained killer.* The deceased did have some neck bruising, as well as some facial injuries. That suggested that she had been struck violently and perhaps grasped at the throat. *So the killer beat her before precisely killing her. Why? To get her to admit where valuables were, right?* Kevin knew that was the logical, most likely conclusion. *That suggested it was a robbery, however. Sure, the purse was taken and the door kicked in. But, the method of killing, the precision of it, was not that of a methhead. Nor of a typical burglar. It was that of a trained killer.*

Kevin leaned back from the desk, using one of his hands to massage his muscular neck. *All the weight training in the world,* he reflected, *doesn't stop me from getting a sore neck caused from bending my head over my desk too much.* Finishing his neck massage Kevin turned his attention back to the case.

"So, if the husband didn't do it, then could he have hired someone?" he said aloud.

Having asked himself that question, Kevin turned his thoughts back to the evidence before him on the desk. *There was no indication of marital infidelity or problems.* Kevin knew enough to know that such things might not surface quite so easily. But, the couple was not buried in credit card debt nor were their bank accounts empty. That took his focus to the phone records. However, he saw no high volume of calls to or from any single number. Unless one of them had a secret cell phone, there was no evidence that either had any extramarital affairs. *All this is making it hard to assign a motive to the husband.*

Kevin was now back to burglary as the most likely cause of her death. Besides the purse, a folder of savings bonds was missing. But, that hardly merited a professional killer robbing the house. Savings bonds were numerically unique and thus quite traceable. The husband had reported that neither of them carried much cash. There had been no activity on her credit card, which Kevin had ensured was kept open.

But if not robbery, then what? Why kill a retired lady who is a genealogist, golfer and gardener? Why a professional killer? Kevin realized the answer lay in him painting a picture of anything and everything Mary had been doing in the days and weeks leading up to her death. His thoughts went to the computer, and he realized he had not yet received a report on the computer contents. He reached out and picked up his desk phone, shoving it over his shoulder and pressing it against his ear. Running his hand down a phone list taped to the desk, he dialed the number his finger found. It rang and then someone answered.

"Information Technology," said a voice on the other end of the line.

"Hi, this is Inspector Kevin Falls in homicide. I need the status on a crime scene computer. Case is Mary Fester."

"Oh, that woman murdered in her home," a young voice replied.

They're all young in the computer department, Kevin thought. *God, I hope somebody who knows the chain of custody rules for evidence is supervising them.*

"Let's see, Myers has that. Hold on, I'll transfer you."

The phone clicked before Kevin could even think of saying thank you. A moment later, it was ringing again. Then another young voice answered. It took Kevin a moment to realize it was a recorded voice.

"Hi," the message began cheerfully. "This is Steve Myers. Can't answer my phone now, so leave a message."

At the beep, Kevin spoke. "Steve, this is Kevin Falls in homicide. I have the Mary Fester murder and I understand you have her computer. I'm definitely going to need to know everything that's stored in it. I'm particularly interested in her email. Please make it a priority and let me know when it's ready. Thanks!"

Kevin hung up the phone and turned his attention back to the files. His thoughts returned to the message from Sean. He flipped though his notes and found his entry. It was from a man identifying himself as Sean who mentions a person named Kim. He grabbed the phone records and thumbed though them, reaching the last page. There, he spotted two received calls on Monday afternoon. One was local. *That has to be the husband calling from the friend's house.* Nevertheless, he wrote it down in his notes for following up. Then he turned his attention to the other number. The area code, 206, looked familiar.

Reaching down to the keyboard drawer, he grasped the mouse wiggling it to wake up his computer. Once the screen blinked on, he quickly launched a search engine, entered "206 area code" and pressed the "enter" key on his keyboard. In what seemed instantaneous, he had a screen full of results indicating the area code was Seattle, Washington.

Now intrigued, Kevin used the mouse to open his browser links and selected a "reverse white pages" website he liked. Once it opened, he typed in the full phone number and clicked on "search." After a few seconds, a screen appeared displaying "no results." The website also offered all sorts of ways to pay money and obtain "more" results. Kevin, however, suspected the number was probably a cell phone.

Instead of following one of the pay links, Kevin closed the search engine window and opened up his contacts list within his email program. There, he found the service he was looking for, a police and official-use-only system where he could look up any phone number he needed. He called the service and, once someone answered, gave his personal identifying code and quickly received a name and address. He thanked the person and hung up.

Pleasingly, the name he had gained, Sean Johnson, matched the name on the answering machine. He lived in Seattle. Kevin found that very interesting. He decided against calling the number immediately. Instead, he re-launched his search engine and entered the name. He typed in "Seattle" for good measure and initiated the search. Within a few minutes he was certain he had found his man. Very interestingly, he appeared to be a reporter or a journalist of some type. Kevin had found a few stories written by the reporter, as well as a few references to the man. *This certainly feels like the right direction,* Kevin thought. *Journalists in Seattle don't call retired ladies in Phoenix for any old reason.* Kevin decided to create a file on the man and run a national records check.

Kevin then turned his attention to tracking down some remaining loose ends. He began by focusing on all out-of-state calls made or received. By running area codes, and going backwards he spotted a call to Kansas City and a call from Knoxville, Tennessee. The city of Knoxville jarred his memory. Kevin flipped through his notes quickly finding what he wanted. Mary Fester had a brother, a professor, in Knoxville. *That must be him.* The husband had reported that she had spoken with her brother the week before, a rare occurrence.

Kevin leaned back again and thought for a moment. His brain felt tired and he glanced at his desk clock. It was early afternoon. Somehow, Kevin had worked right through lunch. He needed a break and something to eat.

Knoxville

It was early evening and the weather was about as perfect as it could be. Sean suspected that late April was probably one of the nicest times in this area. He was sitting outdoors on the patio of a café with the professor due at any moment. The café was perched along a street that plunged down and across the creek which ran through Knoxville. Tall trees towered over the outside eating area. Across the street and to his right, the red brick buildings of the University of Tennessee rose upwards among even more trees. Students were scattered around at the remaining tables. In fact, Sean was once again the oldest person at the café. That was one reason he looked forward to the professor's arrival. He had been there for about an hour, outlining the story some more and just generally relaxing. He spent the better part of the day at the university library reading up on Abraham Lincoln and the city of Denver. The two topics had actually not melded together well. Denver had grown from being a small muddy town into a modern city well after Lincoln had been assassinated. Still, both topics had been absorbing.

Sitting there, Sean considered whether being a reporter and journalist was really a great future. His father had left him with a home and enough money that Sean did not have to earn much to enjoy a decent life. He certainly enjoyed being a writer and investigator. Considering how blue collar and physical his first ten years out of high school had been, it was not predictable he would wind up doing this job. But in

college, journalism is what had attracted him. He had gotten a chance
to write a story that Paul had liked and had purchased. That, he realized, is what cemented his decision. He could see how the internet
was changing the economics of news and information, though. The
industry was globalizing as well, leaving small newspapers and independent journalists behind.

Sean was broken out of his thoughts by the sight of the professor
walking toward him. He smiled and gestured toward the open chair
at the small table. James Enloe smiled back at him and took the seat,
sliding in heavily, as if overly tired.

"Long day?" Sean asked.

"Longer than most. I have two lectures on Wednesdays. I also had
two committee meetings earlier today. Finally, I had several student
meetings on top of that." James looked at Sean. "You, on the other
hand, look very relaxed. Like you've had an easy day."

Sean held up his hands as if in protest.

"Oh no. I've been very busy and extremely productive. The relax-
ation you see in me is entirely the product of sitting at this café in your
fine city, basking in this beautiful weather."

"Fair enough," the professor grunted. He then looked around.
"I think I need a coffee. You want anything?"

"No, I'm good." Sean gestured towards his cup. "It's taking me a
while to get through this."

James stood up. "Okay, I'll be right back then."

Sean watched the professor walk into the café. It struck him that
not only were they the oldest there, they also were the tallest. *Some
of the oldest,* he corrected himself, noting the arrival of another man
about his age. Sean relaxed for a few minutes, letting his mind wander
through his questions again.

A few minutes later the professor returned, carrying a paper coffee
cup complete with a lid. He looked irritated.

"Ridiculous," he declared as he sat down. "Would you believe they
have no real dishes or mugs here? It's all paper. We've become a dis-
posable-recyclable nation. Lost is the simple pleasure of holding a hot
mug in your hand."

"Ridiculous!" he repeated.

Sean laughed gently. "I can attest that there are still places, even here in Knoxville, where they use real mugs and plates. I suspect that the problem is we are at an establishment routinely overrun by students."

"You're probably right," the professor admitted. He took a small sip of his coffee. "You know what I hate about paper? You can't tell how hot your beverage is. And everything is so damn insulated, that it takes forever to cool down." As he finished speaking, he ripped off the lid of his paper cup, revealing the steaming black coffee beneath.

"Ah, this is better," he said.

"So, Professor," Sean intervened. "I told you on the phone that your sister had added new elements to my quest for this story. Mary introduced me to a woman in Kansas City with a story so fascinating, that I flew there to interview her."

"Well, you're fascinated by things, Mr. Johnson, that I find humorous." The professor was being sarcastic, adding a slight humorous tone to his voice.

He's easier to interview in the evening than at other times. Sean stored this observation away as useful knowledge, not only for the professor, but also for all future interviews. *Interview them at their best time of day, not yours.*

"Okay, but I think you'll find this interesting," Sean replied.

"Okay lay it on me!" The professor took another sip of coffee, then looked as if he was ready to listen.

"Well, it begins with this woman, Kim Poole, finding a letter from her recently deceased father. It tells her that her real last name should have been Thomas."

Sean continued, walking the professor through the events of the last week. As he spoke, the afternoon light began to give way to twilight. The professor listened attentively and truly seemed intrigued as Sean brought in the Enloe connection.

"So that's it. I have not been able to speak with Mary since I learned all of this. But, I am curious to pick your brain about what possible events in Lincoln's life could possibly involve the Thomases or the Enloes."

The professor sat quietly for a moment.

"If you weren't so serious I would probably laugh at your story. But

I can tell you are determined. Have you seen the documents?"

"Yes. They are real. This Jacob was clearly afraid of something. I think it's accurate that he was a Thomas."

"Hmm." The professor was lost in thought, so Sean sat patiently. Finally, James brought his eyes down and locked into Sean's.

"The government at the time of President Lincoln was nothing like it is today. The Civil War, of course, made things even more different than you or I could ever truly imagine. Washington D.C. was at the edge of the war zone for quite a while and there were always evacuation plans ready at a moment's notice."

"President Lincoln's assassination changed everything about the approachability of the president. Even during the war, President Lincoln had to surrender his habit of riding back to the White House alone on his horse. Alone! Can you imagine that?"

The professor's voice grew louder as he began to get involved in teaching Sean.

"His assassination came at the end of a terrible, bloody, costly war. The war itself had resulted in a loss of liberty and rights of citizens on a level that we, today, would attribute as being appropriate for the most brutal and corrupt government in Africa. It was a terrible conflict that pitted a nation of free people against itself. In doing so, much of the people's humanity suffered."

"And people suffered. Mothers lost children and husbands alike. The machinery of war improved before and during the war, making killing and maiming much easier. The government did what was necessary." The professor paused. "On both sides too, Sean. Nobody was clean."

"Then, President Lincoln was assassinated. There was a brief burst of widespread panic, that changed over to grief or excitement, depending on perspective."

"There never has been much doubt that Lincoln's assassination was part of a conspiracy. It was carried out and aided by a whole band of southern sympathizers all of whom, or almost all, had been spies for the South. By definition, that's a conspiracy. There is even evidence that the Confederacy could have ordered the assassination. There is strong evidence that the southern leadership did, at some point, try to kidnap the president. There's quite a bit of evidence showing Booth to be a southern spy who, at the direction of the South, formed the band of spies that carried out Lincoln's assassination."

"You may or may not know that Lincoln was just one of four targets that night. He was just the only successful one. And though today we look at Lincoln as a universally loved martyr, he was hated by plenty of people in the North, including some in the Federal Government."

"There was a theory proposed by a chemist in the middle of the twentieth century that the Secretary of War, Edwin Stanton, was involved in a conspiracy to kill Lincoln. About the only motive identifiable is that Stanton did not like or respect Abraham Lincoln, as a person, at all. But, he came to accept Lincoln as the President. Moreover, the logic and the theories proposed by the chemist—his name was Eisenschiml, if I remember correctly—were terribly flawed and misleading. Kind of like the grassy knoll theory in Kennedy's assassination. Ever since then, though, you'll hear people throw Stanton's name out there."

The professor paused and gulped some of his now cooled coffee.

"So if you ask me, this Jacob Thomas had to have been afraid of something associated with the war or the assassination of Lincoln. But, the list of things that it could have been is quite long. On this list of possible fears would have to be that he had knowledge of Union or northern involvement in Lincoln's assassination. Or perhaps he had knowledge of northerners who knew of the plan to assassinate President Lincoln but did nothing."

"Beyond that," James said, sweeping his arms open, "he could have had knowledge of corruption in the government or something truly terrible that the government did."

Sean had listened carefully to this long speech and now spoke.

"So then, and here is the weird part, what is the connection to the Enloes?"

"I don't know," James admitted, shaking his head. "I haven't the slightest idea."

"But do you think it's most likely that this Jacob Thomas was afraid of something he knew that happened during the war or about the assassination itself?"

"Yes, but that is still my conjecture. This is an interesting story, but it's also a bit surprising. I would like to think about this before I give you misleading advice. I'm having a hard time understanding the Enloe connection."

"I understand that completely, Professor. To be honest, this has been a bit of a whirlwind for me as well. My gut feeling is that there is something lurking in this Jacob Thomas fellow's story that would be very worthwhile to figure out."

"Hell, I came out here a week ago to research a pretty simple story, but it has become much more complex and has me rethinking what to make of it. I just don't know."

The professor leaned back in his chair. Sean also relaxed and took in his surroundings. The night was closing in and some students had left or had gone inside.

It was then that Sean caught a simple movement of a man behind the professor that sent a shiver of instant alertness through his body, a programmed and trained reaction. The man he had noticed arriving at the same time as the professor had averted his eyes in a way that Sean recognized from his own training. Sean had noticed the movement in part, because there were less people on the patio and in part, because the man himself stood out, much like Sean and the professor.

As Sean, with his old training kicking in, continued his eye, head and body movements as if he had noticed nothing, his mind raced through the observed motion.

He was carefully listening to us. Sean tried to rationalize it, thinking the professor's speech would have been interesting to anyone. But Sean added up the facts leaning the other way. The man had arrived right after the professor. He managed to never look Sean in the eyes, despite the fact that he was facing them. *And,* Sean thought, as his mind went back though his observations, *he never bought a drink. He never looked like he came here for a reason. Somehow he snuck into the table behind us without me really paying any attention to him.*

Sean decided to look the man in the eyes. His reaction might tell Sean a lot about him. He could remember one of his former instructor's saying, *The eyes are everything Sean. You can read a man, affect his behavior, even defeat him through his eyes. But you can also be defeated yourself, through your eyes.*

Sean focused his eyes at the middle of the man's torso and moved up. *Loose, thick dark jacket,* he observed. *He could be carrying a gun. Dark brown pullover shirt underneath. Stubble on his throat and chin.* Then, he reached the man's brown eyes. They looked away from him briefly, but then came back to lock Sean's eyes in a full stare. He could hear the professor talking again, but his mind was now zeroed in on the man behind the professor. They maintained their stare for at least ten seconds. The man's eyes were cold and challenging. Sean now suspected that his intuition had been right: the man had not accidentally ended up listening in on a conversation, he had intentionally crept in to listen.

Worse, this man was confident and dangerous. Adrenaline began to rise in Sean's body as he felt old skills and teachings trying to wake up from a long slumber. He worked at keeping his eyes locked on the other man's stare.

Sean soon felt overwhelmed. The man was holding his gaze relentlessly and Sean could not mentally clear his mind enough to recall any strategy for what to do from his old training. Sean knew he was rusty. He tried to think of an explanation for the man's presence, something that would give Sean a road map for what action to take, but he could not think of anything. Finally, in need of a chance to think clearly, he dropped his stare.

The man exploded upwards the instant Sean did so. For a moment, Sean was certain he had made a fatal mistake, one that could not be undone. *You're a soft and rusty form of your old self.* But instead of moving towards Sean, the man pivoted backwards and, in a flash, had hurtled out of the patio, down the steps and turned left on the sidewalk.

Sean's mind was stalled for a moment. The shock of the man's action froze him. After a moment or two though, his mind clicked and he recognized a simple truth, *the man was using the element of surprise to execute an evasion. The proper action was to pursue at a safe distance!* Hurtling himself out of the chair, Sean had no doubt he was startling the professor, but he did not even let himself so much as glance down at him. Instead, he hissed at the professor in a very commanding voice.

"Stay right here! Go nowhere!"

Then, Sean was past the professor, his legs extending and pumping as hard as he could. He flew down the steps and turned left himself. The road went downhill, fairly steeply towards the creek, separating the campus from downtown Knoxville. There were few people on the street. *The mysterious man is nowhere to be seen!* He began running at full speed on exactly the same vector that man had taken. Inside his head, he ticked off the time that the man had been ahead of him. As his mental count reached the right moment, a set of steps that cut into the hill appeared on his left and led upwards. He ran past them, then stopped and pivoted. Sean then peeked his head around the corner looking up the stairway. He saw nothing and quickly lurched forward up the steps. It was a path across a lawn, with lights about every thirty feet on alternating sides of the path. As he reached the top, he studied the terrain in all directions.

Again, Sean saw no sign of the stranger. Logic told him the man had come this way. He spotted a hedge running down the hill towards the creek and realized it was the best, and perhaps only, place for the man to have ducked out of sight. Sean turned and flew across the lawn, but stayed on his side of the hedge as he ran along it.

Sean's adrenaline had fully kicked in, but Sean could now feel his lungs heaving and throat burning. Still, as he reached the end of the hedge, he forced his breathing down to slow deep breaths that made minimal noises. He stopped abruptly, trying to listen for sounds around him. Hearing nothing, he dropped low and crept around the hedge onto a paved path that ran along the creek. Again, he saw and heard nothing. The lighting was low here, mostly diffused light reaching across the creek from the various buildings that made up downtown Knoxville. He turned his head quickly back and forth from his low position, looking for movement. He saw nothing and realized the man had to have run up the path. About fifty yards further, there was a divergence in the path. The man could have run across the creek on a bridge or he could have turned back up the hill.

Sean took off again, running at full speed, and when he reached the bridge he suddenly turned away from it on a hunch. He was guessing the man was unsure he could clear the bridge and the open area on the other side before Sean could catch up. Sean turned uphill pushing himself as hard as he could. Now, he knew his reserve capacity was spent and he would not be able to control his breathing at all. So, instead of trying to slow down at blind spots, he ran full speed trying to protect himself with surprise more than caution. As he ran, he thought through his training on search and evasion. *Always anticipate the other person's thoughts, decisions and movements. Use surprise or caution to protect yourself. Seek higher ground, but always take the most unexpected, but safe course.*

The path had reached a street that ran between some red brick buildings of the university. The street probably was gated from vehicles, Sean suspected. He saw none. He stopped under a tree that shadowed him from the light and peered up and down the street, at the buildings across the street, and even back at the path he had come from. He was breathing heavily, but trying to suppress the sound.

Seeing nothing, and realizing that he had clearly lost the man, Sean pulled back farther into the shadow of trees. He stood there trying to catch his breath and slow his heart. He felt the first trembles washing over his body that came from the post-adrenaline surge and began doing the little muscle flexing exercises he knew would suppress the trembling. As he stood there in the dark, his mind raced through the possible implications.

Was I overreacting? No. Everything the man did demonstrated training. And fitness. The man was a professional, as I was once. He was dangerous. Most likely he'd been following the professor or me. He certainly had been spying on our conversation. And, when confronted, he had executed evasive actions. Why?

The question of "Why?" was stuck in Sean's head as he looked about and then began working his way back to the café. His legs felt weak from the unexpected demand he had placed on them and his body felt spent. But his mind stayed sharp. He considered whether the spying man could possibly relate to Jacob's fears and warning. *That's silly,* he told himself. But, in the back of his head, the warning from the grave grew into the only logical explanation.

"Sean, this story has suddenly become very, very interesting," he said aloud.

Chapter Thirteen

Knoxville

As Sean was returning to the café he was surprised to see two uniformed police officers talking to the professor. James was slouched in the chair at the table where he and Sean had been sitting. As Sean was trotting up the steps onto the patio, they all turned to look at him. The police officers' hands shifted to their holstered guns, but Sean noticed the guns were still strapped in, making any effort to draw them futile. Sean perceived there was significant tension in the air. Still breathing hard, he stood there for a moment, keeping his hands wide and open palmed. The more he observed the scene, the more he could tell that something was very wrong. The professor had glanced up at him and the look on his face was one of utter shock.

"Hi. Did the professor call you?" Sean found the breath to say.

One officer just shook his head, while the other moved a little further to Sean's right.

The one moving commanded, "Keep your hands where they are and identify yourself!"

Sean was slightly confused by the behavior, but put it off to the bizarre event that had just unfolded in front of the professor.

"Sean Johnson. I'm a reporter who was interviewing the professor here."

"Thank you," the officer replied. He looked over at his partner who nodded to him.

"Please step over here, Mr. Johnson," the first police officer said, gesturing towards a small table on the far side of the patio. Sean noticed several faces staring out from the café at the scene unfolding in front of them.

"Is there something wrong officer?" Sean asked, still feeling that something was not right.

"Please step over here," the cop repeated.

Sean glanced at the professor still slumping at the table, but the professor continued to ignore him and just sat, slumped at the table. *This is weird. Something has happened. Something is very wrong.*

"Professor, are you okay? Why are these police officers here?"

The professor turned up to look at him. Sean could now see that the man's eyes were bloodshot and his pupils dilated. He was definitely in shock. Sean knew that his sudden action should have surprised the professor, but the reaction he was seeing was something else.

"What? What is it? Tell me what's going on here."

James Enloe looked as if he was going to speak but the police officer gesturing for Sean to step over to the small table intervened.

"Mr. Johnson, I need to insist that you come over here. NOW!"

The cop had raised his voice enough to make it clear to Sean that he was serious and was running out of patience.

"Okay, okay," Sean said, sounding as cool as he could. He began walking to the small table, glancing more closely at the police officer. He looked to be in his later thirties. His belly was pressing against the heavy fabric of his uniform, but his arms appeared well-toned. He had light blonde hair with a matching bushy mustache.

Sean sat down at the small table. His whole body was exhausted from his recent exertion and he sat down harder than he had intended to. *The cop had to have noticed that.*

The officer sat down across from him. Sean took a deep breath and worked on calming down the rising tension in his body. Between the professor's behavior and the police officer's formality, Sean felt he had lost any understanding of what was going on. He felt overwhelmed. Something was definitely wrong.

"So, what is going on?" he asked the officer. "Did the professor tell you what just happened?"

The cop had taken out a small notebook and a pen. Despite the tension, Sean almost wanted to laugh at how much the cop looked like a reporter doing an interview, like himself. *Except I don't have handcuffs, mace, a stun gun, a radio and a semi-automatic pistol strapped to my waist when I do interviews.*

"Kind of, but why don't you tell me what happened."

"Okay. I was interviewing the professor when I noticed a strange man eavesdropping on our conversation. I locked eyes with him for about ten seconds and the moment I dropped my stare, he bolted. I chased him hard, but he disappeared very quickly. Too quickly. In my estimation, he was a trained professional. He knew how to escape."

"Could you describe him?"

"Sure. He was about five foot ten." Sean paused and thought back through his observation of the man. "Strong and athletic, probably about 180 pounds. Brown eyes and hair. Black beard stubble though, or at least very dark. Looked to be in his mid to late 40's. Hair was cut pretty tight. Somewhat like yours."

"He was wearing a dark jacket with no markings, loose dark-colored slacks and rubber soled dress shoes."

"You notice a lot of details," the police officer countered.

"I was trained that way," Sean explained. "In the military. So tell me, please, what is wrong with the professor. He looks like a bomb went off in his head."

As soon as Sean said that, another phrase came to mind. *He looks like someone died.* Then, Sean was struck with the obvious. *Mary! I haven't heard from her for days. She's dead. That's the reason for the professor's behavior.* His mind whirled through the possibilities.

"His sister has been killed," the cop confirmed, watching Sean's face closely. *He's watching my expression and he's wondering if I had something to do with her murder.*

"Murdered?" Sean stumbled on the officer's words. "Mary? In Phoenix?"

The cop nodded. "Yes. Did you know her?"

"Well yes. I mean, not really." Sean's mind was racing. *Murdered? This is quickly getting out of hand.*

"I had exchanged emails and voicemail with her over the last week.

I wanted to meet with her after finishing interviewing her brother here. How was she killed?"

"I cannot disclose that, sorry." The cop looked at his note pad. "You said the man was eavesdropping on your conversation? How could you tell?"

"Okay, listen," Sean felt a surging sense of panic. "A long time ago I was trained in counterespionage and related tactics. Spying if you want to call it that. I left that life behind years ago, but tonight those old skills helped me notice this man. It was his behavior that confirmed he had bad intentions."

Sean looked over at the professor. He was quietly talking to the other cop now. He could tell he was about to leave.

"Listen, I need to talk with the professor, privately."

"Really? What do you need to talk to him about?"

Sean regretted his request, now sensing accusation and suspicion in the officer's voice.

"I just want to talk to him about his sister." Sean started to stand, but the officer jumped up more quickly.

"Stay here for a moment, Mr. Johnson." He held his hand out like he was giving the "stay" command to a dog and afterwards walked over to the table with the other cop and the professor. He hunched down next to his partner and they began whispering back and forth, glancing at Sean periodically.

Meanwhile, Sean could see that the students in the café had not ceased their complete fascination with the activity on the patio. Sean felt like a fish in an aquarium sitting by himself at the table. He also felt overwhelmingly disoriented. He knew the rapid sequence of events was threatening him with shock as well. Again, he focused on calming himself. *Slow, deep breathing. Focus on your inner self. See yourself in the universe with everything as it should be.*

Finally he saw "his" cop disengage from his partner and walk back over to him. He reached Sean.

"My partner is going to escort the professor home. I need to ask you a few more questions, okay?"

"No, that's not okay," Sean said feeling anger rising.

"Professor, professor, will you please speak to me?" he called out.

Sean started to act like he was going to move, but, as he expected, the cop held his hand out. James got up from his table, glanced once at Sean and then started walking out a side exit of the patio. After glaring back at Sean momentarily, the other cop followed the professor out.

Sean noticed his notebook still sitting on the table while his small backpack sat on the ground next to the table. He felt his anger getting stronger.

"Look, Officer…" Sean read the nametag pinned on the cop's chest. "…Murray, I want to know what the hell is going on here! Do you suspect me of killing his sister? Is that it? What are you doing here?" Sean felt adrenaline quickly flowing in his body. But he held himself under control as much as possible.

The cop stepped back a pace and moved his hand back onto his holster. Sean tried to calm himself.

"Okay, look officer, I'm in nearly as much shock as the professor. You have just told me that his sister was murdered. I just chased a very suspicious man away from us. Don't you think those things are connected?"

"They might be," Officer Murray acknowledged. "Can I ask you some more questions?"

"Yes, by all means," Sean said tiredly, feeling his energy now fully drained away. "Ask your damn questions!"

"You recently communicated with Mary Fester. What was it about?"

"Did I tell you that?" Sean asked. He tried to remember what he had just told the cop. Finally, he remembered that he had told the police officer about his connection to Mary. "Sorry, I'm just feeling spent. It was about this story I'm trying to write." Sean felt his mind sharpening. *Keep the facts to a minimum. There's something going on here and until you know what it is, play this close to your chest. Don't tell him about Kim or all the stuff about Lincoln, the Enloes and especially the danger.*

Besides, Sean laughed to himself. *He'll think I'm nuts.*

Sean calmed himself and answered the cop's remaining questions. The officer was not interested in Sean's story about the strange man and Sean suspected he did not really respect Sean's judgment. Sean also provided the police officer his driver's license and the cop jotted down Sean's information.

.....

A few minutes later, Sean had collected his notebook and bag and was walking back to his hotel. As he passed the steps leading up in the direction he had pursued the stranger, he stopped and stared for a moment. Sean mentally replayed the sequence of events from the moment he truly noticed the man until he had given up on the chase. In some ways, the man had been a phantom. From the moment he had dropped out of sight going down the steps, Sean had never seen him again. Sean searched his memory to see if he had missed something. But nothing came to mind. Discouraged, he returned to walking down the hill, across the creek and up to his hotel.

Now, however, Sean was very alert and observant as if he was on patrol. He noticed details about every vehicle and tried to observe features of the drivers of every car that approached him. He constantly scanned horizons and took glances back over his shoulder at random intervals. He thought of James. *The tough professor must be tremendously torn up right now.* Sean wondered if the professor had any other siblings. Something told him the answer was no.

Then, Sean thought of the stranger's presence and Mary's murder and a new thought came to his mind. *James may be in danger!* He pulled his cell phone out of his jacket and called James's office number, the only number he had for the professor. After hearing the message followed by the beep, Sean spoke.

"James, I am devastated that Mary has been murdered. I know this is a huge shock for you. You have all of my sympathy. Obviously, my concern about the story is gone. But I am concerned for you. Please don't hesitate to call me anytime. Also, please consider that Mary's murder and the stranger I spotted at the café tonight could be related. I did not share this with you, but in my past I worked for the government in ways that required my training in special operations, intelligence and espionage. The man that I believe followed you to the café is a very dangerous man. His skill at evading me was quite high. I have no idea if this does or could relate to the Jacob Thomas warnings, but I think you should be extremely careful until we know what is going on.

I hope to God that I'm worried about nothing, but until we know, be very careful. If something seems wrong or out of place, please don't hesitate to call the police. And again, James. Call me soon. Any time, day or night."

Sean repeated his cell number twice and then hung up. He had reached the hotel and stepped into the lobby. Then another thought struck him. *Could Kim be in danger?* He froze in the lobby, running the events through his mind and trying to connect them to various people and events that had unfolded over the last few days. Kim had been in close contact with Mary until she had quit communicating. If Kim was in danger, Sean knew, it could only be because there was truth to Jacob Thomas's warning. So the question was could there be truth in that warning, today, more than one hundred years after it was made?

Sean thought this over and concluded that he had to assume the stranger and Mary's murder were related. If they were, the only logical connection would be the Jacob Thomas letter. Thus, Kim could be in the same danger. He knew he could be overreacting, but his intuition told him he was not. *If I'm right...Kim is in danger!*

Sean turned around and stepped back outside of the hotel, seeking the privacy of the louder outdoor environment. He selected Kim's cell phone number and called her. After five rings, just as he was certain he was going to get her voicemail, she answered.

"Hello?"

"Hi Kim. This is Sean."

"Sean? Hi." She sounded confused and Sean knew she was wondering why he was calling her.

"Hi Kim. Sorry to bother you so late. It's important though."

"That's okay. Where are you?"

"I'm in Knoxville. Listen, I have some real bad news for you. You better sit down."

There was a pause.

"What are you talking about?"

"Kim, Mary is dead. She was murdered. I'm sorry."

The phone was silent. Sean tried to imagine Kim's shock and what she was thinking.

"Wha-what? What are you saying?" she stammered

"Kim, the police here in Knoxville told me she was murdered. They would not give many details. I was with James Enloe, her brother the professor, when they told him. He's pretty beat up over it."

"Murdered?" Kim's utterance turned into a wail. "Murdered?" Sean could then hear another voice in the background. It was Abby, who must have come running when she heard her mom. There was a flurry of voices and then Kim's, sounding stronger, telling Abby to sit down on the bed.

"Sean?" she said returning her attention to the phone.

"Yes."

"I want to know why. Why was she killed? When did it happen?"

"I don't know Kim, but I want to know as well." Sean paused as he tried to determine the best way to explain things to her. "Listen, there is more I need to tell you. Are you okay though?"

"Yes, yes. I'm okay. But it's so awful! She was such a nice lady. And patient and calm." Kim sobbed for a moment and then sounded as if she had gathered herself. "Okay, I'm okay."

"Listen! Something else happened tonight. A stranger was eavesdropping on my meeting with the professor. I could tell that he was a dangerous man. When I noticed him, he bolted away at full speed."

"What? Why?"

"I don't know. One of my deepest fears is that he was connected to Mary' murder. Are you following me?"

"Yes, I think so, but, why would someone want to kill Mary? Why would they care about her brother as well?"

"I don't know, but the coincidence is too great to ignore. If they are related, the only reason I can come up with, no matter how unlikely, is Jacob's warning. I know that sounds crazy, but it's possible and if it is…"

Sean found it hard to go farther. He did not want to scare Kim and found himself questioning whether or not he was overreacting. But Kim interrupted his thoughts, urging him to continue.

"What Sean? What are you saying?"

"If Jacob's warning is real, then you also could be in danger. I don't know why, and I could be nuts, but it's possible."

"No, no…" Kim's voice drifted off.

"Look Kim. I may be wrong, but in the slim chance that I'm right, we need to take some precautions."

"Do you really think they're related?"

Kim now sounded overwhelmed and Sean knew he needed to calm her down and help her concentrate.

"No, I don't think they are. I can't eliminate that chance though. I don't want to scare you, Kim, but, I'm a very cautious man. I don't want anything bad to happen. If you'd seen this man tonight, you would be thinking the same way I am."

"Listen, I am going to head back to Kansas City. Please be careful! Go to work like normal. I'll get to your shop tomorrow as early as I can." He paused and then warned:

"Have your daughter be very careful as well. Both of you be aware of your surroundings. Call the police if anything seems wrong or out of place. Don't hesitate. Promise me. Okay?"

"Okay!" Kim assured him.

"Again, this could all be much ado about nothing."

"But you're worried enough about it to call me, warn me, and return to Kansas City, right?" Kim asked, sounding more like her old self.

"Yes, that's true. I need to assure you, I am a very cautious man. I also follow my instincts and my instincts tell me to be very careful. We need to look again at Jacob and his story. Then we need decide if there could be anything to it or not."

They talked a little more and then Sean hung up, knowing that Kim and her daughter would likely have a rough night. It was time for him to try and see how quickly he could get to Kansas City.

Atlanta

Mike was relaxing in his home study watching the local news channel. He was sunk in his brown leather chair. A glass of scotch dangled in the air from his right hand, which was hanging out past the end of the chair. He was slowly twisting his scotch back and forth, causing a light ringing from the ice as the drink sloshed gently against each side of the glass. He was dressed, as always, in a suit, though the jacket was hanging over a chair by the entrance of the room. His tie was missing, as well. The mahogany room was quiet, except for the murmur from the television. Mike's eyes took in the empty leather chair on the opposite side of the table. He had been expecting a call from his brother this night, updating him on the events to the north in Knoxville. While he truly enjoyed their luxurious home, it was too quiet for his liking. All his staff had left for the evening and Jessica was in Washington D.C. working some political circles for his campaign. The legislative session was over for the year, which meant his duties as a Senator were much lighter.

That's okay, Mike thought, *my campaign is just starting to demand more time. And the emergence of a Thomas lead, completely unexpected, is also quite distracting. After years of protecting the family name, we might be able to go on the offense and put an end to the threat of the Herndon letter once and for all.*

Mike lifted his hand and took a sip from his drink. He turned his attention back to the television which was now shifting into business news. A few minutes later, his focus on the television was interrupted by the ringing from his new, encrypted cell phone which was sitting on the table in front of him.

Mike leaned forward and set the drink down on a wooden coaster that was resting on the table while he picked up the cell with his other hand. He glanced at the phone as he was leaning back into the chair and noted that it was his brother. As he lifted the phone to his ear with his left hand, he used his now empty drink hand to find the remote on his lap to turn off the television. The silence in the room was only momentary as he greeted his brother.

"Hello."

"Hi."

Mike immediately knew that all was not well. He could not remember the last time Terry had given him a one syllable greeting. Mike suspected that Terry's plans had gone awry.

"Speak, brother," Mike intoned. "Tell me what's going on."

"Tonight did not go as I had planned," Terry admitted with an edge of anger to his voice.

There was a silence as Mike waited for Terry to continue. He thought about his brother's failures and wondered about his brother's stability. *He probably killed the professor! My brother is one part too confident and one part too reckless.*

Terry finally spoke, "Our Seattle reporter is as resourceful as I was concerned he might be."

Mike could still detect the anger hiding behind Terry's words.

Terry continued, "He made me while I was trying to listen in on a conversation he was having with the professor."

"Whoa! Wait a minute. The reporter was with the professor? In Knoxville?" Mike's mood had gone from concerned to surprised. "Did he see you?"

"Yes, damn it!" Terry cursed back through the phone at his brother. "I was careless, reckless. All the things you accuse me of being too often."

Mike's mind spun through these revelations. *It's good that Terry is openly admitting his mistakes. But, it's bad, very bad that this reporter saw him.*

"Did he recognize you?"

"No, no I don't think he knew who I was, if that's what you mean, but that's actually worse in a way. I think he spotted me as somebody spying on them. That tells me that his observation skills are good. Worse, he pursued me across the campus very well. I barely escaped without a confrontation."

"He chased you?" Mike was now growing alarmed.

"Yes. I had been tailing the professor from his office on the Tennessee campus. He went to a café where the reporter, Sean Johnson, was waiting for him. I recognized the reporter right away. I made a gut decision to slip into a table next to them. I really did not think the reporter would have any reason to be looking for a tail."

"I don't think he was looking," Terry continued. "They got into a very deep conversation about Lincoln, the Enloes and Jacob Thomas, brother. I was so amazed at the discussion, I think I got a bit careless. Then this guy, Sean Johnson, looks up at me briefly, looks away, then comes back for a full on stare. As soon as it broke, I jumped and ran."

"Right in front of him? Are you nuts?"

"No, no. He made me. This guy showed he's well trained. I saw it in his stare back at me. We were ten feet apart. As soon as he looked away, I knew I had to get out of there. I was right! He jumped up right after me, but I managed to duck behind a hedge in the dark across a street and he ended up running right by me."

There was silence while Mike mulled over Terry's statements. Terry interrupted his silence.

"It gets a bit worse. Cops showed up back with the professor. While the reporter was looking for me, I headed back to look at the café from a vantage point. Just as I did, two campus police showed up on the patio."

"What! What did they want?"

"I don't know for a fact, but it had to have been about the sister. The professor slumped hard after they spoke to him. Then he started talking and gestured towards where the reporter and I ran. I got nervous and left."

And there it is, Mike thought. *My reckless brother kills a woman in Phoenix, probably for no good reason and pays the price a thousand miles away in Knoxville. I've got to get him under control!*

"Okay, look Terry. No more killing! Do you understand that?"

"Yes, I do brother, but don't start telling me what to do." Terry had raised his voice and Mike detected the anger coming back.

"Look Terry, I don't mean to sound like I'm bossing you around, but I'm concerned. We are perhaps on the eve of finally ending the mystery and risk of our family secret ever coming out. We cannot afford to lose this chance."

"I know, I know, brother."

Terry's voice had gone right back to the apologetic and resigned tone. *He is getting more and more mercurial,* Michael thought.

"So do you think this reporter has identified you to the police by now?"

"I don't think so. I'm logged into the police bulletin network. If this reporter had helped the police connect me to the woman's murder back in Phoenix, the word would be out everywhere to look for me. It's all silent on such topics."

"Okay, then. You need to stay low for a while and slip back here in the next day or so. Meanwhile, I have a few ideas."

"Send them at me," Terry said.

"First, let's let this group work on the secret fairly unimpeded. A reporter and a Lincoln professor, who is an Enloe, no less, chasing Jacob Thomas is a good thing, so long as we keep tabs on them and intervene at the right time." Mike could feel his confidence rising.

"Second, in order to keep tabs on them, let's bring a team into the United States to keep an eye on the reporter. You can hand pick them from our European team. Give them a well thoughtout storyline with a pretend client. When need be, we can shuttle them right back out of here with nobody the wiser. It will also allow you to stay behind the scenes for a while."

"Third, start digging and doing complete workups on these two people, the reporter and the professor. We need to know everything going on with them."

Mike paused and Terry spoke.

"Okay. That's all good, but we need to include the woman in Kansas City. She is actually the key. Remember it's her who is apparently a descendant of Jacob Thomas, and it is her who connected the Enloes somehow to Thomas. I can only think of one reason for that."

"You're right, but, if she had the Thomas letters, then she would not be sending out vague inquiries on the internet. Still, we cannot ignore the fact that she might have the letters, or might find them quickly. The net around all three of them needs to be tight. We have to be able to intervene quickly, very quickly!"

"Yes, yes," Terry said enthusiastically. "Very tight!"

"But. you need to stay back. If this reporter has described you to the police, we have got to be very careful."

"Yes, yes brother, but don't worry. If that happens, I should know about it before the police themselves. As you know, our systems and access are very good."

"Okay, but they were not good enough to tell you about this reporter, were they?"

"No, but recall I sensed that he would be more talented and challenging than most." Terry paused. "But don't worry brother, I won't underestimate him again. And yes, I'll be careful."

"Good!"

Terry and Mike said good-bye and Mike hung up. He set the phone down on the armchair and leaned his head back, staring upwards. He noted the intricately carved wood trim running all around the ceiling and tried to recall the first time he had noticed it. *I had to have been pretty young.* He let his eyes follow the patterns. *It's really good craftsmanship.*

Suddenly, Mike got up. He picked up his scotch and headed out of the study and upstairs to his private office. Once there, he went over to a bookshelf, setting his drink on his desk as he passed it. He flipped open a small section of the bookshelf that revealed a very old safe embedded in the wall behind. He quickly dialed the combination, feeling the very heavy tumbler work its gentle spinning magic. Once he was done, he grasped the smooth steel handle swinging it ninety degrees. It always fascinated him how he could never hear or feel the slightest click in the workings of the safe.

With the door open, Mike pulled out a leather pouch that was sitting vertically against one side of the safe. He took the pouch to his desk setting it down while he sat himself down in his chair. He then opened the leather container and pulled out a small set of documents. One was an old letter on yellowed paper. It was this letter that he lifted out of the stack. The sheets were flat, but there was an old crease where they had once been folded. He read the letter through, finding, as always, the writing hard to follow. It had been long enough since his last reading that he had forgotten most of its exact wording.

After Mike worked his way through all the sheets, he set the letter down and stared at a window across the room. It was dark enough outside that the window was a mirror. He could see his reflection clearly. In some ways he looked just as he remembered himself as a young teen when his father had shown Terry and him the letter and other documents. He had told them then all about Jacob Thomas, as well as their history. Michael could remember being awed at seeing a letter written by President Lincoln. But, it had come with a burden, he recalled, and he knew that from that day on his perception of the world was different.

Mike sighed, bringing himself back to the present.

"Well, Dad, maybe I can finally end this." He thought again about how he and Terry had no children to pass anything along. *Why do we work so hard for the future, when we are all that's left?* he thought. He looked again at the letter and continued to think about the future.

Chapter Fourteen

Thursday, April 30
Kansas City

It was a beautiful spring day in Kansas City. Sean had just landed at the Kansas City airport and picked up a rental car. His mind was preoccupied, though, with thoughts about Kim, James, Mary, and President Lincoln. Sean noted that he had slipped into old habits quickly. He was noticing people around him and taking inventory of facts, like what clothes they were wearing, what they were doing, their age, their race, even their hair style. He knew that alertness came with a price, though. It was taking energy and concentration. At the same time, he was trying to make sense of Mary's death and sort out the connection between the Lincoln-Enloe theory and the Jacob Thomas warning.

Sean had been taught a long time ago that you should do your thinking in private rooms and your acting in public. That assumed, of course, that you were on a mission that was planned, one that you were prepared for. He had not been on a mission since the disastrous one in South America. He had no desire to ever return to that life. But now, he felt his training kick in and old familiar feelings returning. Still, he knew he was unprepared. The basic tenet of any mission was to rigorously prepare. Gaining an understanding of intelligence was absolutely required in preparation. But here he was, feeling immersed back on a mission, but lacking any intelligence. He did not know who the enemy was, or even why they were the enemy. He was not even sure if he really had an enemy or was just imagining things.

Last night, after Sean had learned that the next flight that could get him to Kansas City would not leave until the following day, he had checked into a new hotel, then checked out of his old one. More habits, he knew, that just instinctively came to him. By the time he grabbed food and settled down in his new hotel room, it was well past midnight. For a few hours, he reviewed the day's events, as well as the entire week. He went online searching for an article about Mary's murder. He found what he believed was the story, but it had few details, not even the victim's name. *An apparent home robbery?* In the end, he did not get far in making sense of things and began second guessing himself, wondering if he was overreacting.

Sean also knew that fatigue would make him more suspicious and less able to function, so he had shifted into preparation for the following day. He reviewed his schedule, looked up maps and tried to memorize everything. He thought more about what to look for and what to do if unexpected things happened. Finally, he knew he was getting tired, so he quit his preparation and tried to go to sleep. But his short rest had been fitful and poor. When his alarm woke him, he had been dreaming of Jesus dying on the mountain again. The clear overriding theme of his dream had been lack of preparation and helplessness.

So now, as Sean drove towards Kim and her shop, he was trying to suppress his need to examine and solve the mysteries surrounding him, and instead focus on observation and execution. It had been a long time since he had lived that life, though, and he found himself drifting back and forth. He was also tired and he knew that would be a definite problem. If there was a sinister group out there, one that had hunted down Mary and sent the man to spy on his conversation with James, then he needed to focus all of his concentration on being prepared to protect himself, as well as his new companions.

Sean called Kim on his way in and they had agreed to meet at the same coffee shop at one o'clock that afternoon. It was past noon when Sean exited the freeway, reached the trendy shopping area and finally parked his rental car. Sean had managed to park where he could observe the coffee shop and settled in to wait for Kim's arrival. He was across the street and could watch the coffee shop's entrance using his rear view and side view mirrors while he would also be able to see Kim approaching in front of him. As he sat there and watched for anything out of place or suspicious, he ran through things once again.

Mary is dead, most likely murdered in her home on Monday. Somebody was spying on her brother, James, last night. That somebody ran from me and appeared quite dangerous. Kim found a letter from "the grave" claiming that her great, great grandfather had changed his name out of fear that something terrible would happen. This warning was for future generations to wait until the people with the same family name as James and Mary, the Enloes, came forward and told the truth about President Abraham Lincoln. Are all of these things connected?

Sean shook his head in frustration. *It really makes no sense to connect Kim's old warning to what happened to Mary and what happened to James. Instead, what makes sense, Sean, is for you to quit trying to see shadows where there are none.*

But Sean could not shake his gut feeling that things were connected, that he was not overreacting. *And if I am right, what is the next step?* He began to work on that question while he waited for Kim to arrive.

.....

Finally, Sean could see Kim approaching. She was across the street, and though she never noticed him, he was happy that she was acting alert and observant. He watched her as she reached the point where she was even with his vehicle and then was able to see her in his side view and then rear view mirrors. Meanwhile, he scanned the area in front of them. Kim reached and entered the coffee shop, all without Sean seeing anything out of the ordinary. Sean did not move, but instead sat there scanning with his eyes. After several minutes, he finally got out of his car and headed toward the coffee shop. As he walked, he was questioning himself, still, about whether he was being paranoid. Doubts or not, though, he kept alert. He reached the coffee shop, entered and headed to Kim's table while carefully looking about. *It's busier than the last time we were here*, Sean thought, *but that makes sense, since it's lunch time.*

Kim watched Sean approach her while she tried to separate her hands from each other. She kept finding herself squeezing them out of some sort of nervous habit. Sean had come in and spotted her, but his eyes had never locked with hers. Instead, she could see, they were subtly looking about the coffee shop. *He's nervous, too*, she thought. *Is he being paranoid? True, it's shocking that Mary was murdered, but what makes her murder related to the Jacob Thomas mystery?* As she watched Sean approach her table, she also considered whether she should be suspicious of Sean himself. *He came along conveniently. Am I that gullible? But no, I trust him. Besides if he was manipulating me, that means that the Jacob Thomas warning has something real to it. That's what I'm more suspicious of than anything.*

As Kim came out of her thoughts, she realized that Sean had sat down and was now watching her. He had been sitting there for half a minute.

"Sorry, distracted," she said straightening in her chair. "Hi, it's very good to see you."

"Yeah, me too," Sean replied. "I'm so sorry about Mary."

As he said that, he reached his hand out across the table and Kim found herself involuntarily reaching out and taking it. He then placed his other hand over hers. His hands felt incredibly reassuring to Kim.

"You know, I never got to meet her in person, but she was so open, friendly and warm, I feel like I got to know her really well," Kim explained. "It's so terrible that someone would murder her."

As Kim spoke, she thought about the word "murder." *It's a terrible word,* she thought. *But, I don't think I ever really understood just how evil. I feel terrible every time I say it out loud.*

"It's still very surreal. Did you learn anything more about what happened?" Kim asked.

Sean released Kim's hand as he replied. She pulled hers back too, feeling a bit flushed about how comfortable his grip had felt.

"I searched the internet thoroughly last night. I found a story about a retired woman found dead in her home Monday evening, a victim of an apparent robbery."

Sean had pronounced the word "robbery" with a tinge of sarcasm. He continued speaking.

"I don't mean to say that she might not be the victim of a robbery gone bad, Kim, but after what happened last night, I am tremendously suspicious. I spent most of last night and this morning going through things in my head. Murder is not nearly as common as we sometimes think. The chances of a strange and dangerous person spying on her brother right afterwards is even less likely. Still, I feel like I must be crazy to think that a warning from more than a hundred years ago could still be relevant and connected to Mary's murder today."

"What makes you say this man in Knoxville was dangerous?"

"I have not always been a reporter. I served in the Navy and received secret training. I was trained in identifying and dealing with people like the man I saw last night. I also had to do some very dangerous and scary things, Kim."

Sean looked at her square on, his eyes boring into hers.

"I have not seen a man like that guy for a long time, but I assure you, men like him are real and out there. He was a professional and probably more than capable of murder."

Sean held up his hands.

"I'm not saying he killed Mary. I tried to tell the cops last night about him, and they pretty much ignored me. James had called them after I scared him with my jumping up and chasing the stranger. Turns out, they had been trying to find him in relation to Mary's murder. They even had my name already. I think they were suspicious of me, but they were not homicide investigators."

"Wait. They asked about us?"

"Not you. But the police alert had my name. I'm guessing they traced me from the cell phone call I made and maybe my emails to her.

"Oh," Kim started to feel relieved. Then her hands rushed to her face. The timing of their call struck her. "When we called Mary, she must have already been dead!" Her eyes welled up and she felt a shortness of breath as she imagined Mary dead in the house while they were leaving a message on her machine.

Sean's hands reached across the table and grasped hers again, pulling both down to the table.

"I know Kim, I know. Look, right now you need to keep it together, okay? Take a deep breath." Sean spoke firmly, trying to calm and focus her. "Nothing we can do can change the fact that she is dead. There will be time for grieving. But right now, we have got to figure out if there is a danger to James, or to you or to me. We have got to figure out the story behind Jacob Thomas."

Kim controlled herself and then began looking about. She pulled a napkin out of the holder and dabbed her eyes. Kim noticed that Sean was also looking about. Several people were staring at her, but then looked away as she glanced back at them.

"Do you think we're in danger?" she asked.

"I think it's possible. That's enough for me to be very careful. I know it might sound crazy, but the coincidence is just too unlikely to ignore."

Kim and Sean were looking at each other in their eyes and she suddenly felt reassured by his strength.

"Okay, so what do we do?"

Sean hesitated for a moment. Kim could sense he was nervous to say what was on his mind.

"What?" she demanded. "Don't hold back."

"We solve the mystery," Sean said simply. "If we're worried about Jacob's warning being real, then we find his secret. Our other options are to do nothing, or to go to the police. I don't like the do nothing option and I think the police might lock us up for being nuts."

Kim thought for a moment. "Okay, we solve the mystery. Mary would have wanted us to anyway. So what's our first step?"

"I think we need to research two things: Jacob's history and the Enloe's connection to Lincoln. I think you need to go to Denver and get everything you can about Jacob. His will, any land records, news clippings, etc."

"What else?"

"I think I should go to the Abraham Lincoln Presidential Library in Springfield, Illinois and learn everything I can that might connect Lincoln to Jacob Thomas or an Enloe. I think Mary found something. Remember her emails?"

"Yes, she said she figured out one part of the mystery."

"Well, if she found it, so can we. However, she said that it was only part."

Sean paused and looked at Kim for a moment.

"Look, I think Denver holds the key. We need to know more about Jacob."

"Okay, okay. I can do that." Kim noticed Sean looking at her bleakly. "What?"

"I mean that you should go there now. We should not waste any time!"

"I know that. I get what you're saying." Kim grimly smiled at him. "I agree with you. This is too much of a coincidence."

"Can I ask you a personal question?" Sean's voice was softer now.

"Sure, go ahead," Kim replied, her mind wondering just how "personal" the question was going to be.

"Is your daughter's father in the picture?" Sean asked awkwardly. "Does he live around here? Can she stay with him?"

Kim laughed. "Oh, he would like that, for sure." She turned serious. "No, HE is my ex-husband and HE lives in Dallas. HE gets her for two weeks a year. If I let him have her anymore than that, I'll get a court document in the mail within a week seeking to amend the child support and custody order!"

"Sorry, I had to ask. So, if you cannot send her to Dallas, you need to take her with you."

Kim sighed. "I must be nuts to be seriously considering this. Okay. Yes, I will take her with me."

"Great, so how soon can you leave?"

Kim thought for a moment. "Tomorrow, I guess. I'll need to get my store in order. Bridget can run it if she's willing, but I am not sure how easily I will get Abby out of here."

Sean smiled. "I bet you can do anything if you set your mind to it."

Knoxville

James was sitting in his study, with his phone pressed to his ear. After listening for several minutes he spoke.

"Okay Phillip. Keep me informed."

James listened some more and then spoke again.

"I'll be okay. Don't worry. I'm just glad we spoke when we did."

After a few more pleasantries, James hung up the phone and sagged heavily back into his chair. In truth, the thought of his sister being dead, worst yet, murdered, was overwhelming. He could deal with it for a few minutes and then some memory or image of her would hit him and he would need to sit and cry. It had been bewildering since he had received the news.

The thought ran through his head again, of why Phillip had not called him. *I had to hear about my sister's death from a cop, before her husband! That's wrong.* But, James knew in his heart that Phillip was not capable of having murdered Mary. He was too meek and way too kind. So, James was left to consider the image of an intruder entering his sister's house and then brutally killing her. He hoped she had not suffered fear or pain, but he suspected that she had to have endured some horror.

This reminded James of the frustrating police department in Phoenix. Apparently, they had told Phillip next to nothing. When James had finally received a return call this morning from the cop, the cop had refused to tell him very much. He would not even confirm how his sister had died. James could understand withholding from Phillip, as the police had to consider him a suspect. There was no reason, however, not to tell him, her brother, who lived a thousand miles away.

The cop had hinted that, or tacitly acknowledged that, Mary might not have died by gunshot. James knew then, that she must have died by someone's hands or some weapon, maybe a knife. That meant suffering. James did not even have the courage to ask about sexual assault. He simply was not ready for that. He also hoped beyond all hope that if that had been the case, the police would have told him.

"Dear God, please don't let her have suffered." He pleaded aloud. "Please tell me that she died peacefully."

James kicked the table as he got up. He went to the kitchen where he pulled a bottle of whiskey from a cupboard. He looked at it for a moment and considered pouring himself a drink.

"Oh, that's good! I'm drinking to deal with this," he said aloud again.

He shoved the bottle back into the cupboard, half wishing it would break and cut his hand, but he was pleased he had not taken a drink. He used to indulge way too much, he knew, and the last few years he had worked hard to reduce his drinking to near nothing.

James started to wander out of his kitchen, feeling dejected, when his phone rang. It was his cell phone. He quickly sprinted to it in his study and picked it up. It was a Seattle number, Sean Johnson's he suspected. He stared at the ringing phone in his hand, as he considered whether to answer it or not.

The night before had been bewildering, stunning and crushing. First, Sean had leapt up out of his chair right in front of him and chased a man off the patio. Actually, the professor had only sensed that some other man had leapt up behind him and dashed off. A few seconds later, Sean had done the same, saying something to him about staying there. James had decided to call the police and when they arrived they informed him that they had been given notice to inform him of Mary's murder. Everything after that was a blur. The cop had taken him home and he had barely slept all night.

Now, as James stared at the number on the cell phone display, he could not decide whether to answer it or not. He was suspicious of Sean. *No, that's not right. I'm angry with him. He had been talking to Mary more than I had for the last week.* But, Sean had acted very strange last night. He had left a message on his office phone, somehow suggesting that the stranger last night might have been connected to Mary's death, that the Jacob Thomas revelations that Sean had just finished walking James through might be related as well.

James had shut that idea down. He was not ready to deal with such a bizarre theory. The phone ringing in front of him, however, made ignoring too hard. So, he decided to answer. As he brought the phone up to his ear, though it quit ringing. He pulled it back away from his face and looked at it.

"Missed his call," James said aloud.

He decided to wait until the voicemail symbol popped up and was staring at it when it rang again.

"Damn, he's persistent," he muttered.

James reluctantly took the call.

"Hello?"

"Hi James, this is Sean. I'm sorry to bother you like this but I need to talk to you."

"Okay, well you have me," James responded, surprised at the anger in his own voice. "I haven't hung up yet."

"Look professor, I am so terribly sorry about the loss of your sister. She was very polite and considerate in every interaction I had with her."

"You must be calling me for a reason."

"That's one, I want to express my sorrow and sympathy."

There was a silent moment before Seen continued.

"Also, I need to try and ensure that you understand what happened last night and why it's so important. While we were talking a stranger was listening very closely to our conversation."

"Oh stop, Sean," the professor interrupted. "This is ridiculous. My sister was not murdered in some big conspiracy. Somebody broke into her house, killed her and now you are mocking her death with this fancy."

"Professor, wait. At least hear me out," Sean interrupted. "You may be right. God I hope you are. But you don't know everything there is to know about me. I was a Seal in the Navy and was assigned to a special job or two that brought me some specialized training and experience. The man listening to us last night was a very scary person. I know that. There are too many coincidences. I believe that."

Sean paused and hearing nothing asked, "Are you still here?"

"Yes, and I'm listening." Sean could hear a bit less anger and a bit of serious interest in his voice.

"Look, robberies happen all the time. Murders during robberies, however, are much less frequent. Having a strange man showing up to spy on the brother a couple of nights later in an entirely different city is downright super unusual. When you consider that our strange man ran off into the dark when confronted, well that's suspicious. Look, I am not saying it's certain, but it's possible. My intuition says they're related and that somehow the Jacob Thomas warning is involved."

"I think you're nuts Mr. Johnson. Plain nuts!"

"Okay, but what if I'm not?"

"I'm not playing those games!" James warned. "Good-bye."

"Wait!" Sean practically yelled into the phone. "Look, I mailed a copy of the letter along with the old note to your school address this afternoon. It's supposed to be delivered tomorrow morning. Please read them! Also, please be careful. If anything out of the ordinary happens, call me right away."

"To make you happy, and to make you go away, I promise to do both. Now good bye." James abruptly ended their conversation. He pulled the phone away from his head, pressed the red "end" button and hurled the phone into the chair at his desk. *It's bad enough that my sister is gone. It's even worse dealing with this reporter.*

Sighing, and feeling terribly restless, James decided to take a walk outside.

Phoenix

Surprised, Kevin Falls hung his phone up. The Information Technology department had just informed him that the computer had been erased. Apparently, there did not appear to be anything on the harddrive and it wouldn't even start up. They had just thrown him a serious curveball.

However, as he thought about it, it was one that he should have been expecting. Things had not been adding up. The husband appeared to not be involved, but the robbery story was too obvious, too perfect at the superficial level. As he dug deeper, though, it began falling apart. Take the cause of death, for example. It now appeared very certain that the woman had her neck broken very crisply, almost perfectly. Kevin, had actually never seen this before, though he had certainly read about it. This fact went against it being a common robbery.

Instead it looked like a professional hit using robbery as a cover-up. That was bizarre. Why kill a nice, retired lady? He could find nothing that connected her to any illegal activity, or to give anyone a motive to kill her. It made no sense. Finding out during this apparent "normal" robbery that her computer was probably tampered with just added fuel to the fire. In fact, he thought, the computer kids downstairs really sounded stumped. They reported it as if the computer had been intentionally and very completely erased. The husband had said she had been on it non-stop for the last week or so and had even probably been on it Monday morning.

"This case is going to need a lot more of my attention," he said out loud.

As Kevin spoke, he brought himself out of his thoughts and back into the busy commotion in the homicide room where his comment was swallowed up in the usual noise. He looked at the case file he had spread out on his desk and thought about his next move.

First, he realized, he needed some help on the computer issue. He flipped through his contact list and found the phone number he needed. It was the local office, in Phoenix, of the Federal Bureau of Investigation. Last year, the FBI had helped the Arizona police with some digital files in a drug case. The story of their usefulness had spread throughout the force. They might be able to assist him with this case.

Kevin dialed the number. After a few rings a woman's voice answered the phone. He introduced himself and explained what he needed. After she asked a few more questions, she promised to have someone return his call.

Satisfied with that effort, Kevin thought more about what other odd elements had been introduced into his investigation. It did not take him long to home in on Sean Johnson. He had received a report from the campus police in Knoxville that this reporter had been with the deceased's brother last night. He had acted strangely, by suddenly running off only to return a while later. Kevin had asked the brother, James Enloe, this morning on the phone about it and James had confirmed the odd behavior. James believed that the "Kim" mentioned by Sean on the voice message was a woman connected to a story on Abraham Lincoln that the reporter had been working on. But, James had also told him that he had referred the reporter to Mary. He thought that Mary and Sean had not yet met.

Kevin had gotten distracted for a while after that call, but he now considered this information. He decided he needed to consider Sean Johnson a high priority person of interest. To Kevin, it seemed unlikely, but possible, that the reporter might have had a hand in the death. The reporter's story was apparently about Abraham Lincoln though, a topic that the deceased had been researching. Kevin considered the computer and its strange emptiness in light of the fact that the deceased had been hard at work researching something connected to Sean Johnson's story. That made him more suspicious.

So now, Kevin thought, *the question is whether to call Sean and question him or see what else I can find out first.* He decided he wanted to first exactly identify who the woman named Kim was. On a hunch, he went back to the phone records, but found nothing showing a Kim as the registered owner of a phone.

As Kevin thought things through, he decided to contact the Seattle Police and also see what help he could get from the FBI. He turned to his computer to find a number for the Seattle police.

Chapter Fifteen

The Sheriden Corporation was headquartered in Atlanta, in its own building and campus southwest of the city center. It was a two story concrete building that, from the front, looked more like a bunker, or perhaps a jail. Chain link fences enclosed it, complete with razor wire spools running along the top edges. Entering and exiting the campus required passing through a two gate system, whether in car or on foot. But then, such security in post 9-11 America was not that uncommon. It was the norm for companies involved in military or defense, or ones that housed weapons and conducted security. Sheriden Corporation did all of those things, so truth be told, its security was quite normal.

It was the appearance of the security, the daunting look of the razor wire in front of the concrete structure, that made it seem overdone. However, from the rear, the campus looked quite different. Instead of paved parking lots and minimal windows, the back side of the building presented a much more inviting view. There were gardens intertwined with paths. There was also a fitness area with tennis, racquetball and basketball courts, along with a pool. The back of the building also included more windows, and it was easy to assume that Sheriden executives enjoyed some of the larger second floor offices looking out from the rear of the building.

Such an assumption would be nearly correct, but for one exception: Terry Sheriden. His office had always been on the front side of the building, from the first time he had started working for the family company as a young executive up to his current role as President. There was an office on the friendly side for the president of Sheriden. It had been occupied by Terry's father and then by his brother. But when Terry had taken over the company, so his brother could pursue a political career, he had refused to make the move over there. Instead, he had modified his existing area, by adding a second office behind his primary one. He called the second of these two offices his "brains" room. Meanwhile, he let the old president's office become an honorary office for his brother. In fact, his brother's office had not been touched since he departed to his Senate office.

Terry preferred it that way for two reasons. First, he actually disliked being president. So, it was his hope that either his brother's political career would end or they would promote or hire a new president. Secondly, he really hated large, airy rooms with nice views, at least as far as getting work done went. That was why his office at the mansion was down in the basement and that was why his office suite at the corporation headquarters was on the fortress side of the building.

Terry had an executive assistant and an executive vice-president. Between the two, he managed to minimize his presidential duties to official "pomp and circumstance" events, corporate governance meetings or work, and occasional strategy sessions with his executive staff. He would not ever admit it, and probably did not even know it, but in trying to avoid being very "presidential" he was actually running the corporation excellently. He relied on competent people and minimized how much he interfered with their work. Truth be told, most people were a bit scared by him. He had a temper, as most everyone did. He spent large amounts of time out of the office and carried himself with a toughness that exuded "stay away." Terry wanted it that way. He had always felt that it was through fear that one could best control the behavior of others.

Terry had very few important rules and one of those was his "do not disturb" ultimatum. It meant exactly what it implied. He had made it very clear that if he was in "do not disturb" mode, then it was to be as if he was not in the building and not available at all to anyone for any reason. What that meant in practice was that his executive assistant actually locked his door and her own and left a note in the hall that read "DND." She frequently left her office and went down to the lounge, out to exercise, or even out shopping. She never even answered the phones, unless she had work to do. She had learned that her boss was fine with her disappearing. Anybody who was frustrated at not getting a return call or an email answered would come down to Terry's area, see the DND note and turn right around. It just added to Terry's aura of fear.

Right now Terry was in a do-not-disturb mode, and his assistant had left the campus. He had come in very early and simply scribbled DND on a sticky note which he then stuck on her chair. She had come in, seen the note, checked her own calendar, and decided right then and there to simply post the DND sign, lock the door and leave. She could handle her fairly eccentric boss, but most of the building staff resented her for the privilege she enjoyed. Unless she felt like mingling among them and absorbing their stares, it was easier to go shopping for the day. So, that was what she had decided to do.

Terry was back in his "brains" room behind his official office. There were monitors scattered at three desks and on the walls, as well as three televisions mounted even higher on one wall. Terry had a table at the center of the room with a desk light, a phone, and desk-pad/ calendar combination. At this very moment, Terry was at the table in the center of the room with sheets of paper around him. He had been writing for a while. Sometimes, he would flip around to the computer on the desk behind him and retrieve some information and review it. A few times, he had printed documents or sent an email. It was now ten in the morning and he was satisfied that he had implemented a strategy that would please his brother, Mike.

Terry had assembled a talented team of mercenaries. Actually three teams to be exact. Each had been recalled to the United States and would be heading to various locations to receive more instructions. He would be personally briefing each of the teams. He would then be seeing them off to keep surveillance on his three subjects of interest. He was not concerned at all with finding the professor, certain that

James Enloe would either be in Knoxville or at his sister's funeral in Phoenix. He felt equally confident he could find Kim as well.

Terry was more curious about Sean, but hoped that Sean would not be educated on modern electronic spying technologies. If he wasn't, then Terry was certain he could track Sean through his credit card activity. He usually avoided doing that, as it could leave a record that led back to the corporation. So, he had created a bogus client, a confidential and rich individual in Washington state who believed Sean had embezzled funds. He then aligned that client with a shell corporation that then retained Sheriden Corporation. Despite such preparations, he knew that the Sheriden name would still be exposed if and when he ran those searches. That was partly why he had not yet executed the search for Sean's financial trail. Instead, he preferred first to focus on Kim and James and see if they could lead him to Sean.

Terry was planning on briefing each team personally to minimize paper and electronic trails as well. The crews he had picked were excellent at taking jobs for good pay with little questions. He was not about to suggest any of them commit murder within the United States, but he knew there were a couple members who would do that if asked.

Once having started the ball rolling on all the needed preparations, his mind came back to Sean. Terry had driven back down from Knoxville on Thursday and stayed out at the mansion. He had missed his brother who had left for Washington D.C. for a fundraiser set up by his manager, Jessica. Terry did not resent Jessica and, in fact, actually respected her relentless drive and willingness to do whatever was required. He was probably more jealous of Michael than anything. Terry had never managed to have an even slightly deep relationship with anyone besides his brother, let alone with a woman.

Sean Johnson had surprised Terry. Worse still, it was his second mistake of the week, since he counted being seen exiting the Phoenix scene as a mistake as well. Sean really bothered him though. He thought he understood the role of the Kansas City woman. She was apparently a Thomas heir and, as Michael hoped, might have family secrets or clues to lead them to Jacob Thomas's secret. He understood the role of the professor as well. He was an Enloe and a Lincoln historian. So, how could he not end up getting involved at some point in his life. He did not understand, however, how a reporter from Seattle, who just happened to have a pretty extensive background in espionage and counter-insurgency, managed to choose the Lincoln-Enloe story at this very inopportune time? In summary, Terry realized he was extremely irritated that he had to deal with the reporter and preferred to eliminate him instead.

But, Terry also knew that his brother was right. The reporter had the right skills and annoying persistence to, perhaps, help the other two idiots figure things out. Deep inside though, he knew that Sean was a risk. *I may get only one more perfect chance to eliminate him as a threat. So, if that opportunity comes along, I should take it. Michael be damned.*

Springfield, Illinois

Sean was truly feeling his fatigue. He had driven most of the afternoon across Missouri to Saint Louis. There, he had eaten at a freeway restaurant and then crossed over from Mississippi into Illinois where he had headed northeast into Springfield. As near as he could tell, Springfield was right in the middle of Illinois and right in the middle of nowhere. The road leading up to the capital of Illinois had been a long, mostly flat, ribbon of asphalt with headlights and taillights as his only companions. Exit signs had told him of nearby towns and communities, but only once or twice had there been more than a few highway commercial businesses within his sight.

Sean had arrived in Springfield late at night and found his way to a downtown hotel. It looked like the tallest building in town. Finally reaching his room, he quickly fell into another short night of fitful sleep. In the morning, after eating breakfast in the hotel, he had inquired about the Lincoln Library and was delighted to be informed it was merely a few blocks away.

Sean gathered up his notebook and bag and headed straight there. Along the way, he was fascinated by the quaintness of the capital. A large square held the very capital building that Abraham Lincoln had spoken in many times. There were statues of Abraham Lincoln and his family scattered along one edge of the square. At one corner was the Lincoln Herndon law office building, which Sean made a mental note to visit if he could find the time. A block farther he found what he initially thought of as "Lincoln Headquarters." There was a Lincoln archive and library on one side of the street and a Lincoln Museum on the other. Though Sean had been sorely tempted to head to the museum, where most tourists had been going, he forced himself to enter the more prim and sterile library and archives.

Entering the library, he encountered a stern librarian-like woman who seemed to have, as her first priority, the task of directing lost tourists across the street to the museum which was their correct, actual destination. But, Sean had suspected he would need a good scholarly story and had roughly prepared one the night before while driving.

"Yes, well I have actually come here from Seattle, Washington to research unique and hard-to-find records of Lincoln's life for a school program in the State of Washington. I'm a journalist on assignment from Washington."

A ruse, Sean knew, though only barely false. But, it had sufficed. Then, he had stumbled some when he became confused about using only pencils and having to lock bags in lockers. Soon enough, however, he had selected himself a table amidst the single largest and most complete collection of everything Lincoln had ever written and everything written about Lincoln.

Now, even though Sean had only been at it an hour, he felt his eyelids growing heavy and knew he needed a break. He had barely left the table, having spent most of his first hour organizing his plan of attack. He had decided he needed to do several searches: one on Lincoln's early childhood and that of his parents, one on anything Enloe, and one on anything Thomas. So, he settled down with an essay listing documents from Lincoln's childhood and continued his search.

Sean glanced at his watch. It was only eleven o'clock. Too early, for sure, for him to grow this tired. He put his Lincoln library pencil down and pushed his chair back, grimacing at its squeaking noise. He was in a room with about fifteen tables. There were four other people like himself at these tables. They all looked at him when hearing the noise and he truly felt like he did not belong in the room. Nevertheless, he tried to act completely nonchalant about the noise he had made with his chair and exited the room. The archive librarian was at her desk by the stairs going down to street level. She looked up at him as he approached.

"Hello, Mr. Johnson. Can I help you?" she inquired.

"No, no, I just need a break," Sean replied. "Is it fine if I leave everything where it is at my table?"

"Certainly."

"Great! Next question. Is there a good place to find a cup of coffee?"

The librarian smiled at him. "You'll find a great coffee shop out the door to your left and down a block."

He mumbled thanks and quickly headed to the stairs.

Once outside, Sean took a deep breath of the fresh, cool spring air and right away felt more refreshed. He turned left, as instructed, and started walking. As he walked, he pulled his cell phone out of his pocket. Selecting Kim's cell phone number, he pressed the call button and waited to hear it ring. After a moment it did and then he heard a younger-than-expected voice.

"Hello?"

He recognized it as Kim's daughter, Abby.

"Hello Abby, this is Sean Johnson. I'm the reporter you spoke to last week."

"I know who you are," Abby responded back. He then heard Abby speak with the phone lowered, "Mom, it's the reporter."

Sean sighed to himself. He always tried to call himself a journalist, but invariably, it was easier to say "reporter" and most people ended up calling him that. To him, though, there was a significant distinction between the two roles.

Sean could hear Kim express surprise and ask for the phone.

"Hello?" she said.

"Hi Kim. This is Sean. I'm in Springfield taking a break from the archives. How are you?"

"I'm fine. We're on the road to Denver. We should arrive by early afternoon. I already know where I am going today, to the county recorder's office."

Sean could feel Kim's energy coming right through the phone.

"I suspect you and your daughter are having some quality time together on your road trip?"

Kim laughed. "Yes we are. Abby is quite fine with missing a day of school and heading off to Denver for the weekend. It is a good mother-daughter event."

"Okay, well I just thought I would check in with you to make sure you departed okay."

"Okay, talk to you later." Sean could hear the two women laughing as he hung up the phone.

The call had energized him, but he knew some food and caffeine would be more long lasting. He turned into the first sandwich shop he came across.

Phoenix

Alan Nazimi, Special Agent in Charge of the Phoenix office of the Federal Bureau of Investigation, had heard enough.

"Agreed. This case clearly appears to cross state lines. Besides, I have a great information technology team here, courtesy of increased funding after 9-11. If anyone can find anything in that computer, they will."

"Great, thanks," Kevin Falls replied. " I have ten more cases that I'm behind on now, and it appears that I'm at a standstill on this one."

"So, can you have the case file sent over today?"

"It's on its way!"

"If my notes follow, let's see,…the husband probably did not do it, it looks like an apparent robbery, but the method of death, broken neck, and the erased computer, smell of something more sinister. Does that sound about right?"

"You just summarized three days of work in twenty seconds. Yes, that's it."

"And, there's a Seattle reporter who had been contacting Mary about an Abraham Lincoln story, a mysterious woman named Kim probably in the Kansas City area, and a brother who is a professor in Knoxville?"

There was silence for a moment before Kevin replied.

"Yeah. Man, you either have made me feel like I accomplished a lot or nothing."

Alan Nazimi laughed grimly. "You accomplished a lot. Give me the weekend to dig into things and we'll see where we are on Monday."

"Okay, thanks."

"Good-bye."

Alan Nazimi hung up his desk phone and reviewed his notes one more time. He glanced up at the time on the large wall clock above his desk. *Already noon? On a Friday? Why do things like this always come along on a Friday?*

He picked up his phone and dialed a four digit extension. He waited until somebody picked up and then spoke.

"This is Alan. A computer is on its way to you. It was found at the scene of the murder of..." Alan glanced through his notes, "Mary Fester. She was supposedly madly at work on this computer leading up to her death, but its hard drive is strangely blank, as if someone erased it. I want a full meta-analysis of every scrap of information on that computer by tomorrow morning."

Alan listened to the groaning voice on the other end for only a moment.

"I don't care what day it is or how nice the weather is outside. Besides, if you get it done by dawn, you'll have all weekend to play. Once you get the computer this afternoon, give me a quick call to report what it looks like, okay?"

Alan listened for the acknowledgement and ended the call. The complaining by his tech team was nothing new. They were FBI agents yes, but newly recruited ones. They were mostly college graduates who had been computer techies, as well as video game addicts all of their lives up until now. So, he was used to hearing them whine. Still, he made a mental note to talk to the technical division manager next week. They were paid well enough, so there was no room for complaining.

Alan lowered his head and briefly flipped through his notes. His gut intuition told him that the reporter was involved. *It's too coincidental. Yet, the cop says that his story of being a reporter had held up.* Alan checked the clock again and then turned to glance out his window at the city of Phoenix. Their offices were on the tenth and eleventh floors of the federal building and he had a decent view of the skyline.

He could tell it was getting hot, a sign that spring was about over and that summer was arriving early as usual. He actually hated Phoenix. It was too damn hot, and he did not like golf. But, the chance to become a special agent in charge, SIC, of an office was too good to pass up. He could work unfettered by others, mostly, so long as his office got results and did its job on national matters that brought the Arizona desert world into play.

Alan was not a tall or overpowering figure, but he had smarts. He was lightly built and of average height. However, he was fast on his feet and had managed to make SIC when he was forty-two. That was young he knew, and his youth also gave him special status as someone to watch. Other SIC's avoided clashing with him. Still, he did not feel so young anymore. Two much work, he reflected. His long hours were taking their toll. His blonde hair had started thinning, so he now shaved his head. His skin was feeling old and dry and even his eyes were tired all the time. But, he stayed in top shape, exercise being his one escape, his one luxury. Besides daily workouts, mostly early evening, he allowed himself some sports and some weekend adventures, like cycling, when he had time.

It was cases like these that Alan loved taking on and solving. It was cases like these that sometimes also brought recognition. So, Alan was determined to start on it right away. Not wanting to wait for the case file to arrive, he looked though his notes and decided to call the brother in Knoxville. He quickly found the man's office, cell and home phone numbers in the federal database at his disposal and decided to first try the home number. *True, it's a workday but he's a professor and his sister was murdered. That makes it very likely he's at home.*

After a few rings, his logic was awarded by the sound of a voice answering the phone.

"Hello?"

"Hi, is this James Enloe?"

"Speaking." Alan detected a tired man, but one who was also curious about who was calling.

"Hi James. This is Alan Nazimi, Special Agent in Charge of the Federal Bureau of Investigation in Phoenix. Can I call you James?"

There was a pause and then a "sure." Alan was certain James was awake and alert. The effect of having the FBI calling was usually like that.

"Thank you James. I wanted to ask you some questions about your sister's murder. Is that okay?"

"Sure, but the FBI? What has brought you guys into my sister's death?"

"There are a few things about your sister's case that are complex, that make the case more complicated."

"Complicated?"

"Yes. Look James, can I ask the questions here? I am terribly sorry for your sister's death. If you can help me out, I will be closer to finding the person who did this."

"Okay, yes. I certainly don't mean to hinder your progress Mr. ..."

"Nazimi," Alan finished for him, saying it slowly. "Yes, I understand."

"First, let me ask, do you know what your sister was working on before she died? Her husband reported that she had been deeply involved in a genealogy project."

James chuckled slightly. Alan sensed that was all the joy he would allow himself. *A mourner,* he thought.

"My sister was always involved in our family tree, Mr. Nazimi."

"Yes, but was there something special she was doing?"

"Yes, yes there was something. She never told me about it, but I learned about it through a reporter. It had to do with a historical rumor that has lingered for years in our family. It claims that Abraham Lincoln's real father was an Enloe."

Alan was surprised at this comment and sat in silence for a moment. Then he replied.

"President Lincoln?" was all he managed to say.

"Yes, Mr. Nazimi. It's very unlikely to be rooted in truth, but my sister believed it. I really think she wanted to believe it."

The gears in Alan's head were now whirling and clicking. *A family history involving a sordid story of President Lincoln? This case has just gotten quite interesting. But what's the connection to the reporter? Blackmail? Was he offering to sell false information?*

"James, what else can you tell me about her research on this?"

"Not much more. I actually referred the reporter to her to help him flesh the story." James paused. "Look, you don't think this story is somehow connected to her death do you?"

"No, no, I have nothing to directly connect it to her murder."

"Then why does it matter what she was working on before she was killed?"

Alan could tell that James was sharp. *Of course, he's a professor. A history professor, no less.*

"As I said there are some irregularities about this case."

"What kind of irregularities?" Alan could tell that James suspected something, that he had been on the alert for something. There was something James was not telling him.

"Well, first, I have to ask you to speak to no one about the details of this case okay?"

"Yes, that's fine."

"Good. Well, for starters, it appears her computer was erased. That is a very strange and unusual fact. I am learning more about this, but lacking her computer, I am in the dark as to what she was working on when she was killed."

"Okay, Mr. Nazimi, that's fine, but how does an erased computer bring in the FBI?"

"You are observant James. I'll tell you more."

Alan paused before continuing. "Your sister, Mary, was killed instantly from a broken neck. Her spinal cord was severed, caused by a special twisting motion of her skull. There's evidence of a burglary, but the manner of her death is not consistent with a home invasion burglary. Whoever did this had special training."

"I really cannot tell you more than that, James."

There was silence on the other end. Alan took this as normal when a brother hears about the means of his sister's death.

"Look I'm sorry to have to tell you these details. But it's these details that are driving my interest in knowing what your sister was doing." Alan paused to give a chance for the professor to catch up with him. "I understand that Sean Johnson, this reporter, was with you Wednesday night when you were informed about your sister?"

James answered back, but he sounded shocked. "Yeah. Yes, I mean."

"Was he with you on Monday, James? Was he in Knoxville?"

"What?" James exclaimed sounding very confused. "I'm not sure. I need to think for a moment. Let's see..."

There was a pause while James thought and Alan waited patiently.

"No, he was supposed to interview me Monday before heading back to Seattle. He called and told me something had come up and he was headed to Kansas City instead."

"When was the last time you saw him?"

"Wednesday night at the café where the stranger was listening in on our conversation"

"Stranger?" Alan felt his alertness rise. "What stranger James?"

"I told the police all about it. Didn't they file a report?" James sounded irritated.

"I'm sorry. They may have, I don't actually have the case file yet. Can you briefly walk me through it?"

James told Alan about the evening at the café and Sean's bizarre behavior. Alan interrupted him with questions and took copious notes while they were talking.

"So, anything more?"

"No, that's it."

"Can I ask you a question, James?"

"You've been asking them all day."

"Well, this is a question where I want your opinion. Do you understand?"

"Yes."

"Do you think Sean was involved in your sister's death? Could he have been?"

There was silence on the phone yet again. Then James answered slowly.

"No, I don't think so. I don't think he is a killer, Mr. Nazimi. He is a reporter working on a story and my sister's death has stunned him as it has us all."

"Do you know where he is now?"

"I think he said he was headed to Springfield, in Illinois. That is where Lincoln practiced law and it's the home of the Lincoln Presidential Library."

"Okay, thank you for being candid with me. If I have any more questions can I call you?"

"Yes, by all means do."

They said good-bye and then Alan hung up the phone. He cleaned up his notes for a few minutes and sat back thinking about their conversation.

The professor was not telling me everything, but he was being truthful in his opinion of Sean Johnson. What is he hiding and why? Alan's thoughts then turned to the tie in with Abraham Lincoln. *President Lincoln? That's bizarre. Who kills a lady over a story of Lincoln's mother's infidelity? Some odd blackmail scheme? Some weird genealogy spat?* Alan sat in thought, convinced there was much more to the case than met the eye.

Knoxville

James hung up the phone, stunned. *The FBI? Her computer erased? What the hell is going on here?*

He remembered Sean's last words to him, "*If you learn anything out of the ordinary please call me.*" Sitting on the desk in front of James was an opened shipping envelope that he had picked up at his campus office earlier that morning. He had pulled some pages out of the envelope, but had not yet read them.

Was he being manipulated? The thought had already occurred to him, but when the FBI agent had asked him if he thought Sean was involved in his sister's death, he had to think it through. The facts that he had learned about Mary's murder made him rethink his understanding of what had happened. As he thought it through he realized that Mary's computer being erased and his sister being killed in such a specialized way increased Sean's credibility. But, now, James wondered, was Sean masterfully manipulating everyone? Was he a professional killer? The professor thought about this and then found himself trusting Sean. *He's not a killer. He's really trying to help.*

James sat back in his chair as he thought about his sister being murdered. Now, in his mind, he saw a sinister, evil man twisting her head. It was an image he could not bear to think about!

"No damn it!" he yelled at the ceiling. "What's going on?"

He leaned back down and wiped the tears aside that now flowed from his eyes. He then grabbed a tissue from a holder on his desk and blew his nose. Finally, he focused his attention on the documents Sean had sent him.

He noted that one was a letter written to this Kim woman. It was from her dad. He read it slowly. The next was a copy of an old note written with a heavy pen. *This must be the cryptic warning note*, he thought. He read it through once and then again. *It's very odd.* The rest of the pages were printouts from some genealogy program. They provided Kim's lineage.

So Kim Poole was really a Thomas? Her ancestor Jacob Thomas changed his name apparently to protect his family from a danger related to Lincoln. And somehow the Enloes were involved.

James thought this through and then reached a harder topic. *And somehow, my sister might have been killed over this?* He again found himself thinking how preposterous that sounded. This time he noted that, in light of the mystery around her death, this was the only direction that offered an answer as to why she died. He also thought about why he had not told the FBI agent of this information. *Was it embarrassment? Did I not believe it mattered? But do I still feel that way?*

James had been around history long enough to know that governments lied as much as ordinary people did. *Could a secret from so many years ago be worth killing for today?* Why else would Mary's computer have been erased? Finding no answers and feeling restless, James got up and paced his home office floor.

He knew he had to decide on a course of action. Either he needed to drop this entire topic, tell everything to the FBI or pursue it himself or with Sean and Kim. He thought things through some more and finally reached a decision. He would at least consider that there could be something to the Jacob Thomas warning. That meant figuring out what it was that his sister had been trying to solve.

Chapter Sixteen

Denver, Colorado

Denver was basking in brilliant afternoon sunshine as Kim and Abby approached the downtown area on the elevated freeway. Kim had never been to the city before, and like her daughter, she found it fascinating. The skyscrapers were gradually growing in size as they got closer, but it was clear they would never compare to the massive snow-topped Rocky Mountains looming in the west, on the edge of the city. That mountainous backdrop did make the whole skyline, tall buildings included, appear all the more majestic though. Kim was used to the typical Midwest city thrusting up from plains with its buildings being the tallest objects around. Having a mountain range dwarf the buildings gave Denver a humbling appeal, as if it existed at the whim of nature.

Abby and Kim had gotten along very well on the drive. This was remarkable, considering its length and repetitive scenery. It was only as they approached Denver that they could really tell they were getting anywhere. They had started at six that morning and, stopping only for gas and bathroom breaks, had made it in just under eight hours. *And,* Kim thought, *no speeding tickets!*

Kim had known she had to hurry if she was going to get anything done before the weekend began. So, she had pushed Abby to rise early. In fact, Kim considered, Abby had really woken up somewhere in Kansas and had been grumpy for only a few minutes. After that, it had been smooth sailing all the way across Kansas and into Colorado. The scenery had mostly been an endless sea of fallow or recently plowed fields. Kim had noticed that very little of anything had been planted yet.

Along the way, Kim and Abby had talked girl chitchat, as well as some mother-daughter topics. Kim was still suspecting that Abby wanted something, but she had not brought up anything yet. When they had fallen silent, Kim used the time to mull through the events of the last two weeks. It had been very exhausting. Now, she knew, this trip would place a strain on her business as well. Bridget was good, but it was unfair of Kim to dump so much responsibility on her employees. Kim hoped, however, to be back home by Monday night at the latest, so this trip would be nothing more than a four day vacation. *Some vacation. Trying to unravel a mystery dumped on me by my family, a mystery that might have killed an innocent woman in her Phoenix home.*

During the drive, Kim thought long and hard about Mary and her death. She found herself flip-flopping back and forth from thinking she was insane, to believing that what she was doing was logical and important. She also thought about Sean and kept wondering if his efforts at convincing her to head off to Denver were part of some grand manipulative scheme. But in any case, she realized, finding the truth of her great, great grandfather was reason enough to follow this story to its end. However, the idea that Mary might have been killed over it seemed surreal. Sean had her convinced, though, of the reasonable chance that the two events could be related. That had her scared, very scared.

It was for that reason that Abby had no choice about going with Kim on this trip. Kim was not going to leave Abby behind in Kansas City while she, herself, ran off to Denver to find out whether her family was in danger. No, that would have been irresponsible. So, she had brought Abby with her, promising her a "fun" weekend in Denver. Kim knew, however, that it might not be that much fun. She was thus prepared for Abby to be disappointed.

Now, having reached Denver, Kim was very happy that the trip had been quite smooth. She glanced at the time displayed on the dash of the SUV: almost two o'clock. Then it struck her that she had gained an hour by heading west. That meant it was really just one o'clock. That was great news!

"Well, we're here Abby," Kim announced. "Our first stop is the county recorder's office. We're going to get the will of your great, great, great grandfather, Jacob Poole."

"Wow mom, that sounds real exciting," Abby replied, with forced, exaggerated sarcasm.

Kim had not even begun to try to explain everything that had taken place. She had explained a bit more about the focus on who Jacob really was, but she had still not shared the letters with Abby. Nor had she explained how Mary's death might be connected to the quest. Abby had been worried enough about her mother being upset over Mary's murder. *And*, Kim reflected, *Abby would probably tell me that I'm nuts to be running off to Denver if she knew the whole story.* Kim had hinted that they needed to be careful, but that there was no specific reason to think that Mary's death meant that they were in danger.

"Sorry honey," Kim said, glancing at her daughter in the passenger seat. "Today will probably be boring mostly because I have to get the government records research done before everything closes up for the weekend."

" I know mom, I know. But I don't see why I cannot go to a mall or something while you do your errands."

Great, Kim thought, *the honeymoon is over.*

"We discussed this. Denver is a new city, unfamiliar to both of us. We need to stay together today, just to be safe. Okay?"

"Sure, whatever, Mom. Just don't ask me to start digging through boxes of old documents." Kim looked over at her daughter again. *Well, I see a smile on her face, so all is not lost.*

Kim glanced at the driving directions she had printed from the internet and turned right at a massive intersection. She had just passed the convention center, which was also huge. To her left, on top of a ridge that Denver appeared to straddle, was a large building unmistakable as the capital building. The golden dome on its top was shining in the afternoon sun. There were other government buildings surrounding her, and Kim was certain she should take the next parking spot she could find. She turned, passed the capital on her left and then saw a sign for public parking.

Soon, Kim and Abby were on the sidewalk heading to the recorder's building. Several minutes later, she found herself at a counter, on a floor in the middle of the building, talking to the clerk in the county recorder's office.

"What I want is a copy of the will for Jacob Thomas who died on June 4, 1901," she explained. Abby had sat down in a chair along the wall by the entrance. The clerk, a slim, dark haired man in his twenties, pulled a three ring binder from a shelf.

"This is a list of the microfilm records by year and topic," he explained. "You want 1901 probate, which is in…" His fingers were drifting across the page.

"23Y," he announced. He looked up at her triumphantly and Kim gave him an encouraging smile.

"Follow me over here," the clerk said next, walking to her left. She followed him and he stopped in front of a bank of filing cabinets.

"Here are the microfilm rolls. 23Y will be on the other side of this row. You'll find the readers and printers over there," he said pointing to a row of machines along the outer wall of the room.

"Have you used microfilm before ma'am?"

"Yep, this is all coming back to me," Kim responded smiling at him again. "I remember having to bring rolls of dimes to print pages."

"Ah, well no change needed anymore. Count your copies and settle up with one of us when you are done. Cash or check only, I am afraid. No credit cards."

"That's fine, thank you." Kim turned away from him and set her bag on the table in front of the cabinets. She glanced over at Abby, and saw her texting away on her phone. *God knows what she is saying about me to her friends,* she thought. Abby did not even look up at her, so Kim turned back to her task at hand. She unzipped the bag and pulled out a pad of paper along with a pen. Noticing her purse in the bag, she decided it was safe and went around the corner of the microfilm cabinet row to find cabinet 23Y. Once on the other side, she found cabinet 23 and realized that the letter "Y" was the drawer number.

Pulling the drawer open, Kim found five little cardboard boxes, each apparently holding a roll of microfilm. She took the five rolls, along with her pad and pen, and headed to the machines. A few minutes later, Kim had figured out the organization of the rolls. They all contained wills, with the third, fourth, and fifth rolls most likely to hold Jacob's will. Once she had threaded the third roll, figured out how to turn the machine on, and reached the first image, she was delighted to find a typed index in chronological order. Scanning through it, she spotted Jacob Poole fairly quickly and realized the will was on the fourth roll.

A few minutes later, Kim had found the will. She could see the name "Jacob Poole" right up near the beginning of the document and tried reading it on the screen, but found it too difficult. She noted the will was handwritten in a very flowing and old fashioned style. The darkness of the screen compounded the problem, and she gave up trying to read it right then and there and began figuring out how to print it.

Finally, the machine spat out the last of Jacob's six page will and she picked it up, eager to read it. Glancing at her watch, she saw that it was already nearly four o'clock which was the closing time for the records office. So, she ejected the microfilm roll and began putting everything away. Abby was still sitting in the chair by the door, much more slouched than she had been when she had first sat down, but still texting her friends.

Kim grabbed her bag after tossing her materials in it and hustled back to the counter. This time, Kim noticed the name of the clerk on his desk. It was Peter. He looked up as she approached.

"All done?" he asked. "Did you find your will?"

"Yes and yes," Kim replied. "I made six copies."

"Oh, that's right." Peter then hopped up, having obviously forgotten about the need to collect money. "That will be a dollar twenty."

Kim pulled her purse out of her bag, counted out the change, and handed it to him. Peter had been scribbling on a form and handed her the yellow copy of a receipt.

"Okay, that's it." Peter announced and glanced up at the clock on the wall. "And right on time."

Kim noted that it was exactly four o'clock as well.

"Okay, thank you very much."

She turned from the smiling clerk.

"Come on Abby, I'm done."

Abby glanced at her mom and then jumped up, now seeming more alert. They turned and headed to the elevator.

…..

After leaving the parking garage, Kim had driven through downtown Denver, in search of the return address on Jacob's letters. It was an old house in the southeast Cherry Creek area. Cherry Creek was one of two major tributaries that flowed through the city. She was parked in front of the house and had been sitting there for several minutes trying to imagine her great, great grandfather living there. *It must have been a much newer house in a very different looking neighborhood in the 1890's.* Now, it looked more like a very poor and tired neighborhood. She tried imagining the people living in the house now and whether they thought of the people who had been there before them. She knew, though, that they would have no idea who had lived before them in their home. *Nor would they likely care,* she thought. Kim assumed the home was now a rental home that served families for short periods of time before they moved on. Kim could not help but think that it was possible that Jacob had hidden something in the house, in a wall maybe. But after sitting there for a few minutes, with Abby growing crabby, Kim drove away feeling strangely mournful, as if she had missed a chance to meet someone very important to her.

Kim headed downtown and checked into the nice hotel she had booked online the previous night. Once upstairs, Abby had promptly turned on the television and parked herself on the bed in front of it watching an entertainment news show.

Meanwhile, Kim was at the small desk in the hotel room and had just pulled out Jacob's will. She tried again to read it. The handwriting was easier to understand now that the document was printed on white paper. However, the paper that the will had been on when copied had obviously yellowed, which resulted in a light shade of gray in the background of the copy she was now reading. As a result, some letters and words took more time than others to identify. Thus, reading the will was a slow, plodding affair. Impatiently, she skimmed through the pages looking for something obvious, but nothing caught her attention. On the last page, she saw the signature of "Jacob Poole" and the signature of a witness, David Haggard. She wrote David Haggard's name down, thinking it could have some value. A thought struck her and she pulled the note and the letters from Jacob out of her pile of documents. When she compared them against the will, it was obvious that the will had been handwritten by Jacob. It was the same handwriting. She noted that on her pad as well.

Kim glanced over at Abby. She was sprawled on one of the beds watching the television and looking bored. Kim knew she needed to give her some attention, so she put her documents back together, adding the will to the set. She then pivoted in the desk chair to face Abby.

"Hey honey, you ready to go see Denver and get some dinner?"

Abby eagerly looked up from the television. "You bet!" she replied.

Kim was relieved to see her smile. "Okay then, let's go," she exclaimed.

A few minutes later, they were in the elevator heading down to the street.

Phoenix

Alan was just getting ready to head out of the office to the gym when his desk phone rang. He reached over and pressed the speaker button. Calling out "Alan Nazimi," he walked over to the door of his office where his clothes were hanging.

"Hi, Mr. Nazimi. This is Brian." The voice came out of the speaker on Alan's phone.

"Hi, Brian," Alan called back while unbuttoning his shirt.

"I've started in on the Fester computer. You said you wanted an initial impression."

"Yes, that's right. Thank you. Go ahead." Alan pulled his dress shirt off and continued undressing.

"Well, I have to tell you this is not an accidental erasure. Someone has purposely gone through and re-formatted the hard drive. But even that is not entirely accurate. It looks to me like somebody ran a sophisticated disc erase program on this hard drive. When I usually see these, there is a pattern to the reformatting and I can recover much of the data by finding the previous patterns. But, this looks like it has been processed by a program that goes through and randomly changes lots of points making it very hard to find the original organizational structure. It's possible the program reassigned every single spot on the disc."

Alan froze just as he was getting ready to unbuckle his pants. *Very interesting,* he thought. *Stunning!*

"Who has such programs?" Alan asked

"Lots of people really," Brian replied. "What's interesting is that when you find this you know someone really wanted to hide what was on the computer. It also takes quite a bit of time. That's why you almost never see a full scrub. And, finally, it also means that whoever did this used another computer."

Alan started walking over to his desk. It was an involuntary effort that he knew had no effect on his ability to hear or be heard from. For some reason, though, he felt as if it was easier truly engaging a caller on speaker phone if the phone was directly in front of him. Once Alan reached his desk, he stood, arms folded akimbo, staring at the phone.

"Another computer?"

"Yes. To run a program like this you have to free up the hard drive from supporting the computer's operation. Easiest way is to plug in another computer, network them together and then use the new computer to rewrite the hard drive on the existing one."

"So, if this hard drive was erased by the killer, then it meant the killer brought something in with him to do it?"

"Yes. That's a reasonable presumption."

"Thanks, Brian. So, recovering data from the hard drive may be thwarted by this erasure?"

"It's too early to tell. I expect to find some data under the assumption that the killer would not want to spend hours at the murder scene waiting for a full rewrite."

"How soon?"

"Oh, I'll be at this all night."

"Brian, you're my hero!"

"Just doing my job, Mr. Nazimi. Just doing my job."

"Well, I appreciate it." Alan ended the call right after his parting comment and moved back over to the door and continued changing for the gym. As he donned his exercise clothes, he worked his way through the information Brian had just provided.

This was definitely not a simple burglary. This was probably a hit intended to be disguised as a burglary. Somebody has gone to great lengths to cover something up, but why?

Once Alan was dressed in his shorts, tee shirt, and sneakers he went back over to his desk and sat down. He flipped through his Fester notes until he found what he needed. Pulling a shelf out of a slot in his desk, he fingered his way down a set of phone numbers.

After pressing the speaker button and dialing the number, he sat back listening to the phone ring. After five rings, Alan knew the number had flipped over to the agent on call. It was answered shortly after that.

"Agent King, Chicago." It was a brusque, hard voice. Alan knew that the guy could not be happy about getting an evening call on a Friday night.

"Hello Agent King, this is Special Agent in Charge, Phoenix, Alan Nazimi. How are you this evening?"

"Great sir! How can I help you?" Alan was impressed by how instantly the voice had become professional and eager to help him.

"I need to get somebody out to Springfield tomorrow to track down a person of interest in a murder case here in Phoenix."

"That's Springfield, Illinois, right sir?" Again, the sharp professional voice impressed the hell out of Alan.

"That's right, Agent King. My person of interest is named Sean Johnson. He is a reporter researching Abraham Lincoln at the Lincoln Library there. I would like to have him brought into your office in Chicago for questioning."

"Okay, can you send me the file information and details this evening? I will arrange to have two of our agents head down there tomorrow. It's several hours of driving or a one hour flight. How soon do you need us there?"

"Early tomorrow."

"Do we know which hotel he's staying at sir?"

"Nope, I'm leaving that in your hands. I'll have to have the case documents scanned and emailed to you tonight as we've just opened this case and nothing is in the system yet."

"Yes sir, I'll watch for them."

Alan hung up feeling much more satisfied that things were on track. He quickly sorted through and collected several of the documents. He stuck a note on them indicating that they were to be copied, scanned and emailed to "Agent King" in Chicago. He then grabbed the documents, as well as his small travel bag and clothes on the hanger. On his way out he would drop the files with the clerk on duty, leaving them to take care of business.

Atlanta

Terry had been in his brains room all day. After ensuring he had all his men on recall, he began seeing to various logistical details along with needed cover stories, false clients and shell business entities. He had also run full credit checks on all three of his targets, gathering most of their necessary credit card numbers. He then focused on Sean, using a special type of inquiry that would tell him the latest usage location of his credit cards. He quickly found a hotel reservation in Springfield, Illinois. Some quick internet search engine work had shown him that Springfield, Illinois was packed with Lincoln institutions, including the Lincoln Library and document archive.

It deeply concerned Terry that the reporter had gone to such a place and he quickly began routing his first team directly to Springfield. He then made logistical arrangements for them, setting up the covers and providing them their necessary gear. This team would be two men who had been working together in Venezuela on a job for about four months and would thus be a good match. Of course, he was paying them ten times what they had been already making. Finally, he arranged to brief them telephonically mid-morning Saturday, once they were equipped and ready for their task.

It was now pretty late and he was feeling the fatigue of working furiously all day. He had emerged from his office only twice, each time to get a meal in the cafeteria. Now, he sat back and reviewed his plans for the fifth time, making sure every detail was correct. There was no room for error.

Knoxville

James was also feeling fatigue. He too, had been hard at work after having decided to try and determine what his sister had been on the verge of discovering. He had thrown himself hard at his new found quest. He had a good set of Lincoln files in his office and he also had access to several databases online where he could retrieve indexes and sometimes even documents themselves.

So, James had buried himself in his research project, his sister's work. This, of course, had actually begun by studying the Poole letter and Thomas note, and by rethinking his conversation with Sean. He had made note pages of his conversations to reduce everything to writing. Then, he ate a late lunch which included a turkey sandwich on wheat bread with iced tea, as he sat down to think things through. His first task was to evaluate what his sister had been researching. That was a very hard first step, though. He knew that she had been trying to find a connection between the Lincoln-Enloe story and Jacob Thomas. He even considered that everyone was too focused on the Lincoln-Enloe story and was missing some other connection between the Enloes and Lincoln.

That was where James started, with a comprehensive search for any Enloe connections to Lincoln. That had taken him the rest of the day and well into the night. Though he had a list of a few resources that he did not have access to, he was now mostly done for the evening. He knew that to be complete and thorough, he would have to follow up on those resources as well.

Generally, his work had not produced any real results. James had found Enloes on each side in the Civil War. He had found records of Enloes alive at the time of Lincoln, but he found no mention of anything or anyone directly connecting Abraham Lincoln to an Enloe, except for the Lincoln-Enloe theory.

That is why I'm feeling so tired. If I had had some success, I would be more exuberant right now.

James got up from the desk. His study was now a mess with books and files scattered everywhere. He was too tired to clean it up though, and resigned himself to attacking it in the morning. He walked through his house and into the kitchen. This time he did not resist the urge to pull out the bottle of whiskey in his cupboard. He grabbed a tumbler, threw some ice cubes into it and gave himself a generous helping of the well-needed drink. He then walked into his living room where he sat down in his favorite padded leather chair. As he sat there, his eyes were drawn to a picture on a bookshelf on the opposite side of the room. It was a black and white photograph that showed a young boy and girl in their bathing suits with their arms around each other's shoulders. Seeing the photo brought a flood of memories. Tears welled up in his eyes and he lifted the glass up in a toast to the empty room.

"To you Mary. I swear that if you died trying to show the world something, then I will make sure the world gets to see it."

He then pulled the glass back down to his lips and took a swallow, tasting the salt of his tears on his lips combining with the burning sensation of the fiery liquor.

Springfield

Sean, too, was tired. He had spent the afternoon going through documents and reading various essays and reports. In some ways, it had been overwhelming. The body of work that Lincoln had authored or touched was massive. After his assassination, many people had taken a lot of time to write many things about the President. He was focused on finding a Jacob Thomas or Enloe record somewhere in this lot. There was so much to look at though. Mostly, he had gotten caught up in the assassination files. At one point in the morning, he had walked across the street to the museum perused the bookstore. He bought ten different books and then found himself being ushered to a table where it was explained that he should join the Lincoln Museum Foundation because the discount he would get on the books he was buying would make his membership significantly cheaper. He wound up joining, but more because of his admiration for the museum and the work and commitment of the people he saw there. He did not go through the exhibits, but decided to take time on Saturday to fully explore the history on display in the museum, as well as in the downtown area.

Sean returned to the library and trudged up the stairs with his bag of books in tow. Upon seeing his purchase and the little "foundation member" sticker still attached to his chest, the historian in the library smiled. She followed him to his table and asked questions about what he was researching and how she could help him with his task.

That made Sean nervous. He knew he could not blurt out that he was trying to find out whether a story that Lincoln was a bastard was related to the death of a woman in Phoenix. If he had been honest, the woman would have run away in all likelihood and might have even called the police. So, he made up a story on the spot that had apparently worked. He told her that he was researching some obscure aspects of Lincoln's life. He then told her that there were two people who supposedly worked for, or with, Abraham Lincoln during his life. Their names, he explained, were Jacob Thomas and Abraham Enloe. The woman scribbled the names down and hustled off to do some research of her own. She came back a few minutes later, explaining that she did not find anything in their primary data base but that she would continue looking for anything lurking in odd files. Sean had then spent the rest of the afternoon scouring the list of resources and then researching and browsing through some of them. He did not find any specific connections, but by the end of the day, Sean felt he had developed an even better understanding of the various facets of Lincoln's life and his work.

Sean was lying on the bed in his hotel room, wishing that he could make sense of everything. His mind was reviewing the events of the day. He had not seen anyone suspicious or strange, but also knew that he had somewhat dropped his guard. The events of the previous days seemed surreal in quaint Springfield. But in the back of his mind, he knew, he needed to fight to stay on his toes to be alert. He finally drifted off to sleep, with thoughts of his actions for the next day running through his mind.

Chapter Seventeen

Saturday, May 2
Denver

Kim put her copy of Jacob's will down and stood up from her desk chair in the hotel room. She was alone, having sent Abby out to tour downtown Denver earlier in the morning. She was not really comfortable with the idea of Abby roaming in the city alone, but it was the only way Kim could find some peace and quiet. *And some sanity,* she thought. *That girl is going to drive me nuts!*

Kim considered that it might have been a mistake to bring Abby along, and she also thought about leaving early to return to Kansas City. The whole trip was beginning to seem very impulsive and somewhat silly. When she had met with Sean in the coffee shop and they had gone through the documents and discussed the events that had unfolded, it had seemed clear why she needed to act quickly. But now, after only one day of being mostly cooped up with her daughter, she was beginning to question that clarity. *Worse, I've got Jacob's will and it's not revealing any magical secrets about Lincoln or the Enloes, or anything else for that matter.*

Kim thought back to her conversation with Sean. He had seemed very convinced that something important had to be behind Jacob's message. Kim had felt herself agreeing with Sean, but she thought now about how much her cooperativeness had probably come from a need to share the shock of Mary's murder. She also had needed a companion to share the Poole-Thomas revelation and Sean had stepped in for that, too. He had then convinced her of the possible danger that could be lurking from the Jacob Thomas warning. Clearly, Sean was at the core of all of this mess.

So how much do you really know about this guy? First you find a letter from your dad with a strange warning in it. A week or so later, a woman in Phoenix is dead and a reporter with a weird past, from Seattle no less, has convinced you to run to Denver to explore your ancestor's past. He convinces you that you're running, but from what? From some evil department of our government that's holding a 150 year grudge against your family. How crazy are you?

But the letter is real. The note is real. And, if I believe Sean, Mary's death is real and its circumstances are highly suspicious. Also strange is a man in Tennessee spying on Sean and James Enloe. So maybe this is all real? Maybe I'm not that insane.

Kim realized she was now pacing back and forth in her room. She stopped, leaned her head back and took a deep breath, holding it for a few moments before exhaling heavily. That helped her relax. She walked over to the window in her hotel room. She was not on a very high floor, but her room looked west and she could see some of the Rockies located between other tall buildings that tried to block her view. Of what she could see, the mountains looked beautiful. Seeing them gave her some strength. *I'll stick with this. At least through Monday.*

Kim glanced at her watch.

I'll call Bridget in an hour and make sure all is well at the store. Until then, its back to the grindstone.

Kim sat back down at the table and picked up her "translated" version of the will. She skimmed through the pages again and decided to read the will even more closely, looking for clues deeply buried in phrases. Kim was convinced that the will, being handwritten, was Jacob's most likely means of communicating something from beyond the grave.

He must have buried it in the words, or used a code, or did something that could be found, so that a casual reader of his will would not have noticed anything awry. The problem is that the whole will is writ-

ten with a prose and style more common in its time, making all sorts of words and phrases seem suspect.

Kim began jotting down phrases and words that seemed awkward to her. One phrase was, "I told my god true." The sentence did not seem to relate to anything else in the will. This caught Kim's eye. This new task took quite awhile. When she had finally completed the daunting chore she sat back stretching her neck and resting her eyes. She now had several pages of handwritten notes reduced from a six page will. What did this all mean? She still did not know.

Kim took her two pages of notes and spread them out in front of her, lying them on top of her translated will and all the other papers she had now accumulated on the hotel desk. She then went through her notes looking for common phrases or words. She found nothing.

Glancing at her watch, Kim realized that Bridget should be in the store by now, getting ready to open it, on what would probably be the busiest day of the year. Kim decided she would call her and then maybe take a walk downstairs to wake herself up a bit.

Atlanta

Terry put his page of notes down and mentally reviewed his plans. He was back in his brains room for the third day in a row. Being a Saturday, the building was hauntingly quiet and mostly empty. He had seen a few employees come in, apparently working on some project they had not been able to complete during their normal work week. Terry, himself, felt on schedule, but for a while it was a schedule that would require his attention every day of the week.

He now had three teams of people in the country. One team, the one with the most rest, was now in Springfield, Illinois in their hotel room awaiting his call. Terry disliked using a hotel room for their center of operations, as it could be too obvious, especially if activities rose to an extreme level. But, he was also not convinced that the reporter would stay in Springfield very long and thus felt that renting a space other than a hotel room added more complications than it was worth. Springfield, capital of Illinois or not, did not have a Sheriden office. Even if it had, Terry probably would not have used it. Secrecy was of the utmost importance in this operation. By running these teams himself, he was minimizing the people who knew about them. Better, he had limited the involvement of any one Sheriden person, so nobody would ever see the whole picture of who was involved or what was happening. Nobody, of course, but he and his brother. This level of secrecy, however, was tasking. Terry had to create and complete so many layers of paperwork that he was working more as an administrator than as a team leader.

Terry, however, accepted the burden of paperwork and administration as necessary to achieve his goal. He had been burned by the Seal-turned-reporter and was not about to let something like that happen again. This time he would have teams, instead of a single person, to take care of any necessary business. They would also have exit strategies and the ability to take any action necessary. Any action, that is, that they perceived as necessary or that Terry directed them to take.

But for now, their task was simple enough: monitor and observe the target and determine what he was doing in Springfield. Terry wanted to know if and when the man suddenly acted differently, which could be a telltale sign that he had found what he was looking for or had an epiphany. It would be then that the team would need to get real close. They would have to either stick to him like glue or capture him. It was this last task that made Terry the most nervous. If the men screwed something up, it was most likely to occur when they got too close or purposely revealed themselves in order to abduct him.

He is sharp and observant, but he is also out of shape and practice. Terry also had decided that the reporter had little idea of whom or what could possibly be involved. *Most likely, Sean is alerted to the fact that something is going on, but has found no other strange things to keep him alert.* Terry had also been monitoring the Phoenix and Knoxville police "traffic" using the company's various sources. He had not noted anything that told him the police were treating Mary's murder as anything other than a senseless act of violence in a city plagued with them. Nor had he seen any signs that the event in Knoxville had been associated with Mary's death.

Terry completed his mental review of all the parameters that could affect the situation surrounding the reporter and decided that he would deploy this first team. He picked up his file and took it to the center table in the room where he had laid out a large map of Springfield. On it he had flagged the airport, the team's hotel, and points where Sean had used his credit card to purchase items that had been reported with an identifiable business name or address. These points of reference, a hotel, the Lincoln Museum, and a couple of restaurants were all within four blocks of each other. That told Terry that Sean was most likely on foot. Terry's research had also revealed that Sean was in the center of a tourist zone. It was likely to be extremely busy on Saturday and Sunday. Hordes of tourists would help his team blend in nicely. However, those same crowds might make spotting Sean harder. Still, Terry suspected that the reporter would be buried in a stack of books and notes at the museum or library. So, the team was split on its covers. One man was set up to be a student studying. His outfit included the omnipresence backpack and tennis shoes. The other was set up to be a tourist, complete with camera and tour book.

Terry surveyed the map and his plans one final time. He then pressed the speaker button on the phone at one corner of the table and dialed a number from one of his notes. Two rings later, a man answered.

"Hello?"

"Lincoln, this is Master," Terry began the call using the titles he had assigned for the mission. More than anything, this allowed Terry to run the operation without the team being any wiser as to whom was running it. His voice was being synthetically modified to mask its identity. This was particularly necessary since one of the team members had met Terry on a few occasions.

"Hello Master."

"You are instructed to begin surveillance as planned."

"Roger, begin surveillance."

"I have new information to provide."

"Okay, we're ready to proceed."

Terry then began to inform the team of the most recently reported location where Sean had used his credit card. Terry continued with a reminder to exercise extreme caution, to treat the reporter as being a trained and dangerous target. The team acknowledged this last instruction.

Satisfied, Terry released them to begin their work. They would report in if certain events had occurred at six o'clock in the evening, or as soon thereafter as they could. They had no idea who was giving them their instructions. In fact, they believed they were on a leave from Sheriden to work a private job. These layers of protection gave Terry as much assurance as he could ever have, short of doing the work himself.

Terry turned away from the center table and decided it was time for him to begin preparing a team to monitor Professor Enloe. He had another team idling in Nashville that would be ready to deploy by Sunday. But first, Terry would need to complete their necessary covers and plans of action.

Phoenix

Alan had come into the office after his computer guy had contacted him to report that he had finished a full exploration of Mary's computer. Stacked in front of him was every document or file that had been found and re-created. Alan had known from experience that there would be garbled portions within the documents. Such lost data were the result of the traces of the program that had destroyed the file organization and hierarchy within the storage device. Once the documents were returned to their original form, it was usually the case that a team could then figure out what words might be missing.

In this case though, Alan was very surprised by the high level of destruction. It was thorough, very thorough. The technician had explained to Alan that this meant the program, while not taking the time to write over every site in the device, had written over random places, as well as over the organizational hierarchy. That had added time to the task, but had destroyed more content than usual.

Alan had gone through the stack of printed files, making notes as he went along. He began with email. He quickly found some partial emails to and from Kim. He also found the email address for the reporter, Sean Johnson. He focused on their content first. In fact, that had been all he had spotted in all of the email that was of interest to him. The computer's internet browser files had been almost destroyed and Alan did not have much to tell him what websites Mary had been at recently. Within the text documents and other program files, he also had no luck. There had been many documents with family history in them and others had been from a specialized genealogy program. Others had been text files. There had been quite a few picture files that were not re-rendered, however, the file names and their file organization suggested these were family history photos and not worth assigning someone the task of attempting to rebuild each of them into viewable photos. So for now, those would remain a line of seemingly random letters and symbols.

That brought Alan back to the email. Apparently, that would be all he would initially have to go on. Alan did not think that he actually had all of the recent email that Mary had sent. There were gaps and also some replies to email where Alan did not appear to have the original email. That told him that he was seeing a partial record of Mary's email. The email themselves were also damaged, with portions appearing as jumbled random letters and symbols.

Besides getting Kim's email address and her last name, Poole, Alan had also been able to determine that the common element between Sean, Kim and Mary had been an ancestor of Kim's named Jacob Poole. At least Alan believed it was Jacob Poole. There was also a Jacob Thomas mentioned in one sentence that had survived. That email, though, suggested that Jacob Poole and Jacob Thomas might be the same person. Interestingly, President Lincoln also appeared to be involved and there had also been a reference to danger and secrecy.

Alan was thus very intrigued by the computer's revelations. Interestingly, his investigation kept leading back to Abraham Lincoln. *But what's the motive in here worth committing murder for?* That question bugged Alan. He was either on a tangent or missing something that was key to understanding the motive. The more he learned, though, the more he was certain that Sean Johnson was at the center of all of it.

Alan flipped through his file and found the cop's notes on Sean Johnson. He had checked with the Seattle police. They apparently only had a few records on people with that name, and none were likely matches. Alan realized that the cop had not gone farther on Sean Johnson, so Alan decided to investigate the man's past.

About a half an hour later he had thoroughly fleshed out Sean's file. He was a former US Navy Seal with a crisp and clean record and now had a reputation for writing compelling human interest stories. He was born and raised in Seattle and had settled there after his service. His service was classified, but Alan had expected that, since he had been in the Seal program. Alan also knew that his participation in that program meant he was smart, physically talented, and probably very tough. All were good characteristics needed to cover up a murder. He appeared to be living cleanly, however, and his life after the service did not suggest anything other than what he appeared to be: a human interest journalist.

Alan shifted his attention to the woman named Kimberly Poole. He quickly called up her details. She lived in Kansas City, had divorce filings in Dallas, Texas a few years back, and also appeared to have a clean record. She owned a garden shop in a shopping suburb in Kansas City. From the email chain, she appeared to have been communicating with the deceased before the reporter had entered the scene. *That matches what the professor said as well.*

Alan leaned back in his chair and considered his next step. It was Saturday and his first decision was whether to do anything else on the weekend or just let this sit until Monday. His intuition told him that there was something very strange going on that he had not yet figured out. The simplest explanation came back to the reporter killing Mary to cover up some scheme gone awry to extort or trick Kim or Mary out of money. Something did not ring true about that explanation though. *Something is missing!*

The more Alan thought, the more he was convinced there was a larger story involved. *And,* he thought, *Kim might be in danger or possibly even involved.* Alan decided his next step would be to pay a surprise visit to Kim in Kansas City. Then, he could head up to Illinois and question the reporter himself. Alan began making his travel plans, not waiting for Monday to arrive.

Springfield

Sean trudged back down the wooden staircase midway through a
line of tourists doing the same. He was in the Lincoln-Herndon Law
Office taking the standard tour with everyone else while learning all
sorts of fascinating trivia about Lincoln. The tour had been led by an
eager kid in his twenties who seemed very passionate about his job
and responsibility. He had responded to questions with enthusiasm
and energy and a sparkle in his eye. The law office occupied a three
story building on a corner at the heart of Springfield. It was mostly still
sitting the way it had been when Abraham Lincoln had practiced law
there. The federal court had actually used the middle floor during that
time, and that floor had also been arranged accordingly.

Two things struck Sean from his experience in the building. First, it
was fascinating to see how Lincoln still had an effect on people today,
perhaps even more than in the years after his death. He was symbolic
of many good human virtues and America and people flocked to him
and his past. Second, it seemed amazing that Lincoln could ever have
become President of the United States. Once there, it seemed incredible that he could have been equipped with the leadership and organizational skills necessary to do the great job that he did. His life seemed
so unassuming and so burdened with difficulties, that it just seemed
highly unlikely that a man from Illinois, raised in dirt cabins in Kentucky and Indiana, could have risen as far as he had.

Before visiting the law office, Sean had gone through the Lincoln
Museum's exhibits. There, buried among the tourists, he had been absorbed by the program that took him from the beginning to the end
of Lincoln's life. *It's really quite an extraordinary experience*, Sean
thought. *They have done a great job, perhaps as good as can be done,
of letting you walk through Lincoln's life as if you were there.* It took
you from the sleepy little Kentucky cabin replica, through tumultuous
formative years during the building tensions over slavery, through his
successes and failures, and right up to the presidency and the Civil
War. The program at the museum culminated with the sudden assassination of Lincoln. The experience had truly moved Sean. He left the
museum feeling numb and also pathetic that his own life, compared to

Lincoln's had amounted to so little.

So now, Sean stood on a street blocked off from cars staring at a life size statute of Abraham Lincoln and his children walking, as he tried to think of what to do next. There were tourists everywhere. Clearly people descended on the museum from all parts of the country and the world. The fact that Sean was here trying to unravel a mystery about the President, one that suggested, at least in part, that the President's real father had not been Thomas Lincoln, seemed silly.

Sean also felt that he really did not know what he was truly looking for in Springfield, much less, in this mystery. He was searching for Thomas and Enloe references, but he mostly felt like he was shooting in the dark. There was something he was not doing right, something he needed to figure out. The best way to figure it out, he knew, was to get back to work. So, he headed for the library to dig back into the books and records.

Knoxville

James Enloe had figured it out, or at least a big piece of it, he was certain. After working most of the night, taking only a short nap when he could truly no longer keep his eyes open, he had figured out the Thomas connection. Better, he was certain he knew who Jacob Thomas had been. He had not directly worked for Abraham Lincoln. That had been the key reason he, like his sister, he suspected, had not been able to easily find out who Jacob Thomas had been. Jacob Thomas had been an employee of the War Department, assigned to work as a courier to Lincoln.

James had felt he had run through every record he could find and had not found anything. But along the way, he had come across a reference in correspondence to a person, whose name he had not seen in White House records. After having woken up from his nap, he had recalled the odd name and it had struck him that it was a sign that there were other people that had worked for Lincoln who would not show up as being White House employees. James had then started digging into other records and had found the person as being in the Army and assigned to escort the President on a trip out of town. With that revelation, a whole new world of documents had been brought into focus. James did not have very many of them, but the internet had revealed all sorts of sources. A few hours later, he had found a Jacob Thomas employed in the War Department as a courier or driver of sorts. James had sat back in his chair, struck by how easily the information was available. On payroll sheets, Jacob Thomas first appeared in December of 1864 and last appeared in March of 1865.

James had noted the shortness of the employment and had set about searching for Jacob in any other government records. The problem was that James could not simply search by name. Instead, he had to scroll down and search documents page by page. It helped that most of them were in some semblance of alphabetical order, but many were also in some form of chronological order and most were not the best of copies either. His eyes had thus grown tired many times over. He had, in fact, more than once considered ceasing his work from home. He could have packed up and headed to a major document repository. He knew there was one in Richmond, Virginia and one in Washington D.C., but having started on his search in this manner, he had not been able to bring himself to stop. That was one reason why he had worked through the night. Before he had taken the well needed nap, though, he had been feeling somewhat discouraged. But, after the short nap and some light breakfast, he had gone back at it. It was then he had found Jacob Thomas. It had been that simple.

Now, having found the man, James was uncertain what to do next. He believed this had to be the target. His employment put him in the War Department at the end of the Civil War and also just a few months before Lincoln's Assassination. Lincoln had frequented the War Department, so it was very likely that Jacob Thomas had encountered the President. It was possible, if not probable, that he had been assigned more than once to take documents to or from the White House. However, all James had found were payroll records. He suspected that more information would require going to the source, but even that, he was uncertain would reveal more data. If the topic had been Abraham Lincoln, James would have been very knowledgeable of where to go and what to look for once there. But, he was not a Civil War historian and he knew that he was already beyond his normal depth in that subject.

Then it struck James, that, in part, he did know what to do next. After all, the issue was Abraham Lincoln. He needed to know how Jacob Thomas, a war department courier, had come to know President Lincoln. So, his first step was to now flip the task back around and ask how Abraham Lincoln came to know or use Jacob Thomas. That was more along the lines of his knowledge base. As James thought about it, there were two logical ways Jacob and President Lincoln could have possibly connected. Either it had been a casual meeting in the War Department, or Jacob had delivered documents to, or for, Abraham Lincoln. James suspected the latter, that Jacob had been a courier for the president as more logical, since casual meetings would not be likely to create the kinds of burdens that Jacob had later carried. So, James needed to scrutinize the days President Lincoln had visited the War Department. He also needed to scrutinize White House records for the period of time Jacob had been employed to determine when, if ever, he or any unnamed War Department courier had visited the White House generally, or the president specifically. As to War Department visits, James could do that with his resources. But for White House records, though he himself could not immediately search them, he suspected he knew who could. It was Sean. Sean was supposedly headed to the Springfield Lincoln Library which had the most robust set of records of any location.

Excitedly, James searched around his desk for the note containing Sean's cell phone number. He finally found it and pulled the phone closer to him, shoving some papers off the desk and onto the floor. He cared little about the mess, however, and quickly dialed Sean's number. A few moments later it connected and he heard Sean's greeting.

"Hello this is Sean. This must be James. Am I right?"

"You most certainly are. Listen, I have news for you." James was so excited to share his news that he did not pause to wonder how Sean had known it was himself calling.

"That's great. I've spent the morning being a tourist here in Springfield, which was probably more productive than my day before trying to be a historian in the Lincoln Library."

"So, you're still there then?"

"Oh yes. In fact, I am just gearing up to trudge back up to my study location and futilely go through more records."

"Well then my news is both good and timely."

"Oh?" The professor could tell that he had drawn Sean's interest.

"Oh yes," he began. He then proudly blurted out the news. "I know who Jacob Thomas is."

"What? That's great! You found him?" The professor could fully sense Sean's own excitement level rise.

"Yes, yes. I did. He was a courier for the War Department in D.C. from about..." James had to pause and scrambled among the papers on his desk with his free hand to find the right page. "Ah, here it is. Sorry. From about December of 1864 through March of 1865, just before Lincoln's assassination."

"Wow, that's incredible Professor. So, he was right there in the capital?"

"Well yes, most likely," James acknowledged. "Actually, your question hits right at my next topic. You see, we need to now learn more about who and how this Jacob Thomas might have interacted with the president."

"And that means you need me to do something here in Springfield. Right?" Sean had partly interrupted James. Or at least, James felt, he had finished his thought for him. Normally, James would have been moderately irritated by this, but his excitement level allowed him to continue on as if it had never happened.

"Yes, that's right. I need you to scrutinize some White House documents at the Presidential Museum. Some will be copies. Some might even be originals. They might let you see the originals if you have them speak to me."

"Well there, Professor, I might have you beat. I think the ladies upstairs really like me. They might even give me the keys to the whole building if I ask just right."

"Good, well mention my name and title if you think it will help. In the meantime, here is what I want you to do. Can you write this down?"

"Hold on for a moment Professor, and I'll be ready." Sean's voice went silent and James waited patiently. Then Sean came back.

"Okay, I'm ready."

James then gave Sean a list of documents or resources for him to search through. They were mostly White House logs or records kept by several different sources within the Lincoln White House.

"So, is that pretty clear?"

"Yes, I'll get right on it," Sean paused. "So, how did you find this information? Do you think this is what your sister had found?"

They were both silent for a moment at the mention of James' sister. James then realized that he had shoved her out of his mind as much as he could. Having Sean mention her had brought an overwhelming sense of guilt across his psyche, though he knew he did not need to feel that way. He felt himself starting to focus on his memories of Mary, when Sean spoke.

"Sorry, I should be more sensitive when I raise her in this. Professor, please accept my apology. It's just that this really is about Mary now isn't it?"

James sensed that Sean had said it exactly right. It was now all about Mary.

"Yes, you're right. It is. Mary died while trying to unravel this. If she died, for any reason connected to this, then this is all about her. In any case, she would be happy to see that we were completing her efforts."

James paused, then continued, "No apologies needed, Sean. Having found that Jacob Thomas did exist and that his connection to Lincoln appears to be found, I am the one who should apologize for being so rude to you when you last called."

"Nonsense, Professor. I was an annoying reporter raising very upsetting topics." Sean's tone changed slightly. "Understand that I could be very wrong that there is any connection between your sister's death and the Jacob Thomas warning, but in any case, it will be a good thing if we can finish sorting out the history behind Jacob Thomas."

James realized that Sean probably did not know anything more about Mary's death. He had not spoken to him since the FBI agent had called him.

"Listen, has the FBI called you?" he asked of Sean.

"No." Sean's answer was drawn out a bit, showing renewed curiosity.

"Well, they called me. Among other things, the agent told me that Mary's computer was erased in a highly suspicious manner." James stopped speaking to let weight of what he said sink into Sean. After a moment, Sean responded.

"Really. That's very important. That the FBI is involved is also notable itself. But why erase her computer? Especially for a robbery?"

"That was my question back to him, and my point exactly Sean. He had no answer. However, it tells me that there really could be a connection between the two, as weird as that sounds."

Sean's voice took on a very firm tone.

"Well, if that is the case and if you are now suspicious, then that makes two of us. That makes our caution all the more reasonable." Sean paused, apparently thinking. "I will get right to your requested research. I'll call Kim tonight and discuss this with her. She is in Denver researching the rest of Jacob Thomas's life. In the meantime, what are you going to do?"

"I need to scrutinize the War Department side of things more. It's something I am not as familiar with. So I am going to spend some time learning more about the nature of the records, locations of documents, etcetera."

"Okay, well, be careful Professor. And again, don't hesitate to call me for any reason. At any time, okay?"

"Okay."

They said their good byes and hung up. The professor put the phone down and leaned back in his chair to think some more about his sister.

Chapter Eighteen

Springfield

Sean pushed his cell phone back into his pocket after his call with James. He was sitting on the steps of the old Illinois courthouse and legislature building with the Lincoln Library off to his right. He took a sip from the paper coffee cup in his hand and thought about the news James had just shared. He was greatly encouraged that Jacob Thomas had been found. It seemed pretty likely that this courier named Jacob Thomas had to be the same Jacob Thomas that changed his name in Denver some time later.

In fact, the timing is perfect. He's a courier at just the time that Lincoln is assassinated. He appears in Denver and changes his name at some point afterwards. He lives out his life in Denver, harboring some secrets left from his service. That makes the assassination of Lincoln more and more likely to be connected with his fear.

The implications of such a conclusion seemed enormous to Sean. *Could it be that Jacob knew something about Lincoln's assassination?* He recalled that James had explained that the big conspiracy theory had mostly been fabricated a hundred years later by a chemist using very faulty logic. *But what if there is some secret information that has never seen the light of day?*

Sean shook his head. The story seemed to be growing by the minute, at least in his view. First, though, he needed to get the research done for the professor. He also needed to share this with Kim. Perhaps, once done here, he would go to Denver, to help Kim track down and figure out Jacob's life in the city.

Besides, We're still completely in the dark about what this has to do with the Enloes, he thought. *Time to get to work.*

Sean stood up and stretched, noting the tourists flowing through and standing still around the square and the Lincoln complex. He then began walking to the library while gulping coffee down. He smiled at the thought of the librarians panicking if he dared to bring a beverage into the archives.

Denver

Kim used the computer mouse to navigate through the webpage. She was sitting on the edge of a wooden chair in front of a computer at a local internet café. The hotel concierge had given her directions to the business, and she found it easily. It was on a side street to a major pedestrian area at the core of downtown Denver, and was one part coffee house and one part computer café. Kim paid a teenage clerk for one hour of computer use, feeling his scrutiny of her as she asked him questions about how to use their services. *I must be more than a little out of place,* she thought. *Most everyone in here has a tattoo or piercing and looks to be less than half my age.* The thought of Abby finding her mom in the shop made her chuckle. She was certain Abby would be horribly embarrassed to be seen in such a place with her mother. Even if it was 500 miles from their home.

In fact, Kim had called Abby on her cell and arranged to have Abby meet her at the shop around the time her hour would be up. Then, they would go driving together, perhaps down to Colorado Springs. She had decided to find a computer and do some research after concluding that Jacob's will was not going to reveal much more. But in studying the will, she realized that Jacob had to have had a lot of interactions with Denver over the course of his time in the city. So, she had decided to go online and see what records of Denver's history were available to assist her in trying to investigate his life in the mountainous city.

Kim was currently on a web page devoted to Denver history. It was associated with the Denver History Museum, but appeared to be maintained by a separate individual. Her initial assumption was that land and court records and newspaper articles would be her best resources to search. She had settled on the time period of 1870 to 1910 as being her focus. That era probably contained most events, if any, that were recorded and might have included Jacob Poole's life. She had to keep reminding herself to look for Jacob Poole and not Jacob Thomas, though she knew that it was possible he had existed under both names in the city. She mostly suspected, however, that he must have hidden his old name before 1870, as even that date was five years after the end of the Civil War and the end of Lincoln's life.

As Kim worked her way through the website, it appeared that the newspaper records were not online, and were not even indexed. Thus, she realized, researching the newspapers would require days of scrolling through microfilms of newspapers looking for articles of interest. She knew such a search would be like looking for the proverbial needle in a haystack, so she quickly dismissed that tactic. She did, however, jot down the handy list of libraries having microfilm copies of various newspapers.

That brought Kim to court and land records. It appeared there were online resources for these records, and she began by sorting out the various resources. They all appeared to be links to other webpages having indexes of various records. She clicked on each one and made notes about their contents. That took her a few minutes and once done, she glanced at her watch and at the timer on the computer screen. She had about fifteen minutes of research left before her time would expire.

As if on cue, she was distracted from her focus by Abby whispering very quietly over her shoulder.

"Mom, what are you doing here?" Kim found herself mildly enjoying the light embarrassment in her daughter's voice.

"Why? Is there something wrong with your mother using a computer at an internet café?" she responded without looking up from the monitor.

"No, I guess not. It's just weird."

Still without looking up, Kim knew that behind her, Abby was probably looking around at the other kids and trying to see if they had noticed her mom.

"Relax, no one else cares that you're here with your mom."

"Okay, so what ARE you doing here? More genealogy?"

Kim finally looked up from the screen and into her daughter's eyes. She noted an unused chair next to her table and gestured at it.

"Here. Sit down. I'm almost done."

"Okay," Abby muttered as she pulled the chair next to her mom and sat. She leaned in and studied the webpage Kim was navigating through. Kim let her study it for a moment while scrolling down through the records. She then explained what she was doing.

"I'm looking for records about Jacob Poole, what lands he owned, and court cases he might have been involved in here in Denver."

"Okay, that's real interesting."

Abby paused and then began a question in a different tone.

"Mom, can I ask a question?"

Here it comes, Kim thought, there has been something on her mind for a while. "Sure," she replied.

"Don't take this the wrong way, but what are we really doing here?"

Kim was so relieved that her question was not something vastly more difficult to answer that she involuntarily laughed a little. Then she reflected and realized Abby's question was a difficult one to answer. *What am I doing here?*

"It's complicated honey," she began. "I told you that grandpa left me a letter telling me of a secret about our family?"

Kim glanced at Abby again and saw her short nod as she answered "Yes."

"Well, basically, our ancestor, Jacob Poole apparently changed his name from Thomas to Poole because he was very afraid of something that had to do with another family and Abraham Lincoln."

"Okay, so why the sudden rush to Denver? Why's this so important?"

"Good questions honey. It may not be that important, but Jacob was not only worried about something back a hundred and fifty years ago, he warned his son to continue to keep quiet for a long time afterwards. He was also very mysterious and left a puzzling message behind instead of simply telling us what scared him."

Abby giggled. "Oh come on, you're making this up."

"No, no it's true," Kim said carefully. She decided it was time to tell Abby her real reason for urgency, as crazy as she knew it would sound to her daughter.

"There's more. You remember the lady, Mary, that was murdered last week? Sean Johnson, the reporter, called me."

Abby nodded.

"Well, her murder was suspicious. She was helping me solve the mystery Jacob Thomas left behind for us. I know this sounds crazy, but there is a slight chance her murder was related to Jacob's warning. A mysterious man chased Sean a few nights later in Knoxville while he was meeting with her brother." Kim thought for a moment. "Actually, I think Sean chased the man."

"Anyway, Sean and I decided to try and quickly figure out why Jacob changed his name and why he warned us."

Kim stopped speaking and kept her eyes on her daughter. After a few moments, Abby responded.

"You're right Mom. This does sound crazy. We came all the way to Denver for you to chase down some mystery?"

Kim smiled. "I knew you would feel that way. Let me explain things a bit differently. You are my only child. As your mother, I'm exceptionally protective of you. So, I would rather overreact and be a little nutty than let any harm come to you. People don't get murdered everyday. Mary's death is incredibly coincidental. Yes, it's true that this could be 'much ado about nothing,' but I would rather eliminate any danger, especially to you."

"Besides, I thought it would be fun to head over here with you. I get so busy with the shop, we rarely get to do anything together."

"Mom, driving all day to a city so you can spend your time looking at documents and staring at a computer is hardly fun."

"Well, I've got a solution for that, too. Let's head down to Colorado Springs and see the Air Force Academy. Does that sound fun?"

"Better," Abby said trying to suppress a smile.

"What?" Kim demanded.

"Nothing Mom, nothing," Abby replied.

Springfield

Sean had just completed the research James had wanted. After speaking with the same librarian that had helped him the day before, he had quickly found himself buried in files and microfilms. He had begun to go through them methodically, but then had quickly realized that it might take him a full day to truly look at every document that might name a visitor to the White House during the last several months of President Lincoln's administration.

So, instead, Sean had made arrangements to have certain files copied while he attacked the microfilmed records. With those, he also had run into the same issue of the time involved. He also found it tiring on his eyes to scrutinize the screen for extended periods of time. He thus found himself printing page after page of microfilmed records. He tried to be discreet as to the volume he was copying. When he had asked the librarian to copy the main documents, she had indicated that they did not really approve of total copying of records. He had then used the professor's name, trying to talk her into copying the records. She had not known who he was, but Sean suspected that she had accepted his credentials at face value, that James Enloe was a Lincoln history professor. It had seemed to smooth things out, especially after Sean had promised to use bookmarks in the files to indicate specific pages he had wanted copied. With the microfilm, he had printed when he was certain nobody was watching and emptied the printer ejection shelf regularly, shoving the papers into a nearby file so nobody would notice.

It was now four o'clock on Saturday, and the archive was supposed to be closed. Sean was standing in front of a desk while the librarian had left to run his credit card for payment of all of the copies. She returned momentarily, an elderly lady with white hair in a very nice, but plain yellow dress.

"Here you are, Mr. Johnson. If you could please sign this and keep the top copy." She smiled sweetly at him.

"Certainly," he replied.

After signing, he pushed her copy and her pen across the desk towards her and moved to pick up his three inch stack of copies. As he was lifting it, he thanked her.

"Thank you very much for all your assistance. I've been very impressed. Everyone here has been very helpful, everything worked very well and all the documents are so organized," Sean explained. "It's rare these days, you know, to find such organization and professionalism."

The woman beamed with pleasure. "Thank you, Mr. Johnson. It's great to hear that."

She walked him over to the door and unlocked it with a key sticking in the lock. He pushed the door open and, with a short wave good-bye, departed down the steps to the ground floor exit. Behind him, he could hear the lock clicking shut.

Once on the street, holding his copies in one arm, Sean paused, using his free hand to find his sunglasses in his pocket and push them on. The sun's afternoon glare was then much more manageable as he began walking to his hotel. The tourists had thinned quite a bit making the square with the old courthouse much more quiet. He walked along feeling encouraged that there might soon be an end to his bizarre quest. Then, all of a sudden, he felt the same sensation he had felt the previous week while meeting with James.

A man dressed like a tourist, like a father really, had turned his head a certain way, and a little alarm had gone off in the back of Sean's head. Sean was not aware that he had been watching for such behavior, but he accepted his recognition as coming from the programming embedded in his mind.

That "tourist" was watching me. Sean knew it was possible that the man was a genuine tourist who had found something interesting about Sean. *I could be overreacting here.* It had been several days since the chase in Knoxville and he had relaxed from his earlier alertness. Apparently, though, he had still been subconsciously aware. As he walked, Sean tried to think of what to do. He decided upon a simple test of purposely walking around the area and seeing if he could detect whether the man followed him or acted suspiciously. The problem was that Sean could not now see the man and he was unwilling to look back and reveal his own interest. So, he abruptly turned to cross the street towards the courthouse. In doing so, he had a good excuse to look both ways before crossing the street and he did so. He imme-diately recognized that the man had not physically moved from his location, but that his head had turned towards Sean. *That's another giveaway, though it could still be coincidental.*

Sean crossed the street, turned his back to the man and continued walking away. He was now headed right for the coffee shop that he had stopped at several times already. He decided to do so again. The sun would be perfectly positioned so that he could turn and study the street and the man from behind its glass door and windows the minute he got inside the shop. As he walked towards the shop, he tried to fully consider the situation.

Either I'm completely overreacting, or he's working with someone else. Otherwise, he would have had to have started walking after me. Sean began scanning the people in his eyesight, looking for other odd-ities as he walked towards the coffee shop. He saw nothing. Reaching the shop, he pulled the door open and then pulled it shut behind him as he entered. Immediately, Sean spun around and stepped to one side so he could look out the window. The man had moved! He had crossed the street to the side that Sean had been on and was walking in the same direction. In a moment he would reach the intersection. He was not looking at the coffee shop at all and Sean began to relax. *Perhaps you are overreacting, Sean. This has been a weird enough time.* But then, he thought again of the chase in Knoxville and reaffirmed to himself that he should be very cautious, that there was some real threat out there somewhere. Whatever it was, he could not be too careful.

Sean continued to study the scene in front of him. The man had reached the intersection and had begun crossing it looking both ways just as Sean had done. Sean could not be sure, but he believed that the man had let his eyes linger a bit longer when looking towards the coffee shop. He would soon pass out of site to the right side of Sean's vision, and he knew he needed to decide what to do next. Feeling the bulk of the papers in his hands, he decided his first focus was getting back to his hotel room, packing and preparing to quickly exit from town. Then, he could consider trying to confront any surveillance he might have. The problem was that going to the hotel would take him along the tourist's last visible path. Sean thought about this for a moment and then decided on getting a cup of coffee in a paper cup and heading to his hotel as if everything was normal.

A few minutes later Sean exited the shop, fresh coffee in one hand and the pile of papers cradled in his other arm. He walked normally while using his eyes and casual random head movements to scan the scene. He did not see the tourist man, nor anything else that bothered him. He reached his hotel, which was only a block and a half from the coffee shop and slid into the lobby, still on high alert. The lobby was very busy, jammed with a busload of tourists all checking into the hotel. As he walked through, he did not spot anything out of the ordinary. Soon, he had gone up to his floor via the elevator and was in his room packing furiously.

While packing, he thought out a plan. He would take the regular elevator up a few floors and then take the service elevator all the way down to the parking garage. He would then drive some, verify he had no tail, and then come back towards the hotel, parking a block or two away. He could then return to the hotel, and try to detect anybody positioned for surveillance.

Sean completed packing, but only after changing into different clothes and donning a ball cap. He put on his casual walking shoes, that he knew would have a better grip, and then made his exit. He would worry about checking out later, doing it by phone, once he had eliminated his concerns. As he made his way up and then down to his car, he again let his mind consider the situation. *If they're following me, are they also watching James? If this has anything to do with the Lincoln matter, are they also aware of and following Kim? Are Kim, Abby and James in danger?*

Sean decided that the key to answering all of those questions was to determine whether he was really being monitored. If he was, then he needed to call Kim and James immediately. He considered for a moment that he might have detected an FBI surveillance of him. If they had called James, perhaps he had told them about himself and where he was headed. In some ways, Sean felt it would be a relief learning that the FBI was involved, but his intuition told him that was not likely.

Sean reached his car and stored his luggage uneventfully. He did not detect anyone in the garage and quickly drove out sliding his room key into the automated gate releasing the bar. A few minutes later, he was parked about five blocks away, having driven a very circuitous route designed to detect any car following him. As he sat in the car watching for movement around him, he again felt himself questioning his logic, perhaps even his sanity. Again, though, his logic prevailed, and he continued with his plan to reverse things on anyone following him.

After one final glance ahead and behind, Sean quickly slipped out of his car and started walking. He fell in step near a man going in the same direction, towards the side of the hotel. After a few blocks, as the hotel neared, he stopped by a store window and used it to look carefully over the ground he had just crossed. Seeing nothing, he began walking towards the hotel again. As he drew closer, he began aggressively scanning anything that moved. He crossed the last intersection and began walking along the side of the hotel. About halfway, he reached an entrance into a shopping area that shared the ground floor space with the hotel. He took this entrance and then turned again, entering a newspaper, wine and tobacco shop. There, he quickly found a reason to turn back around and monitor the entrance and the hall. A woman in her twenties was sitting on a bench midway down the hall. An older couple were exiting a store across from the woman. The barbershop, located directly across the hall, was empty except for a barber watching a television. Sean pulled a newspaper from a shelf and paid for it. He then exited the store and began slowly strolling up the hall, seemingly window shopping while tapping the newspaper against the back of his legs.

About halfway up the hall Sean could begin seeing the lobby appear around a corner. He drew closer to one side of the hall and walked forward a bit farther, stopping before reaching the point where the wall ended and thus avoiding exposing himself to the whole lobby. He could now see the entrance, the registration desk, and the bellman. He stood there for a moment, as if waiting for someone, and then walked around the corner. On his right, the lobby opened up to reveal the elevators, as well as a restaurant. He saw the suspicious man as soon as he rounded the corner. The man was looking right back at Sean, but it was also as if he were looking right past him. Sean felt his heart pick up speed, and he worked at calming himself and keeping his movements consistent with a casual stroll. Inwardly, though, his brain was furiously assessing his situation. *The same man and he's positioned perfectly to watch the elevators. He showed no surprise at seeing me appear suddenly. If he's a trained pro, he is also trying to assess the situation. I need to force his move, somehow make him reveal himself as well as perhaps reveal who else he is working with in surveillance.* Sean thought carefully and then decided on a course of action. He turned and began walking towards the hotel entrance resisting the strong urge to look back. Instead, he focused on trying to spot anyone else who appeared out of place.

If it's a two man team, the other should be in or near a vehicle. Look for someone parked up or down the block. No, wait! It's a one way street, so they have to be parked to the right.

Sean exited and turned right, following the curved entrance driveway down to the street. A large tour bus was parked directly in front of the hotel and Sean decided to walk directly around it and cross the street. As soon as he had rounded the bus, so that it screened him entirely from view of the hotel, he took off at a dead run across the road into another hotel, this one declaring itself to be The Abraham Lincoln Hotel. He ran into the lobby and immediately turned back around, ignoring the startled expressions of the guests and bellman.

Sean's tactic worked. The man dressed as a tourist came trotting around the bus looking a bit panicked. He saw Sean staring back at him and stopped moving. They stood there glaring at each other for a few moments. Sean absorbed every detail he could about the man. The man was about five foot, ten inches, muscular with a dark complexion and was definitely not the same man that Sean had encountered in Knoxville. Sean suspected the man was carrying a firearm, mostly because he had a windbreaker on that was several sizes too big. Then, the man began slowly walking across the street towards Sean.

Sean instantly took off at a full run down into the heart of the hotel. He figured he had about ten seconds before the man would reach the interior. Guests stared at him, and some half jumped out of the way as he flew along the broad carpeted corridor. Several doors, apparently leading into conference rooms, appeared on his right. He tried the second one and it opened. But, as he burst into a dark and empty room, he knew it had taken too long and that his pursuer had probably seen him enter. Sean glanced around. There were two doors at the back, but also a door leading back into the first conference room that he had passed by. He quickly tried that door and ran through as it opened. Sean's plan was to double back on his pursuer, and it might have succeeded except his pursuer had also developed a plan. Sean was practically run over by the man as he burst through the door into the first conference room at the same time Sean was exiting.

Sean slammed his shoulder into the man, shoving them both out into the corridor again. They tumbled onto the carpeted hallway floor with their hands moving against each other's bodies trying to fend off any attacks, while also creating some space and leverage to launch their own assault. Their actions mostly negated each other, and they began to get up. Sean had landed hard on his knee as they had gone down, and that made him a bit slower in rising. However, his slowness actually gave him an opening, and Sean slung his body in an arch, kicking his leg hard into the back of the first leg to reach full extension on the other man. His aggressor came down hard, right towards Sean, and Sean shoved the heel of his palm stiffly upwards, sharply catching the man's jaw and feeling the head snapping backward. He slid by Sean towards the floor.

Sean struggled to his feet while the other man groggily tried to get up. Noticing that a crowd of people had gathered in the lobby area and were now staring towards them, Sean hatched a simple plan.

"Lookout! He's got a gun!" he yelled as loud as he could.

Sean then took off at full speed back into the conference room. Once inside, he raced to the back and slammed the service door open into a well lit corridor. It was empty. He turned left and headed towards the lobby. Sean's knee hurt badly and his breathing was now as heavy as it could be under the circumstances. He cursed his lack of fitness as he pushed through a door marked emergency exit and then into a parking lot. It was brighter than it had been in the hallway, but the sky was beginning its shift to twilight. He turned and began running to his right, along the sidewalk, trying to circle back around to try and reach the one-way street that ran between the two hotels. He had noted many cars parked along that street, and suspected one of them would be harboring his pursuer's partner.

Sean turned the corner and burst onto the sidewalk. Sure enough, almost immediately, Sean spotted a man in a car look up in his rearview mirror back at Sean. The car had apparently been running, because it lurched forward a moment later, tires squealing, and raced up the street between the hotels. At the corner it turned right, going around the hotel that Sean just ran through.

However, Sean had been able to fully read the license plate and that was what he wanted. He immediately stripped his light blue wind breaker off reveling a dark brown, short sleeved shirt. He bunched the windbreaker up as much as he could in his hand and began walking as normally as he could across the street and behind his own hotel. His chest was straining to breathe, however, and it was all he could do to slow it down enough to make his breathing become silent. Still, he felt no one noticing him as he reached the back of his own hotel and began trotting up the alley to create some separation between him and the scene he was now leaving. Sean would work his way to his car and try to get out of the downtown area as quickly as he could.

Chapter Nineteen

Sunday , May 3
Saint Louis, Missouri

In the blackness, Sean felt terribly disoriented. He quickly reached out with his hands and grasped at the space around him. He felt a leather cushioned surface, and a few moments later, recognition and recollection began to calm him. He had been in the middle of another firefight nightmare, entirely created by the imagination of his subconscious mind. Awakening in the dark, he was, for a moment, stuck between his subconscious and conscious worlds, thinking he was still in some hopeless gun battle. Then, he realized that his hands were touching a leather sofa, which in turn led to the memory that he was at Frank Kelso's house.

Sean groaned, wishing he could go back to sleep, but a mental alarm clock told him it was time to rise, that his body had gotten enough rest for now. As he pushed himself up on the sofa, full recollection of his most recent hours washed through his mind. The day before he had clashed with more suspicious strangers, and this time they had done the chasing. After narrowly escaping them and reaching his car, he had stopped at a highway restaurant to fuel himself and collect his thoughts. He decided to head to Denver by car, assuming that air travel would be too visible. He had called an old Seal buddy, Frank Kelso, who lived in Saint Louis and made arrangements to stop at his house for the night. He then called Kim, leaving her a short message, and then he called James. He and James had talked some, but James had been groggy, apparently having gone to bed very early because he had been up late the previous night. Sean had warned each of them to be exceptionally careful. After reaching Frank's house, very late, he and Frank had talked for a few moments over a beer, before Sean had felt himself dozing off.

In the darkness, Sean had now reached an upright position on the sofa. As he went to swing his legs down to the carpet he felt his right knee twisting against something under the blanket that was wrapped around his legs. He recalled the injury he had caused to his knee while escaping his pursuer. Frank had wrapped it with an artificial ice pack. Though it was no longer cold, the bag was still there, snagging the blanket. He could not yet tell how much the knee itself hurt because the wrapping had fully immobilized the joint. Sean smiled at that memory. Frank had not really been a medic in their Seal unit, but he had always been among the best at general first aid procedures. That skill had not gone away, Sean reflected, as he considered how well bundled his knee was.

Sean glanced at his wrist watch. It was four o'clock in the morning. By Sean's estimate, that meant he had gotten about four hours of sleep. That would have to be enough.

"I see you have finally woken up," a friendly voice came at Sean out of the darkness.

"I probably woke you up," Sean shot back.

A light came on allowing Sean to see Frank standing by the doorway of the living room. *Frank's in better shape than me,* Sean thought, *his job as a cop here in Saint Louis probably fits better with keeping in shape than my job as a reporter. That is until lately. My job has been much more physical recently.*

"How's the knee?" Frank asked walking into the room. Frank was a full head shorter than Sean, but much more muscular. His black hair was as full as ever, but cut very short. He was wearing jeans and a polo shirt. Sean could tell that Frank moved just as smoothly now as he had in the past. In fact, Frank had just snuck up on him in the silent room. That said much about his skills.

"I can't tell. You wrapped it so damn tight."

"Well, let's look at it."

Frank had reached Sean and had begun pulling the blanket off to attack the bandage. As he did, he spoke.

"So, last night you never fully told me what the hell is going on. You were chased for the second time? You're on a hunt for some secret about President Lincoln?"

"Yeah, that's pretty much it." Sean said grimacing some as Frank unwrapped his knee. "It's pretty bizarre and it's getting more complicated every day."

Sean briefly summarized most of the events of the last week to Frank. Frank was one of the few people in the world he knew he could trust completely, even with his life. They had entrusted each other with their lives enough times in the past. Frank mostly listened as he examined and rewrapped Sean's knee.

"So, that's it. That's what brought me to your doorstep pleading for help," Sean finished.

"Hey, I'm glad I'm here to help." Frank was smiling, but then turned more serious. "So, who do you think is following you?"

"I don't know," Sean admitted. Then he remembered the license plate number. "But I have a lead. I got the license plate of the car yesterday. Maybe you can run it?"

"Maybe," Frank said slowly. "But tell me this, why aren't you going to the police. You said the FBI is involved, right?"

"Well, first I don't know what is really going on yet. No offense, but I don't have much faith in the police, especially the FBI. These people are very sophisticated and very good. They have the same skills we had. I think the police would make it harder to protect ourselves. Mostly, though, I think bringing law enforcement in would slow us down too much in trying to figure out what is going on. I also can't shake the suspicion that our own government might be involved."

He looked at Frank. "You and I have seen enough to know you can never trust the government. Yes?"

"Yes, yes," Frank replied studying Sean for a moment, as if making a decision. "Okay. For you, I will see what I can dig up on the license plate number. Meanwhile, I think your knee is just sprained. You barely noticed me wiggling it around, but you might have torn a ligament. Keep it wrapped well for a few days, icing it if you can. If you feel any sharp pain, better see a doctor."

Frank paused as he rocked back on his heels and pushed himself up. "I'll give you a bag of ice and some tape so you can ice it while you're driving."

"You can tell I'm about to leave?"

"You told me last night."

Sean was surprised at himself. "Really? I must have been tired, I don't remember at all."

"You're going to Denver?"

"Yeah. How long will it take me?"

"Twelve hours probably. You should fly."

"No. Whoever it is that found me in Springfield clearly has some ability to follow me. I think flying may be too obvious."

"Credit cards," Frank said quietly, mostly thinking out loud.

"What's that?" Sean asked, not certain what Frank had said.

"Credit cards. They can track you based on credit card use. I can request credit card companies to give me a report on recent usage of a credit card. The credit card companies don't let just anyone do that though. Police mostly. So, I hope that whoever is following you is the government, for your sake. If it's not, it's somebody with a lot of influence or access."

Frank looked at his watch. "I'm getting more interested in your story the more I learn. It will be interesting to see where your license plate number leads."

Sean thought about Frank's explanation. "Well then, I think I'll pull some cash out of a bank today and use it for gas and the like."

"Yeah well, you'll soon see that you cannot travel that much without using a credit card." Frank had started to leave the room but he stopped and looked at Sean. "Are you sure you don't want to come in with me? I can protect you, you know that."

"I do know that, Frank, but you can't do much about my friends in Denver or Knoxville, and I would be essentially stuck here. You know that, too."

"Yeah, I do." He smiled. "Okay, come on. I've got to head in for my early shift, and you need to hit the road. Follow me and we can stop at my favorite coffee shop."

Sean laughed. "Tell me it's not a doughnut shop."

"Yeah, it is. Don't start either. I know what you're thinking, cops and doughnut shops, but I don't eat that many."

Sean pushed himself up, laughing with his friend. He tested his knee, and followed him out of the room.

Atlanta

Terry was furious. He had stayed in his office overnight, sleeping some on the sofa, but mostly doing damage control. His men had screwed up badly, and it was very upsetting! Either this Sean Johnson was even more formidable of an opponent than even Terry had conceded or his men were that much more inferior.

He had gotten a call in the evening from the duo in Springfield. They were enroute back to their hotel. They had quickly explained to Terry what had happened and how they had barely escaped from being detained by the police. Worse, Sean Johnson had to be on full alert at this point, making tailing him futile.

Terry had decided on the spot to withdraw his Springfield team and set about making that happen. After routing them through two private couriers to mask their movement, they would be boarding a flight out of the country. He had arranged a different person to collect their belongings and otherwise shut down the operation in Springfield.

Now, Terry was in his brains room stewing over what to do. The reporter would no doubt have alerted Kim and the professor. Surveillance was, realistically, no longer an option. His choices were to leave them alone, capture and interrogate them, or eliminate them. He knew his brother would never go for elimination, and even Terry knew that too many deaths would attract unwanted scrutiny. He also did not like the idea of capturing them, or at least not the reporter. He was too dangerous. Terry considered that perhaps capturing one and using that person against the others would be best. *Or, leave them alone, at least for a while.* He wanted to call his brother, but he knew how early it was and did not wish to wake him with such bad news. Besides, Terry felt a certain responsibility to resolve the current situation and decide what to do without burdening his brother. *This is my job!*

But the pathetic failure of his men to trail and monitor the reporter was infuriating. *That's the problem with relying on others to do your own work. I should have been there.* Terry knew, most importantly, that he needed to ensure the trail did not lead back to them. If those men had been detained by the police, he would have had a much harder time extracting them without leaving a trail back to him and his brother. Even if the men had talked, though, they barely knew enough to connect their tasks to Sheriden.

Terry knew that Michael would barely tolerate these types of risks, and in fact, Terry agreed with him. Thus, he decided to keep his other teams back for now and use remote monitoring techniques. He needed to know where they were going and have some idea of what they were up to, but do it without direct surveillance. The answer was, of course, to watch their credit card use. The problem with that though, Terry knew, was that too many credit inquiries could raise the suspicion of the credit access that Sheriden enjoyed by virtue of its federal security services. So, Terry needed to be discreet and selective as to when and how often he pulled those credit use reports. He would also rotate the inquiries, both in terms of who he inquired about and which Sheriden subsidiary made the inquiry.

Having settled on a plan for at least the next few days, Terry decided he needed to burn off some of his anger. *I need a good workout.* He stood up and headed for the gym.

Springfield

"That's right ma'am, that is exactly who I am interested in," Gerald King explained patiently. "I apologize for having you come in here on a Sunday, but it is extremely important that I know what Sean Johnson was doing here."

The elderly lady in front of Agent King looked a little intimidated, but also seemed to be comprehending why the museum had called her back on a Sunday morning. He smiled.

"It's nothing dangerous, ma'am. I can't really discuss why I need to know this information, but rest assured, it's very important."

"Very well young man," the lady said, now smiling. "I can explain to you exactly what he was doing, after all, I helped him. He was a very nice man, though. It's hard to imagine what he could be caught up in that would raise your interests."

With that comment, the lady proceeded to explain to Gerald all about Sean's research. Once she was done and Gerald had completed his notes, he thanked her and headed back down to the street. His partner was interviewing staff over at the hotel where Sean Johnson had stayed. They had arrived in Springfield Saturday evening and quickly encountered a police investigation at a hotel near the Abraham Lincoln center. There had been a fight of some sort and Gerald had quickly determined that one participant matched Sean Johnson's description. After a little more investigation, it seemed pretty obvious that Sean Johnson had been involved in the fight, but had then left town. Gerald and his partner had decided to stay the night and fully investigate what had happened.

Agent King was comfortable that he and his partner would now be able to prepare a good report for the Agent in Charge in Phoenix, but the whole subject was very bizarre. *A reporter researching the end of President Lincoln's life is attacked by another man?* But that was not his problem. He would complete the report and then they could head back to Chicago.

Denver

Kim had awoken Sunday morning and made some coffee using the in-room coffee pot. She had tried studying the will some more and had also pulled the letter and note out. Mostly, though, she found herself staring at them. Sean's voicemail had upset her more than she was willing to admit, she realized. He had left a voicemail on her cell phone, which for some reason had not rung when he called, explaining that he had been chased by a man in Springfield and that she needed to double her caution. He had promised to call Sunday and also said that he would be driving to get to Denver by nightfall. It had all seemed so bizarre to Kim.

In the morning, when she awoke, it seemed even worse. She found herself suspicious of Sean again. *After all, he's the only one who sees all these strange men.* But the fact that he was driving all the way from Springfield to Denver as quick as he could had convinced her that his concern was as real as Jacob Thomas's had been.

So, feeling too distracted and worried to focus on Jacob Thomas, she had given up being productive and had taken Abby to breakfast. Then they had gotten in the car and headed up into the Rocky Mountains for the day. The day had turned out beautiful and the fresh air and blue skies had lifted her spirit significantly. Abby was also in a pretty good mood.

It was now midday, and they had just finished exploring some back roads through old mining towns. Kim found it fascinating to imagine miners struggling to live and work in the high country, on the steep mountain slopes. Even Abby seemed intrigued by that concept. Kim had not told Abby about the call from Sean, but she knew that Abby had sensed her increased tension.

Kim was pulling back onto the highway and looking for a decent place for lunch, when her cell phone rang. She was expecting Sean to call, but when she lifted her phone up she was surprised to see her business phone number on the screen. Bridget was calling for some reason. She pulled the phone to her ear while trying to drive safely along the curves of the mountain highway.

"Hi Bridget, is everything okay?"

"Hi Kim. Yes, the shop is fine." Bridget's voice, however, told Kim that something else was amiss.

"What is it?"

"I wanted to tell you that an FBI agent was just here, asking for you."

"What?" Kim swerved the car in surprise and immediately began pulling the SUV off the road. "The FBI?"

"Yes, but it's okay. They only wanted to talk to you," Bridget explained. "Actually it was just one man. His name is Alan Nazimi. He's the 'Special Agent in Charge' in Phoenix."

Kim had parked the car. Abby had begun to ask her what was going on, but Kim had held out her palm to her, silencing her.

"What did he want?"

"All he would say was that he wanted to talk with you. I asked him if it was about the woman who died in Phoenix. He looked a bit surprised, but just repeated that he wanted to talk with you."

"What did you tell him?"

"That you were on a short vacation. I wouldn't say where you were. I also wouldn't tell him when you would return. I just said soon. He was a little irritated with me I'm afraid." Kim could detect some pride in Bridget's voice.

"You acted that way to an FBI agent?"

"Yes. There was something about him. I didn't like him. He finally thanked me and left," Bridget explained. "He left his card. Said you could call him anytime."

"Wow! Thanks Bridget. I'm sorry you had to deal with that."

"Oh it was no problem. It was kind of fun. But it was odd, too." Bridget's voice lowered. "Why would he come all the way from Phoenix to talk with you. Don't you think that's odd?"

"Yes, I guess so." Kim answered. "How's the store?"

"Busy as ever, but don't you worry. It's all taken care of."

"Thank you so much. I should be back Tuesday at the latest. I'll call tomorrow to update you, okay?"

"That's fine." Bridget's voice shifted to a more conspiratorial tone. "Have you been talking with the reporter?"

"Yes, some. He's supposed to call me soon. I had expected it was him when you called." Kim paused. "But don't you start on that. We're purely professional."

Bridget laughed. "Aren't we all."

"No, we're not," Kim protested. "Good-bye."

"Good-bye."

Kim hung up the phone and sat still for a moment. Her attempt at thinking was interrupted by Abby's concerned voice.

"The FBI Mom!" she exclaimed. "Is everything okay?"

"Yes, dear." Kim turned her head to look at Abby. "An agent was asking to talk with me. Probably about Mary."

"What are you going to do?"

Kim thought for a moment and then turned to look out the window. "I'm going to get some answers soon," she said seriously. "Or else I'm going to snap."

Then she turned to look at Abby. "But right now I'm hungry. Let's find someplace decent to eat."

Abby looked relieved as she nodded. Kim pulled her car back on the road. As she continued driving down the highway, though, she was anything but relieved. *This is not normal. Why does the FBI come all the way to Kansas City to talk with me? Why not call and make an appointment?* She resolved to get some answers from Sean when he reached Denver.

Kansas City

Alan Nazimi also wanted some answers. He was in a visitor office at the Kansas City FBI headquarters. Though it was Sunday, the office seemed full of people. *Clearly Kansas City has a lot going on,* he thought. *Nothing like my office.* As a visiting "SIC," he was given the best temporary office available and a secretary had checked in on him twice already. *All of this on a Sunday!* He had connected his laptop, logged in and had just finished reading the report from the agents in Springfield.

He was impressed by the report's thoroughness and completeness, especially given the short turnaround. Mostly, though, he was considering its implications. Sean Johnson had been peacefully, but busily, studying Abraham Lincoln. He had seemed rushed at the end of the day on Saturday. But then, he was chased out of his hotel and into another one and there he briefly fought with another man. Then he disappeared, completely, despite the fact that the police were on the scene very quickly. *The other man that fought with him had also evaporated. What's going on?*

He leaned back in his chair and looked out the window at the Kansas City sprawl. The office here was high enough to provide a decent view of the city and its rivers, but Alan was not here in Kansas City for the view. He was here for an odd case that kept getting odder.

While Sean Johnson is running around Illinois, Kim Poole is gone on a 'short vacation' and the woman she left in charge refuses to answer my questions. As Alan thought about it, he realized that "refuses" was not right. He had not pressed the woman. But he had asked.

What the hell is going on? All his senses told him something much larger than a woman being murdered in Phoenix was going down, yet he had no idea what it was. It did not really smell of blackmail, extortion or some other nefarious scheme. *But what? Who was the other man in Springfield? Why did Sean Johnson fight with him?* Alan realized that the Springfield events gave credence to Sean's story of what had happened in Knoxville. *Was that the same man?*

Clearly, Sean was increasingly at the center of the unfolding events. As Alan stared out the window, he decided upon a course. He would stay in Kansas City for a few days. He would have the office run a credit card activity report on Sean and Kim and figure out where they were. His highest priority would be Sean, but he continued to believe that Kim played a very important role in this whole debacle.

There was one other thing on Alan's mind. He had, so far, kept this case close to him. Truthfully, he was tired of the FBI and his quest to climb the ladder. He sensed that he would be stuck in Phoenix for a long time. A big case could benefit him professionally, maybe give him a shot at moving up. Playing it close would give him the best chance to be the center point of a big case. Better, this case might even offer him a chance to benefit personally. *You deserve better than you're getting. Something important is at play here and you need to be there when it goes down!* Smiling, he resolved to continue pursuing the case personally.

Denver

Kim's phone rang. They were on their way back towards Denver. Abby had fallen asleep in the passenger seat, but the ringing phone woke her. Kim picked it up from the slot in the center console and saw that it was Sean.

"Hello?" she answered.

"Hi Kim, it's Sean." Kim could tell from his voice that he was very tired.

"Hi, where are you?"

"Oh, somewhere in the middle of Kansas, still several hours out of Denver," Sean replied. "Where are you?"

"I took your advice and got out of town for the day. Abby and I are just returning to Denver now."

"That's good. How are you?"

"I'm okay." Kim was keeping her voice steady but now she felt its calmness cracking apart. "The FBI came looking for me at my shop today."

There was a pause, then Sean answered. "Interesting. They called the professor, too."

Sean paused again. "Damn, I forgot to give you the news. I was tired and very distracted when I called last night. I'm sorry."

"What news?"

"James Enloe has found your Jacob Thomas, or at least the person that was most likely him, before Denver."

"What?" Kim swerved for the second time that day, though less than the first time. "What do you mean? Where?"

Sean laughed, "Wow, I knew it would be good news, but not this big. But yes, it's a huge breakthrough. It appears that Jacob Thomas was a courier for the War Department in D.C. for about four months leading right up to Lincoln's death."

"Really?" was all Kim managed to say back, as she began to think her way through what Sean had said.

"Yes. Because of his discovery, Professor Enloe gave me a research assignment at the Lincoln archives. I had just completed my work when all the crap went down yesterday. I shipped him an overnight package of papers earlier today that will hopefully reach him tomorrow."

"Wow, a courier for the War Department. So, Jacob Thomas probably never was from Denver. He came here after the war."

"It looks that way, Sean replied. "But listen, I stayed at the house of an old Navy buddy of mine. He is a cop in Saint Louis. I was not there long, but we discussed the situation."

"He really wanted me to go to the police, but I convinced him that it would still be premature, and that I would feel better if I reached you in Denver first. We talked about who could have found me in Springfield. I've been thinking things over, too. I'm pretty sure whoever it was, they're not cops or the FBI. My friend thinks the most likely way they found me was by tracking my purchases on my credit card."

Sean paused to let that sink in.

"To do that, they have to have a lot of connections within law enforcement circles. I am growing increasingly worried about our safety, particularly yours."

He paused again.

"I want to reiterate, keep a good eye on your surroundings. As you get back into Denver, stay with crowds. If you see anything wrong at all, call the police immediately. I will get in tonight. I'm driving to stay off the grid. Can you rent another room for me in your name? Better, put it in Abby's name, to throw anyone off that is looking for you or for me. Can you do that?"

"Okay, I can. But this seems a little extreme doesn't it?"

"No, not to me. Believe me Kim, these people are serious. I know their type. Once we truly know what's going on, we can decide what to do next. But, I just don't trust anyone right now. I'm going to call you when I get to the hotel. We can meet in the lobby, okay?"

"Okay," Kim agreed, though inwardly she could feel her stomach twisting.

"Tomorrow, we need to get to the root of your Jacob Thomas. James is working the Washington D.C. end of things. We need to focus on Denver. My gut feeling is that Jacob left something for you to find in Denver."

"I know. I feel the same way, but I've gone through his will ten times over already. All I have found is some odd phrases, but they don't say anything or create a riddle or anything like that."

"Okay, well we'll tackle it together tomorrow, okay?"

Kim could tell that Sean was trying to build her confidence. *It's working*, she admitted to herself.

"Okay," she replied back. "Bye." Kim ended the call.

"Now what Mom?" Abby asked.

"A professor in Tennessee, Mary's brother, has figured out that Jacob Thomas worked in D.C. during the war. For the first time, I have some sense of who he was, where he came from." Kim had gotten excited as she spoke.

She looked over at her daughter to find Abby staring at her as if she was mad.

"What? Don't look like that," Kim protested with a smile. "Some-day you'll be glad I've learned so much about our family."

Chapter Twenty

Monday, May 4
Kansas City

Alan now knew that Kim had gone to Denver. He was back in the visitor office reading the credit card activity reports he had ordered on Kim and Sean. The transactions on Kim's credit card included a hotel and several restaurants within that city. As Alan launched an internet browser to get more precise information about her hotel, the bright morning sun was just rising above the eastern horizon outside his window. The city had been dark when he had walked over from his downtown hotel with just a hint of the coming dawn showing in the eastern sky. Now, half an hour later, morning was breaking. Alan barely noticed, though, focusing instead on the credit activity reports and now his computer monitor.

The internet browser opened and Alan quickly entered the name of Kim's hotel. Shortly, he was at its website. He jotted down the basic information in his notebook and then thought about what to do. If it was truly necessary to find and interview her, he could deploy agents from the Denver office or he could go himself. The last credit card activity for Sean was in Springfield, Illinois, but that was the charge for his hotel that the agents had verified he had checked out of Saturday evening. *So where are you, Sean?* Not knowing Sean's whereabouts, his only option was Kim.

Thinking again about his decision to keep the case fully under his control, he decided against using agents in Denver, and decided instead to go there himself. His intuition also told him he needed to make his work on the case less transparent within the FBI, that he would be better served if he began following the case a little more quietly, with less reliance on other offices. Should the case present the right opportunities, he would have an easier time leveraging them. If the potential for personal benefit never surfaced, he could always finish the case publicly, claiming credit. But Alan smelled something lurking in the case. *There's just too many people involved and too many strange things happening. Somebody wants something very badly.* Alan knew that when people wanted things badly, there was usually opportunity lurking.

Atlanta

"What's the news brother?"

"Not what you want to hear," Terry replied to his desk speaker phone in the brains room. "The first deployed team was monitoring Sean Johnson in Springfield, Illinois. They're good men and I carefully briefed them. Still, they managed to screw things up and I have extracted them."

"What happened?" Tension and concern sounded in Michael's voice.

"Relax, we were not exposed. Not at all. However, it was a close call."

Terry proceeded to brief Michael on the events of the weekend. As he explained things, Michael seemed to regain his composure.

"Okay, so now we're back to monitoring from afar?"

"Yes, that's right. I have two more teams, six men in all, but I'm keeping them back until I see a cleaner or more specific opportunity for us."

"I agree with that brother." Michael growled a bit. "But the last two weeks have not exactly been going as planned have they?"

"No, they have not," Terry conceded, feeling some anger well up. "But, I'd challenge you to do a better job."

"Relax brother, I'm not accusing you of doing anything but the best job possible. What I'm trying to say is that we need to think farther ahead of this trio, particularly the reporter. Maybe we need to dig up some protection, some insurance. We have to be able to find something to give us an advantage over one of them."

"Good point," Terry replied. "Since I'm not running any active operations on them, I can devote some time to truly spying on their lives."

"Anything else?" Michael asked.

"Do you think that we're risking their discovery of the truth?" Terry asked back. "If we let them run with whatever clues they have, assuming the clues lead to whatever Jacob Thomas left behind, will they go public too fast?"

"That is possible," Michael admitted. "But, there's no guarantee that any active intervention by us might not risk that anyway. Still, I think we do have to be ready to move quickly."

"I agree brother. I'll keep a pretty close watch on their activities. If things seem to be accelerating or changing, we can decide to move in."

"Good. Good-bye."

"Good-bye," Terry replied, ending the call.

Denver

Kim and Sean were settled at the table they had been assigned at the historical archive. Kim had brought all of her documents with her. The room was a large glassed-in space with about twenty tables. Outside of the glassed-in room was the reception desk and a general reading room. The reading room contained several tall rows of shelves, filled mostly with books of general interest. There were also several computer stations linked to an index of every file in the archive. One archivist, a middle aged woman, was sitting at the reception desk. From her perch, she could monitor the glass room quite well.

Kim and Sean were not alone in the room, despite the fact that they had shown up right when it had opened. Three other men, all of them looking to be in their fifties, had been waiting as well. The archivist had given all of them the same routine speech and then sent the three men into the room to their assigned tables. The speech had explained how to get documents, where to leave them, and how to handle them. The archivist had then helped Kim and Sean register and create a copy account. She had also reviewed a few more rules. The rules were similar to those Sean had gotten used to in Springfield, such as no ink pens. Then, she had assigned them a table and sent them on their way.

Earlier in the morning, Sean had met both Abby and Kim for breakfast in the hotel. It had been the first time Abby and Sean had met, so Kim let them visit. Abby had seemed to like him and Kim had been impressed at how well Sean talked candidly and made her daughter feel comfortable. Abby had then headed back to the room. Kim had given her some specific instructions on safety and let her go free for the day. Abby planned on visiting the mall and then possibly catching a movie.

Kim and Sean had then discussed the events from the previous days and tried to formulate a plan. For all their efforts at trying to get organized, though, they had really concluded that they needed to do two things: learn everything else there was to learn about Jacob and scour everything he had written looking for clues about something he had left for them to find. So, they had settled on coming to the archive simply because it would be a good place to set up camp for the day. On the way over, Kim had noticed that Sean was limping and had been alarmed to learn of his injury. She had calmed down after he explained that his friend had thoroughly examined him. They finished the walk and now found themselves at a table in the archive.

"Okay, what now?" Kim asked with half a grin on her face.

"I don't know. I had not thought beyond getting here," Sean said smiling back. They were across from each other and spoke quietly, so as to not disturb the three other men who were already deep into files.

"Well, let me show you what I've learned about Jacob," Kim began.

"That sounds good," Sean replied. "Let me come around to your side, otherwise, we may get in trouble for talking too loud."

They grinned at each other as he got up and walked around the table now settling in next to Kim.

"Okay, let me have it," Sean said after sitting down.

"Well let's see...," Kim paused while she opened her notepad. "The earliest record I have found for him was from 1871. He apparently bought a parcel of land somewhere in Denver. He sold it two years later in 1873. He married Olivia White in 1882. Abraham was born in 1883. Olivia died in childbirth in 1885. Jacob died in 1901. He is buried at the East Gate Cemetery."

Kim looked up. "That's about it. Oh, wait, the will. It has a witness, David Haggard."

Sean thought for a moment, "So, no other land records? We don't know where he lived?"

"I have an address from the letters. Abby and I visited it. It's an old house in a poor neighborhood. Beyond that, nothing more. Of course, all I really did was search via the internet."

"Okay, then let's do this," Sean said, starting to get up. "You work on learning about David Haggard. I'll see if the archives can reveal anything more about Jacob."

Kim smiled. "I knew this would be easier once you got here. Sounds like a great plan."

.....

An hour or so later they sat down together at the table. Both of them had been busy moving about, talking with the archivist, scouring books, and looking at microfiche and paper files brought out by the archivist.

"So what have we learned?" Sean asked.

Kim began. "David Haggard was a physician. He was born in Denver in 1873 and lived his whole life here. He is well known because after his death in 1939, he donated his estate, his father's actually, to the city. The house remains as a museum to this date. His father was John Haggard, also a physician."

"Was David Haggard Jacob's doctor?" Sean asked.

"Not that I could tell," Kim replied. "But that seems logical. How about you?"

"Jacob is in the census for 1870, 1880, 1890, and 1900," Sean summarized from his notes. "No more land records that I could find. His death certificate lists 'groundskeeper' as his occupation. That's it. That is all I could find."

They looked at each other briefly, sharing a sense of frustration. Then Sean spoke.

"Well, we've learned some new information. It may help. Let's turn to the will."

Kim shook her head a bit. "Right. Listen, maybe we can get a cup of coffee first?"

"Yeah, a break would be good," Sean agreed.

They got up and headed downstairs to the ground floor. There was a café in the entrance lobby of the building. Sean noticed that the hustle and bustle of the lunch crowd was just getting started.

"Maybe we should get a bite to eat as well?" he suggested.

Kim agreed and they ordered sandwiches and lattes from the woman behind the counter and then settled in at a small table. They were silent for a moment, as they both seemed to be having a hard time finding the right thing to say. Finally, Kim spoke.

"So, this has been a weird couple of weeks, huh?" she asked.

"It has," Sean agreed. "I left my house two weeks ago for a short three day trip to investigate a story about Abraham Lincoln. Now I'm in Denver with a woman from Kansas City helping her try to find a secret left behind by her great, great grandfather, all the while, being chased by strangers."

"Tell me more about what happened in Springfield," Kim prompted him. "To be honest with you, it seems like you're the only one dealing with mysterious strangers. You keep telling me to be careful, but nothing has happened to me."

As if on cue, Sean glanced around for a moment, observing the various people in the café and building foyer.

"I understand that feeling entirely. If it wasn't for my past, I would not believe it myself. I certainly never would have even noticed them."

Sean told her the whole story about Springfield. How he had noticed the man, how he came back and spotted him, how he left and the man followed him, then chased him. Once he finished explaining his Springfield ordeal to her, Sean waited for Kim to comment.

"So, this man still could have just been curious about you, right?"

"No, he was chasing me, at full speed!"

"What if he was a police officer and thought that you acted suspiciously?"

"Well, he never said anything like police normally do. Still, I've actually considered that these men might be some type of law enforcement. That actually does not make me feel any better." Sean paused and looked away for a moment.

"I was a Navy Seal, trained to be a commando. You know, storm the beach, slip in at night, all that kind of stuff. I was trained to kill people, to spy on them and do whatever it takes to get the mission done. Then, I was recruited into a special operation run by another branch of the government."

Sean had avoided saying 'CIA', but it seemed obvious to Kim that he was implying that agency.

"They trained me to be a spy and joined me with a special unit. We did an operation in a classified location. I was there for quite a while. It ended badly. I'm telling you this so you'll understand my distrust of government. Most everyone is honest, but they all follow orders. All it takes is one person with power giving the wrong orders and things can happen that shouldn't have happened in the first place."

Kim studied Sean as he spoke. She wanted to ask him for more details about what kinds of things he had done. She wanted to ask him if he had ever killed anyone. But she sensed that such questions would probably go unanswered.

"So how did you end up being a reporter?"

Sean smiled. "I am actually a journalist, or at least that is how I define myself. I studied journalism in college after my service. I loved it. My father died and left me a house and enough money so I tried being an independent journalist. In the last few years, I have managed to write quite a few stories that made it into print, both newspaper and magazines."

"So why are you helping me so much? Why not turn this over to the police and go home?"

"Well, mostly because this has kept going and going and I just found myself deeply imbedded in it before I realized what had happened. But, also because, at this point Kim, I sense that you and James are not entirely safe. I know that better than anyone else involved. I want to see this through to the end."

Kim considered his comments for a moment. "Do you really believe all of this? I keep thinking that we're seeing phantoms created in our minds."

Sean sighed. "Yeah, I keep thinking the same thing. But then I realize that it's just my disbelief of the logical and factual things that have been happening. Your letter and that note are real. Now we know that there was a Jacob Thomas close to President Lincoln. We know that there was a connection between the Enloes and Lincoln, or at least a theory that acts like a connection. We know Mary was killed under very suspicious circumstances. I know very well that dangerous men have been spying on me and perhaps James, too."

He paused as if summing it all up in his head.

"So, I conclude that something is happening that is real."

Kim nodded, then laughed. "That makes me feel better. Unless we're both insane."

Sean laughed as well. "That's the risk of relying on your own logic. If you're crazy, then you won't know it."

The waitress brought their sandwiches and they both ate while Kim gave Sean a summary of her thoughts about the will.

"It's a six page will. I have some notes of things that seem odd, but nothing really stands out."

"You say you spotted some odd things in it?" Sean asked.

"Yeah, it's in Jacob's own handwriting. The will does not really ramble. One thing I did notice, though, is that the will contains funny phrases and sentences that seem unnecessary. It was hard to spot them though, because the will is full of unfamiliar expressions that we don't use today."

They finished eating and headed back up the stairs to the second floor. The building they were in was relatively old and the marble staircase was broad and covered with unique and intricate details that new architecture often lacks. Their footsteps echoed up and down the stairwell as they climbed.

Once upstairs, they settled back at their assigned table. Sean noticed that the three men were all now gone, probably at lunch themselves. Thus, they had the room to themselves, for the moment. Kim spread two copies of Jacob's will on the table and pulled out her notes. Sean retrieved his notebook and flipped to a blank page.

"Okay," Kim began. "The will gives everything to his son Abraham. My first thought was to ask why six pages were needed when he ends up giving everything to his son? Plus, there are the odd phrases. Here's one."

Kim had been flipping through the will while looking at her notes. She read a line from the will out loud to Sean.

"I told my god true."

She looked at Sean. "What in the world does that mean? I did an internet search for that phrase and found nothing. So, it seemed to me that it must be a clue. There are more, too. They also seem to be nothing more than an incomprehensible mush of words."

"What page did you find that phrase on?" Sean asked, flipping the pages of his copy of the will.

"Third page, uh…five lines down," Kim replied.

"Okay, got it." Sean studied the page for a minute. He looked for something odd about the writing, its position, or any obscure marks, but found nothing.

"Hmm, I don't see anything odd, but you're right. The sentence seems like it was added for some odd unknown reason. It does not flow well with the sentences surrounding it."

"Okay, try this one. It's near the bottom of that same page." Kim read a second sentence out loud.

"I have forever will to be."

Sean found the sentence and studied it.

"Again, nothing odd about the writing, but it seems out of place." Sean thought for a moment. "Maybe the sentences are a riddle?"

Kim sighed. "I have thought about that too, but most of the sentences are vague, not like clues or anything remotely suggesting a clue."

"Yes, but even 'I told my god true' could be a clue hinting at something like a church, or some other place where you could communicate with God." Sean scrutinized the page for a moment more. "But that would also be too obvious, wouldn't it?"

"Maybe," conceded Kim. "But, I see your point."

They fell silent for a moment as they both looked at the will.

Then Sean spoke, "What's the next one?"

"Okay, let's see…," Kim said as she looked at her notes. "Next page near the top. "Always his I wanted the most.""

"Got it," Sean said looking closely at the sentence. He was silent for a moment and then started to say something but stopped abruptly in mid sentence. "Okay, whaa…."

Kim looked over at him. "What?" she demanded.

Sean was silent though, holding up a finger to ask her for a moment. He flipped back to the previous page and then back to the fourth page. He repeated the flipping of pages back and forth two more times.

"What?" Kim pleaded. "What do you see?"

"Well," Sean began slowly, clearly still thinking. "For both of those sentences from page three there is a word repeated on page four in the same exact location. You know, line number and word number." He looked up at Kim and then slid his copy closer to her. He gestured towards it.

"See, here on page three is the word 'my' in the sentence "I told my god true?"

"Yes," Kim replied.

"Okay and it's the fifth line, and the seventh word right?"

"Okay." Kim mentally counted off the line and word number. "Yes, yes."

"Okay then." Sean flipped to the fourth page of the will. "See here on the fifth line, seventh word? It's 'my.' The sentence reads. 'My answer is always the same.' Do you see? The word 'my' is in the same place, the fifth line, seventh word."

Kim paused for a moment and then nodded. "Sure, I see it, but that's probably coincidence."

"I thought that, but look again."

He flipped back to the third page.

"Here's the next sentence you spotted. Note the word 'was' is the twelfth line, third word." Kim nodded and Sean flipped to the fourth page. He dropped his finger just below a spot on the page.

"Here it is, the word 'was'," he said emphatically.

His finger sat there for a moment while Kim studied it. She was deep in thought for a moment. She then turned her head to her notes.

"Okay, if that works, let's check more of them."

She looked up the next sentence and together they worked their way though them. Her notes were not actually in order, so they had to jump back and forth. Soon they had found ten words repeated perfectly in the same exact location. Kim wrote them out in order and then read them out loud.

"Okay so its 'my, was, have, will, his, can, and home.' That's our word set."

She finished reading and sat back. "Well, that doesn't make much sense," she said disappointedly.

Sean was deep in thought, though. Kim studied him for a moment and then asked, "What now?"

Sean shook his head. "Sorry, I was thinking that maybe the words spelled something, you know the first letter or last letter of each word. But it's just a bunch of mush."

They sat there for a full minute, both lost in thought. Then it was Kim's turn to speak suddenly.

"What if...." Her voice trailed off as she studied the list of words and then started flipping the pages of the will, noting other words on the page. Sean watched her for a moment, noting the new words she was writing down on each side of each of the extracted words.

"These are the words before and after the second repeated word," Kim explained. She finished and read them. "Oh it's still mush."

Then she stopped and ran her finger down the list. "But wait..."

"Lant," she continued.

"What?" Sean asked.

"Well, the first letter of each of the words following the repeated word spells out 'lant'" she explained. "Actually, it spells 't, l, a, n, t, g'."

"Not much better than mush," she conceded. "But it's something?"

She looked over at Sean, as if begging for support.

Sean was silent for a moment with his fingers at his lips. Then he nodded.

"Yes, it is something. It might be more than just mere coincidence." He looked at her and smiled. "It's more than mush."

They looked at their notes for a moment. Sean continued speaking.

"Let's scrutinize the second, third and fourth page. I will read out the word and you note the matching word on the following page. Every time it's a match, you underline the word. Okay?"

Kim nodded. "I'm ready."

"Okay then, page two, first line."

He proceeded to read the will one line at a time, announcing each line number. Out of the corner of his eye, he noticed Kim occasionally underlining a word. It was all he could do not to stop and see what she had found. When he finished, he looked over at her.

"Okay, that's it for page four."

Kim was already studying the will. She flipped back and looked briefly at the fourth page.

"Okay, so the next earlier one was 'follow' and the following word was 'and'. So it's an 'a' not a 'g', which makes...." She froze as the word seemed to jump up from the page. Both she and Sean simultaneously said it out loud at the same time.

"Atlanta!"

They looked at each other and then back at the word and then back at each other. Both of them were visibly excited.

"My God," Kim finally said. "Is this real?"

"Yes, there's no way that happens by chance." Sean said firmly. "But we're not done. There are more pages for us to do. If we find more, that will prove it's not coincidence."

Kim nodded. "Right," she said, just as firmly.

They then continued, excitedly pulling out the letters they identified. When they were done, Kim read the result out loud.

"inned but Atlanta gold," she said with a tremble in her voice.

"Gold?" she repeated in a whisper, suddenly looking around remembering they were in a public room. The other researchers had not returned. "Is this about gold?"

Sean seemed stunned and sat there looking at the words. Kim looked at him, then looked down at the papers.

Sean shook his head. "Amazing. I think this is real. We need to do the entire will."

"Okay, let me start with a fresh page," Kim replied without looking up from her notes. She flipped over to a brand new page in her note pad and flipped the will to the beginning. "Ready," she announced.

Sean watched her and laughed. Kim looked at him. "Now what?"

"Sorry, it's just that…," Sean said chuckling. "That you're very amazing. You have a determination about you."

Kim briefly smiled, but then became serious.

"If you're done staring, let's get started."

Sean laughed again. "Okay," he said. "Page one, line one…"

Sean then read through the other pages of the will. As he did so, he noticed one of the researchers return. He looked at Sean and Kim oddly, but Sean gave him an intense stare, all the while quietly reading the will and the man wilted, turning his head away. As Sean continued reading, he made a mental note that he and Kim needed to talk seriously about safety and secrecy.

Sean completed reading and then watched as Kim went back to the beginning and began jotting down the repeated words and the following words in two columns. He was mentally spelling out the words that the first letters of the following words spelled as she went. When she had finished writing the words, he had already read the sentence they created. *Really, it's a set of phrases.* He thought. *In fact, it's a riddle.* He began pondering its meaning while Kim wrote out the letters in a third column. She then read it out loud.

"Nation sinned but Atlanta gold saved look beyond." She said slowly, word by word. Then she repeated it adding some implied punctuation. "Nation sinned, but Atlanta gold saved. Look beyond."

She looked at it some more, "What does it mean?"

Sean looked down at the page. "It's a riddle that tells us why Jacob was hiding and perhaps what he was hiding." He thought for a moment. "Or it tells us something he learned. I think he is clearly telling us to 'look' somewhere else, somewhere beyond this will, for answers."

Kim was too stunned to speak. Sean, however, suddenly felt very insecure. He looked carefully around the workroom, noting the one returned researcher and the archivist on the other side of the glass.

"It tells us something else, too," he said quietly with a very strong determination. "It tells us we really are in danger. Someone else who is alive today already knows some of this. I suspect that is all they know. They are watching us to see where we go and what we do."

"If it's gold, that's worse. Men will do anything for gold. It means we need to think very carefully about our next step." Sean started sweeping the papers together. "Let's get out of here right now!"

Kim sat for a moment digesting his words and then said "Right!" She jumped up, glanced around as well, and then began helping him assemble their papers and documents.

.....

A few minutes later they were out on the street, Sean having put all of their papers into his knapsack. He had slung it over his shoulder, Kim had noticed, and was now walking more carefully. They had walked about ten blocks from their hotel that morning, and now they began walking back. As they approached an intersection, Sean casually spoke.

"Turn right here, let's take a different path back."

Kim looked about. "Why? Is someone following us?"

"No one that I have seen. I'm just being careful." He looked over at her, but she could see that his eyes looked behind hers towards the corner they just turned when they began to walk. "In fact, we're going to find a good spot to stop for a cup of coffee and talk."

They walked for a bit, mostly in silence. Kim was starting to feel exhausted. The stunning words they had found buried in Jacob's will had practically drained her. Now, she felt scared and nervous. She glanced at her watch. It was two o'clock in the afternoon. *Still very early,* she thought. She glanced at Sean. *He has to be way more tired than me. And his knee hurts. But his limp has disappeared and he's walking firmly.* She realized that Sean was showing some of that other person inside of him. *The spy, or commando, or whatever he was trained to be.*

She herself, had not been paying attention as they walked. Suddenly, he nudged her arm and spoke.

"Let's stop here," he said simply.

It was a corner restaurant, not too fancy, but with large clear windows. She realized that he liked it because of the view it had to offer them. It was also very busy.

They went inside and quickly were seated at the last open table, a small table along the back wall. They sat down with Sean sitting with his back to the wall. He quickly told the waiter who had sat them that they just wanted coffee. He frowned a bit, but then went off to get their drinks.

"So what now?" she asked.

"Well, I think we now know why there has been interest in this and us. I have no idea how they found us. There is still a lot left unexplained."

"Yeah, like why the Enloes are involved," she interrupted. "We still have no idea why Jacob refers to them." Kim thought suddenly of Mary.

"Oh my God! Was Mary killed over this?"

Sean reached across the table and took her hand, holding it firmly.

"We don't know that, but I think it's highly likely. They must have thought that she had found the answers to all of these mysteries and riddles. But right now, we need to think about 'how' as much as 'why.' How did whoever it is find out about Mary, James and I? Either they had been watching one of us, or maybe even you, for a long time and the sudden activity alerted them. Maybe it was something that we did that alerted them."

"The internet?" Kim asked. "It's totally public."

"Right," Sean nodded. "That's the most likely answer."

They sat for a moment while the waiter brought them their coffee. He put the check down firmly by Sean, a clear hint he would prefer that they drink up and leave so a better paying customer could have their table. Sean glanced around, studying people.

"Okay, here's my plan. First, we need to call James and discuss this with him. I trust him, plus I feel we need to warn him. He needs to be careful. Then, I think we go to Knoxville and sit down with him. He is more capable of solving this than us. Plus, three heads are better than two. Also, I hate to do this, but we need to travel incognito. We need to drive. We need to be impossible to track."

Kim shook her head. "No, no. I have to get back to my shop. Also, Abby needs to get back to school."

Sean squeezed her hand.

"Kim, I know this is all very fast, but you have got to understand that whoever is following us will find you, if they have not already done so. We won't be safe until we solve this mystery. We might be safe if we simply go to the police and explain it all, but I'm not sure they would even take us seriously. Also, I'm not sure our own government isn't involved in this mess."

"Look, just for the next few days, we need to stick together and work very hard to solve this mystery. If we don't get anywhere, then our next step is to go to the police and tell them everything. Give them everything. For now though, we need to think of safety and our next plan of action."

Kim was silent for a moment. "Okay, maybe I might go to Knoxville. Bridget will kill me, though! There's no way I am taking Abby with us." She looked down for a moment.

"I could send her to see her father. She wants to go anyway. She would miss school, but she would be safe." She looked at Sean. "He's in Dallas though."

"Well, we could fly her to Dallas while we drive to Knoxville." He stopped for a moment. "Wait, let's do this. I'll return my rental car and then join up with you and Abby. We'll drive back to Kansas City, where we would go anyway if we were driving all the way to Knoxville. Then, we can send Abby flying to see her father while we continue on to Knoxville. Maybe we'll just fly too. We can decide once we get to Kansas City."

Kim thought for a moment. "Okay," she announced. "It's a plan!"

Chapter Twenty-One

Knoxville

James went to the university early in the morning. He cancelled his classes and then descended on the library. After speaking with a librarian for a little while, he left with an armful of books on the Civil War, the War Department and its records. Upon returning to his house, he quickly cleared the dining room table of its ornate candelabras, dishes and tablecloth and then set up his research. Besides arranging the table, he also set an erasable white board on a buffet along one wall. He then went to work studying the Lincoln White House during the Civil War. Around midday, the package from Sean arrived. He opened it and soon had documents spread out all over his dining room table.

The package from Sean had given him some source material related to one aspect of his research, the White House records. So far today, though, he had spent most of his time focused on the other aspect, the War Department. He had skimmed through a chronological history of the Civil War and had created a bullet list of details about the growth, organization and players in the War Department. He had taken a break and had eaten a bowl of cereal and some fruit for lunch, but was now back at the tedious research job awaiting him.

He turned his attention to the documents Sean had sent. James was pleased to see that Sean had sent copies of some original documents that showed contemporaneous logs of activities. Sean had also made some notes from other documents. It was a large quantity of files, and so James began by organizing them. Once that was done, he turned to information about President Lincoln's White House meetings. Many of these were notes made each day by his secretary, John Hayes. The documents covered December of 1864 and January through April of 1865. James decided to work backwards and started with the day before Lincoln had been assassinated. He read and then made a few notes, gradually working his way back through March. On some days, he noted, there was much detail, but on others, practically nothing was noted.

As James was preparing to attack February, his phone rang. He got up from the dining room table and went into the kitchen to grab the cordless. Once he reached it, he picked it up from its cradle and answered.

"Hello."

"Hi James, this is Sean and I'm with Kim Poole, the woman in Kansas City that started all of this."

"Hello, Sean. How are you?" James replied.

"I'm fine Professor, but I need you to do me a favor. Can you give me your cell phone number? I want to call you back on that, okay?"

Puzzled, James said, "Sure." He provided Sean with the number, hung up the cordless, and went to find his cell phone, unsure of whether it was in his coat, in the foyer, or in his office. Before he had reached the foyer, however, a ringing sound emanating from the dining room told him it was probably in his coat which was hanging on a chair there. He briskly walked to his coat and fumbled for the phone, deep in a pocket, feeling a certain irritation that he always felt about cell phones. He found it and answered.

"Hello again."

"Hi, Professor, thanks."

"So pray tell, Sean, why did you insist on calling me on this quite inferior device," James said with a satirical tone. "And where are you? It sounds like you're inside a washing machine."

"Okay, hold on," Sean replied.

A few moments later the background sounds dropped.

"Is that better?" Sean inquired.

"Yes, thank you," James said. "Now, where are you?"

"I'm in Denver, with Kim. We have some amazing news."

"I could use some. Please go on." Sean was getting to know the professor, he decided, because he could now tell when the professor was putting up his grumpy front more as a joke than when he was seriously grumpy.

"Okay, well, here it is. This is no joke. Okay?"

"Yes, yes," James replied, now truly sounding irritated.

"Jacob Poole's will has a hidden message using a sequence of words that spell out other words. It says 'Nation sinned, but Atlanta gold saved. Look beyond'." Sean fell silent, waiting for James to speak. He finally did so.

"You're serious?"

"Completely."

"Well, well, that's certainly interesting," James muttered. Then he asked again, "You're entirely serious about this?"

"Yes. Do you know what it means?"

"Well yes, at least I think I do, as to part of the message." James paused. "I'm not sure what nation sinned refers to, but most likely it's a reference to a war atrocity. I say that in part because Atlanta gold must refer to one of the Atlanta treasure legends."

"Atlanta treasure?"

"Yes," James affirmed. "Again, this is outside of my field, but there are several legends, or theories, that the confederates, as General Sherman was bearing down on the city, spirited a large cache of silver, gold, jewelry and the like out of Atlanta. Some stories claim it was hidden and then forgotten. Others claim it was stolen. I don't know much more than that off the top of my head."

"Could the stories be true?"

"Well yes, sure. Jacob's will might be the best proof of that." James paused. "This is pretty amazing, but it might connect nicely with Jacob Thomas. He may have learned of the gold somehow. He was working for the War Department after the taking of Atlanta and all through Sherman's campaign from Atlanta to the ocean, across Georgia and South Carolina. The whole campaign is considered an atrocity by some. To others, it was a war necessity."

"Professor," Sean spoke seriously. "If some treasure is really involved and somehow some very capable people have been waiting for someone to come along and find it, then we are all probably in real danger."

"Maybe you're right Sean, but a few things do not fit here. First, how are the Enloe's involved? Did they bury the treasure? And second, what was Jacob so afraid of to have changed his name? I think the first words in the message are about that. You said 'nation sinned' right?"

"Yes, that's it," Sean affirmed. "Nation sinned, but Atlanta gold saved. Look beyond."

"Hmm, hmm," the professor seemed truly at a loss for words. "I've got to mull this over. The Civil War is clearly involved."

"Okay, but listen Professor, this is very important. Be absolutely careful. Don't talk about our findings around others. Trust only those that you have known to be trustworthy for quite sometime. Don't be alone too much and don't be too predictable. Drive rather than walk places."

"You're taking this all very seriously."

"Professor, your sister might have been murdered because of this secret."

There was a long silence. Sean was sure he had gone too far in making his point. But the professor responded with a serious and heavy voice.

"I see your point. I promise I'll be careful."

"Good. I'm sorry to have to have brought up Mary like that, but I am serious about this." Sean paused. "Would you mind if Kim and I come to see you? We'll bring all of our documents. I would like your help in figuring out what we still don't understand. Clearly, 'Look beyond' tells us to find something else."

The professor's voice perked up. "Visit me? Do I mind? Not at all. In fact, until you show me this riddle you've found buried in this will, I don't think I'll really believe it."

"I'll call you tomorrow with our exact plans. We'll probably get there by Wednesday."

James indicated his understanding and they hung up.

Denver

Sean hung up his phone and then turned to Kim. They were tucked inside the indented doorway of a closed shop along a street in downtown Denver. As they continued their walk to the hotel, Sean filled Kim in on the phone call to the professor.

"He seemed to have a hard time believing me, but once he took what I had to share with him seriously, he was extremely cooperative. He says that there are stories of treasure being hauled out of Atlanta before it was taken by the northern troops. Some stories hold that the treasure was lost or hidden."

"Really?" Kim seemed amazed. "So it's real?"

"It may be," cautioned Sean.

"Now wait a minute," Kim sounded playful. "First, the big reporter spends every chance he gets trying to convince me this is real, and now, when I finally believe it, he's trying to talk me out of it?"

"It's not that," Sean explained. "It's just that we can't take anything for granted, at least not at this point." He turned and looked at Kim, grinning.

"Besides, I haven't been on a treasure hunt since I was a kid. I think I'm a bit rusty."

Kim was about to reply when Sean's cell phone rang. He pulled it out of his pocket and glanced at it as they crossed an intersection. He then answered.

"Sean speaking."

Frank's voice greeted him on the other end. "Hi Sean. How are you feeling?"

"Frank," Sean said, happily glancing at Kim. "My knee is doing better. Please tell me you found something on that license plate."

There was a pause, and Sean instinctively knew that Frank was hesitant to tell him.

"I did. It was hard though. It was a rental car rented by an agency. An agency not in Springfield, mind you, but Columbus, Ohio. I had to threaten to drive there myself before they would tell me who rented it. All they would tell me is the name of a company. I traced it as best I could." Frank paused. "I'm pretty sure this is right, mind you, but I had to make a few assumptions."

"Look Frank," Sean said impatiently. "Don't baby me, just tell me."

"Well, I think it was rented by a shell company that is ultimately controlled by a giant security services company called Sheriden Corporation. They're based out of Atlanta and do defense department contracting, if you get my drift."

Sean stopped walking, causing Kim to look at him.

"I do get your drift. You said Atlanta right?"

"Yeah," Frank affirmed. "Oh and there was a police report filed on your chase and fight. They have no names and no information, but the report mentions that the FBI showed up afterwards asking around."

"The FBI?"

"Yep, so you, or whatever it is you're caught up in, have clearly gotten someone's attention."

"Okay. This is really good information. Thanks again, Frank."

"Listen Sean. Are you sure you don't want me to do something on my end?" Frank asked.

"No, not yet. I've learned more about what is going on here and I might still call you yet. For now though, I prefer to keep this completely confidential."

"Understood. Okay, gotta go."

Sean said good-bye and hung up. He glanced around.

"What's going on Sean?" Kim asked, sounding scared.

Sean explained what Frank had just told him and then added, "They sound exactly like who I was afraid was involved in this mystery. Somebody too connected to our law enforcement and government. So, we were right to be cautious."

He started walking again. "Come on, I shouldn't have stopped while taking that call. We need to keep moving." He took her hand and stepped out into the street.

"Let's double back the other way."

Kim pulled her hand free. "I don't get this. The hotel is right around the corner."

Sean kept walking as his eyes were looking around. He spoke once she had caught up with him. "This Sheriden Corporation is just like the ones I worked for in my Navy days. We need to be extra careful. That's all."

He then looked at Kim as they walked some more. "I'm sorry, I don't mean to scare you." Sean was surprised to see Kim smile at him.

"With you protecting me, it's not fear I'm worried about. But I'd hate to know how long it would take for us to walk somewhere really far away. My feet are killing me and we only had about ten blocks to walk."

Sean laughed. "Well, I can help you pick out some better shoes for these types of situations."

He turned serious again. "I want to readjust our plans. When we approach the hotel, I'm going to fall back and watch you enter. I'll tail you in lightly, just to make sure I don't see anything out of the ordinary. Then, I'm going to go return the rental car and come back and meet you. You can check out for both of us. Call me when you are ready to leave the hotel. Check out using the phone, not at the desk."

"Okay," Kim said mockingly. "Anything else Commander?"

"Yes, we need a duress code word. When you use it after being asked how you are, it means that something is wrong." He thought for a moment. "How about 'suitcase'? It's a word you might normally use. You understand?"

Kim nodded.

"Just slip it into a sentence if you are trying to tell me something has gone wrong. You get it?"

Kim nodded again. Sean glanced at her and could see she really did look a bit scared.

"Don't worry. It's probably never going to be needed. This is just basic routine stuff." He looked up. "Okay, I'm going to drop back now."

Kim nodded one more time.

"Okay, I'll see you in a little while. I'll call you once I'm ready to leave," she replied. "Right after I see a shrink."

Sean laughed at her as he pulled off to the side of the building they had been walking along. Kim continued on towards the hotel. He watched her until she was a full block away. He then turned and looked around before falling in stride with another woman headed right towards the hotel.

Knoxville

James hung up the phone from his call with Sean and Kim and walked back to his dining room research area. He sat in his chair and jotted the words down that Sean had provided him.

"A riddle," he muttered aloud. "A riddle about Lincoln and the Civil War."

James stared at the words for a full minute, reading it through again and again. Finally, he shoved it aside and focused back on his review of the White House records. The riddle told him that he was right to start focusing on the War Department, the Civil War and the later months of Lincoln's presidency. Sean's pointed reminder that his sister had been murdered only a week before and that her murder was still completely unsolved, brought him back to a core question. *How does my family name fit into all of this?* He thought of his sister for a few more moments, but then, before melancholy could overwhelm him, he shifted his focus back to the last days of Lincoln's White House.

James pulled a book from a stack on the table and flipped through it. He found what he was looking for after a few minutes. General Sherman captured Atlanta in November of 1864. His march across Georgia and South Carolina was over by Christmas of that very same year. He glanced up at the portable whiteboard he had perched on the buffet. Jacob had started working for the War Department in December of 1864, or at least James guessed that Jacob had started then. By the time Lincoln was assassinated on April 18, 1865, Jacob had also disappeared. Now, he knew that Jacob had moved to Denver and, at the end of the century, had left a message behind saying "nation sinned" and "Atlanta gold saved." So, the key was to try and detect what the young Jacob might have discovered that had bothered him so. It seemed logical that his discovery came at, or near the end of, Lincoln's life.

The problem was, James knew, many people had scoured the documents and records from that period. Lincoln's assassination made that period highly scrutinized. Still, he reflected, it was not entirely organized and documented. The mid-twentieth century chemist who was able to establish the Stanton conspiracy theory, despite the numerous records that should have instantly shown the theory's flaws, demonstrated that lack of complete organization. Also, James reflected, most people were completely focused on Stanton or Lincoln and not on an obscure courier working for the War Department. Having thus thought things through, James turned back to his task of going through the communication and meeting records of Lincoln.

A few hours later, James had found one thing that bothered him. It appeared that a page from John Hayes's notes was missing. It covered part of the afternoon of April 10th, eight days before Lincoln was assassinated. A document listed Hayes's notes for that day as being five pages, but only four pages were in the file Sean had sent. Normally, a gap might not have caught his attention, but James had noted that an index made by John Hayes, himself, indicated that it had been five pages. So, it appeared that a record of part of the afternoon of April 10th was missing. Abraham Lincoln had visited a military hospital that day, having made a trip by train down to Richmond. A thought occurred to James and he sorted through a few books, finding what he was looking for a few minutes later. *Sure enough,* he thought, *the hospital was full of casualties from Sherman's army.*

James jotted down these notes and went back to work. It grew dark as he worked and finally he had to concede he was going to get no farther without a good night's sleep. He stood up from his table and headed to the kitchen to see what kind of dinner he might cook before retiring for the night.

Denver

Kim stood by her hotel door and examined the credential that had been passed though the crack created between the door and the door frame. It told her that the person on the other side of the door was Alan Nazimi, the Special Agent in Charge of the Phoenix office of the FBI. She stood there trying to think what to do next. Part of her wanted to trust the man and tell him everything that was going on. Another part of her, though, was totally focused on Sean's guidance. She could instantly recall Sean's chilling words to James, *Trust no one that you do not already know.*

"Well, do I look legitimate?" the man on other side of the door said. "It's really me, Alan Nazimi."

"Yes, you do Mr. Nazimi," Kim began. "But, I am not used to having FBI agents show up uninvited at my hotel door. Especially one all the way from Phoenix." Kim was trying to create some conversation while she thought things through. *He seems legitimate, yes. But why not have the hotel call up? Why not call me up first himself? Why not come up with a hotel escort? It made him seem secretive, like he wanted no one to know he had come here.*

"I apologize, Ms. Poole. You have been hard to find and I was concerned you might slip away again."

"I'm not sure what you mean by that. I have not been hiding from you, if that's what you are inferring." Kim turned to look back at Abby, who was standing between the bed and the dresser looking equally shocked and surprised. *I'm sure its more about how I'm acting than who is at the door.* She gestured to Abby to remain quiet and then turned her attention back to the door.

"Look, Mr. Nazimi. I'll meet you down in the lobby. How's that? I'm not running or anything. I'm just not comfortable opening the door to my hotel room to a stranger, okay?" She tried to put on the best "single woman in strange city" tone she could find. There was silence for a moment before the FBI agent spoke.

"Okay, I'll do that Ms. Poole."

"Great," Kim said. "Give me five minutes."

There was another period of silence, then the voice said "Uh, Ms. Poole, if you can just give me my ID back?"

"What?" Kim said startled. "Oh yes, sure." She handed the ID back through the chained door and then closed it. She turned the dead bolt over, and then put her eye up against the peephole in the door. She could see a man in a dark suit walking away. She watched until he disappeared from her view and then waited another full ten seconds. Then she turned around. Immediately, Abby blurted out.

"Mom, what are you doing? That was the FBI!"

Kim put her hand out, palm up silencing her daughter.

"Stop. There is way more going on than you know," she said firmly.

"I'm simply being very, very cautious. It's for the both of us."

Kim then looked in the mirror and straightened her blouse and hair. Before leaving, she grabbed her purse. "Don't open this door for any- one except me. Do you understand that?" She looked seriously at Abby who had now crossed her arms and was seated at the end of the bed.

"Sure I understand," she said, trying to keep her voice from crack- ing. Kim could tell she was about to cry, though, and quickly sat down next to her. She put her arm around her. "Listen, I know you think I'm acting weird. I would think the same thing in your shoes." She squeezed her shoulders.

"I will explain this soon enough, but don't be afraid. I'm just being extra-cautious. Besides, I have some news for you."

Abby looked at her. Kim could see that tears had indeed welled up in her hazel eyes.

"Sean and I discussed how unfair it was to drag you along on this work of tracking down Jacob's mystery." Kim had been about to say 'quest' instead of 'work' but realized it would not come across to her daughter the right way. "I decided to send you to visit your father for a few days. Is that okay?"

Abby instantly brightened up. "Really? Have you asked him?"

Kim shook her head. "No, but I have no doubt he'll say yes."

"Wow, Mom." She wiped her eyes. "I'm okay. This has just been a weird weekend, you know?"

"I know kiddo," Kim laughed and squeezed Abby one more time. She then stood up and headed to the door. "Okay, lock this behind me. Chain and deadbolt, and..."

"I know, I know, don't open it for anyone but you," Abby interrupted her with a smile. "You'd better go. I don't think you should keep the FBI waiting!"

Kim smiled, then turned and left the room. She waited in the hall by the door until she heard the deadbolt click. She then looked around and headed to the closest elevator.

.....

A few minutes later, Kim was sitting uncomfortably on a massive chair in the hotel lobby. A toned and very good looking man, a bit younger than herself and dressed in a dark blue suit, was sitting at a right angle to her. *Classic FBI look,* she thought. They both were anxious and Kim noted to herself that the hotel lobby chairs seemed to be made for somebody about three times larger than the average person. Both she and the agent were perched at the end of the chairs, using only a small portion.

He handed Kim his card and she read it briefly and then set it on the glass table in front of her.

"So, how can I help you Mr. Nazimi?"

"I'd like to ask you a few questions about Mary Fester," he explained.

"Yes, she was murdered right?"

"Yes. How did you know that?" he promptly asked right back.

Kim immediately panicked and tried to think of how she knew that information. *Sean told me.* She was not willing to tell Alan anything at all about what she was doing and why she was in Denver. Thus, she was afraid to even open up the topic of Sean. However, she decided that she could perhaps flip the interview around if she played her cards right.

"Sean Johnson told me." She said simply. She noticed his eyes flicker some and realized he was mildly surprised by how easily she had said that.

"Do you know Mr. Johnson?"

"Why, is he a suspect in Mary's murder?" Again she saw a flicker of surprise in his eyes. *So far so good,* she thought.

"I am not at liberty to discuss the particulars of my investigation, Ms. Poole."

His tone turned serious and she could tell he was trying to regain control of their conversation.

"Well, I just asked. Am I a suspect?"

Alan leaned a bit farther forward and closer to Kim. "Ms. Poole, I need to ask the questions here."

"I don't know about that, Mr. Nazimi. If that's who you really are. I'd like to know how you found me here? And why you felt it was okay to interrupt my vacation. My store manager told me that you, or someone else just like you, showed up unannounced in my store yesterday. She did not tell you where I was, Mr. Nazimi. So how did you find me? Was it legal?" Kim felt like she was starting to tremble, but she also felt a quiet rage taking over her emotions.

"If you really are an FBI agent, then I also want to know why you're investigating the death of a nice woman in Phoenix supposedly murdered during a robbery. And I'd like to know why you're being so secretive and somewhat surprising. Those are things I would like to know."

Kim had crossed her arms while she talked and now she sat there, upright, trying to stare at him strongly. He appeared extremely uncomfortable and almost seemed to squirm within his suit.

"Look, Ms. Poole, I'm sorry if I've made you uncomfortable but I'm simply doing my job." He looked around a bit. "Mary Fester was murdered under very suspicious circumstances. I can tell you that. I'd like to know more about your relationship with her. What were you doing with her before she died? I understand she was helping you discover some secret that had to do with President Lincoln and a possible connection to your family. Is that right?"

It was Kim's turn to try and hide her surprise. *He must have read our email, but I thought her computer was erased? Did he erase it? Did the FBI murder Mary?* The thought was terrifying. She decided to try one more time to flip the interview around so she could end it.

"Look, Mr. Nazimi, I still don't feel comfortable talking with you. Let me ask you this. How do you know anything at all about what Mary and I might have been working on together? Our email?" She caught a slight nod of his head.

"Well then you know everything don't you?" Kim was ready for the interview to be finished.

"I had nothing to do with her death." She stood up. "Are you through asking me these questions?" she asked, her anger now showing.

"Ms. Poole, if you'll just sit down," he began.

Kim had already decided to leave. "No, I won't Mr. Nazimi. Next time, call me first. Make an appointment. I will gladly come in, with my lawyer beside me. But don't keep sneaking around spying on me. Is that understood?"

All Alan managed to do was nod. Kim could see, as she retreated, that he was getting angry himself. That knowledge actually calmed her. She turned her back on him and headed to the elevator. She could feel her legs getting weak and it was all she could do to maintain her posture while walking away. She entered an open elevator, punched the button for her floor and then held down the "door close" button.

As soon as the door closed Kim leaned against the side of the car while pulling her cell phone from her pocket. To her surprise, it began ringing as soon as she had it out. She looked and saw that it was Sean. With a sigh of relief, she accepted the call, and put the phone against her ear.

"Sean?"

"Yep, it's me. I watched your whole meeting. Great job. That must have been the FBI?" he asked.

"What, you did? How did you find me? Where were you?" Kim started firing questions at him.

Sean laughed lightly. "Relax, I'll explain later. Are you ready to leave?"

"Uh, no. I will need a few minutes. Did the guy leave yet?"

"Oh yeah. He stormed out of here looking very pissed. I haven't seen someone that mad since my military days." He paused. " Okay, do you remember the parking garage floor where you parked your car?"

"Yes. Third, P3"

"Okay, I will meet you there in thirty minutes. Until then, I'll keep an eye on things down here and call you if you need to do anything differently, okay?"

"Yes." Kim had reached her floor and got out, standing by the elevator to finish her conversation.

"Oh and listen, you're going to hate this, but I think we need to drive all the way to Dallas."

"What? Are you sure?"

"Yep. If this FBI guy has found you, then obviously lots of people are also tracking us. We really need to disappear for a while. It'll make it much harder for them to keep up with us."

"Okay, I guess. I have not even asked Abby's father yet. He's going to have a field day with all of this!"

"It'll be over soon, one way or another, I promise. Let's get Abby out of the picture and put her in a safe place. That will give us a chance to think things through and tackle the remaining mysteries."

"Or give up trying," he added as an after thought.

"Okay, see you in thirty minutes then. It's a silver SUV," Kim replied.

"Got it," Sean said as he hung up his phone.

Kim looked at her phone for a moment and then returned it to her purse. She headed to her hotel room, trying to think through her call to her ex-husband.

Chapter Twenty-Two

Tuesday, May 5
Dallas, Texas

Sean rubbed his eyes with one hand while he kept his other firmly on the steering wheel of the SUV. He had napped for about four hours while Kim drove and then had taken over the driving at three o'clock in the morning, somewhere on the western edge of Texas. It was now seven in the morning. The night sky had given way to a light blue hue of early dawn and the headlights of oncoming cars no longer hurt his eyes.

He was feeling fatigue, though, and needed to work even harder to stay alert. Sean was convinced that they had not been followed when leaving Denver. He had withdrawn as much cash as his debit card and his credit card would allow him to while still in Denver, and they had used cash to refuel before leaving and again when they swapped driving positions. Abby was spread out on the rear seat and had been sleeping solidly most of the trip.

Like only children can, he thought. *We adults, on the other hand, feel all of the burdens of life so much stronger that I don't think many of us get even a single night's sleep as good as most of those we once had in our youth.*

Sean also knew the importance of sleep. He had been taught that sleep was a reservoir, just like strength. It was something you called upon when needed, but eventually you had to refill it. Worse, lack of sleep degraded all of your other resources, including your thinking and strength.

Sean looked over at Kim who was asleep in the passenger seat. Unlike her daughter, she had been sleeping fitfully. Sean thought again about how well she had handled the FBI agent. It had impressed him. The woman could be funny and soft one moment, but could suck it up and be tough when needed. *This has to be more bewildering for her than me,* he thought. She had also placed tremendous trust in him, and that was something he was determined to uphold.

They had talked some, mostly trying to guard their words until Abby was asleep. It was Sean's experience, as a child himself in fact, that kids learned a lot by listening to adults talk while they pretended to be asleep. So, Sean half expected that Abby had learned some of the day's events while faking her slumber.

Kim and Sean had discussed the FBI presence. Sean had explained that he was confident that Alan really was an FBI agent. Nevertheless, they both felt that the agent was acting odd. Kim had not trusted him at all. They also talked about the presence of the Sheriden Corporation. Sean had not yet had a chance to get his computer online, but planned to do so at the very first opportunity that presented itself. He wanted to know more about who they were and figure out who might have hired them to watch Sean and James so closely. They had both agreed that it was awfully coincidental that the company was headquartered in Atlanta and that the riddle had told them of Atlanta gold. However, Kim and Sean had mostly been left with a dissatisfying feeling that they were chasing something far more dangerous than they were prepared for.

Sean reached over and gently nudged Kim on her shoulder. She failed to wake, so he tried again a bit harder and gently said "Kim." Her eyes fluttered open. She looked at him for a moment as he smiled and gestured, with a nod of his head, that it was time to get up.

She gently leaned her torso forward and began pulling herself upright in the car seat. After a minute of stretching, she looked somewhat more awake.

She glanced at her watch and then asked, "Where are we?"

"Past Fort Worth, approaching Dallas I guess. I get the feeling the two cities overlap to the point of being one giant metropolis. We passed the Dallas Fort Worth airport a little ways back."

"Oh, I see," Kim yawned. "I guess I should wake sleeping beauty."

Kim glanced back at her daughter while Sean watched through the rear view mirror. As Kim prodded Abby to wake her, Sean spoke.

"You wanted her there by eight and it looks like we'll make it. Probably not in time for more than a quick freshen-up at a gas station."

"That's fine," Kim said. She wound up waking Abby in much the same way Sean had woken Kim, except with Abby it took more time and more prodding.

.....

Sean pulled the SUV into the driveway and then came to a halt. Abby opened the passenger door and hopped out. A brown haired man in a blue striped suit came out of the door of the house and called her name. A wide grin was on his face. He smiled much like Abby did, Sean noted, realizing that they shared numerous facial features.

"Abby!" the man exclaimed, opening his arms.

"Dad," Abby called back to him. She ran up to him and they hugged. They said a few things that Sean could not quite hear. They were standing on a stone path that curved from the driveway to the front entrance. It was a nice suburban house in a nice neighborhood. The lawn looked immaculate and colorful flowers seemed perfectly arranged, giving the home a sense of perfection. *At least from the outside.*

Sean shifted his gaze to Kim who appeared nervous. She had a smile on her face, but Sean could see her hands clenching the edge of her seat. She muttered something that Sean could not quite hear. Then, Kim got out of the car.

As Kim approached Abby and her father, a woman came out of the house. She was blonde and younger than the father by at least a decade, Sean guessed. She was dressed in a sweater and long skirt, but Sean suspected that she normally dressed a lot more risqué. It was something about the way she walked. The dad had obviously gone for the stereotypical younger woman, Sean decided. Seeing Kim falter a bit as she saw the woman come out of the house, he decided to hop out and give some moral support.

As Sean approached the group, now standing next to the driveway at the end of the stone path, they all looked at him. Abby, he noticed, was at least smiling at him, *She must like me at least some.*

"Jason, Brenda, this is Sean," Kim said. "Sean, this is Abby's dad, Jason, and his girlfriend, Brenda." Sean detected only the slightest hint of distaste in Kim's voice as she pronounced "girlfriend."

"Hi," he said offering his hand first to Jason and then to Brenda. "Very nice to meet you." Jason's handshake seemed overly strong, like he was trying to impress Sean with his strength. *Save it,* Sean thought.

Brenda, however, seemed to cling to his hand a little too long, and Sean immediately suspected she would run off with him if the opportunity presented itself. He felt sadness for Kim, but perhaps more for what Jason and Kim must have had once. *They must have loved each other, but I can't tell what she ever saw in him.*

"Abby, I'll grab your bags," Sean said, thinking anything he could do to shorten the time Kim talked with them would be a good thing. He looked at Jason as he turned away and made sure that Jason could see that Sean was not the slightest bit intimidated.

A few minutes later, Kim and Sean were back in her car. He was still driving and it was silent for a while as Kim sat quietly looking out the window. He let her have some peace while he focused on what they were to do next. He was bone-tired and hungry, so stopping for breakfast and getting some coffee was first on his list. A glance at Kim told him that she would feel the same way. So, Sean watched for a decent place to stop while he navigated back to the freeway.

After we get refueled, I really need to hit the internet for a while. He wanted to research the Sheriden Corporation and learn more about his opponent, but as he thought about the coming drive all the way to Knoxville, he felt trapped, with not enough time to do everything he needed to do. *We could fly to Knoxville, leaving Kim's car here in Dallas. But that increases our chances of being tracked. Unless we pay cash for the airline tickets.* The idea of paying cash for their tickets, however, made him smile. He could visualize the airline employee staring at him as if he were a terrorist. He shook his head at the idea. *We'd draw more attention paying cash than simply using a credit card and letting them notice it.* Sean also expected that the credit card system had a delay in it. So, they might not even know until tomorrow, at some point, that they had traveled to Knoxville. By that time they might be ready to leave anyway.

Sean was just reaching the freeway when he saw a likely place to eat. He tapped Kim on the arm.

"Hey, you hungry?"

Kim looked at him and smiled. "You bet."

.....

Over breakfast they had agreed to fly to Knoxville. Sean insisted on paying for the flights as he felt responsible for having led Kim down to Dallas by car. He also knew that she would have to pay to park her car in Dallas and then later, have to drive it back up to Kansas City. Furthermore, he had no idea if he would be around to help with that. Kim had given in to that argument.

After eating, they walked across the street to a coffee shop that Sean knew would have a wireless internet. Together, they then researched Sheriden. Sean did not like what he learned, as Frank had known would happen. Sheriden had a worldwide presence. They had bought a company that provided security services in South America that Sean recognized as doing CIA work in the eighties. He had not worked for it, but had been alongside some people who had. Sheriden and its subsidiaries were currently providing all sorts of armed escort and security services for both United States agencies and departments, as well as for all sorts of foreign governments. *They reek of danger,* Sean concluded. He also realized that they would have a tremendous level of access to networks and information.

Sean discussed Sheriden with Kim and told her more about the kind of things he had done in the past. He avoided any specifics, as always. For him, avoiding specifics was not only an obligation he had to the United States, but it was also quite therapeutic. His last operation had been brutal enough, that he preferred to avoid thinking about his past life. Frank, who had survived that same disastrous mission, appeared to act the same way. They had not mentioned one specific thing about their past when they had been together briefly.

Finishing the Sheriden research, they then reserved airline tickets for late that afternoon, flying from Dallas to Knoxville. Sean explained that by reserving them, they could hold off paying for them until the last minute. He hoped that paying for the tickets as late as possible would delay their pursuers from learning where they had gone. They then called James and left him a message saying that they would call him the next morning before coming over.

With all of that done, Sean and Kim set out to find a cheap, but secure place to park Kim's vehicle. They would then head to the airport to leave for Knoxville.

Atlanta

Michael sat in his desk chair staring out at the fields behind the mansion and thinking carefully about the events of the last two weeks. A growing feeling gnawed at his mind telling him that he and his brother were losing control of the circumstances. Being out of control was a feeling he had never liked, and candidly, was not very familiar with.

My brother and I control a giant company capable of deploying so much physical power and political influence, yet we're stymied by a reporter, a single mother and a professor!

Michael also knew that if the situation was bothering him then his brother had to be infuriated. Michael, however, increasingly believed that Terry was part of the problem. His brother had gotten too caught up in the situation and was losing his vision of the forest and instead seeing only trees. He, on the other hand, had been busy working on his campaign and had mostly kept a distance from the unfolding events. He had been relying on Terry to make decisions. But, Michael had to admit to himself, Terry had pretty much screwed up every single event.

Terry's first foul up had been killing the Enloe woman in Phoenix. Terry had always been prone to violent resolutions to all problems. He was good at such violence. However, killing that woman had been unnecessary and had led to events that were jeopardizing their family's century of vigilance. If it weren't for the killing, it would be unlikely that the trio they were now following would have any idea that he and Terry were so interested in their results. Instead, at this point, the reporter/ex-Navy Seal had to be on very high alert and all three of them must be looking over their shoulders.

Michael also had to admit, however, that without the intelligence that Terry had gained from the Enloe woman, he and Terry might not even know of the three people and the accomplishments they had already made in solving the mystery of Jacob Thomas.

Michael sighed. *My brother is sometimes too much of a ruffian, but he does get results. It's been a full week since he has been trailing them, however, and they must be getting closer.* Michael considered that the secrets might never be discovered. The problem was that the trio could discover what happened to Jacob Thomas and his pouch, and that was a risk he and Terry could not endure for much longer. It was not about the fortune involved, if that part was really true, but was instead because of his career. Now that Michael was a prominent politician, there was no way he could survive the scandal that would envelop him should the truth come out about the Sheriden family. For that reason alone, they had to ensure that if this was the time for the lost letters to surface and the secret to come out, that they had to intercept them. If the stories were true, and there was a fortune waiting as well, that was all the better.

Of course, Michael considered, they could silence the secret and then reveal the fortune as a public service. In either case, if the trio were going to find the letters, then they would have to be silenced.

He sighed again. *More killing.* Not that he was afraid of it, but any killing risked detection or more complications. There was no more room for any mistakes. If it appeared that the trio were getting much closer, then it would be time to treat the situation as all or nothing. He also knew that his brother, thanks to his predilection towards violence, would go right along with such a decision. Michael was concerned, however, that Terry would not be able to see the larger situation. Terry had taken things personally and now wanted to "defeat" Sean Johnson. He would want to find the letters, not only as a means of protecting the Sheriden family, but also as a means of "winning" his competition with the reporter. That was a problem. If it came down to it, Michael would be fine with destroying any chance of the letters ever surfacing. Terry on the other hand, might be unwilling to accept such a resolution.

Adding it all up, Michael concluded that he had to get much more involved in the final days of this chase. That meant less involvement in campaigning and politics.

He swung his chair from the window view to face his desk squarely. He punched the speaker button on his desk phone and then one of the preset numbers along the side of the phone. He then waited while the call went through. Within two rings, he heard Jessica's voice.

"Hello there. Everything okay?" she asked in her professional voice.

"Yes, completely, but I want to discuss a matter with you this afternoon," Michael said into the phone.

"Okay. You are completely free today, so we can set the meeting for anytime you like."

Michael thought for a moment and smiled. "Let's go with four o'clock. You can stay for dinner."

"Of course, I'll be there then." She paused. "What are your plans otherwise?"

"I'm going to work on my speech for a while yet this morning and then go hunting for a few hours."

"Okay, then, I will see that your calendar stays clear through four. Happy hunting."

"Great, thank you."

Michael hung up the phone. He then repeated his dialing and waited for his brother to answer.

"Hello brother," Terry repeated his favorite greeting.

"Hello," Michael replied back. "How are things?"

"My research is complete. I have not found any useful leverage on the trio, and both the professor and the reporter have no close family members so there is not much there. The woman is divorced from a lawyer in Dallas. They had a child together and she has primary custody. I have been able to determine that the daughter is traveling with the mom. They checked out of their Denver hotel yesterday. I haven't spotted them since. It's probable they went back to Kansas City."

"Where is the reporter?"

"I don't know," Terry admitted. "I suspect the Springfield incident probably caused him to become much more careful. There has not been any credit activity since Sunday. I'm trying to see if I can get access to his cell phone data, but that does not look promising. It's a company in the Pacific Northwest that we have no relationships with. The professor is in Knoxville. He cancelled classes yesterday."

"Brother, as always, you impress me."

"I try," Terry replied.

"I'm calling to discuss the larger strategic situation. I have thought things through carefully. I believe we need to treat this situation as an all or nothing gambit the minute we see signs that the trio is going public or getting too close to learning too much. Do you agree?"

Without hesitating Terry agreed. "Of course. I'm in full agreement."

"Good. I am going to clear my political schedule somewhat beginning later this week. I've been asking too much of you, brother, and staying too detached. Given the importance of this matter, I need to give it my highest priority and minimize how much help we use outside of the family."

Terry laughed. "You want to go into the field brother?"

"I always want to go, you know that. But I rarely have the time these days." Michael paused. "Also, I am going to brief Jessica on this somewhat. I won't tell her everything, but I will need her help if I am to be involved and she'll probably end up knowing everything anyway."

"Do you think that is wise?"

"Yes, and necessary," Michael replied. "Besides, her career is completely intertwined with mine."

"She's intertwined with you in many ways brother, but I respect your judgment as always." Michael detected a smugness in Terry's voice.

"Okay then, please keep me updated on what you learn."

"I will do so."

They hung up and Michael thought for a moment before returning to work on his speech.

Phoenix

Alan Nazimi was still fuming. He had returned to Phoenix the night before and was now alone in his office after morning briefings on the status of various efforts and cases. He was certain his mood had been obvious to the entire staff, but he cared little. Kim Poole had managed to insult him, offend him and make his two-city effort to track her down and get some answers about the case a waste of time. Sean Johnson had disappeared after leaving Springfield before the agents got there. Alan wanted answers as to who Sean had been fighting with and why. He was not even certain that Sean Johnson was alive. The same question just kept coming to his mind in this case: *What in the hell is going on?*

Alan worked on calming himself for a few minutes and then started working through things logically. *What makes a single mother, a shop-keeper, stand up to an FBI agent who calls her out of her hotel room? Why does somebody else chase a reporter who was researching the last years of Abraham Lincoln's presidency? Why is a woman murdered in her own city while doing the same research? Why is her brother stalked in Tennessee?*

For not the first time, Alan considered whether a spook agency, his nickname for the CIA and all of its secret groups, was involved. He again concluded, though, that if that was the case, his inquiries on the woman and the reporter would have triggered a call or he would have encountered a red flag. It was clear, however, that part of Sean's naval service history was blocked, telling Alan that Sean, as a Seal in the Navy, could have been involved with CIA-based operations. That, however, would not explain why there was someone else chasing him. *There is someone else out there chasing him and I don't have a clue who it is,* Alan concluded.

With nothing else to go on with the reporter, Alan returned to evaluating Kimberly Poole. He had managed to learn a lot about her. She had divorced a few years ago in Dallas and had taken her daughter to Kansas City. There, she had opened a shop. Her remaining parent, her father, had died back in December. He left some kind of mystery behind that she had communicated to Mary Fester. Mary had been researching Lincoln when she was murdered. Kim was also communicating with the reporter. After leaving her hotel yesterday, she had not yet appeared. The latest credit card use report showed no activity at all, much like Sean's had after Saturday evening. It struck Alan that the reporter might have gone to Denver after his encounter in Springfield and connected with Kim. If so, then they were now purposely hiding their movements.

Then, Kim's behavior at her hotel room door came to mind and Alan silently cursed as he realized that Sean Johnson had probably been in her hotel room when he had knocked. *Damn, I'm just not thinking well on this case.* He considered creating a team centered around the case and finding the duo, but again, he decided that his best chance to ensure he received the maximum career enhancement was to continue to run it himself. A team would draw in other offices and some other SIC would get credit. *No, I need to run this on my own for now.*

Alan studied Kim's dossier some more and decided to try calling her ex-husband. *He's probably paying way more in alimony and child support than he wants to. He could be very useful.* Alan decided to get the ex-husband's phone number and give him a call.

.....

Alan hung up the phone stunned. *Gold? A civil war treasure? That's what all of this is about?* He realized that it made complete sense. Men had always been willing to kill for gold and treasure. *The reporter, the woman, and the professor are all on a treasure hunt and someone else was either trying to stop them or harness their efforts.*

The ex-husband had been more than willing to talk. What a tale he had to tell! Sean Johnson and Kim Poole were running around trying to find a treasure supposedly hidden by Kim's ancestor. The father had been furious that his daughter had been pulled out of school and driven around the country. Sean and Kim had driven all night, from Denver to Dallas, to drop the daughter off at the father's house. The girl rambled on to her dad about how her mom was on a treasure hunt and that some bad men were chasing them. Alan would not have believed a word of it, if it were not for all the things he already knew that fit perfectly with the tale. The father clearly believed that his ex-wife had gone crazy and was preparing to take full advantage of the situation.

Alan leaned back in his chair, finally cooling down from his rage. A large grin spread across his face as he realized just how wise he had been to keep the case very quiet.

Knoxville

James returned from a day at the campus library feeling tired but still excited. He activated his home alarm system once he was inside the house, another new habit Sean had talked him into adopting. He dropped his bulging briefcase on a chair in the research room, formally known as the dining room, and headed into the kitchen. Shortly, he had put together a hot stir fry with vegetables and steak. He settled in at the small table in his kitchen and quickly downed a large portion of the food. Then he made a pot of strong coffee and headed into the dining room. Within an hour though, he moved to his home office to use his computer. The riddle in the will had turned his attention to the stories and history of the taking of Atlanta. He also wanted to be fully versed when Kim and Sean arrived.

James was really looking forward to the duo's arrival, as he was feeling lonely. He had had a close talk with a couple of friends in his department, but even though he did discuss his loss over Mary's murder, he did not tell them all of the surrounding events and news, partly out of caution and mostly because he was afraid they would think he was truly losing it. With Kim and Sean's arrival, he would have a chance to openly discuss and go through all of the information and events surrounding Mary's death. He was truly looking forward to that.

His research on Atlanta at the library had been educating, but he had found few specifics on any stories of gold or treasure. Online, he found a few websites containing stories about Confederate treasure, but even those lacked many citations or references to any highly reliable sources. So, he was left with the same fuzzy knowledge about Atlanta's treasures that he explained to Sean the day before.

James was more convinced than ever, though, that 'nation sinned' had to refer to Sherman's march across Georgia and South Carolina. There were all sorts of scholarly works on whether Sherman's campaign had been ethical. The reference to Atlanta gold clearly suggested the Sherman Campaign as well. A treasure, though, was unlikely to have made a young courier so upset that he would describe it as the "nation's sins." James had certainly found nothing worthy of hiding a secret in a will. So, James was left with a vague sense of progress about that piece of the riddle.

Finally, he was not getting any farther on the Jacob Thomas connection either. He had read and studied enough to have verified that Lincoln had relied upon War Department couriers regularly. James then developed a premise that Jacob had been entrusted to deliver something to, or for, Lincoln and that he had read it. It had then upset him enough that, after Lincoln's death, he had probably spoken out about what he had read and then felt threatened. But, that hypothesis failed to explain why the treasure never surfaced and why Jacob had a fear for his life that lasted decades. James had thus developed an alternative thesis that Jacob had read the documents and then ran away with them when Lincoln was assassinated. That fit with the facts better, but it was still far from a complete connection. James felt very incompetent, as a historian, as he called it quits for the night.

Chapter Twenty-Three

It was nine in the morning. Sean and Kim had arrived in Knoxville the night before. They had taken a cab from the airport to the downtown area. There, they had quickly found a room with two double beds at a small motel next to the freeway that crossed the metro area. Kim was learning, by watching Sean, how to move about very quietly: use cash everywhere, obtain transportation or accommodations that do not require identification and use quick thinking and explanations when someone asks to see a driver's license. At the motel, Kim had watched as Sean had taken a few minutes to find his license when asked and then had put it down on the counter for only a moment before picking it up. The trick worked. The clerk checking them in had never even noticed that the name on the license did not match the name that Sean had provided.

After they had gone to their room, Kim and Sean had talked for a while. It had actually been a little awkward until they were both settled in their beds for the evening. Both had been averting looking at the other and very aware of the intimate nature of sharing a hotel room. Kim actually would have been fine crawling in bed with Sean. He was attractive, and what mattered most, she was becoming more and more attracted to him. However, she was also very tired and looking forward to a good night's sleep on a real bed for a change. She was also terrified at the thought that she might make an advance towards Sean only to have him rebuff her. He was so serious about taking good care of her, that she had a hard time thinking he saw anything in her at all beyond their quest. Still, they had held hands quite a few times, and were exchanging plenty of smiles, as well as candid friendliness. So, Kim had stuck with her own bed. After she had called Abby and made sure that she was fine at her dad's, she and Sean had talked for a while and had, at some point, fallen asleep.

In the morning, Sean had awakened before her and quickly and quietly showered. She awoke to Sean saying her name quietly. He had then headed out for coffee, a morning newspaper, and a look around. Kim knew enough to know that his last purpose meant some discreet surveillance of their surroundings. He had returned after she was dressed. They had then called James to get directions, but James had insisted on picking them up. They had agreed to meet at a coffee shop located near the motel, and that was where she was now.

She and Sean had entered the coffee shop with their luggage in tow, ordered lattes and settled down at a table. Kim noticed a very tall man pass through the entrance door and she immediately knew he was the professor. He was taller than Sean, but otherwise might have had a similar build if he had exercised as much as Sean clearly did. He appeared to be in his late fifties or early sixties, with graying hair and an older looking face. He looked tired, she thought. What clearly gave him away as a professor was the brown woven sport coat and slacks that just screamed "professor" to Kim. She smiled at him and she felt Sean start to rise next to her. The man's face flashed recognition and he walked towards their table.

"Hello," he said to Kim, ignoring Sean. "You must be Kimberly Poole."

Kim felt herself blush somewhat as she felt his smile washing over her. "Yes, that's me." She offered her hand as she said, "Very nice to meet you, Professor."

He laughed lightly. "Oh no, I get called Professor enough by girls much younger than you but not nearly as beautiful. Please, call me James."

Kim smiled back blushing even more. "I will…James," she said forcing herself to try his first name instead of the more comfortable title of professor.

James then turned to Sean. "Well, at least this time you brought somebody better looking than you!"

Sean took his hand and they shook firmly, Kim noticed.

"It is very good to see you again," Sean said.

"Likewise for me," James replied. "Shall we head to my home?"

Kim and Sean nodded their heads in agreement. He turned around and started leaving. They quickly followed him out, Sean rolling his luggage and Kim carrying her large gym bag over her shoulder.

......

The trio were now spread out in James's living room. It was almost noon and they had just finished a basic review of facts and events. Kim had begun the discussion with a summary of her family history. Sean had then summarized the events that had occurred over the last two weeks. He very delicately discussed Mary's murder and explained his encounters with their pursuers. He finished with a synopsis of the Sheriden Corporation, mostly for the benefit of James. Kim had then walked James through the will and their deciphering of the riddle within it.

It was James's turn. He stood up and walked around the table to a large window looking out on the street in front of his house. He turned back to face them and began speaking, much like he was giving a lecture, with Sean and Kim as his students.

"The riddle suggests to me that Jacob Thomas had information about some particular atrocities committed by some or all of the elements of General Sherman's army as it left Atlanta and proceeded across Georgia and South Carolina. Understand that Sherman was now in the underbelly of the Confederacy and largely unopposed. In general, there was a great sense of need to punish the South for the uprising and for all the death and destruction it had triggered."

"Sherman is criticized for ordering his forces to scour, without strict supervision, in and around the army's path for all of its food needs. Thus, the foraging troops not only plundered food, but took hoards of items of value. They also murdered, raped and burned; more of this apparently occurred farther away from the army, where senior officers would be less likely to observe inappropriate behavior."

"I am left, however, with some doubt that the information that Jacob might have had would have been 'secret' or 'stunning.' He would not have been greeted with much enthusiasm, though, if he had expressed sympathy for the South. Still, that hardly seems the grounds for him to hide in the far west under an assumed name."

James took a moment to clear his throat, then continued.

"As to the Atlanta gold phrase, that is one reason I feel that 'nation sinned' must be a reference to Sherman's time in Georgia and South Carolina. But, reference to 'Atlanta gold saved' also clearly suggests a second or perhaps more important reason for Jacob's secrecy. There is, as I told you two days ago, no shortage of stories and theories about valuable metals and jewelry being lost during, or after, the taking of Atlanta. Some stories even suggest there was a large amount of gold coins. I found some analysis suggesting that a large quantity of gold was never accounted for in the accounting of the Confederacy's finances after the war."

"I have not found many first person accounts of treasure, gold or coins so far. Most stories that have some reference or support are either inferential, that is they logically demonstrate that some gold is unaccounted for or missing, or they are founded upon old, unsupported articles in newspapers and books from that age. Of course, this is not my area of expertise and I do not feel that, at this point, I have a very good grip on the treasure history."

"Jacob's riddle is still the strongest confirmation that I have seen that there is, or was, some 'Atlanta' treasure. However, it does little to tell us where to go, or where to look, other than the last phrase 'look beyond.' Thus, the riddle leaves us with only hints of what it's talking about and a very vague direction of where to go next."

"Meanwhile, regarding Jacob Thomas and his Washington D.C. connection, I have noted that there are some missing notes and logs from the end of Lincoln's presidency. Besides confirming that Jacob Thomas was indeed a courier in the employment of the War Department, I have been unable to confirm anything about what he did, where he went, or who he met. He disappeared as quickly as he appeared, around the same time as Lincoln's assassination."

James paused and walked over to his whiteboard which was still sitting on the buffet. Sean had to get up and move to a chair on the other end of the table. Once he was seated, James continued, gesturing at his whiteboard.

"Here is a chronological map of sorts. Time progresses from the left to the right and events occurring at the same time are vertically aligned. Lincoln's presidency is on top, the Civil War is next, and Jacob Thomas is on the bottom. You can see our interest begins in November 1864 as Sherman overtook Atlanta. In December, as Sherman marches across the south, young Jacob Thomas shows up on War Department payrolls. The months of January, February and March are blank. April has Lincoln's assassination, the hunt for James Booth, and the disappearance of Jacob Thomas. The other two dates in the president's row are dates where something looks wrong with Lincoln's records. This could mean tampering, or maybe it's just lost documents."

James looked at Sean and then at Kim. "I don't think I will get any farther on Washington D.C. There is, however, more for me to explore regarding Atlanta, Sherman, and treasure theories."

James sat down in his chair, his long legs folded and pushing his knees nearly as high as the table. "But I think our best efforts would be spent on the riddle itself, paying particularly close attention to the 'look beyond' phrase."

He then sat there silently, once again looking at Sean and Kim.

Kim was the first to speak, after glancing at Sean who seemed lost in thought.

"Okay, so I have thought a lot about that phrase. I think 'beyond' means 'beyond his will." Kim stood up feeling a need to move around. "That phrase makes me think of his letters to his son, Abraham, more than anything."

Kim had reached her gym bag in the corner of the room. She pulled a thick clump of papers and files out of the bag and set them down on the table. She then grabbed a notepad and began flipping through a few of its pages.

"Abraham was born in 1883. When his father died in 1901, he was only eighteen. Apparently, in the fall of 1900, Abraham went to work at a mining camp in the mountains. He would have been seventeen years old then. Jacob sent four letters to him over the course of two months. Here they are." Kim held out a stack of papers. "They are all addressed to the same little mining town. It's a ghost town now."

"I remember when I found these letters, my first thought was how fortunate it was that they had survived. Now, I don't think it was a coincidence at all. Though, I certainly don't know how they came to last so long. I think Jacob buried the answer to his riddle in these letters and, one way or another, ensured that they would be around for his family to read later on."

Sean and James were both looking at Kim with rapt attention. James spoke. "Well, then let's do some investigating, shall we? Each of us should take a letter. Let's do the first three letters first. I suppose we should look for the same pattern that you found in the will?"

"Yes, but let's also keep an open mind about what else seems odd or perhaps different," Sean said. "I suggest we read the letter the first time and then go through it again looking for words. When we did this two days ago, we did it as a duo. I think that worked much better. So, maybe after reading, we should take turns teaming up with one of us reading the first page while the other follows along on the next page."

They all agreed and set to reading the letter they had selected. It was oddly quiet for a full ten minutes or so in the living room as each of them read their letter. James finished his letter first, picked up the fourth letter and began reading it as well, making notes on a sheet of paper as he went along. Then, Kim and Sean finished their letters. Kim got up and headed to the bathroom while Sean stood and went to the window to stare out at the street.

About five minutes later, James was through with the fourth letter and Kim was back in the room. They sat around the table and James started the conversation.

"The first letter is dated September 7, 1900. It is eight pages long. I found some sentences that seem odd, but not significantly out of place. The fourth letter is dated October 25, 1900. I did not spot any repeated phrases or sentences as compared to the first letter." James stopped but then continued. "Oh, the fourth letter is nine pages long."

"The second letter is dated September 22," Kim explained. "It's nine pages. It is clearly not as filled with odd sentences as the will. Nothing stood out." She looked to Sean, who spoke next.

"The third letter is dated October 10. Like both of you, I found nothing odd. It is eight pages long."

They each looked at each other for a moment. Then Sean spoke. "Why don't you two do the first letter, doing the repeated word comparison. I'm going to take a walk around the neighborhood." He looked at James. "Can you turn off the alarm long enough for me to leave? Then turn it back on once I'm outside. I'll knock when I return."

"Sure," James said getting up. "The code is 1-0-1-9, in case you need it."

Sean laughed, "Tell me that's not your birthday."

James looked back at him innocently. "Why yes. It is," he said.
.....

"We're not doing something right," Kim said showing her frustration. "We've tried all four letters, and found nothing but gibberish."

She put the pages she was holding down on the table. "And that's only when we actually find a repeated word, which is not that often."

James looked at Sean. Sean, in turn, looked at Kim.

"We need to take a break," Sean said. "We need to allow our minds to back off and take a look at the big picture. We're too focused on each page and each letter."

"That's a good idea," James chimed in. "In fact, I think we need to eat something more than the snacks we have been munching on."

They both looked at Kim expectantly, but she was frozen. She was staring down at the letters on the table.

"Of course," she said quietly. "We're being too simple. We only tried to replicate the pattern we found in the will in the letters, but there's a big difference."

She looked at Sean and James with a triumphant expression on her face.

"What's the difference between the letters and the will?" she asked excitedly and demandingly.

James started to answer, "Well, the will is a legal document, the letters are personal correspondence." He looked at Kim, but she just shook her head. She then looked at Sean expectantly.

Sean laughed. "Oh no, I'm not even going to try and keep up with your mind. Come on out with it. What are you driving at?"

Kim smiled and said simply, "There's four of them."

There was a momentary pause before the faces on both men lit up.

"Of course," James muttered. "How stupid of me. We're focused on each letter as being a clue of its own, but we have not tried connecting the letters."

They looked at the table for a moment and then Sean spoke.

"So, what's the first step?"

"Well, we need to compare the letters to each other. Look for patterns, maybe the same repeated word clues," James began. "But there could be all sorts of other ways to hide clues in a set of parallel documents."

Sean and Kim smiled, knowing the professor was just getting started.

"Okay, so Sean, you take letter number one," James continued, ignoring the smiles from them. "Kim, you take letter number two. I'll take letter number three and number four."

James continued giving instructions and the three of them settled in on the task. It took them several hours to find the pattern. They also discovered that Jacob had devised a backup plan. He had created the pattern between the first and third letters and the second and fourth letters. They all agreed that had probably been in case one of the letters was lost.

Each set of two letters followed a pattern similar to the repeated word trick that Jacob had used in the will. The pattern in the first set began with just one slightly odd sentence in the first letter that, in retrospect, they all felt they should have spotted. It read:

"*My son, this letter will tell you much of what you need to know.*"

The pattern in the second sentence had begun with a more innocuous sentence. In both sets of letters, the pattern was the same. Jacob had duplicated a word at the same point in both letters. The word following the second word was the key word. Again, as in the will, the first letter of the word had been used to spell out words. This time, however, they had only found two words: *final home.*

"Is that it?" Sean asked, feeling very tired despite the excitement at having uncovered some more words. "Is that all Jacob left us?"

"I think so," James replied. "Though there are probably still some ways to compare the letters that we have not yet thought of doing. But, I think the fact that the phrase is repeated two times probably tells us that we have found all of the clues."

"So, does it mean his burial place?" Kim asked. "Do we have to dig him up?"

"If that is what it takes, then yes, that is what we will do," Sean said. "What do you think Professor? What else could he be inferring?"

"Well, I think his grave or his crypt is the most likely place. But how would he have been able to ensure the letters got there?" James replied. "Did he bury anyone else?"

"Yes," Kim said excitedly. "His wife Olivia."

James looked at Kim. "Okay, maybe that is the more likely spot, followed by his own grave."

He thought for a moment. "After that, maybe the clue is not a riddle, but is simply saying at the final house he lived in."

Sean had sat up and was leaning on the dining room table with his head now resting in both hands. "Maybe, but a grave would certainly be more permanent," he said. "That gives us three places. Anything else?"

They looked at each other, but no one had anything to add. After a moment, Sean spoke.

"Well then, for now anyway, let's finally take a break." He smiled. "And eat please, I'm starving!"

....

After James had cooked some food and Kim and Sean had cleared some space on the cluttered dining room table, they sat and ate.

"This is great chicken, James," Sean said between bites. "Is this an Enloe recipe?"

"No, just good old southern cooking 101," James said jokingly. "But you just reminded me of a topic that is bothering me. Maybe we don't need to solve it. Maybe what we find, if we find anything, will solve it. But, my question is, what is my connection to all this?"

James stopped eating and put his fork down on his plate. Sean and Kim stopped eating as well and watched him. James began speaking without looking up.

"We are all avoiding this topic, but it's okay, I can handle talking about it. The big question is, why was Mary killed?" He now looked up at them. "I think we're working from the idea that she was killed by somebody who wants to stop us from finding the answers that Jacob left for us. That raises all sorts of questions too. Like, how they noticed us and why they are still around 150 years later. But, the question I truly care about is why it had to be Mary, my sister, an Enloe, that was involved? "

"That's why I'm here. Sure, maybe I'm useful as a professor and a Lincoln historian, but the only reason I got involved..." He paused and looked at Sean. "In fact, the only reason that you got involved, Sean, was the Enloe connection."

"So, you should know that the question I keep coming back to is why Jacob tied this warning to the Enloes? I have lots of theories and they mostly all connect to my theories about Jacob. I think that somehow the Enloes were involved in trying to tell us something about whatever 'nation sinned' means or about the lost treasure. But, in the end, I find it very odd that the same family, connected by rumor to Lincoln's birth, would also be involved in some grand scheme near the end of Lincoln's life."

"So, I've developed another theory. This one fits the facts much better. Kim, your ancestor was extremely smart. He did a great job leaving things to be found and in creating a delay in time. My theory is this. I think that Jacob also knew something about the Enloe theory and used it as an hour glass of some sorts. Probably as another example of his "back-ups" in action. By the time the Lincoln-Enloe story came out, he knew enough time would have passed."

James looked at Kim. "Kim, Jacob was intelligent, and he knew he was leaving behind a fairly young son. He knew he could not tell his son everything, because he knew that his son did not have the full wisdom needed to know when to act. So, he left riddles for his son to follow, along with a very strong warning."

James looked over at Sean and then smiled.

"Sorry, I didn't mean to rant. It's just that you two are the only ones I have to confide in about this theory that has been dying to get out of me."

"I think it's solid," Sean announced. "At least as solid as anything else we have to go on in regards to this mystery. There is also something about family history and knowing who our ancestors were that I cannot quite figure out. American's care about their ancestry, but I don't know why."

Sean turned to Kim. "You and Mary cared a lot about your ancestry. That's the reason that this secret has come out of hiding. You were determined to discern all the facts about Jacob. Mary was very committed to the entirety of the Enloe family history. I believe that Mary was killed by these thugs that have hounded James and I."

Sean now put his fork down and stared at the papers and books scattered around the room. "That brings me to my main point. We now know much more about what is going on than when we started. Thanks to the license plate, we even have an idea of who our foe probably is that's causing all of these problems."

"So my question is. What do we do next? Do we continue to chase this down on our own, or do we take this to law enforcement and turn it over to them to handle?"

Kim spoke up. "I'm not ready to let this go. Sean, you yourself said that the Sheriden Corporation might even be in league with some element of our government. Also, they should be considered very dangerous. Hell, we're assuming they killed your sister, James!"

"Also, that FBI guy that showed up at my hotel room in Denver, the same one that appeared at my shop in Kansas City the day before, was slimy. I don't trust him, but who else do we go to for this? The story is running us halfway across America. So, if we go to local law enforcement, it will end up being an FBI case. I definitely don't trust them at this point. No, I think we need to go at it alone and see this through to the end."

Sean looked at the professor. "James?"

James thought for a moment. "I agree with Kim. But, let's not fool ourselves here. This could be extremely dangerous!"

He looked at Sean. "And you may need to be a grave robber. Are you ready for that?"

Sean shrugged. "Yep, as I said, I'll do what it takes. For what it's worth, I feel the same way as both of you. I used to be a part of the government. I don't wish to turn this over to them just yet."

"Then it's settled," James said. "Good. This old professor needs some excitement in his life. I assume you two will head back to Denver?"

Sean looked at Kim, who nodded. "Yep, I guess so," he replied. "I'm thinking we should fly again. It may tell everyone we've headed back there, but it's a big city so I bet we can stay hidden pretty well. Can I use your computer for a bit to check flights?"

"Sure," James replied.

"Do you want to come to Denver with us?" Kim asked.

"No, I have some ideas of how I can be more useful here. Since Jacob's mystery is pointing us to the Civil War and the South, I think I need to focus on that. I haven't studied Civil War campaigns that much. I'm going to start with Sherman, his taking of Atlanta, and then his march through the South."

James got up and headed out of the dining room. "Come on," he called to Sean. "I'll get you set up on my computer."

Sean looked at Kim and they laughed together.

"I'll see what I can figure out for travel plans," Sean said. "You want to tidy up our notes and the papers we'll need?"

"Sure," Kim replied.

.....

Sean started the car, put it in reverse and backed out of the garage and onto the street. He then shifted it into drive and looked up at James. He sounded the horn and drove off with James waving at them from his garage. The car was a ten year old white Sedan that James had never sold after he bought his current vehicle, a mid-sized SUV. He had insisted that Sean and Kim take it after Sean concluded their best way to get to Denver was to drive to Nashville and catch an easy commuter flight from its airport the next morning. Sean had reserved a hotel room with his credit card, knowing that they would be long out of Nashville before the transaction ever reached the eyes of whoever was following them.

But, the question of 'whoever' continued to nag at him as he steered the car out of the suburban neighborhood and into the heart of the city. It bothered him to think that the FBI might be involved. *If they are, it's more likely that they're just following orders.* Sean looked over at Kim who was talking with Abby on her cell phone. *Her intuition is good. The FBI agent that showed up in Denver was acting suspicious. There's nothing as protective and alert as a mother protecting her daughter.*

But, as Sean watched her talk to Abby, he realized it was more than that. She was a very tough and very adaptive woman. The last two weeks had been amazing, even to him. They had to be overwhelming to her, yet she did not show it.

Almost on instinct, Sean reached out and placed his hand on hers. She looked up at him, somewhat startled, as she finished her call.

"Okay, bye, I love you too." Kim lowered the phone never taking her eyes off Sean. She dropped the phone in her lap and placed her second hand on top of his.

"Thanks," was all she said before turning to look out the window. She left her hands together with Sean's for several minutes before he delicately pulled it out and put it back on the steering wheel. Soon she was deep asleep. He would try to keep her that way all the way to Nashville.

Nashville

It was a comfortable and simple hotel room adjacent to the airport. Sean bounced up and down lightly on the edge of one of the two beds in the room and then stood up as Kim walked towards him from the bathroom smiling. She was wearing a beige bathrobe tied across her waist. Sean had felt bone tired as they pulled into Nashville, but now, watching her approach him, his fatigue was gone. He reached out and took her hand as she stopped before him. Kim giggled ever so slightly, showing embarrassment at his open stare.

Sean reached up and curled his other hand behind her neck, sliding his fingers beneath her hair and against the warm skin of her neck. She arched slightly at his touch as he pulled her lips to his.

Their kiss was passionate and it multiplied into many kisses. Sean's hand gingerly began touching her shoulder and then began pushing the robe off and onto the floor. They then slid down against the bed, wrapped in each other's arms. Both of them poured all of their tension and the stress of the previous two weeks into their lovemaking, quickly and satisfyingly exhausting themselves.

Later, and for the first time in a long while, Sean fell asleep feeling very relaxed, with Kim on his chest and his arm curled around her shoulders feeling the warmth of her bare skin radiate into his hand. It was a night with no nightmares.

Part Three

Hunt

Chapter Twenty-Four

Thursday, May 7
Denver

For the second time in both their lives, Kim and Sean arrived in Denver. This time they did so together. Also, for the first time, they flew there instead of driving. Sean slept hard for the whole flight, his head pressing against the window of the packed jet. This had surprised Kim. She had tried to replace Sean's usual vigilance by constantly looking around at suspicious looking people. The problem, she had noticed immediately, was that they were clearly on a commute flight with a plane full of men dressed in suits. So, they had all looked suspicious to her. Kim had eventually given up her vigilance and fallen asleep against Sean's shoulder, her hand happily resting on his arm.

After landing, they had taken a shuttle bus about three miles away from the massive tent-like Denver International Airport to the rental car area. Sean rented a car for a week. He explained to Kim that renting the car for a week, even if they only planned on a day or two in Denver, might help throw off the people who were trying to track them down. Kim had already figured that out though, and was pleased with herself when Sean confirmed her logic.

They were now driving the car, a gray economy model, towards the city of Denver. Kim had a map unfolded on her lap and was consulting it. A note pad was flipped open on top of the map.

"Okay, the cemetery is in the same southeastern area of Denver that

I visited last week," she said. She told Sean the name of the exit to take to skip going all the way into Denver. "We can drive down east of the metro area and probably miss the morning traffic jam."

"Sounds good," Sean grunted. "You know, there is something else I need to do soon."

"What's that?" Kim asked.

"Laundry," he said simply, smiling. "I left home more than two weeks ago. I've had hotel service do it twice, but I think going forward we are going to stick with motels and bed and breakfasts, staying only one night at a time. So, no laundry service will be available. I also think I need to do a little shopping.

"Yeah me too. I've been gone almost a week." Kim replied, laughing. "It's the little things that are the hardest to get done."

"Or we can just buy underwear and socks," Sean added. "It may sound crazy, but we'll spend more money and time doing laundry than you think."

"Is that what you learned in your special school?" Kim mocked. "How the professional spy stays sharply dressed for under ten dollars a day?"

Sean took his eyes off the road and looked at her through his sun glasses. "Don't laugh, believe it or not, I recall a class on dress, toiletries, and hygiene while going incognito."

Kim laughed again and then went back to studying the map. After a few minutes, they reached and took the exit she had indicated. She then navigated Sean to the cemetery. It was a large area, replete with a wrought iron fence that ran parallel to the street for several blocks. When they reached the end, Sean turned right, following the streets and the iron fence around the cemetery. Finally, he saw a building that appeared to be the administrative center and turned into the driveway. He parked the car in one of several available parking spaces.

They got out of the car and Kim could feel the cool, mid-morning mountain air gently blowing on her face. *Right off the Rockies,* she thought, looking up at the magnificent mountains rising up in the distance on the other side of the downtown area.

Sean reached into the car and grabbed his hardbound notebook. He then shut the door and locked up the car and looked around the cemetery.

"I don't like this place. The trees are old and pruned really high. We'll be visible if we come back tonight to dig up Jacob's grave if he turns out to be in this large flat area," he said. "Not to mention that digging up a grave has got to be really hard work and noisy, and it's going to take a while."

As they were walking towards the office, Sean continued. "We've also got to be careful not to give them our names. If they come in tomorrow and find a grave dug up, we don't want it to be tracked to us."

Kim began to feel queasy at the idea of digging up the grave of her great, great grandfather or grandmother. Up until now, she realized she had been ignoring the image of a moldy body resting in a casket. Essentially, her imagination had stopped at the point of staring at a tombstone and had not gone any further.

"Okay, I'll let you do the talking," she said, finally shaking off the gruesome images in her head.

"Yeah, that's a good idea. I'll act like he is my ancestor," Sean replied. "That'll make it harder still, for anyone to track down who might have dug up a grave."

They had reached the glass door of the sixties-era building. Sean pulled it open and entered, letting Kim follow behind him. Except for a four foot wide break that allowed people to enter the rear areas of the office, a wooden counter spanned the width of the room, wall-to-wall. On the left, a large color-coded map was posted on the wall. The cemetery was broken up into about ten sections, each with a color and a large letter associated with it. Sean looked at the map for a moment and then walked to the counter. Kim slid off to one side to look more closely at the map. She purposely tried to act disinterested, thinking it better if it seemed that this was Sean's family visit and she was just accompanying him.

"Hi," Sean said amiably. "Do you have information on grave locations? I'm trying to find the grave of a couple of ancestors."

A woman was sitting at her desk behind the counter focusing on a computer monitor. She had glanced up at Sean as he approached the counter, peering over her reading glasses. He sensed she was in her fifties. After a moment's scrutiny of Sean, she got up and approached the counter.

"Yes, in fact, it's fully automated," she said, gesturing at a computer sitting in a carrel on the wall to Sean's right. "You can search by name and date of death. There's a form there for you to jot down the location."

She pointed at the map on the wall. "Graves are identified by their section. They are designated by the large capital letters you see on that map. For newer sections, the map shows burial sites by number within that section. Here's a smaller version of the map."

The woman pulled a colored piece of paper out of a shelf under the counter and handed it to Sean.

"Thank you much ma'am," Sean replied, making his voice sound southern. He took the map, went over to the computer carrel and sat in the rigid wooden chair in front of it. A few minutes later he had found Jacob and Olivia Poole's burial plot. He jotted down its section and number. It surprised him that the location included a number after the letter since the woman had indicated that the newer sections were the ones with numbers. But because he did not want to draw attention to himself nor their site of interest, he decided not to ask the woman anything else.

"Okay, got it," he said to Kim who was watching over his shoulder. He stood up and together they left the office with Sean waving briefly to the woman. She did not bother to look up.

A few minutes later they were back driving in the car. Sean stopped in the middle of the section that they would be located. It was on a sloped area leading down to a gulley that bordered the western side of the cemetery. They got out of the car and Sean took a moment to scan the horizon in every direction.

"Perfect! I don't think anyone is even aware that we are here. Certainly, nobody is watching us."

"Well, let's go then," Kim said, sounding eager.

"Okay. It's section C, number 13," Sean announced, reading from his notes.

Kim studied the map in her hands and, after orienting herself, pointed out to the middle of a broad, smooth, lawn area containing only the type of headstones that were flush with the ground.

Sean frowned. "That can't be right. That's a new section."

Kim looked at Sean briefly, then out at the area, and then back down at her map. After a moment, she confirmed the location.

"No, section 13 is definitely right there." She started walking out into it. "Come on."

Sean followed her into the sloped, grassy area, reading headstones as he passed over them. They walked their way through the section, and a few minutes later, Kim called out, "Here it is!"

Sean trotted over to her. At her feet was a stone reading exactly what Kim had learned from a data base. Sean read it out loud, "Jacob Poole. Born 1848. Died 1901." Next to it was a stone for Olivia.

"Wow," Kim said, feeling a bit overwhelmed. "This is cool. These are my great, great grandparents."

Kim and Sean stood there in silence. Kim was staring at the headstones. Sean, though, was looking around and frowning. Finally, he broke the silence by clearing his throat and spoke, "This is cool. But I think we have a problem."

Kim looked up at him and he continued.

"I don't think they were originally buried here. I think they moved them here."

"What?" Kim asked, sounding startled. She looked around and then at Sean.

"Look at this section," Sean said waving his arm wide. "Everyone here died more than a hundred years ago, but every headstone is the same modern design."

"What are you saying?"

"I think they changed this part of the cemetery. Who knows why, it should not look so crisp and new."

Kim looked around and then back down at the headstones. "You don't know that. They might have just remodeled."

"No, I don't think they can do that," Sean replied.

Kim looked around and then lowered her shoulders in surrender. "So, how do we know these are really them?"

"We don't." Sean sighed. "I know how we find out. We go back and talk with the lady in the office. We need a story though."

He paused and looked around. His eyes locked in on the grave next to Jacob's plot.

"Let's give her this guy's name, Jeremy Moore. He died about the same time."

"I don't get it. They can't just move people around and rebury them." Kim was standing over Jacob's grave, her arms crossed. She certainly looked irritated. "So, if they moved them, does that mean we're wasting our time?"

"I don't know," Sean admitted. "I guess it depends on how and why they were moved. We don't really even know what we are looking for either. I've been thinking it's some letter or object buried with them. I was also hoping there would be some clue on the headstone, so maybe we would not have to dig either of them up."

He looked at Kim for a moment.

"Don't get down. Nothing is ever as easy as planned. Come on. Let's go see what we can find out from the lady."

Sean took her hand and half-pulled her away from her ancestors' grave. They walked back to the car.

.....

A few minutes later they were back in the office. Sean had explained to the lady that they were uncertain why the graves looked so new and so organized in that area. She immediately answered.

"Oh, well you see, we had a mudslide on that slope about fifteen years back." She paused and looked at them. Sean was certain she was trying to decide whether they would be difficult people to deal with or not, so he tried to look as casual and easygoing as he could. He must have passed her test because she continued.

"It was really kind of unpleasant. A lot of graves were exposed and some slid down, disintegrating." She looked about and lowered her voice, even though it was clear that they were the only people in the room. "Truthfully, I don't think we really know who was who in some cases. Those were old coffins and they had mostly come apart and gotten mixed up."

"You mean you don't know who is buried in my great, great grandfather's grave?" Kim suddenly blurted. "How can this be?"

The lady pulled back and a serious look came over her face. "I'm sorry ma'am. I just thought you should know."

Sean grabbed Kim around the shoulders and started turning her away from the lady. He could feel her tension, but she let him push and steer her towards the door.

"Thanks," he said over his shoulder. "We understand."

As soon as he got her outside he let go of her.

"Sorry, but the last thing we want to do is make a scene in there," he explained. "Let's get out of here and go think."

"I'm sorry," Kim said. "That was so irritating. Here I was staring at what I thought was my ancestors' graves only to find out it could be anybody."

"I understand. Do you want to go back over there?"

"No," Kim muttered. "I just want to be done with this whole thing and go back to being ordinary Kim, single mother and business owner."

Her voice tailed off as they reached the car. After piling in, Sean started up the car and they drove off in silence, each deep in their own thoughts.

Knoxville

James was cheerfully typing and clicking away on his keyboard in his campus office. He had spent the last several hours devouring a few history books about Atlanta and the Civil War, as well as making a list of several other books that he wanted to research. He had found more stories of Civil War treasures, including some Atlanta-based ones. He was enjoying the challenge in part because it was different than his usual scholarly work. Instead of preparing a paper rehashing many of the same old stories and themes of the Civil War, he was instead on the trail of something totally new to him. He also appreciated that it was helping him do something with all the anger he felt over Mary's death. In short, it was extremely therapeutic.

James was now searching the internet for other sources of information that could help him. One thing had become fairly clear. He needed to go to Richmond, Virginia, to a Civil War museum and library located there. It had the original, or copy of, nearly every book or record he could possibly want, including details about Sherman's campaign across the South. Better, an old colleague of his ran the place, so James was certain he could get first class treatment there. He had made a tentative plan to head to Richmond early Friday morning and work there through the weekend.

James was also interested in more unique resources. The Civil War fanatics and treasure hunters, he knew, could probably teach him more than he could ever learn through official records. *Somebody has probably re-enacted Sherman's siege of Atlanta and could walk me through every little known aspect of it,* he thought. He remembered seeing a re-enactment of a civil war battle in Virginia several years back. The soldiers had worn authentic looking uniforms and even ran around with guns dating back to the Civil War. He supposed that some of the guns had been replicas, but some certainly looked real. The battle had been planned to the smallest detail to replicate the actual battle that had occurred earlier in history. *That's what I need to do,* he thought, *re-create Sherman's campaign and the taking of Atlanta.*

His eyes caught a story posted on a webpage about a hunt for Civil War gold in North Carolina. He followed the link on the webpage and found himself at a website run by, what appeared to be, a Civil War treasure buff. The person's name was Kurt Cathey and he appeared to have devoted a substantial amount of his life to the topic of Civil War treasures. Intrigued, James clicked on a link that would allow him to send the person an email. He then typed out a short note explaining that he was interested in learning more about theories of treasure surrounding Atlanta and its capture. He then sent the email and returned to the webpage. James tried to learn more about the man's exploits, but they were hard to really decipher, so he left the site and returned to his core search.

He spent another half an hour exploring webpages, as well as notes. He was then satisfied that he had done enough along those lines and turned his attention to planning his Richmond trip. He needed to think through where his focus would be, once he was at the library. Taking a lesson from Sean, he decided to drive there and to also find an old hotel once he got there. The "spy stuff," as he called it, was partly amusing to him; at least until he thought of his sister. Then, it felt a little unnerving.

With most of his plans made, James decided to head down to the faculty technology office and see about getting a laptop to help him stay connected on the trip. He got up from his desk, put on his sport coat, and headed out of his office.

Atlanta

Terry had decided that it was time to do something. He was back in the brains room after taking a day off out at the mansion to somewhat unwind. He now had in front of him the latest credit card activity report. It showed that Sean Johnson had purchased two tickets, one way, from Nashville to Denver. Nashville had surprised him. He had seen the flights to Knoxville that the duo had taken from Dallas, but then nothing showed up at all until the tickets from Nashville to Denver. Terry closed his eyes and ran through the facts in his head.

They're traveling together. They went to Knoxville to meet with the professor. Then, they suddenly appear a few hundred miles west and fly to Denver, the same city where this Kim woman was last week.

It seemed obvious to Terry that something had happened. *Either they figured something out or they found something. But why Denver?*

It was also clear to Terry that Sean Johnson was now traveling more cautiously. *But then why telegraph the flight? He had to have known I would spot the tickets and know that they went to Denver. Is this a red herring? Is he trying to trick me, or does he truly not care?*

As Terry thought through the facts, he concluded that it was most likely that Sean simply did not care about his trackers knowing he was in Denver. He would, no doubt, stay entirely under the radar screen and be invisible once there. For that reason, Terry suppressed the urge to send a team to Denver. He knew it would most likely be a waste of time and effort. It could also result in the exposure of yet another team.

But that left him in a quandary. His options were limited and he could not just sit back while Kim and Sean deciphered the mystery. *What should I do? Is it worthwhile tailing the professor? Is he worth interrogating?* Terry asked himself those questions and then worked through an analysis of the professor's role. As with Kim and Sean, he decided not to send a team to Knoxville. Instead, he concluded that what he really needed was control over them.

That was when the perfect idea struck him. *Of course! Nothing better to play off of than a mother's love of her daughter.* He needed to strike some fear into the Kansas City woman. Better, he needed to control her and force her to come to him. That meant using her daughter, Abigail as the bait. Terry also suspected that he knew exactly where the daughter was. *Why else would they show up in Dallas?* Satisfied that he had a plan, he knew he needed to fly it by his brother. He picked up the phone and called him on his cell. In a few moments, Michael answered. Terry summarized the latest intelligence report and then made his proposal.

"Kidnap her?" Michael had asked him. "That's a high risk operation."

"Look," Terry explained. "We don't have any other choice. Sean Johnson is too difficult and too dangerous to tail or track. I'm certain they've figured something out. They could be on the verge of figuring it all out. We need an insurance policy. The professor may not do us any good at all. The girl is perfect!"

Terry had noticed that Michael had not seemed that upset at the idea of kidnapping, so he continued.

"It will force them to come to us with whatever they find. We can terminate their entire exploration and gain all of their intelligence by doing just one thing."

There was silence before Michael responded.

"Okay," he said. "But this has got to be done perfectly. No screw ups. This will also mark the point of no return, brother."

Michael paused and thought for a moment. "Are we using a team to do this?"

"I'm not sure," Terry admitted. "I would need to have the girl transferred to me to be useful, and this type of a crime would be highly visible. I think it needs to be a personal effort. That way there won't be anyone left alive that knows what happened.

After a pause, Michael agreed.

Phoenix

Alan was also studying the credit card activity report and fuming. He was more certain than ever, that there was something enormous at stake. But his trips to Denver and Kansas City had been thwarted and had been an absolute waste of time. Kim and Sean were making a fool of him. He also sensed that there was someone else involved.

Alan slammed his fist on his desk. *They're back in Denver! No more mister nice guy!* He took a deep breath and looked around him. He had closed his office door, so nobody had noticed his outburst. After taking a moment and calming himself, he came up with a plan of attack. He would go back to Denver, but this time he would find them and get some answers. He would also now go fully private on the case. *Whatever this is, I deserve it. If it really is a treasure, well then, what the Bureau doesn't know won't hurt them.*

Alan got back to work on his computer. First, he changed the status of Mary Fester's murder investigation to "terminated." That meant it would roll back to the local cops and was no longer an FBI matter. Next, using a fictitious name, he created a new investigation file. He restricted all access to the file except for those with the special code he had created. Alan knew that would keep the file inaccessible until he closed it later. In the meantime, he could use it as the purpose to continue his surveillance of the people and events of interest. It would also let him travel and move about without anybody really being able to scrutinize him and his whereabouts.

Satisfied, he began arranging his travel plans. *Time to go back to Denver,* he thought, as he smiled grimly.

Denver

Kim was rapping her fingers on the small table in their hotel room. Sean was seated across from her. Various files and documents were strewn across the table and the bed behind them. Kim considered how pathetic the situation really was for them.

I'm in a seedy hotel room, in a strange city, with my hot and handsome new lover. But am I actually using the bed for its more romantic purposes? No! Instead we're sitting around going through documents, trying to find a secret clue that we missed. I'm pathetic!

The room was actually not as seedy as she had thought it was going to be when Sean had pulled the car into the parking lot. But, it also was not luxurious either. It was fairly clean though, and Sean had been satisfied that their presence would not be noted by whoever was trying to track them. Kim watched as Sean picked up another pile of papers and began sorting through them.

"I think we're wasting our time," she finally said. "We've gone through this stuff fifty times in the last five days."

Sean looked up at her and then sighed.

"Maybe you're right. I just cannot escape the feeling that we've missed something." Sean put the pages down and looked up at the ceiling, his eyes noticing the popcorn coating stained with years of smoke and who knew what else. "Jacob was smart. He left clues and warnings in place to get us to this point. But he had to have known that burying…"

Sean's voice stopped and he dropped his eyes down from the ceiling and looked straight at Kim. She immediately knew that he had thought of something.

"What's wrong?" she said excitedly. A small smile crept over Sean's face.

"I think we were on the wrong track," he said simply.

"What are you talking about?"

"Try this. Something was buried in Jacob's grave right?"

"Right," Kim said slowly sounding slightly irritated.

"And we think it was probably lost or destroyed when his grave went downhill in the mud, right?"

"Right. What are you getting at?"

"Bear with me. And we have no idea where he or Olivia is actually buried, right?"

"Right." Kim's voice was showing irritation.

"So, we're left with his house, which seems unlikely."

"Yes, yes, now tell me where you're going with this."

Sean smiled more fully. "We asked ourselves the question that if it had been buried with him how did it get there right?"

"Well, he buried…" Kim stopped speaking as it struck her. *Of course, he could not bury it with himself, he was dead. So someone else had to have put it there. But who?*

Sean interrupted her train of thought.

"So, if he's dead, and he did not put it in his wife's grave a decade earlier, who did he trust to put something in his grave."

Kim looked at him, trying to think of who was left. "It wouldn't be his son right? He was trying to hide it from his son, at least for a while."

It was Sean's turn to agree.

"Right. So, who does that leave?"

Kim suddenly knew where Sean was leading her. "The witness guy? What was his name?"

"Exactly. He was David Haggard, a doctor."

Kim was shuffling papers around on the table. She finally found the file. "Here it is."

She flipped it open and spoke as she went through it. "He was a doctor. His father was John Haggard, a doctor also, who is famous because David donated his father's estate as a museum and park." She looked up suddenly.

"Is that where you are going with this?" she demanded.

Sean held his hands up. "I'm not sure where we're going. I just felt that Jacob had to have planned something better than a gravesite in a cemetery. We would have to assume though, that there is some connection between the Haggards and Jacob."

Kim suddenly smiled back at him. "There is." She handed the file to him pointing at a spot on a page. "Look there."

Sean took the file and looked at it. She was pointing at a summary of the museum. It was Kim's turn to tease Sean.

"So, what do you see?"

"Let's see, description of the museum, history, etcetera."

"What else do you see?" Kim was truly enjoying turning the tables back against Sean.

"The address, its size, when it was built..." Sean looked at her. "What?"

Kim pointed at the page again. "Look more closely at the address," she said quietly.

Sean did and then it struck him.

"1905 Sherman Street?"

"Yes. That's it, but maybe not for the reason you're thinking, that it's Sherman's name."

"Then for what reason."

"Because..." Kim said pausing to savor the moment. "I've seen that address before. It's the address listed on one of the census reports."

Sean looked at her, stunned. She continued.

"There's more.That census lists his occupation as a groundskeeper."

A light bulb finally went off in Sean's head.

"You think he tended what is now a museum and hid his secret there somewhere?"

"Yes," Kim said calmly.

Sean stared back at her and together they studied each other's faces as they each digested their new ideas. Gradually, their expressions went from ones of consternation to smiles. Sean finally spoke.

"Okay, so we need to know more about John Haggard and the museum. When did John die? Before or after Jacob?" His questions were rhetorical though, as he was now studying the file Kim had handed him while looking for answers. Kim had also printed the museum website pages and he dug through those too.

"Says here that John died in 1890, that's eleven years before Jacob." Sean stopped reading and looked up. "Of course."

"What?" Kim demanded. She stood up and walked around the table. She then leaned over Sean, placing her hand on his shoulder. She could feel herself getting distracted by the close, physical proximity of Sean's torso. But, she willed herself away from such thoughts and focused on the page he was holding. She read it for a few moments."

"Final home," Sean said simply. "But not Jacob's. No digging either. It all makes sense. Doesn't it?"

Kim sat on the arm of the chair next to Sean.

"Yes. If he really was the groundskeeper he would have had free range of the estate. He could have easily planted something in the home later. He wrote the letters and the will eight years later. He would have had plenty of time to think through his plan for placing clues and riddles."

"We need to visit a museum," Sean added.

Chapter Twenty-Five

"Well, it's definitely a beautiful place," Sean remarked, as he parked the car on the street outside the museum and estate.

The street was shaded by massive ash trees with roots that were pushing at the sidewalk, as well as the roadway. An eight foot high stone wall ran the length of the block, past their car. It was interrupted only by an iron gate that provided the entrance to the museum. The gates were open and Sean had parked the car just past the entrance along the street next to the stone wall. The combination of the old trees and the stone wall created an ambiance of old elegance that Sean expected to find more in upstate New York or thereabouts.

"Mmm hmm," Kim mumbled as she studied a map of the museum she had printed out the night before. "It takes up half a block. Looks like there is a servant's entrance located off of the alley in the back."

"Let's go in the normal way and be tourists," Sean said smiling. He reached his hand over and placed it on hers for a moment. Kim looked up from the map and smiled at him.

"I'll be good this time. No blowing our cover," she said.

"I know," Sean replied. "I just felt like touching you."

They got out of the car and joined up together on the sidewalk. Sean ran his hands across the stones in the wall.

"These are massive stones. It's old. This wall must be original and yet it barely shows its age."

"The Haggard's were pretty rich," Kim replied. "If you had paid more attention to my lecture last night and less attention to me, you might have remembered that."

"Every spy needs to take a break." Sean smiled. "I don't remember you complaining."

"Hey, I'm just trying to keep you focused."

Kim laughed at her own joke, but noticed that Sean had slipped into his "spy" mode and had barely heard what she said. He was scanning the streets, the cars, even the windows in the building across the street. It took him about 30 seconds, she guessed. *Probably just memorized the plates on every car on this street.*

Sean seemed satisfied that all was well. He glanced at Kim with a smile and they started walking towards the entrance.

"So, nothing weird?" Kim inquired.

"Nope, though that's not exactly what I was looking for."

"So what then?"

Sean glanced at her. "I was really just doing an inventory. If things go wrong, or even as a way to know when they have gone wrong, you have to know what your surroundings are like. If we had to come running back out here, I would have a better chance of spotting new cars or other changes. I could also tell you that we could enter that tan building across the street and probably exit at the back."

Kim shook her head. "You're weird. I'd love to become as good as you at all this stuff, but I think it's way beyond me."

"Trust me, you really don't want to. I spent the last decade or so trying to forget all of it." Sean shrugged his shoulders. "I guess it's like riding a bike. You never forget."

They reached the entrance in the stone wall and turned to enter. There was a small parking area right next to a tall and elegant home. It was white with tan trim and stood three stories high. The wood detail and patterns showed it to be an old house, clearly from the 1800's. The whole area around the home, along the walls and throughout the grounds, was lusciously landscaped. Tall trees, more ash mixed in with some oak, hung over the house and yard creating a shady, cool area on the grounds where all sorts of green and flowering plants were growing. The house retained an estate-like feel to it, while officially looking like a museum. Directly in front of them, what had probably once been a side room was now a modern looking museum entrance.

Kim paused and looked around at the foliage, "So, my great, great grandfather, Jacob, was the groundskeeper here," she murmured. "This was his work." She swept her arms widely, encompassing the whole area.

"A few of these oak trees look well over a hundred years old," Sean replied. "He must have cared for them, maybe even planted them."

Kim took a deep breath. "It's overwhelming, like a piece of me is here that I am only now finding."

"I can understand that. But let's keep our cool here, right?" Sean looked at her and reached out to hold her hand again.

Kim looked at him and smiled. "Yes. I'm okay."

They held hands as they crossed the paved area and entered the museum. They found themselves in a large atrium. A high counter with brochures and various magazines sat along the wall to their left. To the right, lay an entrance to the house itself. In front of them, sat a low glass top counter, fronted by white, painted wood. The walls were painted white as well. Two women sat behind the counter. One, an elderly lady with white hair, looked up and smiled at them.

"Hello and welcome to the Haggard Museum," she announced.

Sean replied and quickly engaged her in a friendly conversation. He wound up paying for two admissions. The lady provided him with a pamphlet and Sean and Kim set out on a self-guided tour.

They crossed the doorway and entered the first room, a large sitting room. A red carpet led through the room and velvet ropes along each side made it clear that staying on the path was expected. Kim glanced at the brochure, looked up, and then looked back down at the brochure to read.

"Dr. Haggard entertained guests here," she announced in a lecture-like voice. "The furniture is not original, but is from the same period and typical of what you would have found had you been a guest of Mr. Haggard." Kim glanced at Sean and found him staring up at the ceiling, running his eyes from one corner to another. They then ran down to the floor. He looked over at Kim.

"I think the building has been massively rebuilt," he said. "It looks so crisp and new."

"Yes, recall I told you that the museum re-opened a few years ago after a long and intensive remodel." Kim had shifted to her mother-like, scolding voice.

"Right, but it's really becoming clear. So much work makes it hard to believe there would be anything hidden that would not have been found."

Kim had nothing to say in reply and after a few moments, they moved into the next room. Their pattern continued. Kim read a bit from the brochure and then they moved to the next room. The path led upstairs, through a few bedrooms and then back down to a study at the back of the home.

Kim continued her reading. "Dr. Haggard wrote letters and also maintained his records in this room. It says here that the desk is original."

Sean perked up a bit and glanced around the room. Seeing no one, he nimbly stepped over the velvet rope and to the desk. Going around it, he began opening the drawers.

"Sean!" Kim said, louder than she wanted. She began glancing back towards the entrance and out the windows behind Sean where more manicured lawns and plants surrounded a rear courtyard.

"What?" Sean replied. "I'll be fast. Just keep an eye out for anybody."

Sean did not even look up as he continued opening drawers and examining the desk. Kim started to utter a protest and then thought the better of it and stood on the carpeted aisle glancing about. Sean seemed to be inside the ropes for an eternity, but eventually he finished his searching and hopped back over the rope after closing the last drawer.

"See anything interesting?"

"Nope. Worse, the desk looks like it was restored as well. But, I'm not sure I could find a secret compartment, even if there was one." Sean sounded dejected. "I feel like we are fumbling about, not really getting anywhere."

"Yeah, I feel the same way," Kim replied. "We are also not even seeing half of the building. I bet there is a basement and an attic."

"I don't think it matters. This building was clearly overhauled."

"Just like the cemetery then," Kim was beginning to feel Sean's gloom. "Even if Jacob left a clue, it's probably been lost or destroyed."

Kim noticed Sean flinch a tiny bit at her words, something about him she had become more perceptive of since spending so much time with him. Sean rarely gave away his reactions with his eyes, nor did he often give his thoughts away with obvious body language. He had this habit, she had found, however, of slightly shrugging the muscles at the base of his neck when he had suddenly shifted this thinking. Kim had thought about telling Sean of her discovery, but then decided it was better to keep her secret to herself. She waited for a moment as he stood in thought, and then she began slowly walking towards the exit, a large door that led out to the courtyard in the rear. As she reached the door, Sean finally spoke.

"It's the same issue. Either Jacob was smart enough to anticipate the risk of his clues being destroyed or he wasn't. Everything we have found so far shows him to have been very savvy and extremely careful. So, just like we realized that he would never have put something in a grave, and could not have put something in his own grave, he had to have been smart here as well. We came here because the clues he left pointed to Haggard and this home. His role here makes it clear that this is the place. So, we need to think better than him and definitely better than ourselves. Where would he have put something he wanted to stay safe for a long time?"

As Sean spoke, Kim had turned to watch him. He looked determined, but he also seemed to have no idea what to do next. Kim looked about the room. They had seen all the main rooms.

"Well, I cannot imagine him leaving something outside, despite the fact that he was the groundskeeper. Nothing outside would be as safe as inside, and certainly not survive a long time."

"How long do you think he imagined his secret would stay hidden?" Sean inquired. He asked it more to the room itself than he did to Kim, but she answered it anyway.

"I think his words suggest he knew it might be generations."

"But Lincoln was dead, the Civil War was long over," he objected.

"Sure, but if that was all that needed to happen then he could have brought it forward himself," Kim fired back. The room they were in had high ceilings and was large enough that their voices had a bit of an echo to them. "The very fact that thirty years had passed and he felt compelled to hide his information in layers of secrets tells us that he had to have been thinking it might be thirty or more years."

Sean had turned to look at Kim as she spoke. His face went from seriousness to containing a light smile.

"You're right. You would have made a great professor."

"Sure, but right now we're both amateur sleuths and we need to figure this out." Kim felt frustrated. "Or at least I do."

"No, I'm in this until the end, Kim." Sean paused and smiled just a bit more slyly. "And maybe longer."

"Really, Mr. Johnson?" Kim said loudly and mockingly. "And what makes you so certain you would be welcome around here once this mess is cleaned up?"

"Just a feeling."

"Well, keep your feelings under control then." Kim shifted to a lecture-like voice. "Right now, face it, we're stuck!" She looked about, feeling a warmth inside that told her she felt as Sean did, but she also felt a coldness stemming from their failure to figure out where to look, or what to look for to solve the mystery.

"Yes we are," Sean admitted, feeling his own frustration. "This certainly felt like the place we were supposed to go, but I don't think we were ready. We could spend weeks tearing this place apart and not find anything. And besides, something else tells me that our Jacob would not have entrusted his secrets to a mere wooden house. He was too meticulous."

"Okay then, what's next?" Kim asked.

"We go back and think things through again," Sean said grimly. "We just keep throwing our brains at this."

Sean walked over to Kim and took her hand and they walked out the exit to the courtyard.

Richmond, Virginia

James walked across the aged wooden floor. It was polished and had obviously been restored, but that just helped it show its age even better. It had a dark color and was speckled everywhere by even darker spots where something had gouged or scarred the wood years earlier. James recalled that the building had once been a market and storage place, built before the Civil War. It had held offices of the Confederacy during the war. *The wood is very old and many people have walked across it. Probably Jefferson Davis himself.*

James was in the Civil War museum in Richmond, Virginia. He'd been driving since very early in the morning to reach this place before they shut down for the weekend and was relieved to have made it with plenty of time to spare. Besides noticing the floor, James also felt the refreshing cool air in the building wash over him. Just from walking from his parking spot to the building, a walk of only two blocks, he had worked up a sweat. His heavy tan sport coat probably did not help much, but he had hardly ever felt the need to wear a summer suit coat this early in May.

James reached his destination, a counter on the far side of the building from the entrance. He was in a wide, but deep, entry room. The walls between which he had just walked were coated with framed portraits and photographs from the Civil War. The counter at the end had a computer monitor sitting atop it with a young man with short hair sitting behind it. Behind him, above a doorway, loomed a large painting of a Civil War scene. James identified it instantly of the burning of Atlanta. *How appropriate*, he thought, *for my visit.*

The young man behind the counter glanced up at him and then tried to discreetly look at his computer, clearly looking to see the time. *He was hoping he would have no more visitors today.*

The young man spoke first.

"Hi, can I help you?" His voice was polite and helpful, showing no signs of being disappointed at having a late Friday visitor.

"I think so," James replied. "Professor Enloe here to see my old friend, Butch Jones."

The man's face shifted slightly and he stood up sharply.

"Oh Professor, Mr. Jones told me you might visit today. One moment while I get him."

The young man then spun around and walked out of the room, under the painting of Atlanta burning. James watched him turn right and disappear into a hallway and then turned his attention back to his surroundings. He had not been here for probably ten years. The place appeared in much better condition, something James took to be a sign of good times for Butch and his museum. James set his briefcase down at the foot of the counter and began walking back along the hall, staring at the portraits. He did not get past the first one, a picture of a gaunt, young confederate soldier staring at the camera, when he heard footsteps behind the counter. He turned to see a wiry man, somewhere in his seventies, with thinning gray hair. He had a big smile on his face.

"James, James," he exclaimed, walking around the counter. "I hung around here late just hoping to see you."

"Well, here I am," James replied. "Older, fatter, but still kicking."

James took a step towards Butch, and they shook hands firmly, both smiling.

"Come on back to my office," Butch gestured towards the rear doorway.

His drawl made the word "office", sound more like "orifice" and James chuckled. "You still sound like the South Carolinian that you were when you taught me a few decades ago."

"That's nothing. You should hear my sister talking." At the word sister, James shuddered, suddenly remembering why he was here. Butch must have noticed, because he looked at James briefly and spoke.

"Did I say something wrong?"

"No, just something familiar," James took on a serious tone. "I'll tell you more in your office. I am here with a purpose."

"Okay, okay," Butch smiled. "Come on old friend." Before James could do it himself, Butch picked up the professor's briefcase. James was happy to see that Butch showed no signs of his age, easily hefting the thick, stuffed bag. He did comment though.

"What do you have in here, James, a whole library?"

"Something like that," James said, chuckling again.

A few minutes later they were sitting comfortably in Butch's office. Like the entrance, the office was also tastefully remodeled with more Civil War paintings and photos surrounding James. Butch had gotten them both glasses of water and James took several large swallows, feeling himself finally cooling down.

"So, what brings you to town?" Butch inquired.

James had thought carefully on the drive over from Knoxville just what he should and should not say. He drew the line at lying to his old friend, but he also knew he had to keep him somewhat in the dark, perhaps more for his own protection than for reasons that benefited James.

"As I mentioned, I'm conducting urgent research for a team investigating a story about Sherman's march to the sea. It's a personal family issue, but it's incredibly urgent. I'd like to work through this weekend, researching in your archives."

James had given his story with a straight face, in part because it was not a false statement. However, he could tell from the look on Butch's face that he was not buying the explanation.

"Look James, don't give me a song and dance," he began, looking mildly offended. "I can smell government cover up a mile away. Some spook in D.C. wrote that script for you. Am I right?"

James sighed. "Look, you're a good friend. You know me. I'm never going to lie to you. You are right to be suspicious of my story. It's the stuff I'm not telling you that makes it misleading. Trust me, Butch, I have very good reasons. You'll find out later. I'll personally tell you."

Butch looked at James for a long moment, then broke into a grin. "Just promise me you're not off on some fool's treasure hunt and I'm fine."

James barely concealed his surprise. *What's Butch know about treasure?* He could feel his suspicions rising.

"You get many of those these days do you?"

"Yeah, and they are all fairly nutty," Butch replied. "You on the other hand, are a genuine scholar, though you're a bit out of your normal topic."

"Well, actually," James jumped in, happy to have the topic off of treasure hunts, "it connects to Lincoln."

James smiled at his friend and Butch grinned again. James could see that Butch's teeth had become perfect in his old age. *Dentures! Butch is wearing dentures!*

Butch stood up. Come on, let me show you the office I have for you and then show you around the museum. It's changed a lot since you were last here. I've got to get a key and pass code for the alarm for you as well. Then, once we have you settled in, tell me you will at least take the time to enjoy dinner with me. Yes?"

James had stood up while Butch was talking. "That's a deal. I drove through lunch, so I'm starving."

Denver

Sean pushed himself up from the chair where he had been sitting. Kim remained seated, across the bed from Sean. Laying on the sheets, were various stacks of papers. Sean walked over to the desk where his laptop sat plugged-in and online. He sat down heavily in the desk chair and sighed, staring at the fuzzy art painting on the wall.

"We're not getting anywhere," he said, more to the painting on the wall than to either himself or Kim.

He stared at the painting for a few more moments. Kim waited patiently, mostly because she had nothing to say. They had spent the last few hours going through the documents and the clues, trying to figure out what they might have missed.

Sean spun around in the chair. "Let's go through it again."

Kim paused, always amazed at how quickly Sean could find a burst of energy and start anew as if nothing had been dragging him down.

"Okay," she finally said. "Let's see. We have a note left by Jacob Thomas, only I knew him as Jacob Poole. He apparently came to Denver after the Civil War. He lived out his latter years working for a prominent doctor named Haggard. Jacob's note tells us to look closely at his words. We find, in his will and in a series of letters, two coded messages that suggest he hid some secrets about the Civil War, Atlanta and treasure. We suspected his grave, but it was destroyed or washed out in a mud slide. We refused to accept that he would have been dumb enough to bury it in the ground, so we turned to the man for whom he worked and the grounds he cared for. But they're enormous and it would be like looking for a needle in a haystack."

Kim stopped her monologue because Sean's eyes had taken a sudden squint.

"What?" she demanded looking right back at his stare.

"We did not ignore Jacob's grave simply because we thought he would be too smart to put something underground. We gave up because he could not bury something with himself."

"Okay, smarty pants, thanks for correcting me.k" Kim smiled. "As I was saying…" But Kim stopped again as Sean's stare continued and a grin began to form on his face.

"Kim, what if we had the right idea about a grave, but the wrong person?"

"Huh?" she replied, her brain trying to think of who Sean was thinking of. "Not him, not Olivia, then John Haggard?"

Sean nodded. "Yes, he died when?"

Kim sat for a moment and then leaned forward and pulled a stack of papers from on top of the pillow. "Let's see, 1890." She looked back up at Sean.

"You don't think…"

"Sure! He was Mr. Haggard's close friend, groundskeeper and what sounds like, almost a butler. Haggard died before him, sufficiently before him that Jacob could have had lots of time to figure out how to leave clues."

"But then we're back to the question of being buried underground."

"That might be true, but I don't think so."

"Okay, I'm lost. Was Haggard buried in the 1800's version of a watertight coffin?"

"Not exactly," Sean smiled, and then shook his head. "Actually I am guessing now, but I noticed something that I think you did not."

"Sean, just tell me okay?" Kim pleaded, feeling her excitement and impatience threatening to take over her emotions.

"When we left the Haggard Museum earlier, I saw a crypt. Actually, I did not think of it at the time as a crypt. I was just noting the structures in the backyard."

At the word crypt, Kim's brain started racing through the implications. "If Haggard were buried there, then Jacob might have had plenty of access later, long after the burial. He could have placed a clue, or anything really, at any point."

Sean smiled, "Exactly. So, is that Haggard's burial crypt?"

"It has to be," Kim muttered as she grabbed a folded up map of the museum. Unfolding it, she laid it on the bed, on top of the various stacks of paper. A smaller map of the exterior areas was in the bottom right hand corner. Within that map, she quickly spotted the structure that had to be the one Sean had noticed.

"Number eighteen," she muttered, quickly running her hand down the index. It froze next to the number 18 on the map.

She looked up at Sean. "Mausoleum," she announced happily. "But it does not say who is in it. Hold on."

Sean watched her as she looked around the bed and found a file. Her hair was bouncing on the top of her head and she had regained her energy and enthusiasm.

"Here it is," she said. "Copies from a book on Denver's old buildings and homes." She began thumbing through it while Sean waited patiently, deep in his own thoughts.

After a couple of minutes, Kim found what she was looking for.

"Yep, it's him. John Haggard is resting there." She looked up at Sean. "Do you think...?" She let her voice drift off, not wanting to put words to her new found hope.

Sean had been deep in thought, as if in a trance, but he lowered his eyes from the ceiling and looked at her.

"I do. It makes sense, total sense. It's above ground. It's the structure that is never touched. Jacob himself probably had a hand in building it, so he would have known how well it was built. He had plenty of time to recognize the opportunity and plan for it. That must be it. And it's a 'final home' as per Jacob's own words."

"Or his own clues anyway. However, that begs the question of what to do?" He glanced at his watch. "It's four o'clock, and it's not like we can simply walk in there and ask to see the body."

Sean grimly looked at Kim.

"Oh no," Kim said, shaking her head. "We are not going grave robbing. Sean, this crazy quest has taken me to a few places and made me do a few strange things, but I'm not going to break into a museum and then into a crypt and then rifle a dead body."

Sean smiled at her. "You're right. You never asked for that. I'll take care of it."

He stood up. "Just stay here and wait for me. I should be back by two or three in the morning."

Kim leapt up herself. "Oh no. You are not going alone. If it has to be done, then I'm going with you."

"I thought you just said there was no way you were going grave robbing."

Kim looked at Sean for a moment.

"Damn," she exclaimed. "You walked me into that. Okay, you win. We're going grave robbing." She looked around the room.

"But there's one problem."

"What's that?" Sean looked over at her, slightly alarmed.

"I don't have any tools," Kim said laughing. "Gotcha!"

They stood there for a moment looking at each other and laughing. They could both feel an exhilaration, but for Kim it was tempered by a sense of foreboding about what she was getting herself involved in. *This is really it. There's no turning back now.*

Sean glanced at his watch again. Kim could practically see his mental gears clicking away.

"Okay, it's Friday. That's good. The place should empty out quickly. It's also four o'clock. That's bad. We need to hit a hardware store, or better, a home improvement store. We need to dress like we are working on a home project, but bring along dark clothes that we can change into later. We'll catch a nap after we shop and do a recon of the place."

Sean paused and looked at Kim. His lips pursed and he almost looked like he was going to pout.

"What now? Am I sounding like a spy again?"

Kim struggled to suppress her laugh. "Recon?" she said in a mocking voice. "As in reconnaissance? Nap? You think I'm going to be able to sleep while waiting to break into a crypt? I think I'm beginning to really like you, but sometimes you are so funny."

Sean laughed at her. "Laugh now. You'll wish you had napped by the time we get in at five or six in the morning."

Chapter Twenty-Six

Dallas

Terry was once again in his element. Darkness had descended on the neighborhood and he was sitting in an auto parts delivery van parked along a residential street. He was shaded from the street light by a large locust tree looming over the van. *The situation's good,* he thought.

He had stolen the van to help cover his trail. He would switch over to his rental car, thus ensuring that, even if his vehicle was noticed here at the scene, it would not lead to him. He had flown to Dallas in a small jet under a false name on a ticket paid for by an offshore slush fund buried beneath layers of secret records. His rental car was even rented under the fake name. *Zero traceability, that's the name of the game,* he thought grimly.

As Terry sat alone in the van in the dark, he focused himself on his plans. He knew that kidnapping someone was probably the most risky operation he would ever accomplish. Killing someone could be quick and silent. Breaking into an empty home or building was also easy and relatively safe. However, taking a person out of a house against their will, that was something else entirely. Too many things could go wrong or differently than expected. *You can't plan for everything,* he reminded himself. *All you can do is be prepared for anything.* He searched his memory to try and remember where he had learned that. After tracing his way through his past, he concluded it had been from a counter-intelligence agent that his company had hired for operations in

Asia. Terry had spent two entire months with him, learning many new skills and techniques for times like these.

Terry shook his head briefly, as if to shake off his reverie. He knew he had to stay alert and ready. The girl was most likely not home. He was even more certain that the father was not home. The house was dark and had not shown any signs of activity for nearly an hour. It was getting late enough that he would soon have to leave and come back in the middle of the night. That would create new uncertainties. It was never easy entering an occupied home, especially when he would have no idea of the situation inside the house. He could not stay in this location forever. Every minute he sat parked curbside increased the chances that someone would notice and remember too much.

Fortunately, the father did not live on a cul-de-sac or court so there was a decent amount of regular traffic. Terry knew this meant that the residents would not be suspicious of activities on their street. That was good, but it also meant that there were more people to drive by and perhaps notice something. Terry also knew that, while his stolen van would help protect him, every clue that might get put together after-the-fact could undermine even the best protective steps. So, the more cars that passed by, the worse his chances.

He tensed slightly as headlights turned onto the street from behind him. He kept his head down, knowing that the bill of the hat he had on and the lowered angle of his head would ensure that no one would notice any of his features. The brightness of the headlights grew, and then the car passed. Terry watched the red taillights until they turned at the next intersection.

Relaxing slightly, he allowed himself to look at his watch. It was eight-thirty at night. He decided he could only allow himself another fifteen minutes. Then, he would have to leave and return much later and in a different vehicle. He looked up slightly as a car turned onto the street in front of him. Its speed and lack of caution suggested to Terry a teenage driver was in control. Terry's intuition was rewarded as the vehicle stopped in front of the house he was so closely watching. Inside, he could see a teenage girl, the driver, saying good bye to her passenger, another girl who matched the description of his target. *Abigail Wilcox, you have finally come home.*

The girls finished their good-byes and the car pulled forward while Abigail started walking up towards the front door. Again, Terry lowered his head enough to ensure his facial features were hidden. The car roared by him, the girl driving like a stereotypical teen. The moment it was past him, he looked back up towards the house. Abigail appeared to be unlocking the front door. Terry noted that her hand never strayed from the door knob itself, which meant that there was probably no separate deadlock and was probably an easy door to pick. He should be able to execute a quick and damage free entry at the front door. He slid his hand down the column to the ignition where he had inserted a special tool that replaced the usual key.

As soon as the door closed behind the girl, he started the van. He noted the time on his wristwatch and slid the gear selector on the steering column to drive and eased forward with his headlights off. He glanced at the homes on both sides as he drove, knowing that if anyone saw his vehicle out their windows he would look very suspicious. He saw no one, however, and shortly had pulled the van up to the curb and between his target house and the house next to it. He stopped the van there, knowing it was facing the wrong way, but also knowing that he would be there for only a few minutes. He sat for a moment in the seat, scanning his mirrors and windows for any activity. He saw none and knew it was time.

.....

Inside, Abby had set her bag down on her bed and then headed to the bathroom. As she sat there relieving herself, she thought again about the weirdness of the last few weeks. Her mom was running around with a reporter trying to find some family secrets and had dumped her to stay with her father. He had proceeded to almost immediately ignore her, letting her do as she pleased. Tonight, she suspected, he would probably visit his girlfriend and get home in the middle of the night. She was missing class and her friends back home, but she had managed to reconnect with a girl she had met the summer before. She was a year older than Abby, but very cool and extremely fun. She knew her mom would never approve, but she had given up worrying about what her mom might think. *Especially, when she's obviously not worrying about me anyway!*

Finishing her bathroom business, she left the room and headed to the kitchen. *One thing cool about dad,* she thought, *his kitchen is always well-stocked.* She exited the long hallway, turning right into the kitchen, hitting the light switch as she entered. Abby made a beeline for the fridge and bent down as she opened it. She had just finished lifting a can of soda from the bottom shelf when she felt her back bump into something. Instinctively, she half turned as she continued to stand back up. Before she could even get her body turned slightly, her head was suddenly pulled back sharply. A spasm of pain from her scalp told her that her hair was being yanked down viciously, confusing her. She was trying to figure out how she could have caught her hair in the refrigerator door so painfully, when suddenly a voice hissed in her ear.

"Don't make a sound and you won't get hurt. Don't make a move either." The voice practically spat in her ear and she could feel warm breath on the skin of her neck. Her head was pulled down hard, canting to one side and she instinctively reached behind her with her free hand. Before she could move it far though, an arm flew over her head and caught her neck in the crook of its elbow. She saw a gun flash by as the arm came over her and realized that the bump she had felt in her back had been the barrel of a gun. Abby's whole body froze with fear as she felt her body tensing.

Just as quickly though, she was lifted backwards and off her feet by the arm pinning her neck against the intruder behind her. He whispered again.

"I said don't move. Don't move at all!" He paused and then said in a less menacing voice. "Try not to panic. You will be okay, as long as you do as I say. Understood?"

Abby tried to nod her head but it was pinned so badly she could barely move it. So, instead, she tried to speak.

"Okay, okay," she stammered.

She felt her body being gently lowered back onto her feet as the pressure on her neck began to somewhat relax.

"Put your hands behind you," the man commanded her. Abby had still not even seen the man's face, but did as she was told. Quickly, she felt metal bars clamping down on her wrists by the hand that had been pulling painfully on her hair. The man was strong and quick. *Handcuffs! What's going on?* She involuntarily released the soda that she had been clutching and it fell down onto the linoleum where it bounced without rupturing. Her mind raced to try and keep up with the sequence of events, but she mostly felt a cold panic coming over her. The man jerked down on the handcuffs checking that they were secure and then just as firmly spun her around to face him. She found herself staring at an olive skinned man in a dark suit and black ball cap. His eyes were dark as well and they piercingly stared at her, sending cold chills down her spine.

"Abigail, I am not here to harm you and as long as you cooperate, you'll be fine," the man spoke smoothly, as if he did this all the time. "Don't speak unless spoken to."

Abby lowered her eyes and noticed a black hand gun in one of the man's hands. It was lowered, pointing at the floor. The man obviously noticed her glance because he lifted the gun and inserted it into his suit jacket, finding a holster that she could not see.

"I won't need my gun either, as long as you cooperate." The smoothness of the man's voice bothered her. He spoke so easily and casually she was certain he was lying, or at least that his words meant nothing. There was little she could do about it.

"Okay," Abby stammered.

"Lead me to your room," the man commanded.

Walking awkwardly, with her hands held behind her back by the handcuffs, Abby did as she was told. As she walked, she tried to figure out how the man knew her name. She certainly did not know him. Then it hit her. *Mom! This has to be about mom!* She started to say something to the man walking behind her, but thought the better of it. *You're in deep enough as it is. Just stay quiet and do as he says.*

They reached her room. She went in and turned around observing the man as he entered. His gun was still put away. She noticed that he had gloves on his hands. His eyes roamed her room briefly and then settled on her.

"You're doing great. Keep it up. Now you're going to help me pack for you." He pulled the suitcase from her closet where she had left it sitting there after unpacking.

"This yours?" he asked.

Abby simply nodded.

He tossed it on her bed and gently pushed her backwards so she fell against the bed, next to the suitcase. As she fell backwards with her hands held behind her back she began feeling panic. Abby tugged on her arms wanting to use them to break her fall, but the bed caught her. She fell sideways somewhat and then struggled for a few seconds to pull herself upright. She then sat there on the bed staring at the man. He had watched her for a moment and then turned to the chest of drawers on the wall by the entrance to her bedroom.

Within a few minutes he had packed her suitcase, pausing only to ask her a few questions. He even went into the bathroom and grabbed her toothbrush and makeup. He then pulled her up by one arm and shoved her in front of him. Out of the corner of her eye she could see him grab her suitcase and purse. Abby could stand it no longer.

"Where are you taking me, what are you doing?" she cried out, trying to turn slightly to look at the man. As she finished her sentence, though, a blow struck the side of her head and face, and she felt his open hand slide across the back of her neck. He had slapped her.

"Next time, you will be unconscious, if not dead," the man's pleasant voice was gone, replaced by his angry hiss. "Don't say another word!" He shoved her hard and she fell forward against the door frame. Abby scrambled to keep her feet and barely avoided falling to the carpet.

"To the front door," the man commanded.

Denver

Kim glanced at her watch. She was both excited and terrified. She and Sean were dressed in black slacks and shirts. Sean had a dark blue windbreaker on over his shirt while Kim had a dark brown sweater pulled over hers. Their car was parked on a street, just before an alley that led to the back entrance of the museum. Kim was sitting in the driver's seat.

The hours leading up to this point had been frenzied. After driving by the location a few times, they had then gone shopping. Sean's usual paranoia required that they do both their clothes shopping and hardware shopping in multiple locations. Then, they had returned to the room and Sean had prepared a bag of supplies and devised a final plan. After Sean had gone through the details with her several times, Kim was so nervous that she thought she would never make it through the ordeal.

Sean had sensed that though and had then shifted gears, giving them a break from the upcoming action. His massage had turned into soft and gentle lovemaking. The end result was that Kim had finally felt relaxed, and they had napped until midnight.

It was now two o'clock in the morning and, according to their plan, it would be time for Sean to exit the car, move to the alley and then signal her with a hand behind his back as he rounded the corner into the alley. She was to wait four minutes and then get out and follow him.

As if on cue, Sean spoke.

"Time to go. I'll see you in a few minutes if all looks good." He smiled at her and then reached across and caressed her cheek. The caress was still tingling on her cheek after he had gotten out of the car, as if he had sprinkled some magic dust on her. Kim shook her head to focus on the task at hand.

"Get a grip," she said quietly, almost whispering. "This is no time to be thinking of love."

Kim watched Sean turn the corner. As he told her, he turned widely and just as he would have slipped from view his fisted hand went behind his back. If it had been an open hand she was to wait ten minutes and then drive away to an all night coffee shop they had designated, unless he came out in those ten minutes and told her otherwise. But it had been a fist. That meant that the alley was deserted and quiet. The last thing she saw was the pack on his back as it slipped from her view.

Kim looked down at her watch and waited patiently. Periodically, she scanned the mirrors, windows and windshield. The street was quiet. Finally, four minutes had passed. She got out of the car and quietly closed the door. Then she simply walked to the entrance, turned, and walked into the alley.

The alley was dimly lit, containing only the light that filtered in from each end. There had been a small light over the door that led through the wall, but it was now out. *Sean did that.* As she approached the door, she could see that it was open. Just as she reached it, Sean leaned his head into the alley and smiled.

"So far so good," he said. "The door was easy and there does not appear to be any type of security system connected to it."

Kim felt relieved as she reached him. "That's good. Let's do this and get out of here."

Inside, her stomach had begun to feel a bit queasy. She walked by him and into the rear courtyard. They were under a tree that was growing next to the wall and it shaded them some from the light on the back of the house.

"Remember, don't look at the lights. Look around them, but never at them. It will ruin your night vision."

"Too late," she replied, but she smiled as she spoke. She had, in fact, not looked at the light.

"Well, your eyes will adjust," Sean replied, missing her joke. Sean closed the door they had come through, even locking it from the inside. He then turned and led her toward a dark structure they knew to be the crypt. As they approached it, Kim found herself half expecting a mummified man to come bursting out of the door. It was an iron door though and looked very heavy, like it was rusted in place.

"Is that thing actually going to move?" she asked in a whisper.

"If not, we'll make it," Sean replied grimly.

Sean reached the crypt and set his pack down next to the door. He pulled the pouch open and then moved up to the lock. Kim could tell he was holding some object in his hand. It looked like his makeshift picking key.

Sean's other hand removed a can of lubricant from the pack and he sprayed some into the lock mechanism. Then he slid his tool in and began jiggling the lock as he gently twisted. Kim was surprised to hear an audible click as Sean's hand turned ninety degrees.

Sean pulled his hand from the lock. "Just as I expected, just a simple lock, even a screwdriver could do this one."

He put the tool in his bag and then stood up and sprayed the door hinges with the lubricant. After doing so, he swapped the can of lubricant for two short, flat prying bars. He stuck one bar under the lower edge of the door and the other one on the side, near the bottom.

He began gently alternating between lifting and pulling on one, then the other pry bar, getting a rhythm going that he continued for about twenty seconds.

"It feels loose," he grunted. "This may open easily."

Sean stood up. Kim had moved in close to him and he almost collided with her.

"Sorry," she mumbled, backing up a step.

She watched as Sean inserted both bars along the vertical edge, one above and one below the lock, and then gently pried them outwards. It didn't budge. Sean relaxed for a moment and then pushed on the pry bars even harder. This time it moved, making a very distinct creak that sounded terribly loud to Kim.

"Hmm, more lubricant," Sean muttered, more to himself than to Kim. He grabbed the can and sprayed the hinges some before returning it to the bag. He paused and looked at Kim over his shoulder.

"I'm going to open it this time, even if it's loud. It's better to have one single loud noise than a series of them, so don't panic."

Kim nodded glancing around her. The light on the back of the house provided only moderate light, but she saw nothing unusual and nothing moving.

As good as his word, Sean inserted the two pry bars, tested them and then pushed heavily. The door opened with a loud, groaning, screech. Kim wildly looked around for a moment. Sean had opened the door about four inches. He put the crowbars away and pulled the can of lubricant back out. After spraying some more, he used his hands to wiggle the door a bit and then was able to open it about ten more inches. This time it barely made a noise. Behind the door was pitch black darkness, and Kim felt a deep shudder go through her body.

"Okay, that's good enough," Sean commented casually, as if he had just hung a picture frame on the wall. "Time to go in."

He turned and looked at her. "Are you ready for this?"

"No, but I'm going in anyways," Kim said quietly with a bit of determination in her voice.

"Good, here's your light."

He handed her a small flashlight with red tape covering the lens.

"Remember, never point it back towards the house or on the walls.

Just at objects in the crypt."

"Right," Kim muttered. "And I won't look at it either."

Sean smiled and then turned to enter. He did not turn on his light until his arm had extended into the crypt. Then he turned sideways and slid in, pulling his bag behind him. Kim stayed right behind him. Shining her flashlight on the ground in front of her. She could see Sean right in front of her and she turned to slide through. She tried not to touch the sides, but in the dark, she failed. She felt the edge of the door push across her chest and tried not to imagine what kind of bugs were jumping off onto her.

Once inside, she shined the light around. It was dusty, but there were only a few cobwebs. Sean could stand upright only if he slightly bent his head. He turned his light off. She watched as he kneeled down to reach into his bag. She followed with her light, helping him see what he was doing. He pulled a pry bar out and half stood. She lifted her light and shined it past him. A few feet beyond was the casket. She supposed it was made out of wood, but could not tell because it was covered with a thick layer of dust. Sean answered her thought by taping lightly on the casket with the pry bar. It made a gentle thud, confirming that it was indeed made out of wood.

"Shine the light along the seam," Sean directed.

She did as she was told and shined the light back and forth from one end of the casket to the other. Sean then reached out and began inserting the pry bar into the seam in the middle, so she kept the light shining there. He pushed it firmly in and lifted it up a bit. It appeared to move and some dust slid down. Sean reached down and grabbed the other pry bar and inserted it next to the one already stuck in the seam. He pushed it much farther in, though, and it seemed to Kim that he had lifted the lid up enough to get it all the way through. Sean then lifted gently with the bar and shortly had his hands under the edge of the lid. He pried it up farther, revealing, to Kim, what looked to be a human waistline. Sean inserted one pry bar vertically to hold the lid open about ten inches.

"That thing's heavy for wood. It's thick, too."

Kim barely heard him as she had followed the torso up and had locked her light onto what she could only describe as being a mummified face. It was sunken and bony. *Thank god the mouth is shut*, she thought. *If it wasn't, I don't think I could stand here staring at it.*

Sean had reached back into his bag and pulled out his flashlight. He shined his light up and down the torso and then up at the underside of the lid of the coffin. Seeing nothing he brought his light to bear on the man's chest.

"Can you shine your light there? I'm going to see if he has anything in his jacket."

"Sure," Kim said, happy to have a reason to keep her light off the face. She realized she was sweating and breathing heavily, even though she had hardly exerted herself. She began trying to breathe slower. *At least my hand is steady.*

Sean had put his light away and was now reaching into the coffin. He lifted the jacket up with one hand and pushed his other hand underneath it, feeling the pocket area. After a moment, he rotated his hand and felt along the torso of the mummy. All Kim could think of was to make sure that Sean washed his hands before he even came close to touching her again.

"Ah, what's this?" Sean asked, his hand pausing. He moved it very slowly for a moment and then withdrew it. Between two fingers he was tugging what looked like folded cloth. *It's too stiff to be cloth. It's probably leather.* It was a little over a foot long and six inches wide. Sean gently slid it out and held it with both hands as he turned sideways and then set it on the ground next to his bag.

Kim found herself trembling now, and the light wiggled slightly as a result. Sean did not seem to care though, as he leaned his face closer to inspect the pouch.

"It's folded leather. Feels like some papers are inside."

"Well open it," Kim said impatiently.

"Okay."

Sean lifted one edge of the leather and flipped it over. Inside was another fold of leather, that he nimbly gripped and flipped open the other way. As it fell open, Kim's light revealed a yellowed envelope. It looked to be one of several yellowed envelopes stacked on top of one another. Sean paused for a moment and then reached down and touched one corner of the top envelope. He then pinched it briefly.

"Seems to be in pretty good shape." Without looking up at all, he continued. "I think we found what we're looking for. Let's fold this back up, check the body for anything else and then reverse our tracks and take this back to our room."

"Yes, okay," Kim replied, trying not to sound disappointed at having to wait further before knowing its contents. His comment reminded her of where she was, though, and leaving suddenly sounded like a very good idea.
.....

A few minutes later, they had exited the crypt and begun the process of returning to their car. A few minutes after that, with Kim nervously glancing everywhere, they reached the car and drove away. Sean took over the driving and they reached the hotel room without any incident. All the way there, though, Sean had been on total alert. Although he had never acted like he saw anything out of the ordinary, it made Kim feel terrified that the police, or someone worse, were going to come around every corner to stop them. Finally, though, they had retreated to their room. Sean left everything in the car except the folded leather and its contents.

Now, back in their room with the leather pouch on the table in front of them, they both sat looking at it. Sean had pulled a beer from the fridge and was sipping it, while looking thoughtfully at their triumph. Kim had a soda in her hand, and was thinking of how to best open the envelopes.

Sean broke the silence. "Okay, you're our historical documents expert, so have at it."

"Should I cut the envelopes? It seems like a sacrilege. They're so old."

"Well, the way I figure it, they're yours. Your ancestor left them for you. So do with them as you please."

Kim thought about that for a moment. "You're right. But I don't have a knife. What do we have that is sharp? I don't want to just tear them open with my finger."

Sean looked around and then picked up the combination beer and wine opener he had bought with their groceries. "Here, use this. It has a little flip out knife for cutting the foil on wine bottles."

Kim took the tool and sat it on the desk. She lifted the first envelope. It was yellowed with age some, but not completely. It felt surprisingly soft. She flipped it over and examined the other side. It
was blank. She repeated the procedure for the other two envelopes.
They felt thicker, like another envelope was inside them. They too,
though, were blank on the outside. She decided to start with the top
one. She lifted it up and used the knife on the opener to cut into the top
corner and then carefully cut across the top of the envelope. Setting
the tool down she gently pulled some folded sheets of paper out. She
set the envelope down and then opened up the paper. She recognized
the handwriting immediately.

"Oh my god, it's a letter from Jacob," she said breathlessly. A
wave of relief washed over her as she realized that she had not truly
believed, up until now, that they had found the right thing. She laid it
down on the table and began reading it out loud.

To Who Find These Letters,

*My name, my real name, is Jacob Thomas. When you read this
letter, I will have left the earth as Jacob Poole. This letter and the
two other letters with it were left for my family to find when they
realized it was time to follow my final instructions. I am assuming
that it is my son, or his son, or his son after that who is reading
these letters. I, Jacob Thomas have left this burden for you.*

Kim paused and looked up at Sean. "Guess he didn't expect a girl,
huh?"

Sean smiled back at her. "Different era. Girls played with dolls,
remember?"

Kim went back to reading the letter.

*"I was born to John Thomas in Baltimore, Maryland. At age
18, during the Civil War, I joined the Union Army as a courier and
came to work for our great president, Abraham Lincoln, in the White
House. Near the end of the war, when the outcome was certain,
President Lincoln dispatched me to his hometown of Springfield,
Illinois. I carried with me two letters. One for his law partner,
Thomas Herndon, and one for his stepmother. It was odd that he*

used me to deliver such letters, as these would have normally gone by regular mail.

I was attacked in Cincinnati on the same night that President Lincoln was assassinated. It was only by sheer luck that I killed my attacker. On him, I found a note describing me and my destination. I also found his Union Army identification papers. I realized the Army had sent him to kill me and stop the delivery of these letters. Appalled, I decided to examine the two letters.

The letter to Mrs. Lincoln was an inquiry about another family, the Enloes. President Lincoln had apparently been visited by Isaac Enloe who claimed to be his cousin. He claimed that it was his grandfather who had sired Abraham Lincoln. The president had felt truth in the man's words and also noticed a significant resemblance. He decided to ask his mother, who of course was really his step-mother, if she knew of any truth to the story.

The other letter, however, is more sinister. President Lincoln explained to his former partner that he had spoken to an injured captain, Captain Greene, at an army hospital outside of Richmond following the president's visit there. Captain Greene, had told the president of a group of high ranking officers in Sherman's cavalry that had been taking land from Confederates using murder and forced signatures. They were amassing an empire to profit after the war. He had discovered it and suspected he would soon be dead from his injuries. He told the president that he had hid his evidence in a cave that Confederate soldiers had been using to store "treasure" spirited out of Atlanta before its fall to General Sherman. President Lincoln was warned that the conspiracy reached the top ranks of the Army. He provides some crude instructions on where to find a map of the location of the cave.

The next morning, I learned of the President's assassination. It was a dark day for me and I was filled with anguish. I did not know what I should do. My duty was to deliver the letters. But I was certain I would be killed before I could fullfill my duty. For the same reason, I was certain I could not return to the Capital. Thus, my only choice was to hide.

I decided to head as far west as I could and find gainful

employment under a new name. Hence, I changed my name from Jacob Thomas to Jacob Poole. I went to Denver where I settled and began my life anew.

For decades, I have wondered if I could come forward with the letters and tell my story. Nothing was ever revealed about the accusations raised by Captain Greene though and I have always worried about how the assassination affected things. I have wondered if the assassination was part of a larger conspiracy, so I remained silent and hid the two letters.

Now, by you reading this letter, I have told my story. It is in your hands to properly reveal the truth. I apologize to my family for deceiving them. I did it to protect them far more than I did it to protect myself.

Kim completed reading the letter and sat there staring for a full minute. Sean also sat and absorbed the implications of the letter. Finally, it was Kim who spoke.

"Baltimore. My great, great grandfather was Jacob Thomas and he came from Baltimore. My three-times great grandfather was John Thomas." Kim sounded thankful. She looked at Sean. "If we learn nothing else from all of this, I am happy to know the truth of my family name."

Sean looked at her and smiled. "I am happy. Really happy for you. All we've got to do now is unravel the sinister side of this. Jacob was right, we have inherited his burden."

Kim nodded her head, her mind now digging into the rest of the information in the letter.

"Okay, well, according to Jacob, the letter to Herndon is one of these letters." Kim gestured at the two other envelopes and continued, "and it's going to tell us where to find directions to a cave somewhere."

"Jacob also explained to us more about what his reference to 'a nation's sins' was about. It was a Union Army conspiracy during Sherman's invasion of the South to take land away from southerners." Sean frowned. "Is it possible that this is who is pursuing us today?"

"Or is it the Army itself?" Kim asked, suddenly growing very afraid. Sean shook his head though, helping her feel somewhat relieved.

"I would have a hard time believing that today's Army is involved. But, could the Army have left information behind and thus some branch of the government is trying to cover it up?" Sean asked rhetorically.

He answered himself, "Sure, that's possible. And they both mean the same thing."

"What's that?" Kim asked, certain she knew the answer.

"We need to find the cave and the evidence and bring it forward," Sean replied. He looked stern, but a twinkle appeared in his eyes and he smiled. "And find some treasure while we're at it."

Chapter Twenty-Seven

Saturday, May 9
Richmond

The ringing phone was behind him, but no matter how much James turned around, he could not find it. It was maddening. Suddenly, he was awake and realized he had been dreaming of his cell phone being lost while ringing. Then, he heard the ringing continue and realized that his real cell phone had actually been ringing and had invaded his dreams. It was pitch black around him, and it took a few moments for James to remember his location. *Richmond. I'm in my hotel room.* Once he got himself oriented, he reached up and turned the light on next to his bed and then fumbled for his cell phone under the sudden bright glare of the light in his face. It was still ringing as he spotted it on the bedside stand below the lamp and pulled it to his ear while answering.

"Hello," he said, intentionally trying to sound disturbed and tired. He heard Sean's voice answering.

"Professor, this is Sean and Kim. Sorry to wake you, but we have important news."

James digested this information for a moment while trying to shake off his sleepiness. "Go ahead," he said into the phone, using his free hand to push himself upright in the hotel bed.

"Okay." Sean sounded eager to James. "The quick version is that we found three letters hidden in the tomb of John Haggard. One is a letter from Jacob Thomas to whoever found it. The other two are letters from Abraham Lincoln that were never delivered to their destination."

James was startled and did not speak for a moment. Then he simply managed to utter, "Letters from President Lincoln?" He looked over at the clock on his bed stand. *It's six thirty in the morning and Sean is telling me he found lost Lincoln letters?* For the second time, he found himself trying to discern between dream and reality. He quickly realized that he was awake and that what he was hearing was real. He shook himself and began climbing out of bed while holding the phone to his ear.

"Yes Professor. They were letters that Jacob Thomas had been in the process of delivering when Lincoln was assassinated. Jacob explains that he was attacked by an agent of the Union Army." Sean's voice sounded patient, as if he understood that James was trying to wake up. "Oh, and Jacob confirms what we suspected, that he was the courier whose records you found."

"I see," James said, seating himself clumsily on the desk chair in his room. He used his free hand to turn the light on at the desk. He considered what he had just been told. "You said there were two letters from President Lincoln?"

"Yep," Sean confirmed. "In fact, it's the contents of one of them that Jacob was giving us clues about. It seems that a cavalry captain under Sherman told Lincoln about a conspiracy happening in Georgia to take land away from the southerners."

Sean explained the contents of the Thomas Herndon letter. He finished by reading the instructions that Captain Greene had given to the president who had, in turn, provided to Thomas Herndon:

"Captain Greene informed me that he placed a map in the grave of a Confederate soldier named Jeremiah Clarke in a small cemetery east of Athens, Georgia. That map shows where to find a sealed cave located on a river to the east. There, the captain placed evidence of the Army officer conspiracy amidst Confederate gold and valuables taken out of Atlanta before its fall.

I respectfully ask you, and personally appoint you, to discreetly investigate this story, and if upon finding it to be true, to report such results directly to me and the Secretary of War."

There was silence as James absorbed the information. Then he spoke. "Wow, this is truly incredible. You said there's a second letter?"

"Oh yes," Sean responded. "Sorry. It's a letter to his stepmother. This is where you Enloes fit into this mystery. President Lincoln was visited by Isaac Enloe, the grandson of Abraham Enloe. Isaac claimed to be a cousin of Abraham Lincoln. Apparently, Lincoln was so taken by the man and by their similarities that he wrote a letter asking his stepmother if any of it were true."

James thought for a moment. "I don't understand. How does that relate to the army conspiracy?"

"I have no idea, maybe it doesn't," Sean admitted. "I think it was just coincidence the two letters were together."

"But why…" James's voice dropped off for a moment as he thought things through. "Okay, if you're right Sean, then maybe Jacob tied his message and its timing to the Enloes as a measuring stick, a way to ensure that enough time had passed."

"I don't know," Sean replied. "Kim and I think that idea is plausible. It was all we came up with as well. In any case, I think our path forward is clear."

"Yes, yes. I think it is."

"Kim and I plan to head to Athens. It's east of Atlanta. We're going to drive and stay as far off the radar screen as we can. It's going to take us at least a day, so we won't get there until sometime on Sunday."

"I know Athens well. It's the home of the University of Georgia. Hmm." James let his voice taper off again. Then he spoke firmly. "Okay, I am headed into the archive as quickly as I can. I'll learn everything I can and then head home. Then, I'll head down to Athens as well. It will take me 'til Sunday night, I suspect, to get there."

"Okay Professor, that sounds like a plan. Remember to be very careful. Don't drop your guard for anything. Go to public places with a decent amount of people if you feel threatened."

"Yes, Mr. Johnson," James responded in his professor voice. "I shall be very careful."

…..

An hour later, James was in the archive and giddy with excitement. *Lost, hidden Lincoln letters! Treasure! Amazing!* His brain felt like an old vinyl record with a scratch. It kept playing the same lines over and over again. After Sean and Kim hung up, James had found it practically impossible to sleep. Instead, he had gotten up and headed down to the archive building, just as the sun was rising. Not needing any coffee, he immediately wrote down his task list. First and foremost, was to collect records and maps of General Sherman's march to the sea from Atlanta. Second, was to learn about any treasure rumors out there that matched the story they had unearthed. He was going to give himself until early afternoon to locate any of this information. Then he would rush back to the hotel, check out and then head back to Tennessee.

.....

It was now eleven in the morning and James had collected a good amount of maps and journals, as well as some scholarly work on Sherman's march. He had become quite adept at using the copier, especially the oversize one. Keeping his material organized had been his hardest task. He had managed to find a box of folders and had used a marker pen and those folders to create a fairly organized set of documents. James's stomach was now growling at him, as he had been going non-stop since being woken up in his hotel room. The archive, closed to the public on weekends, was empty. Butch had told him to expect as much at dinner. There were no other visiting scholars or researchers camped at the archive right now, so it was expected to be deserted all weekend, except for James. He felt like a ghost walking the halls, opening file drawers and disturbing their contents.

The map room had been the eeriest. It was constructed with dark red stained oak paneling. The map drawers squeaked lightly as James pulled them open. Capping it off, were the yellowed, original, old maps laying in the drawers. Some felt and looked so old, he almost expected to see a bloody finger print on them, as if a soldier had held that very map in his hands during the war.

Now, though, James was in his guest office, with a stack of folders and a pad of notes. He thumbed through them for a moment and then leaned back in his swivel chair, staring up at the ceiling. *What next?*

He had precise maps and data of where Sherman had marched. He had copies of journals, letters and other records commenting on various encounters with Sherman and his army by the residents along the route from Atlanta to Savannah.

Treasure! That's what I need to dig into next. I need to get back to my study of lost treasures. As James reviewed his treasure research files, he quickly concluded he needed some expertise. He dug out his previous research and flipped through his notes and printed webpages. His eyes quickly fell upon the southern treasure explorer he had noticed earlier, Kurt Cathey. He noted Kurt's phone number and quickly picked up the phone and dialed it. After a few rings, a rough voice answered.

"Hello?"

James thought the voice matched the photo that James had in front of him. *Just like a gruff army man.*

"Hi! Is this Kurt Cathey?"

"Speaking." The voice already sounded impatient.

"Hi Mr. Cathey. My name is James Enloe. I'm a professor at the University of Tennessee." James paused and considered how to best warm up the man on the other end of the line.

"Uh huh," Kurt answered back.

James hurried to get something going between Kurt and himself.

"You may recall, I emailed you the other day. I'm currently tracking down a lead on a lost confederate treasure and have identified you to be the most experienced confederate treasure hunter out there. You've seen quite an abundance of action."

"That's right. Well, I mean, thanks for the compliment. I like to just think of myself as having been lucky enough to be in the right place at the right time."

James sensed a complete change of tone in the man's voice and was confident he had warmed the treasure hunter up. He considered, for a moment, that he should be cautious about how much he revealed, given the circumstances they were operating under. He also knew, however, that he had to give information to get some in return.

"Well, you certainly deserve the accolades and attention Mr. Cathey. I'm helping a couple try to find a treasure possibly taken away from a confederate city before it fell to invaders."

"Sounds like the Atlanta treasure to me."

James was shocked at the quick and accurate conclusion that Kurt had made. He stumbled somewhat.

"Uh, yes." James paused trying to think how and whether to go farther. "I'm hoping you can tell me more about what we're, I mean they're looking for. Is this coins, art, candlesticks, etcetera? If you can point me at any sources, that would also be great, however, I have to inform you that I'm short on time."

"Heading off to dig it up right now are you?"

"No, no. Just other deadlines. I'm in Richmond, not too far from you, I believe, down in Norfolk. I'm heading back to Knoxville shortly."

There was a pause and James was sure the man was trying to take his measure. *He's wondering if he can trust me, whether to help me.*

Kurt finally spoke.

"Okay, well let's see…what did you say your name was?"

"Professor of History, James Enloe, University of Tennessee. I emailed you."

"Okay Professor. Well, you're either after the biggest lost treasure of the Civil War, or the biggest myth of the war. Most of the information about it is secondhand, but there are so many stories, I think it is very likely that there is something to them. Whether this treasure was truly lost and never found or simply stolen, that's another question."

"I see. What do you know of its supposed contents?"

"Most stories say that when it became clear that Atlanta was going to fall, Richmond ordered all valuables to be collected and brought to Richmond. Supposedly, there was a faction within the confederacy, connected to the Knights of the Golden Circle, that had become very disenfranchised with the war effort and its leadership. They organized a group of their sympathizers to capture the treasure as it was being taken out of Atlanta. They did just that and took it to a temporary hiding place located in South Carolina. However, they were never heard from again and the treasure never reached Richmond."

"Uh huh." James was scribbling notes, while holding the phone between his shoulder and chin. "Do you think the Knights of the

Golden Circle were real?"

"Oh they were real all right, but I think they were not as organized or as large as many have tried to make them out to be. They firmly believed in the importance of a separate state for the South, a separate country. Some think that they secretly advanced the cause of the Civil War, but they were as decimated and as dismantled after the war as the confederacy was itself."

"So you believe the story of the Atlanta treasure?"

"I believe we do not know what happened to it. I have never seen any first hand accounts that it was hidden away or even that it was intercepted by the Knights."

"I see." James thought for a moment. "Any information on how large it is."

"Atlanta was a booming economy during the war and considered to be a very safe location, much more removed from the front lines than Richmond. There were coins and gold stored in banks there. Apparently, the order to collect the treasure was taken seriously and family gold, silver and jewelry were added. Some art and historical items were added to save them from what was expected to be the Union Army's destruction of Atlanta. Maps, paintings and the like were supposedly saved."

"You said South Carolina?"

"Yes, one widow wrote that she overheard a conversation in her Atlanta parlor that the selected interceptors were to catch the treasure as it headed northeast, ideally as it crossed the Savannah River. They were supposed to head to an agreed-upon location in South Carolina near a river. However, even that information is second hand. It's in a small self published book from the late 1800's and it's based on the author having read a letter from the widow to her sister."

"Savannah River. Hmm," James was pondering the significance of this information. Kurt took the opportunity to respond with a question.

"So Professor, can you tell me what has caused you to take up this mission? Have you uncovered some information about the treasure?"

James brought himself back to the present task at hand. *Best to back off now and downplay my interest.*

"Not really. This is mostly a theoretical effort on my part. You've helped me more than enough for me to make my report. Thank you Mr. Cathey."

James, satisfied that he had learned enough, ended the call. He hung up the phone before he could be asked any more questions. *This was probably all the man knew.* He glanced down at his notes and pondered what new maps or information he could put together based on the phone call. *Maps of the Savannah River.* He looked at a map he had laid out. Athens, he noted, was probably right on the old route between Atlanta and Richmond. *But how does a Union officer end up being involved with the interception of the treasure long after the fall of Atlanta?* He felt like he was missing one key fact, one that he could figure out with logic, if he had enough time. *That's one thing I don't have, time.*

James jumped up from his chair and headed back to the map room eager to begin his new mission.

Norfolk, Virginia

Kurt hung up the phone in his kitchen. He looked down at the notepad on his counter. He had scribbled "*Prof. James Enlow, UT, Knoxville.*" Picking up the pad he turned and sat down in a chair at his kitchen table. His blond hair was rumpled and he was wearing only a pair of shorts. The professor's phone call had woken him from a deep sleep on his sofa after a night of heavy drinking. The professor's words had awoken him and shot straight through his hangover-induced haze to start his mind working. He stared at the note pad for a full minute as his brain rehashed the phone call. *Damn, I'm too old to drink like this and still be able to think in the morning. This, this is big!*

Kurt settled on a course of action. A phone call, some aspirin, coffee and then packing. He sat up and turned back to the phone on the counter. Picking it up, he dialed a number from memory. It rang and then an equally hungover-sounding voice came on the line sounding downright hostile.

"Yeah?"

"Pack your bags and head to Knoxville right now! Call me in two hours and I'll give you your instructions." Kurt spoke sharply, but slowly, making sure his full message was understood.

"Huh? What the hell Kurt…"

"No, Bill, tell me later, but do as I say. I think we may be about to nab the biggest treasure we will ever see."

Kurt waited until he heard an acknowledging grunt and then hung up the phone, satisfied his companion would do as instructed. He was not as smart as Kurt, but he was much tougher. Kurt on the other hand, knew he desperately needed some aspirin, some coffee and some food.

I-70, Kansas

Sean had long since concluded that Kansas consisted of endless rolling corn fields. Since sunrise, that was mostly all he had seen. There was a dark band of pavement protruding in front of him out over the last visible rolling hill, and then there were young corn plants. That was it. The number of fellow cars on the road had increased somewhat, and they had provided some distraction. Behind him, laying down in the back seat, Kim was sound asleep. He tried to keep the driving even and steady so as not to wake her. Their plan was for her to take over the driving at some point in the afternoon while he slept. He would then take over after midnight.

So far it had gone well. They had bought a thermos of coffee and some sweet rolls and then set off from Denver with a full tank of gas. They were now well into Kansas. Sean expected to turnover driving duties when they stopped for gas in Missouri. He was driving just a little over the speed limit, having observed that most other cars on the road did much the same. Sean also recalled his drive on this very highway, but going in the opposite direction. It had been a whirlwind of cities, days and weeks. Somewhere in that time frame he had even discovered romance. He snuck a glance over his shoulder, but Kim had pulled her head under a blanket to keep it dark, so all he could see was the outline of her head.

He brought his vision back to the horizon and smiled to himself. *What a trip.*

His cell phone vibrated in the center console beside him, and he reached down for it with his right hand. Grabbing it, he looked at the screen but saw that it showed "private number" giving him no clue as to who was calling. He thought for a moment and decided not to answer, uncertain if answering might give, whoever their pursuers were, more information. The call died away and he put the phone back in the console. As expected, it vibrated again a minute later, and Sean picked it up again, expecting to see the screen show him that he had a voice mail. Instead, it continued vibrating and the screen showed "private number" once again.

Sean thought again and decided to answer it.

"Hello?" he said quietly, trying not to wake Kim.

"Hello, Mr. Johnson," a calm voice with a southern drawl greeted him.

"Hello, yourself. To whom am I speaking?" Sean worked to try and place the voice or even the accent. It reminded him of someone he had served with, but nothing came to mind. The tone of the voice also threw him. It had a serious sound to it, conveying a distinct sense of superiority.

"You'll learn soon enough. I am calling to discuss our common interest. Your success in solving an age old secret."

Sean reeled at those words, with a flood of thoughts racing into his brain. He fought the surge of thoughts back and answered clearly and instinctively.

"I see. So then, am I to assume that you are my shadow?"

"Maybe I am."

"Well, since you know my name, it's only fair I know yours."

The voice chuckled. *Super confidence,* Sean thought. *Either he's crazy or he really has us beat.* Sean tried to think what to say or do. Before he could, though, the voice on the phone continued.

"Mr. Johnson, you will find out who we are when we want you to. Until then, you'll do as we request."

Sean felt an alarm going off in his head. *Confidence and arrogance. I'm about to find out something I don't want to know.* He tried to maintain a posture of confidence back, but he knew it was a front that "they" would see right through.

"And why would I do that?" he asked calmly.

"Because that is how you will ensure that little Abigail comes out of this unharmed and intact."

Sean swerved the car some as he felt himself stiffen up and push back against the car seat. *Abby, they've taken Abby! Shit. This is getting way out of hand.* He looked over his shoulder and found Kim looking up at him from the back seat. Her face showed alarm too. *She must have woken during the call and sensed that something was wrong.* He gave her a strong but grim smile.

"I see. In that case, you are probably right." He tried to answer back in a way that would not alarm Kim. He needed to break this to her under better circumstances than driving down a highway with murderous thugs on the phone. His muscles had gone tense and it was all he could do to keep the car steady and talk on the phone at the same time. He began watching for the next exit, knowing he needed to take it.

"Good. Where are you?"

"I'm in a car headed to Georgia." Sean had quickly decided to tell the man on the phone as much accurate information as he could. There was a long pause, and Sean immediately sensed he surprised the person on the other end of the line. He had told him something he was not so ready to deal with. Finally the man replied.

"Why are you going there?"

"Because a long lost letter told me to." Sean felt that somehow he was gaining some ground with the caller. There was another pause.

"Do you have the letter to Mr. Herndon?"

Sean was surprised at how quickly and sharply the man had brought the conversation back to his advantage and also focused it right on the point at hand.

"Yes I do," Sean replied simply. Kim had scrambled up to a sitting position and was leaning over the front seat looking at Sean with a questioning look on her face. Sean's mind raced, trying to think of what to do next. He was torn between telling Kim immediately or holding off until he finished the call. In either case, he knew Kim would go nuts. He concluded that he needed to do something to ensure Abby's safety. Regardless of whether that meant having a crazy mother in the car with him. He could see an exit coming up and he accelerated towards it. The man on the phone had been silent for a notable period. Sean waited him out while trying to give Kim a calming, but serious look. He sensed he was failing at both measures. Kim could tell something had gone very wrong.

"Your candidness may save Abigail's life, Mr. Johnson. Drive to Atlanta. Bring all that you have found. We will call you on this number when we are ready to meet with you."

Sean thought for a moment. *It's now or never. Either I confront him now and upset Kim at the same time, or I hang up and tell Kim I just talked to her daughter's kidnapper, but did nothing.* He decided he had to do something.

"My candidness is what you will get if you treat her well and deliver her safely to us, but it has to be a clean exchange. Letters for the girl and in a public place. I'll expect your call."

Sean hung up as he heard Kim gasping for air. He had reached the exit and began a sliding turn on the off ramp pulling into the gravel of a truck stop located next to the exit. As the car slid to a stop, Kim was finally able to speak.

"Did you just talk about Abby? Is she okay? What's going on Sean?"

To Sean's surprise, Kim was not screaming. However, her voice got progressively less under control as she spoke. He turned his body as he slammed the shift lever into park. He reached out with his hands grabbing at Kim's.

"Yes, I did. Listen. A man just called on my cell. He said he had Abby and that she would be okay if we cooperated. I am certain it is the same people who have been shadowing us. He told us to meet him in Atlanta and to bring the letters."

"Oh my God, Sean!" Kim turned and frantically fumbled for her cell phone. "This can't be!" Sean's hand grabbed hers over the back of the seat.

"Yes, it is. It is happening Kim. Stop and listen." Kim's head whipped up to look at Sean, fierce anger replacing her shock.

"Don't you tell me what to do. This is my daughter, GOD DAMN IT."

Sean sighed. "I won't tell you what to do, but listen for a minute. Before you call anyone, let's think this through. We need to make sure that whatever we do does not harm Abby. We need to do what we think best helps her, okay?" He clenched her hands tightly.

Kim looked at Sean defiantly for a moment, and then the anger in her face was replaced with grim determination. Sean could see suspicion in her eyes. *She doesn't know who to trust. I don't blame her.*

"Okay. You're not sure who to trust or what to do. Right?"

Kim nodded at him so he continued.

"We need to call her and maybe your ex-husband and confirm she is not there, but let's assume it's true and she is not there. What then? Do we tell your ex some, or all, of what is going on? Do we call the FBI? Or do we keep silent and try to make a swap for Abby?"

He paused and looked at her. "That's what it comes down to, but we have to figure out our plan before we call anyone."

Sean sat silent letting her absorb his words. She stared back at him for at least ten seconds. Finally, she spoke.

"I don't trust the FBI. I even think they could be behind this. Can we make the swap Sean? Can we get her back?"

"You heard what I told him. I fired back at him with my terms. If they meet those, then yes, I think she will be fine. They clearly want these letters and we can give them up. But, if they won't do a public exchange, then we need to bring in help."

Kim stared at Sean again, and then nodded her head in agreement.

"Okay, I'll go along with your plan. You are the only one I trust. You'll tell me the minute you think it's going wrong?"

Sean nodded. "Yep, the very second."

Kim nodded back grimly.

"Okay, I'll call Abby's cell, then the house, and then my ex-husband."

She thought for a moment and then continued. "But what if he has already called the police? Or even the FBI?"

"I don't think that has happened yet. The man on the phone sounded in control, as if this is part of his grand plan. Plus, I would think you would have been called immediately by your ex, or law enforcement if they were aware. If they are aware, though, we need to play dumb, right? Act like a terrified mother and learn what you can."

Kim nodded grimly again. "Right, that'll be easy, playing a terrified mother."

Chapter Twenty-Eight

A red dawn, eventually being replaced by a blue sky, had crept up over the edge of the highway as Sean and Kim approached Atlanta. Kim had woken early, if she could call any of her time during the night sleep. She had mostly just lain in the back seat and tossed and turned. The few times she had fallen asleep had been terminated prematurely by a nightmare involving her daughter. So at dawn, she had crawled up into the front seat of the rental car and settled in next to Sean. They had tried to make small talk, but the underlying tension of the coming day made it impossible.

Kim watched the sun rise in front of them as she considered the past day's events. After the shocking call and her discussion with Sean, she had called Abby's cell and gotten her voicemail. She had called the house and gotten the answering machine and then talked with Sean some more. Then, she called her ex-husband on his cell. She had tried to ask him casually if he knew the whereabouts of Abby. His answer had nearly set her off into a fit of rage. He had replied that he had not "noticed" her the night before or even in the morning. It was his tone that had really upset Kim. He sounded irritated to have to think about keeping tabs on his daughter. Kim had kept her cool, though, and had gently asked him if the house had seemed fine when he came home.

Looking back, she was certain that was where she had gone too far.

He had become suspicious of her call at that point, and after they had hung up, had tried to reach Abby with no answer at his home or on her cell. He had then gone home to discover Abby missing. Kim knew all of that because he had called her back. She had not answered that call, but instead had waited and listened to the inevitable voicemail. He reported he had no idea where Abby was and was worried.

Kim's mind was stuck on those two words: "noticed," and "worried." They told the whole story as far as her ex-husband was concerned. He never paid attention to things that he truly cared for until they were gone and then, that was all he could think about.

Kim and Sean had talked more about the situation. They were both convinced that someone from the Sheriden Corporation kidnapped Abby, and had driven or flown her to Atlanta. Sean had noted that the Sheriden Corporation was headquartered in Atlanta. That city was increasingly becoming the common thread.

That was where things would have been for Kim if it had not been for something Sean did the previous day. At a fueling stop, before they hit the road again, Sean called someone with his cell phone. It was fairly quick, but he had started the call while she had been in the bathroom. When she returned to the car, he abruptly hung up. Kim had asked Sean about it and he had given an odd answer about "covering all their bases." While Kim had been driving from late afternoon until midnight, the mystery of Sean's call gradually evolved into suspicion. Thus, while Sean had driven, she had tossed and turned with images of betrayal, even by Sean himself, haunting her and her dreams of Abby.

Now, they were stopped at a highway strip mall. Sean was eating a breakfast sandwich and was clearly trying to get her to eat something as well. Her stomach was tied up in knots, though, and she refused. Kim was certain she would throw up anything she ate.

They were waiting for his phone to ring, signaling that they might be able to move forward towards Atlanta itself and Abby. As Kim sat there, one question kept returning to her mind. It was one she could not answer. *Was I right not to go to the police?* Deep inside, she was worried that she had made a mistake that would harm Abby.

"Do you ever worry that you've made a mistake, like chosing the wrong tactic?" she asked Sean.

Sean looked up from his food and the map of Atlanta he was studying. "You mean during an operation?"

At Kim's nod he replied. "All the time. That kind of worry is good because it keeps you on your toes. It helps you recognize when you need to change tactics. The hardest thing though, is keeping on your original course when all you have is nagging doubt. That's why you make a plan beforehand, so you make decisions when you have the clearest head."

"So, do you worry that maybe we should have gone to the police?"

"Does that doubt nag at me? Yes. Do I truly think that we've made the wrong choice? No. I still think we have the best chance to recover Abby from these criminals, because we have what they want. The FBI may not be trustworthy, and even if they turn out to be, they might not be able to save Abby."

Kim sighed and pulled her knees up against her chest. "God, I want you to be right."

Phoenix

Alan finished dialing the number and waited for the man to answer. *Kidnapping? It's going to get hard to keep this one under wraps if this is true.* A man answered the phone.

"Hello?"

"Hi. Mr. Wilcox?"

"Speaking." Alan could tell that the man on the other end of the line was stressed and worried.

"This is Alan Nazimi, Mr. Wilcox, from the FBI. We spoke a few days ago when I was trying to track down information about your ex-wife's whereabouts."

"Oh, yes. Listen. Thank God you've called. I reported a possible kidnapping late yesterday. It's my daughter. She's…"

"Mr. Wilcox," Alan cut him off before he could finish his sentence.

"Yes?"

"I know all about it. That's why I'm calling. I have your daughter, you and your ex-wife listed in my file. When the police reported this to the FBI, I received a call immediately. We are on it. Okay?"

"Thank God." Alan could hear the man's breathing. It was short and heavy, indicating to Alan that the man was working himself up into a frenzy. "Listen Mr. Wilcox, please take a moment to relax and sit down, okay?"

"Okay, okay."

"Good, now can you walk me through what you know in case the report I got could possibly be missing anything? Try not to leave anything out?"

Jason Wilcox then did. Upon sitting down, he explained to Alan how it began with a telephone call from Kim, his ex-wife. He explained that he went home and found no sign of Abby in the house. He was thinking she had stayed at a friend's house for the night, so he called that girl's house. A little while later she called back and told him she had dropped Abby off the previous night.

Alan had heard it all before and this was not too different than so many other cases he handled. It sounded like the girl had runaway. With all that the mother had been involved in recently though, Alan was on the alert for all other possibilities. In the end, he concluded that he could justify reporting it as a runaway, not a kidnapping, and no-one would be the wiser. He thanked the father, told him not to panic, and to stay home by the phone in case his daughter called the house.

After hanging up, Alan smiled and looked back down at the cell phone use report he had in front of him. Thanks to the status of a possible kidnapping, he was able to obtain the cell phone report. The report was through late evening the night before. Kim had been heading east out of Colorado, with calls from near Topeka, Kansas, and from somewhere in Missouri. He leaned back at his desk and let these observations sink in while he tried to piece together what was happening. *Had the girl really been kidnapped? Were Kim and Sean close to finding out something important? Who was trying to stop them from doing so?* His reflections gave him little satisfaction, but they did help him decide that he needed to get closer to the action. That meant heading to Nashville because that would put him in the center of Sean and Kim's travels giving him the best chance to be there if they truly found a treasure.

Knoxville

James had woken up after a lousy night's sleep. Worse, it was the second night in a row he had not slept well enough or long enough to help him recuperate from the previous day's activities. This time, his sleeplessness had been because of worries about Kim's daughter. Abby's plight had brought nightmares about his sister, Mary. The worse nightmarish memory had been where Kim's daughter and Mary had been holding hands at his door, but he could not unlock the screen and help them. That one had caused him to wake in a sweat, panting uncontrollably.

Now, James was grimly going about packing his SUV for a mission he hoped he could handle. He loaded shovels, a pickaxe, buckets, rope, a tarp and other odd supplies. He added his camping gear as well. *I haven't been camping in a long while.* The thought made him want to smile, but the circumstances on his mind made that impossible. Instead, he wore a grim, determined expression.

He worked as quickly as he could and finally felt that he had packed everything he could think of as being important. James went into his house and grabbed his duffel bag of clothes and his box of maps, notes and other documents and carried them out to his car. His bag went on the backseat, and the box on the front passenger seat. He stood there for a moment trying to think if he had forgotten anything, but nothing came to mind. Satisfied that he was ready, he went back into his house and headed into the kitchen. There, he grabbed his hat and a bottle of water. He then punched in the alarm code to arm his home alarm system and finally headed out the door.

A few minutes later, James was on the road and headed south on the highway towards Chattanooga. From there, he would turn towards Atlanta. He glanced down at his cell phone to make sure it was on, so he could be reached if needed. He prayed that it would ring and that it would be Sean calling to tell him that they had Abby and that everything was all right. So far though, the phone just sat there as if it was staring back at him. Glumly, he turned the radio on at a low volume and focused on the road ahead.

James had failed to notice the car that had been following him from his house. It had dropped back on the highway, but was now steadily pacing him. Had James not been so preoccupied with packing and thoughts of Abby, he might have noticed the vehicle when he drove right past it on the way out of his neighborhood.

Atlanta

The phone finally rang as Kim and Sean sat in their car in a gravel parking lot next to a coffee shop. Sean looked at it and then nodded at Kim. He then put the phone up to his ear as he answered it.

"Sean speaking."

"Hello Mr. Johnson. Have you two arrived in Atlanta?"

"Why don't you tell me where I am, whoever you are. Don't you already know?" Sean felt a need to assert himself somewhat.

"No, I'm not that good, Mr. Johnson."

"We've met before, haven't we?" Sean was now associating the voice on the phone with the face of the man in Knoxville.

"Perhaps we have. You and I have some common background you know."

"Yeah, well that's as far as we go. You're doing something entirely different with your skills." Sean intentionally tried to make his voice sound exasperated. "Listen, we've got your letters and we're ready to make the exchange. I don't know what your interest in this is, but all we care about is Abby. You give her to us, and you get the letters, no tricks. I promise."

"I hope you're right Mr. Johnson. For your sake."

"Yes, well that makes two of us." Inside, Sean was boiling with rage towards the man on the phone. He had not killed anyone for a long, long time, but he was more than ready to change that. Right now, he cared more than anything, that they get Abby back. The voice had a calmness to it that sounded icy and cold, given the surrounding circumstances. It made Sean more convinced than ever that he was right to not trust the FBI to get Abby back.

"Well, if you are ready, I will give you your instructions," the man said.

"I am," Sean replied. He then listened and repeated, out loud, the man's instructions. Kim jotted down the address and intersection he provided.

"Just the two of you will come," the man finished with.

"We're all there is," Sean had replied. However, he heard nothing from the other end.

The man had hung up. Sean then hit the "end" button on his phone. He put the phone down and looked over at Kim.

"Are you ready for this?"

Kim nodded. "Yes, I've never been more determined in my life. You want me to take over driving now?"

"Yes, that's a good idea. Let's swap now before we leave here. I need to use the bathroom before we leave though."

They got out of the car and headed back into the coffee shop they had left earlier. A few minutes later, they were back in the car, Kim now driving. She pulled out of the parking lot and began taking directions from Sean. As he told her where to go, they discussed their plans.

"We'll drive around the place completely. You'll park where you can see what's happening. Keep the car running. You'll have 9-1-1 entered in your cell phone, so you can quickly call if anything goes wrong. Follow Abby no matter what else happens, but don't get too close. Your job will be to bring the police to you while you follow Abby."

Kim kept nodding with a grim look covering her face. Sean reached over and touched her cheek as he spoke.

"You are the strongest mother I have ever known. Did you know that?"

A slight smile appeared on Kim's mouth.

"There, that's better. Don't forget how to smile. That was the best advice I ever received. I can remember sitting in an airplane, waiting to jump out, smiling."

"I'll smile now, for you, but when we get Abby back, you'll see the biggest smile you'll ever see." Kim turned her eyes back to the road with her dismal thoughts returning.

"Good. You remember our rendezvous point if we get split up?"

Kim nodded. "Roger that! Twenty minutes after the second full hour passes from the time we split up. It's the truck stop we passed five miles back."

"That's it." Sean nodded. "We're ready."

They drove on, with Sean giving her directions until they finally reached their destination. It was a large shopping mall next to the freeway. Even as they approached the exit, they could see the department store sign marking their target. Sean pointed.

"Drive that way. We can do a full circle before reaching the parking lot where they told us to meet."

Kim acknowledged, feeling butterflies in her stomach as she did so. Her mind was locked on her task, though, and she fought down the urge to start franticly looking for Abby, even though she knew that was what she really wanted to do.

They drove around to the other side of the mall. It was a large shopping structure, two stories, rising out of a sea of parking lots like an island. It was just before noon and a decent number of shoppers had arrived, but it was not full by any means, judging from the number of empty parking spaces. Kim could see Sean's eyes raking their surroundings. He asked her to drive a bit slower. She could see that he was turning his head, trying to absorb every detail he could. They came around the far end and were now driving in front of the parking lot they were instructed to go to.

"Turn in here," Sean said suddenly, pointing at a doughnut shop across the road from the parking lot, tucked in next to the freeway.

Kim wanted badly to keep going, to look for Abby, but she did as Sean had said and turned into the doughnut shop.

"Park right here." Sean gestured to a spot that would point them towards the parking lot. She did so. Sean, in the meantime, had pulled out a small set of binoculars. Using them, he scanned the area, pausing in different directions to study cars.

"There is a car with deeply tinted windows over there. Can you write down this license plate number?"

"Sure," Kim replied, letting go of the steering wheel and grabbing her pad and pen. "Go ahead."

Sean read the number out loud, and then began slowly moving the binoculars again. "Here's another. It's a white van." He read off another license plate. Kim wrote it down.

Sean scanned for a short time longer and then put the binoculars down. He turned to Kim.

"I really think that one, or possibly both, of the those vehicles are involved. I'll get out and then cross the street. I'll then walk straight into the parking lot. Once I get out of the car, pull out of here and drive past the parking area and pull into the lot maybe 100 yards past it. If this works, Abby will walk to you and get in. Once she does, take off. Understand?"

Kim nodded and Sean continued.

"By splitting up, we force them to give us separate control over Abby at the same time they receive the letters, but this will only work if you leave. If, by chance, I'm able to walk with Abby to the car, I will. If not, don't worry, I'll get out of there and somehow see you at the truck stop."

Kim nodded. Sean picked up the envelope containing the letters and leaned over towards Kim. She looked at him and then they kissed for a few long seconds. Sean smiled.

"See you in a few and don't worry."

With those parting words Sean got out of the car and walked into the doughnut shop. Kim took that as her cue to leave. She started up the car and backed out of her parking space. She then put the car in drive and pulled out onto the one-way lanes of traffic going around the parking lots circling the mall. She could feel her hands trembling as she drove by the designated area where they were to exchange the letters for Abby. She had to use all her willpower not to turn and look. Once past it, she steered the car into the lot located about 100 yards away just as Sean had said. She selected a space that allowed her to use her rear and side view mirrors to see most of the parking lot. Kim put the car in park and settled in, discreetly adjusting the mirrors.

Soon afterwards, she spotted the white van Sean referred to and tried to imagine Abby inside. Then, suddenly, she remembered instructions about having 9-1-1 dialed in advance. So, she picked up her phone, pressed 9-1-1 and set it on the dash so it was ready to go. Turning attention back to the mirrors, she remembered Sean's instructions carefully watch in all directions for anyone else who could be approaching the car. *Nobody suspicious within thirty feet,* she reminded herself. Grimly, she set about scanning the horizon and then using the mirrors to scan the area.

After what seemed like an eternity, She spotted Sean walking into the area. He was holding the envelope in his right hand. He had it between his thumb and forefinger and was holding it upright, like a manila colored flag. He walked closer and began getting partially obscured from Kim's view by other cars. She forced herself to pull away for a moment to scan the horizon yet again. Then she brought her eyes back to the mirror. She could see that Sean had stopped, but could not tell if he was speaking because of the distance between them. He stood there and slowly lowered the envelope. *That means he has made contact,* she thought nervously. She began scanning around, almost franticly, looking for Abby to emerge.

Then, just like magic, she did! The side door of the white van slid open and Abby stepped out. She was dressed in jeans and a sweatshirt and appeared fine. She had a small backpack over her shoulder. A surge of relief swept through Kim, but only for a moment. She remembered that Abby was a full 100 yards from her and not yet safe.

Abby turned her head and focused back on Sean. Kim realized that he must have been calling to her. She started to move, but then stopped and looked around, her eyes locking on Kim's car. As instructed, Kim tapped the brakes twice. Abby looked back at Sean and then, after a pause, began walking towards Kim's car. Kim felt another surge or relief. *So far, so good.*

Kim watched as Abby began walking faster and faster. She shifted her vision back to Sean and could see that he was bending over to lay the envelope on the ground. He stood back up and began backing away. Kim checked on Abby and could see she was getting closer. She looked back towards Sean and could now see that another man had emerged. He was holding a bag of some type and Sean had froze.

Even as Abby was getting closer, a new fear raced through Kim. *The man has a gun!* She knew that Sean had warned her of this and then remembered again, his instructions, to keep watching her own surroundings, as well as to focus on getting Abby. She did as she was told and scanned her area again as she rolled down her window. As she stuck her arm out, Abby broke into a run towards her. Kim put her foot down on the brake and then put the car in drive. Abby was close enough now that Kim could see her clearly. She used her hand to gesture towards the passenger side of the car and saw Abby swerve to head towards it. Kim took a last glance in the mirror for Sean. He was still standing there, frozen. That was all the time she had.

Abby burst into the car, out of breath, saying, "Oh Mom, oh Mom!" Kim wasted no time!

"It's okay," she replied. "Shut your door." Kim did not wait for Abby to comply, though, and stomped on the accelerator causing the car to surge forward. The door practically shut itself as they hurtled out onto the perimeter road. She had no time to try and look back at Sean, but she came up with a better idea.

"Abby!" Kim found herself yelling, but only out of excitement. "Turn around and look back. Tell me what's happening to Sean!"

Abby immediately spun around in her seat trying to steady herself against the rocking, jerky motion of the speeding car.

"He's standing there near the man that grabbed me," she said. "Wait, a car just slid up next to him. The man dropped his bag."

Abby's voice tailed off as she lost sight of the parking lot behind a building. She spun back around.

"What, what happened?" Kim demanded while aggressively cutting around a car and entering a freeway on-ramp. At this point, Kim did not even know what freeway she was approaching or even what direction she was heading.

"That's all I saw, Mom." Abby sounded close to tears and Kim looked over at her. She realized she needed to calm herself and Abby.

"That's okay, you're here. That's my first concern. Are you okay? Did they hurt you at all?" She reached her hand out and put it on Abby's leg. She looked Abby over, and saw nothing amiss. *Her hair's messy, that's about it.*

"No, I'm okay Mom. But I was so scared. That man was very cruel, Mom, I think he's crazy. I really thought he was going to kill me."

Anger rose in Kim. "Not anymore, he's not. You're safe now. I am so, so sorry for letting this happen to you. Until this is over, you're not leaving my sight."

"What is this Mom? What's going on?"

"It's very complicated and scary. I'll tell you everything soon. Right now, I need to find out how Sean is doing. She looked for her cell phone but it had, of course, long since left the dashboard of her car.

"Honey, can you look around your feet for my cell phone?"

Abby bent over and quickly retrieved it.

"Here Mom," she said, handing it over.

Kim took the phone and looked at the screen. No missed calls were showing. In bouncing around, the phone had added a few numbers after the 9-1-1 she had entered earlier. She cleared the screen and set the phone down once again. She thought for a moment. Until she knew Sean was okay, she couldn't really do anything, but if he was not okay, then she should be calling for help right now.

"Honey, I need to ask you a question. This might sound strange, but it's important. While you were being held and taken here, did you get any idea who it was that did it? What I really want to know is if you think they were from the government, maybe like the FBI."

"What?" Abby seemed genuinely surprised. No, they were definitely not FBI. I only saw three people, Mom. There was this guy, the dangerous one. He broke into the house and took me away. He was like some kind of super criminal. Later, somewhere, I was transferred to a van driven by two men that acted like they worked for him. I was blindfolded and handcuffed most of the time. They were polite. I kind of thought the two men did not like being involved in kidnapping me. Well, they talked like they didn't anyway."

Abby paused and looked around at the scenery. "Where am I anyway?"

"You're in Atlanta, honey. Atlanta, Georgia."

Kim was trying to think what to do next when her cell phone rang. It was Sean. Nervously, she answered it.

"Hello?"

"Hey there, I'm fine. Is Abby okay?" Sean replied,

"Yes, yes. Oh, thank god!" Kim felt another wave of relief surge through her. "Where are you?"

"Headed to the truck stop." Sean replied. "How about you?"

"Oh, shit." Kim exclaimed, realizing she was driving aimlessly.

Then, she looked over at Abby, who never heard her use words like that so often and easily. "Oh, sorry honey. It's been a rough couple of days."

Kim looked at the freeway signs.

"I think I'm headed the wrong way. I'll figure out where I am and head there. What happened?"

"I'll explain later. I'm with a friend."

Kim was puzzled. "A friend? What do you mean?"

Sean laughed. "I'll explain later. Let's just say I was covering my bases."

"Okay," Kim felt unsure of herself. She remembered the car that Abby had seen pulling up. "That's who you were talking to yesterday!" she said accusingly.

"Like I said, I'll explain when we get together. Call me the instant you see anything amiss. I'm going to call James and let him know everything is okay."

"Okay."

They hung up, and Kim set her phone back down.

"That was Sean. He's fine," she said to Abby. "We're meeting him at the rendezvous spot."

Abby laughed. "The what?"

Kim smiled at her. "Don't start. Sean is infectious. I really like him. Even his military talk is getting into me."

Kim finally saw a sign she recognized and realized that she was headed towards the truck stop after all. She thought for a moment.

"Listen, Abby," she said, sounding as firm as she could. "I need you to do something for me okay? It's going to sound weird, but just trust me okay?"

"Okay Mom," Abby replied looking at her.

"I need you to call your dad and tell him that you're fine. Tell him you caught a bus to meet me in Atlanta."

"What?" Abby protested. "Mom, I was kidnapped!"

"Yes honey, I know. But, there is much more going on that you don't understand. I promise you will understand as much as we do in a little while." Kim paused, thinking some more. "Tell him I was sup-posed to call him at work and tell him that I forgot. Act surprised when he acts upset and relieved to hear from you." *He deserves it,* Kim thought, recalling again that he did not even notice Abby missing.

.....

A few minutes later, they reached the truck stop and Kim saw Sean and another man standing next to a car talking. She approached cautiously, until she could see that Sean was truly relaxed and smiling. She pulled her car up next to them and got out.

"Kim, meet Frank Kelso. You may remember he was the cop in Saint Louis that put me up for a night?" Sean gestured to the man standing next to him.

Kim remembered the name and then the story. "That's right," she said. "Very nice to meet you." She shook his hand and then turned and punched Sean on the shoulder.

"Ow," Sean cried out half mockingly, as he reached up and rubbed his shoulder.

"That's for not telling me you called him," she said seriously. "Don't you trust me?"

"Man, I hope you never hit me in the face." Sean looked at her, returning the serious look. "Standard procedure. You did not need to know about him, and if you were caught you might eliminate his surprise value. Sorry. I thought about it, I really did. But I thought it was best. You have never had to perform like you just did. I really thought you would do fine, but I was not sure."

Kim reached to rub his shoulder and then let it become a hug. As she let go of him, Frank spoke up.

"Okay, so you two adults need a room, I can tell."

Abby had gotten out of the passenger side of the car. "Uh, that's gross. At least they're not kissing in front of me."

Sean turned. "Abby, I've always been glad to see you, but never as much as I am right now." He walked around the car towards her. "You get a hug too."

Abby was a bit taken aback, but then found herself opening her arms and returning his hug. "Thanks," she said. "I'm not sure what's going on, but I'm grateful for your help."

"Help nothing, Sean engineered this rescue," Kim said. "But it's my fault that you were ever in danger."

"No, it's not," Sean countered. "It's not your fault that your father died and handed you this mess. And it's not your fault that some criminals are running around murdering and kidnapping. I'm the most at fault here, but even I won't accept it."

Frank spoke up. "Well, I'm glad I was able to help. You owe me now, Sean."

"I've always owed you, but you're right. It's even more so now."

Frank turned to Kim and Abby. "I've got to catch a flight back to Saint Louis, before my night shift. It's been nice to meet both of you." They both waved good-bye to him.

Frank turned to Sean. "Sorry, I can't hang around. But if anything else comes up, you call me. You're right not to call the police. The FBI posted a revision to the earlier alert that was posted on Abby, declaring it to be a runaway family matter. That did not happen by accident. Someone in the FBI, someone with control over this matter, deliberately covered up Abby's kidnapping."

Frank glanced around at all of them. "I would not trust anyone on this until you get to the root of it." He reached out and shook Sean's hand.

"See you amigo."

"See you," Sean replied.

They watched as Frank hopped in his car and drove off. Sean then turned to Kim and Abby.

"Well, we've got some catching up to do," he said. "First, though, we probably need to report that Abby is safe and sound."

"Already done," Kim said. "Even better, Abby did it herself. She called her father and told him that she took a bus to meet me."

"Wow," Sean was truly surprised. "The Poole, ah Thomas, women continue to amaze me."

"Thomas women?" Abby interjected. "What's he talking about?"

"We have lots to tell you honey," Kim said. "But let's do it over some food, I'm starving."

Chapter Twenty-Nine

Athens, Georgia

Kim's phone rang as the three of them sat at a wooden picnic table at a highway rest stop just before Athens. They had just finished eating some take out Chinese food they had nabbed at the last exit and were languishing at the table while finishing their drinks. Kim looked down at her phone resting next to her. She frowned.

"I've seen that number before," she mumbled quietly as she tried to prod her memory. She could not place the number, though, and decided to not answer it. She looked up at Sean and Abby who were seated next to each other.

"Where is area code 602?"

Sean looked over at Kim and thought for a moment.

"It's Phoenix, I think. Is that where the call came from?"

"Yeah," Kim replied, watching the screen on the phone for a sign that a voicemail message was waiting. Instead, after a few moments, the phone began ringing again and showed the same number.

"Whoever it is, they're persistent," Kim announced. "Think I should take it?"

"Might as well," Sean said. "I don't think we are that hidden right now anyway."

"Okay." Kim sounded a bit uncertain though. She answered the call and held the phone up to her ear.

"Hello?"

Sean and Abby watched her listening to the caller.

"Well hello, Mr. Nazimi," she said next. "How can I help you today?" There was another pause while Kim listened. She looked over at Sean for advice. Sean drew his hand across his neck in the universal symbol for turning it off. Kim nodded.

"Look Mr. Nazimi, Abigail is right here with me. She's fine. She called her dad. I'm not about to let her talk to you. In fact, I have no desire to talk to you. Good-bye."

She pulled the phone away from her ear and pressed the button to end the call. Once she was certain it was disconnected, she looked up at Sean and Abby.

"He said he still needs to talk with me about what I'm doing. He asked why I was dragging my daughter into it as well." Kim sighed. "He was implying I'm doing something wrong. I think he was fishing for information about us, like where we are."

"He spoke to Abby's dad?" Sean asked.

Kim nodded.

"Did you guys tell him we were in Atlanta?"

Kim thought for a moment, but Abby answered for her.

"I did."

"Well then, it's likely that he told Nazimi, right?" Sean asked.

Kim and Abby both nodded.

"So, we should assume he knows where to find us," Sean concluded. "Not that I care," he added, after a moment's reflection.

"I just don't trust that guy," Kim shuddered. "He's slimy."

"So, what are we doing here?" Abby interrupted. "I thought you said we're hunting for a treasure."

Sean answered. "First, we need to connect with our wayward professor. We also need to go get a couple of rooms in town. The professor will debrief us on his findings. He'll probably want to read the Lincoln letters as well, or at least my copies."

"I cannot believe you gave them up." Kim said, sounding sad.

"Hey, it was Abby or some old letters from a president." Sean tried to sound serious, but they could tell he was joking. "Besides, I kept the original letter from Jacob. And I did not give them the key page in the Herndon letter that has the directions on it."

Sean stood up and stretched. "I'm really beat. Let's head into town and see if we can find a decent motel. I could use a nap before the professor gets here."

Kim followed him in rising from the picnic bench. "I second that. It has been a long day."

"I can't believe it," Abby said. "We're about to go find treasure, and you two want to nap?"

Nashville, Tennessee

"That's right, I need another report on that phone number," Alan explained. "The suspect just completed a call. She claims to be somewhere in the Atlanta area. You have the federal authorization from the last request, right?"

"We certainly do, Mr. Nazimi. I will run the inquiry and get it to you right away," the cellular company employee replied.

"I'm headed into the field, but I will be getting email. So you can send it to me electronically."

"Certainly, we're always glad to be of service to the Bureau."

"Thanks," Alan replied, hanging up the phone. He leaned back in his chair, placing his hands on the back of his head. He stared out the glass window that separated his Nashville guest office from the hallway and thought about the recent events. *First, the girl is kidnapped. Then she is miraculously returned? Meanwhile Kim and Sean disappear in Denver and reappear in Atlanta?*

Alan knew that something was getting ready to happen in his special case and he planned to be there. He decided it was time to head out on a few days of "vacation" and see what he could stir up.

"I hear Atlanta is nice this time of year," he said out loud. Then laughing, he started making his travel arrangements.

Atlanta

Terry drove his sedan up to the mansion and stepped out. He was seething inwardly, but fought the urge to let his anger show. In his left hand was the manila envelope that he had obtained in exchange for

Abby. He was angry, though, that he had failed to capture or eliminate Sean. It was the second time that Sean had directly defeated his efforts and that really made his blood boil. It was also the second time he had met Sean face to face and both times he was left feeling that he had been defeated, that he had failed. He pulled a small device out of his jacket pocket and glanced at it. The distraction helped him calm down a bit and he smiled. *The game is not over, Mr. Johnson.*

Terry had parked in his space on the side of the mansion. It was adjacent to a side entrance that led directly to his study. He went through the door, but instead of heading straight to his office, he turned left and headed up the carpeted stairs towards the study where Michael was waiting. Reaching the top and walking down the hallway, he entered the room and shut the door behind him. He glanced about, only briefly, as if to verify that he and his brother were alone. Michael was sitting in one of the deep chairs fronting the low mahogany table. Terry tossed the envelope onto the table and it slid neatly towards Michael, stopping just as it reached the end of the table.

Terry, meantime, shed his light jacket and hung it over the back of the empty chair across from Michael.

"So, this is it?" Michael asked, as Terry turned towards the bar.

"Yes," Terry growled. "There looks to be two letters in there." He reached the bar and pulled a short tumbler forward. While placing ice cubes in it, he continued.

"No Sean, no Abigail, no Kimberly." He sounded bitter, as well as slightly sarcastic. "He had a surprise waiting for me and had planned the exchange very well."

Terry had finished using silver ice tongs to add cubes to his glass and now poured himself a nice slug of whiskey. He picked it up and spun around to look at his brother. "That man is really pissing me off."

Michael smiled. "But you're much better than him, are you not? You have held your temper in check, knowing that we still control the situation."

Terry had walked over and sat himself down across from Michael.

"Yes, but it was not easy at all." Terry then smiled fiercely. "But, knowing that I will call the last shot is enough to see me through such a challenge."

Michael smiled back and opened the envelope, spilling out its contents, two folded letters.

"Remarkable. After nearly 150 years we have the loose thread that our ancestors could never find."

"We may have that thread, but we have three, maybe four loose cannons running around Georgia," Terry growled before taking a hefty sip of his drink.

"Patience my brother, all things in time." Michael had lifted up the first letter, unfolded it and then set it down. He did the same to the other. He leaned forward and compared the two letters for a few minutes and then picked up the second one. He began reading while Terry sipped his drink and watched him. Michael finished the first page of the letter and flipped to the next. After a moment, he paused and flipped to the third page, then the fourth and, finally, last page. After a moment, he flipped back to the first page. After another moment he set all five pages down next to each other on the table and studied them. He looked up at Terry and frowned.

"I believe that your Sean Johnson has retained a page of the Herndon letter for himself."

He picked up the other letter and flipped through its four pages. He then reached down and lifted the second page from the Herndon letter and inserted it into the letter in his hand, leaving only four pages on the table.

"In front of me are four pages of a five page letter that President Lincoln wrote to Thomas Herndon about Captain Greene. Of course, the missing page probably contained directions to where Captain Greene hid his documents and his find." Michael looked up at Terry. "You're right, Mr. Johnson is quite the pain in the ass."

Terry squeezed his drink tighter but said nothing. His boiling anger was surfacing again. Michael picked up the four pages and leaned back to read them. Terry sat in stony silence, his glare directed out the window at the meadow and lake visible through the glass. It had been a long two days, and he knew he needed some sleep.

After a few minutes, Michael had completed reading the Herndon letter and set it back down.

"Yes, it's the letter, and President Lincoln does indeed tell Herndon to go forth and follow Captain Greene's directions. But, the page with the directions, and, I suspect, a summary of most of the president's conversation with Captain Greene, is missing. In its place was a page from the other letter to Lincoln's stepmother."

Terry slammed his free hand against the leather arm of the chair. "It won't happen again." He reached over his shoulder and pulled his windbreaker into his lap. Reaching into a pocket, he pulled out his small computer device and looked at the screen.

"They're in Athens," he announced. "Next to the highway leading into town."

Michael leaned back in his chair and thought through the situation.

"We cannot allow them to get too far, nor go too long. You should head out there tonight and tag their vehicle with a better tracking device." Michael gestured at the device in Terry's hand. "That device will work for a day or two, at the most. That's assuming they don't find it. You yourself said that putting it in her purse risked discovery."

"That's right," Terry replied. "Battery life is 72 hours, but I wouldn't bet on more than 24."

"You should get some rest, then head out tonight," Michael repeated. "I'll follow tomorrow with a situation trailer. Just the two of us from here on out. We give them a day or two to think they are free from us. If they have not centered in on the location, or if they start to leave, we take them."

"You don't want a backup team in place?" Terry asked after finishing his whiskey. "If they run, we'll have a hard time catching all of them. It's best to outnumber your prey two to one, minimum."

Michael thought for a moment more. "Okay, two teams, one here in Atlanta and one in the east, maybe Columbia. Is the professor with them?"

"I don't know," Terry admitted. "We pulled back our surveillance. He certainly has not surfaced."

"Did the girl ever see your face?"

"With a disguise," Terry replied. "But it does not matter. They will not live that much longer either way."

Michael sighed. "Yes, you are right, brother."

"The death of someone else does not concern me," Terry said smiling. "It's my own death that I wish to avoid."

Athens

James cleared his throat. "Remarkable," he said. "So my ancestor visited President Lincoln? There's no such record of his visit. And President Lincoln was so moved that he wrote his stepmother? I guess it was just a damn coincidence that the letter was in the same pouch with the Herndon letter."

James was seated on a sofa in the room he was sharing with Sean. It was a kitchenette with a large round kitchen table and a bar to spread out their documents. James had taken the Jacob letter and Sean's copies of the Lincoln letters and gone over to the couch to sit and read.

"More than coincidence, maybe," Sean interjected. "First, his stepmother was near the same location, so it made sense to send it with the Herndon letter. Second, old Abe might have wanted to keep his inquiry discreet. His famous quote about his family history was the 'annals of the poor,' so perhaps he was embarrassed."

"You misunderstand that quote. He meant it as a statement of humility and also as a way to downplay the importance of ancestry, of breeding, if you will. Abraham Lincoln saw himself as a servant and, I think, was awed that he, a poor farmer's son, could rise to be president. But it never went to his head. So, when confronted with the fact that he could even be a bastard, like his mother was, and still rise to be president, I think it impressed him all the more."

"But he wanted confirmation." Kim objected. "He was not convinced."

"His name had been Lincoln all of his life. To have himself confronted by a man who convincingly tells him that he is an Enloe had to have been shocking." The professor looked around at them.

"But we digress. My point was that the Enloe connection was just that, a connection to a deeper and more fantastic story. That there might be a lost trove of gold, silver, jewelry and art buried about somewhere."

"Is that really possible?" It was Abby's turn to interject. James smiled. He had clearly been taken with Abby from the minute he had met her. She was sitting next to the professor on the couch.

"I mean, even if it really was buried or hidden, wouldn't somebody have found it by now?"

"Maybe so young Abby, maybe not." James said looking at her. "But that is why we are here, to find out."

Sean was sitting at the bar, on one of the vinyl covered bar stools.

"That's right. Your ancestor, Abby, your great, great…" He trailed off for a moment trying to make sure he got it right. Abby finished for him.

"My great, great, great grandfather," she said.

"Yes. Well, that guy," Sean said smiling. "That guy was almost murdered over it. And he left a deeply buried secret just in the hopes that his later generations would find it and track it down when the time was right. That's why we're here. I have to tell you though, that if those letters ever surface, they alone are priceless."

"We have copies," Kim protested. "And one of the original pages. Isn't that proof?"

"Proof yes, and valuable yes." James said. "Priceless, no, but still incredible."

James got up and walked over to the kitchen table. He pulled a file out of his box and set it down on the table. From it, he pulled out a map and began unfolding it and spreading it out next to his other items.

"Here is what I think will be our best resource," he explained as he finished laying the map out flat. "It's a Civil War history map of the area. It shows Civil War battle sites and the location of Civil War cemeteries."

He gestured south of Athens. "Sherman's army hacked and slashed its way quite south of here actually. There is a record of a skirmish a bit south of here, but most records of the small fights along Sherman's path simply were never made. The farms and plantations were staffed only by women, children, elderly men and slaves. They mostly hid in fear. Soldiers roamed in bands, taking food and supplies in a broader swath than the army itself had done. That was necessary to feed and supply the army and it was at Sherman's order. That was the order that mostly gives rise to him making his famous 'war is hell' statement. It certainly has created a cruel and tough image in history for Sherman."

James paused and looked around the map. "You can see some cemeteries marked on this map. Mostly, the dead were buried near where they died. By my count, there are at least ten cemeteries in this area to visit."

While James had been talking, Sean, Kim and Abby had gathered around the table. It was dark outside and they had all the lights turned on in the unit to make it easier to see. James reached into the file and pulled out some printed sheets. I found grave listings for some of the cemeteries, but, to tell you the truth, it's hard to be sure which list corresponds to which cemetery, so we probably need to check them all."

Kim spoke. "We're looking for Jeremiah Clarke. It's supposed to be east of Athens."

"Yes, and that worries me some," James said. He had been hunching over to reach the table and now leaned back and stretched his back. "It was probably a village cemetery or even a plantation cemetery. I'm worried that it has been lost, or that, even if it still exists, that there is no longer a marker or something to tell us that Jeremiah was buried there."

"Didn't people use headstones," Abby asked.

"It was the war, and it was a long time ago. The poor had little money to spend on stonework. The Civil War and, even more so, Sherman's campaign, had left people starving and having to use all their time just trying to get by. But even if the Civil War was not involved, many small local cemeteries have been swallowed up by trees and bushes. Stones have become buried, cracked or even stolen."

"So, then we might not find anything?" Kim asked. "Then what?"

"I'm not sure. We might be at a dead end." James looked over at Sean.

"I don't have any ideas either," Sean said. "Do we have any clues or stories to connect the treasure to?"

James retrieved another folder from his box.

"We have several varying stories or versions of the same story about an Atlanta treasure. You recall that Atlanta gold was one of our first clues?" He looked about at the three of them like they were students in one of his lectures. They all nodded back.

"Well, there are various stories about Atlanta treasure or gold being taken out of Atlanta before it fell to General Sherman." James flipped through the pages in the folder he was holding. He pulled some notes out and glanced at them.

"One decently matches Captain Greene's story as recorded by President Lincoln. It holds that a group of the Knights of the Golden Circle, a separatist group that supposedly survived the war, used the chaos of the fall of Atlanta to capture a collection of coinage, bulk gold and valuables being taken to Richmond. The group they sent to intercept the treasure was never heard from again."

James paused and read some more.

"It matches our story because they were supposed to intercept the treasure as it crossed a river. Captain Greene talks about a cave on this river."

James looked up. "But without better information, I'm afraid we'd be wasting our time."

There was a silence while the group stared at the map of the Athens area.

Sean broke the silence. "Let's talk a moment about what has happened in the last few days."

"Abby was kidnapped. We think someone else had knowledge of the existence of the Herndon letter. In fact, we know that. They are very dangerous and willing to kill us. But we don't know for sure who is part of the group pursuing us. It may include members of the federal government, perhaps even the FBI. We just don't know."

"I have a hard time believing that some conspiracy about treasure would survive more than 150 years, so I am assuming it relates to the other thing that Captain Greene spoke to President Lincoln about, the land grab conspiracy."

Kim nodded, "It makes sense." She was now leaning against the bar, her arms crossed on her chest. "But there's another angle, Lincoln's assassination. Couldn't this be connected to the assassination?"

James spoke up. "It's certainly possible. The Herndon letter speaks of corruption and conspiracy within the Union Army under Sherman's command. The attempt to murder Jacob and stop the letter from being delivered suggests War Department level involvement, someone in D.C. If they were willing to kill Jacob, could they have been willing to kill the President?"

James sighed. "But that is just conjecture. The Herndon letter does not suggest that Lincoln was afraid for his life. It comes across, instead, that Lincoln wanted to avoid a public spectacle, or at least, not have one until he knew for certain it was true. But what if the conspirators in the War Department knew that Captain Greene had informed Lincoln? They might have been uncertain what to do. But when Lincoln was assassinated, it made killing young Jacob and stopping Lincoln's letter to Herndon as the only thing they had to do to put an end to the risk that their scheme would be disclosed."

"But, what if they were involved in a conspiracy to murder Lincoln?" Kim persisted. "Then the government today could have a reason to keep this conspiracy a secret. That would explain why the FBI and maybe CIA are involved."

"Maybe," James admitted. "But we would be speculating about Lincoln's assassination to defend a theory about why our own government appears to be involved. That's a fairly strained analysis."

Sean smiled. "That's too much logic for me. But here's what we do know. Besides a southern land grab conspiracy that may have happened right where we are standing, we also know that the Sheriden Corporation is somehow involved. Their headquarters are here." Sean paused and briefly looked at the three others listening intently. "So, my point is that we have walked ourselves straight into the enemy's camp. This is their home turf and we are the intruders. Only one of us has the right accent to fit in down here." He nodded at James.

"You're saying we are in danger and need to be careful," Kim commented.

"Yes, well, I know I have been saying that a lot lately, but now I'm trying to emphasize it. But there's more."

"You see, I think they want us dead. We are the only ones that know about the letter. In fact, I don't think they can risk letting us live much longer with what we know. We might share the information with others. Somebody has a lot to lose if this story gets out."

Kim dropped her arms, "Yes, but if we go forward with a copy of a Lincoln letter and one original page of the Herndon letter, neither of which offers proof or even names a person, how dangerous is that?" Kim asked. "Do you think they are so concerned about allegations?"

"I admit, there is a chance that they think that we can no longer hurt them and maybe they have backed off. But we should not assume that at all. I want to do a few more things."

"First, let's pair up. Kim and I will travel as companions." Sean paused and made a face at Abby, "You can pretend we are pretending." Abby made a face back at Sean before he continued.

"James and Abby, you'll travel as grandpa and granddaughter. We need to try and stay under their radar."

"We also need a duress code word. A word that if any of us is in danger, caught or something else where you cannot talk candidly, you can use that word in conversation and it tells the other person to get help."

"Let's use Mary," James suddenly offered.

Sean looked at James for a moment and then spoke.

"Is that fine with everybody?" Seeing nods, Sean continued. "Okay so only use Mary from here on out if you are threatened, captured or the like. If you hear someone use the word Mary while talking to you, don't say or do anything, but disengage as quickly as you can and then go to the local police and tell them everything. Is that clear?"

"I've done something else. I put copies of the letters in the mail to my editor, and to a couple of friends. I've told them to hold the documents and if they don't hear from me in a week to go to the police."

Sean paused and looked at all of them.

"That just leaves reminding everyone to stay on their toes and to watch for cars or people following them. We'll pick up some of those two way scrambled radios tomorrow and use them when and as we need to."

Kim smiled. "You've forgot one thing."

"What?" Sean asked, looking quizzical.

"Dinner. We need to eat!"

Sean smiled back. "Oh yeah," he said. "So what does everyone want?"

"Pizza!" yelled Abby. "We want pizza."

"That makes two of us," James added.

Chapter Thirty

Monday, May 11
Athens and Seagraves, Georgia

Terry felt fatigue relentlessly trying to take over his body. It was six o'clock in the morning and he had slept only two hours. He had found Sean's car in the parking lot of a motel right next to the University of Georgia campus. He felt a need to be extremely cautious and so he had retreated and returned after midnight to place a tracking device on the vehicle. That had taken him a full hour, because he carefully and patiently surveyed the area and eventually moved in only when he was as certain as he could ever be that he was not being watched. It had been extremely difficult because there had been many students out and about after midnight, despite the fact that it was a Sunday night.

Finally, after getting a hotel room, he had allowed himself to sleep a couple of hours before rising, preparing and hustling back out to a strategic spot to await movement. He was parked on the street two blocks away from the motel. The car tracking device showed the vehicle to be stationary. The purse device had not shown any movement either.

The car tracking device was displayed on a laptop that was sitting in the passenger seat of Terry's vehicle. After napping the previous afternoon, he had picked up a Sheriden "secure" vehicle at one of their generic storage locations. It was a greenish-grey, two door sedan that looked completely unremarkable. The vehicle was registered to a "shell" company that was managed by a fictional person and owned by a fictitious company in Scandinavia. Only by accessing private offshore bank records, could the car be traced to Sheriden. *Perfect for tailing and tracking without being noticed. Better, the car comes with a fully equipped trunk, having most any tool I could possibly need.*

Still, Terry was not taking anything for granted and would give Sean the longest lead possible. Thanks to the vehicle tracking device, that was possible. Terry glanced at his watch and decided he could take a quick break and get some coffee and possibly a doughnut. He had seen a shop half a block behind him. So, he got out, locked the car, and then headed off for his breakfast. In his pocket was the purse tracking device.

A little while, later he was back in his car. There still had been no detectable movement of anybody on his devices. In a way, that made the waiting harder. The devices were his only "eyes" on the scene. The longer he stared at them, the more he questioned whether the devices had been detected and left behind at the hotel *But,* he told himself, *that's unlikely and expecting them to move before eight in the morning is unreasonable.* So Terry sat and waited. At seven thirty, his cell phone vibrated and he tapped the headset to answer the call.

"Yes," he said plainly.

"Good morning brother," a cheerful and rested Michael responded.

"Maybe for you, but not me. It won't be until Sean is six feet under, the rest of his group eliminated and we have the treasure and records in our hands."

"Ho there, brother, don't get too testy or upset," Michael sounded truly concerned for his brother. "You'll be happy to hear that I am on my way now to pick up a trailer. I should get out there by early afternoon."

"You're right, I am upset," Terry replied. "We'll have two back up teams staged, as requested, by four o'clock today."

"Excellent," Michael drawled, a rare moment where he let himself sound quite southern. "I'll call again when I'm on the road with the trailer."

"Good," Terry responded and tapped his headset to hang up. He looked back down at the device and then the laptop, and then reached for another doughnut. *No wonder cops get fat,* he thought.

.....

"Sean?"

Sean picked up his radio and pressed the side response button. "Go ahead."

"We're going to break for lunch," Abby's voice was barely recognizable over a hissing background noise.

Sean looked at Kim. "A lot of static. They must be at the edge of the range of these radios."

Abby's radio call to Kim and Sean capped off a mostly unproductive morning. After rising and eating the free breakfast at their motel, they had driven over to a giant mega-store by the highway where they had bought some supplies, including four bright yellow radios. They had checked out of the motel, deciding that it was better that they not be tied to any one location. They split up in the parking lot, James and Abby working a southern area east of Athens and Kim and Sean working the northern area.

Sean and Kim had found it slow. Their first cemetery was supposed to have been on a farm along a road that went around a hill. They drove on the road around the hill, seeing no farm, just pastures, crops and an orchard. Once they had decided they had gone far enough, they stopped to consult the map and the notes on the cemetery. They had then driven back, looking for old roads or turnoffs that might have been a driveway in days past. Once they thought they finally had found one, they parked, got out, went through a gate and walked up a muddy, gravel filled pathway. It went over a rise and ended at a pond. Some cows had seen them and then had started wandering over to them.

"Great," Sean had muttered. "We're probably trespassing, cows think we're going to feed them and all we've got is mud stuck to our shoes to show for it." He looked down at his shoes. "Well, at least I hope it's mud."

Kim had said nothing and they trudged back. They both decided that trying to find every single cemetery might take a week or more. So they had given up on the first cemetery on their list and moved on to the second one. By the time Abby had radioed them, it was almost one o'clock in the afternoon and they had seen two cemeteries and given up on two more. Of the two they had found, one had some nameless old stones mixed in with a few actual headstones. The other had markers noting the burial locations of a couple of civil war soldiers. All in all, Kim and Sean had a sinking feeling that they might never find the grave where Captain Greene had placed his map. Or, stated better, they might pass right by the grave and never know.

"We'll join you if you're not too far away," Sean replied to Abby after seeing Kim mouth the words "let's eat" while rubbing her stomach. Abby relayed her location, and they decided to head to a main road that lay between them and then meet at a restaurant somewhere in that area.

. . . . .

When the two tracking devices first showed movement, Terry did not catch the fact that something was amiss. The purse device had a pretty low accuracy and so Terry expected to see some differences in their readings. Moreover, the two units displayed their results on two different devices. So, Terry had to switch back and fourth from the small screen of the purse device to the larger screen of the laptop to compare the two. They had headed down to the highway, and once they were a good five blocks ahead of Terry, he had turned down a side path and started paralleling them.

Driving while following another moving object on a scrolling map was challenging, and it was all Terry could do to stay out of traffic accidents, yet still monitor their progress. The two devices had showed they had stopped near the highway, so Terry had stopped as well and parked under a nice shady oak.

Then, the devices had started moving again and he quickly spotted the issue. *They're not on the same path. One is heading due east, the other is turning back up north from where they came.* That told him that they either had two vehicles or that they had found one device and attached it to something or someone else. He suspected the former, but that was just his gut feeling. Terry had decided to stay in between the two sources for a while.

He had parked in a gravel lot next to a warehouse and watched the screens while he ate an apple. All morning, the two sources both had exhibited similar behavior of meandering for a short time and then stopping for a little while. By noon he had figured out what they were doing. *It's a quadrant search and either they split up or they have help.* He considered that it could be the person that had driven straight at him in the parking lot the day before, forcing him to dive, and then scramble for his life. He also considered that it could be the professor or some other friend. What he concluded is that he had to know how they were now organized, how many people were involved, and who they were. So, when the two vehicles started converging, he decided he had to take a try at observing them.

They were actually converging right on top of him and he considered simply sitting in his car, but he knew that would make it too easy for Sean to spot him. So, instead, he started his car and began driving east. The source coming down from the north was now behind him, while the source coming up from the south was just ahead of him. He slowed and pulled into a gas station. He quickly drove around behind the building emerging out the other side. He stopped the car with the station shielding him from the west, where one source was, but giving him a good view of the east, the purse source. *I should see the girl.*

He sat there for about a minute watching his two screens. Then as the purse device showed him that the car should be coming into sight, he lifted his vision and began scanning the cars coming along from the east. Five cars later, he spotted them. *The professor has returned! And he has the girl.* Terry smiled. *So far, so good. Now to spot Sean.* He eased the car forward and reached the edge of the street. He checked both screens and could see that Sean's car had stopped and that the professor's SUV was halfway to them. He quickly pulled out and turned left, running about an eighth of a mile behind the professor. He decided to quit trying to watch the movements on his tracking screens as it might make his head move too much, something that Sean might spot. So, instead, Terry focused on driving along in the flow of traffic while casually looking about.

After a short time, he spotted the professor turning right into a gravel parking lot of a restaurant. Terry maintained his natural back and forth scanning which forced him to look away. When he came back to look at the right side, he got a good solid glimpse of Kim and Sean standing by their car waiting for the professor to finish parking. Terry was careful to not look Sean in the eye, but instead to turn away and keep driving down the road.

…..

Over lunch, the foursome shared their experiences. Abby and the professor had done better than Kim and Sean, having found three of four burial spots. They were now in the community of Seagraves, well east of Athens, and James was hopeful that they would shortly strike gold. When the food came, they all dug heartily into their choices. Sean had decided to try some catfish which, he admitted to the other three, he had never eaten. He loved it.

After lunch, Sean headed outside to look around. Kim took that as his version of making sure they were not being followed. She watched as he stepped out the door and then moved to one side and stood there, looking about at the surrounding area. Kim and Abby headed to the bathroom, as did the professor. Kim followed Abby into the room and waited while Abby used the only toilet in the room first. Once Abby was done, Kim went in the stall. She could hear Abby at the sink when suddenly she heard Abby say "Mom?" in an alarmed voice. She immediately began finishing her business.

"What honey?"

"Uh, well, I need you to look at something…on my neck. I think it's a growth."

Relief washed over Kim. Relaxed, she stepped out of the stall to find Abby holding a small black device in her hand while holding her other hand up to her lips as if to say "silence!" Kim was startled for a moment and then noticed Abby's purse on the counter with a few of its contents laying next to it. *That thing came out of her purse! It's a bug!* Kim went from relief to shock to revulsion in one gasp that she cut off realizing she would be heard. She stood there for a moment and then nodded her head. Abby, for her part, did not look the slightest bit scared. *I guess when you've been kidnapped, a bug in your purse doesn't really phase you.*

Kim gestured for Abby to put everything, including the bug, back in her purse. Abby did so and they left the bathroom. Seeing Sean still standing outside scanning the horizon, she gestured to Abby to walk ahead of her and keep going. Kim then followed Abby out of the busy restaurant and stopped next to Sean. Once Abby was most of the way to the car, Kim spoke.

"Abby found a bug in her purse," she said simply.

Sean turned and looked at her and then over at Abby who was now standing in front of Sean's car.

"Really?" he asked. He then looked up again and began scanning the horizon while walking towards Abby. He gestured to Abby to open her purse and show him. She did so and held out a black plastic device, about as big as a pack of cigarettes but half as thick. It had a wire wrapped around it. He took it from Abby and studied it for a moment, sensing Kim walk up beside him.

Suddenly he spoke, breaking the silence.

"I've got good news and bad news. The good news is that this is not a bug. The bad news is that it is a tracking device."

He looked around again. "Damn, I've been too relaxed again. I should have known things have been too easy." He looked at Kim and then at Abby, and then came up with a plan.

"Okay, I have an idea. Let's continue like nothing has changed. Whoever finds the burial site, assuming we find it, leave and keep going to another location where you will stop. The device can actually help us fool them if we use it to our advantage. Okay?"

Sean looked around. The professor had joined them and gotten the gist of their conversation. His eyes dropped to the black device.

"Tracking device?"

"Yep," Sean replied. "It was in Abby's purse."

They conferred a little more and then set off on their afternoon routes.

The road Kim and Sean were on was narrow with curves every hundred feet or so, or at least it felt that way to Sean. They came around a bend and found an old farm house set back about fifty yards from the road.

"Should be on the right about now," Kim said looking up from the map.

Sean spotted it immediately. "There it is!" He pointed to the right at a small cemetery on a slope. It had, what looked to be, about thirty burial sites, most with headstones. It looked extremely old. The headstones were upright, though, with the weeds and growth under control.

"Somebody cares for that cemetery," Sean said looking back to the farmhouse on the other side of the road and then scanning the entire area around them.

Kim pulled the car over to the side of the road. "Should we go ask the farmer if it's okay if we look at it."

Sean looked up at the farmhouse again.

"No, let's just walk out there quickly and look around. There's no fence, signs or anything and it's not on the same side of the road as the farmhouse anyway."

"Okay," Kim said dubiously. "But if I get shot with a load of rock salt you're picking it out of me."

Sean laughed as he hopped out of the car. "Nobody does that anymore." He looked around. "At least I don't think anybody does that anymore."

Kim had gotten out also, ignoring his joke. She led the way. The cemetery was about fifty feet from the road. There were pine trees located behind it and to one side, creating a natural corner for the dated cemetery There was a path through the weeds to the lot. Kim completed the path and came upon the first stone.

"1867. That's a good start," she called out.

Sean walked off to the left and began working his way down a row next to Kim.

"Here's one dated 1865, that's even better!" Sean called out. "Sherman left Atlanta in November of 1864."

He heard nothing in reply and kept scanning. After a moment though, he sensed Kim had stopped moving and turned to look at her. She was standing in front of a small stone, her hands at her sides. Her mouth was open, but nothing was coming out. Sean hurried to her side.

"I'll be damned," he said. "Clarke, 1864."

"Is this it?" Kim finally managed to mumble.

"It's gotta be. I bet this is not the original stone though. Maybe by the time it was replaced his first name was forgotten." Sean, too, was stunned at the simple sight of something that a 150 year old letter had said would be right where it was found.

He stared for a moment more and then finally spoke.

"Okay, let's look at the rest of the stones. Could be another Clarke here. Then, we'll get out of here before we end up talking to somebody."

Kim nodded her head in agreement. "Right."

They checked the rest of the stones, but found no more Clarkes. Sean then searched the horizon in all directions. Kim was sure he was trying to figure out how they were going to sneak into the cemetery at night. She was sure it would not be easy. It was a quiet country road. Whoever lived in the house across the street would be quick to hear any car.

They reached their car and got into the vehicle. Sean started the engine, put it in gear and pulled back onto the road.

"Whew," Kim said. "I felt like I was holding my breath back there."

"Me too," Sean said. "Let's drive this area some and see if we notice any other roads or approaches to the area we could possibly use at night."

A few minutes later they were parked about a half mile south of the cemetery in a wooded grove off another road. Sean pointed north.

"The cemetery should be straight over that ridge," he said. "We can come back here tonight and hike over to it. Nobody will even notice our vehicle back in here."

"I guess," Kim said less than enthusiastically. "I'm beginning to picture the night's work ahead of us. Hiking half a mile in the dark, digging with minimal lights and praying that we don't hit rocks and stones. Then finding a corpse and hopefully something with it. Then, finally, running back at top speed as a farmer with a shotgun chases us through the woods."

"That's pretty much it," Sean admitted.

"Great!"

.....

Terry pulled up to the white trailer. It was the fifth wheel variety, and inside it would have everything necessary to be the mobile equivalent of a command center. Sheriden used these for the center point of large security details, but it was a perfect fit for their needs here. *Perfect in particular because it has two bunks in it.* Terry was bone tired and knew he needed some sleep. His fury over his previous failures and the importance of what they were now doing, were all that were keeping him going.

Michael had parked the trailer at a truck stop along the freeway. It was a busy area and the trailer was unnoticeable amongst all the trucks and RVs in the area. Michael himself was standing on the trailer door-step as Terry got out of his sedan and waved to him.

"Hello brother," he said simply.

"Hello," Terry responded. "Tell me you have food in there."

"Oh, but of course," Michael said stepping aside and ushering Terry into the trailer. "The finest chow found along America's highways."

Terry stepped in with a grunt and looked around the inside. He was in the front portion which was the command center portion. A large table with several chairs dominated the very front. The area where he had stepped in was filled with counters, drawers and several moni-tors. One muted monitor displayed a twenty-four hour news station. Another showed an internet-based weather overview for their area.

"Seagraves," Terry muttered, noting the name at the bottom of the screen.

On the table were some plastic food containers and bottles of spring water. Terry knew that the doorway to his left would lead to a small living quarter consisting of two beds and a shower. Right now, he wanted food, but first he needed to put the movement of Sean's vehicle up on one of the monitors. He pulled out a keyboard drawer and typed for a moment. Michael entered behind him and closed the door. Terry finished and a third monitor lit up with a map showing the area. It contained a blinking square showing Sean's location. They were back at the motel they had stayed at the previous night. *Back for the night,* Terry hoped.

"There," he said. "There's the tag I put on the vehicle that Sean appears to be driving. The professor's here and I have not yet tagged his SUV, but as luck would have it, the girl is traveling with the professor and her purse unit is still working."

"You think they're in for the night?" Michael asked.

"Hope is a better word for it, I need some rest."

"Well, I'm here as well, so I can cover this for a while brother. You get some sleep," Michael said. "I'd like to stay out of the way during the day as much as possible, just so I'm not recognized. Monitoring in here and covering night time operations, is perfect."

"Good," Terry grunted. "I'm going to get some sleep after eating something."

.....

The plan was ready for execution. Sean waved at the professor and he waved back. Sean then started up the SUV and drove off with Kim in the passenger seat."

"I hope they'll be fine," Kim said wistfully. After having Abby kidnapped once, it was hard to see her being left behind at night to play the role of rabbit, while she and Sean went undetected.

"They've been well briefed," Sean replied. "It shouldn't be a problem."

"I know, I just worry."

"I'm worrying too," Sean said. "There's no way I'll allow her to fall into their hands again."

Kim reached across and stroked Sean's forearm with her fingernails. "Thanks," she said.

Sean glanced over at her and smiled. "You're welcome, but thanks are not needed. I care about her as much as I have come to care about you. These past several weeks have been crazy. When it's all over, I am hoping we can find a way to stay connected and see if we're just as compatible when we're not running around the country on a treasure hunt."

"Me too," Kim said. "Me too."

They drove in silence for a while. Sean could feel the fatigue setting in and hoped that they could get this task done quickly. He had never dug up a grave before, but suspected it would be a huge amount of work.

.....

Abby glanced at her watch.

"Time to go," she announced.

"Okay," James responded cheerfully. "Let's begin making our run."

He started up the car and began driving. Their job was to drive a slow, random pattern through the countryside until Kim and Sean called them to tell them to stop and where to go from there. James suspected it was going to be a long night.

.....

Inside the trailer, Michael noticed the movement of the car. He glanced over at the device and compared the two displays for a minute. They seemed to be showing the same path. He thought about it for a moment and decided against waking his brother. *So long as they don't stop in one place for too long. If they do, then we get in gear.*
.....

Sean and Kim had reached their destination, parked, unloaded their gear, and begun their tedious hike to the cemetery. Besides shovels, a pick, a hoe and a big pry bar, they had dark colored sheets to lay around for dirt and the same red flashlights they had used in Denver. Sean had most everything in a small backpack and they each carried a shovel and one of the other necessary tools.

Kim felt like a miner headed off to work. She had a shovel in one hand and pickaxe in the other. Her flashlight was shoved in her jacket pocket. They were darkly dressed and Sean had found two dark beanies to add to the their stealth clothing collection. Their dress certainly was not going to win any fashion contests, but it was practical for the task at hand.

The hike was uneventful, and they soon found themselves sneaking down the hill to the cemetery. The farmhouse across the road was dark and silent. It was a still night, so Kim walked as quietly as she could. Sean was doing the same thing in the lead and, as a result, they approached the cemetery slowly. By agreement, they would only speak if absolutely necessary. Sean had reminded Kim at least five different times to never, ever shine her red flashlight at the farmhouse.

Soon, they reached the cemetery and Sean quickly walked over to the Clarke headstone. He carefully set his tools down a little distance away from the marker and then pulled his backpack off his shoulders. He removed the two sheets from inside the pack and laid one out on each side of the grave. He then gestured to Kim to set her own tools down and shine her light on the spot where he was digging. She put her shovel and pick down and pulled her flashlight out of her jacket pocket. Turning it on, she shined it down on the shovel tip that Sean had now rested in the soil. She watched as he tried to push it into the dirt just by stepping on it. It barely moved. Sean backed up and set the shovel down and then went over and grabbed the pickaxe. He came back and swung it gently into the soil. The ground gave way more easily. He repeated the pickaxe swing a few times and then switched over to the shovel.

It worked out to be a pattern that went on for an hour. Kim stood there shining her light, cringing at every sound Sean made, and occasionally looking back over her shoulder to see if there were any signs of activity at the farmhouse. It had stayed silent and the only real break had occurred when her batteries ran out and she switched over to Sean's flashlight. She knew Sean had extra batteries in his backpack.

Sean was sweating profusely now. He had dug quite a ways down. Just like in the movies, Sean swung his pick axe for the thousandth time only to hear a different sound. The noise had a much softer, muffled sound to it. Sean put the tool down and picked up the shovel. He gently pushed it into the earth and lifted. A heavy fabric came up, pulling some soil with it. Sean repeated the process a bit farther down and got another section of fabric. Kim kneeled down, while keeping the light on Sean's work area and felt the material with her hand. It felt like an old, thick blanket that was just beginning to rot away to nothing. *A horse blanket* she thought.

Sean put the shovel down and pulled out a screwdriver and trowel. With one in each hand, he was now on his knees loosening and moving dirt around. Suddenly, he stopped as the screwdriver appeared to be stuck in something. He used his fingers to dig into the soil and a minute later pulled a rectangular shaped object out of the earth that looked like something folded. Sean set it down at Kim's feet, and she kneeled back down to help him examine it. It was leather, she realized, like an old saddlebag. Sean gently pried the top flap open. What looked to be the remains of a rusted buckle fell away. Inside the pouch, rested a clean looking, folded roll of leather. Sean gingerly lifted it out of the pouch.

"I think this is it," he whispered. It was the first words spoken in over an hour and they sounded shockingly loud to Kim. She simply nodded.

Sean pushed the leather back into the saddlebag and handed it to

Kim. She then stood there, holding the ancient saddlebag, while Sean continued probing and prying with the screwdriver and trowel. A few minutes later, he put the tools aside and proceeded to try and undo his hour's work, shoveling the dirt back into the grave. It went a lot faster, but when he was through, it was pretty clear that the grave had been disturbed. Besides being freshly turned soil, it was now mounded much higher than the surrounding soil, making it look like a truly fresh grave. Kim looked at her watch. It was four o'clock in the morning.

Sean set about repacking the gear. He took the saddlebag and placed it in his backpack as well. Once it was tightened up and on his back, they picked up their tools and started the trip back to their car. As they left the site, Kim was trying to imagine the shock and confusion that would confront someone the next day when they saw the disturbed grave.

Chapter Thirty-One

Sean stood, like a sentry, outside the copy shop, watching the street. Behind him, inside the store, Abby, Kim and James were preparing to open up the folded leather satchel and look inside at its contents. It was now six-thirty in the morning. Sean was becoming so fixated on preventing their quest from being derailed by their pursuers that he had chosen to stand outside and guard the others. He was standing still, under the large canvas awning that fronted the copy shop with his back against the stone front of the building, well hidden in the early dawn light.

After Kim and Sean had reached the car from the cemetery, Sean had called the professor and told him to drive to the motel parking lot and stay there. Sean and Kim had then made the drive back, resisting the urge to open the folded leather parcel.

James had called to report that he and Abby were parked in the motel parking lot. When they got near the motel, Kim had dropped Sean off a block away so he could scout around the motel looking for anything suspicious. Finding nothing unusual, Sean had called Kim to come to the parking lot, and then walked over to the car containing James and Abby.

After showing James and Abby the leather parcel, they had decided to leave the cars in the lot and walk the block and a half down the road to the 24-hour copy shop that Sean had seen earlier. They had purposely left the small tracking device in one of their cars.

Sean felt a deep tension driving him and knew that he was getting weary. *You're near the end of this though, Sean old boy. Just stay alert for a day or so more and this will be all over.* As he stood there, he thought about whether it was time to go public by trying the local police. As he reflected though, he realized that they would have to defend their recent conduct, which now included grave digging and breaking and entering. *And wouldn't the cops think we were nuts?* He concluded that they might come out okay, but also that there was a good risk that going to the police could endanger them. *No, you're going to have to stick this one out. Protect your unit until the end.*

It bothered him, though, that they seemed to have gone past the point of no return. If they failed to find any hidden treasure or documents, then they would have nothing to come forward with to the authorities. If they did not come forward, however, their pursuers would continue to hunt them. They were screwed in either case. *We just need to find the treasure. If we do that, we'll be fine.*

While Sean was outside guarding them, Abby, Kim and James gathered around a small work area in the self-service copy area. Kim was gingerly unfolding the leather package. The leather itself was still fairly pliable and was not breaking as much as she thought it would when touched.

"Okay, that's the first set of folds," she said. The package had been about a foot long and half a foot wide when they had found it. She had unfolded the first two outer flaps and now the leather covered a much wider area. Another set of folds, laying in a perpendicular direction to the first set, were now visible. Based on the thickness, she suspected that this was the last set. Whatever was in the package would most likely be resting directly behind the two flaps that would fold up and down.

She peeled the top one up and peaked beneath it to see if any paper was sticking to it. All she saw was more leather, so she steadily lifted the flap up and then flipped it over. Next, she grabbed the flap that was now exposed and repeated the same investigative procedure. This time, when she peeked inside, she saw what looked like yellowed paper.

"There's something under this flap," she said excitedly.

"Be careful Mom," Abby said quietly. James stood there smiling.

Kim began lifting the flap. The paper did not appear to be sticking to it, so she lifted it fully off the paper and flipped it down. The leather now looked like a large, unfolded, rectangular envelope with a sheet of yellowish brown paper sitting in the middle of it. On the paper were lines and words that took a few moments to register.

"It's a map," Abby cried happily. Kim looked at her sharply as a reminder for her to watch how loudly she spoke. James had leaned in and was now studying the map.

"Yes, it is Abby," he said slowly. "It's a map that shows, what I believe to be, the Savannah River and the precise location we seek on that river."

Kim looked around the shop. She was nervous about doing this in such a public area, but had agreed it was the best they could do this early in the morning. All Kim saw were a few desperate college students in the computer center and two employees working on a copy job. She could not see Sean through the window, but she intuitively knew he was out there, watching. She turned her attention back to the map.

"Do you think we can copy it?" she asked.

James nudged a corner of the paper. "I think it may fall apart on us if we try to move it off of the leather. Perhaps, if we're extremely careful, we can lift this whole thing and set it face down on a copier?"

"Good idea," Kim said.

"Of course we could try and hand sketch it first," James continued. "Just in case we ruin it trying to copy it."

"I think I want to get out of here as fast as we can," Kim replied. "Now that we have this thing, I'm feeling really jumpy. Let's all study it closely for a minute and try to memorize the information. Then we'll try to copy it. Okay?"

Abby, though, had already grabbed a piece of paper and a pen and was furiously making a sketch that showed the shape of the river. She was even including the other landmarks on her drawing. Kim and James studied the map while Abby hand copied it. Kim noticed a mill drawn on the map downstream from the location. There was an annotation by the spot where an "X" was boldly marked.

It read, *"White Cliffs 60 yards above river."*

After a full minute of studying the map, Kim broke the silence.

"Okay, let's go," she commanded.

She and James lifted the leather up cautiously and shifted it over to the nearest copier that had its cover flipped open. Abby kept scribbling on her makeshift map as they moved it.

"Let's just smoothly and gently flip it over onto the face of the copier," Kim said as they reached the machine.

"Okay," James replied. "On three. One, two, three."

With a smooth plop, the map landed nicely on the copier in the right location.

Kim walked over, grabbed one of the hanging key cards from a nearby rack, returned, and stuck it in the slot on the copier. She then made a few selections on the control panel and hit the copy button. In a few seconds a shrunken copy, of almost the entire map, emerged.

"Not bad, Mom," Abby said comparing the copied map to her sketch.

They continued copying for a few minutes, carefully and delicately nudging the map around. Finally, Kim managed to make a copy with the entire map shrunken down and fitting on a single sheet of paper. She made several copies. Then, they picked the leather back up, flipped it around, and folded it back up. James went over to pay with the key card, while Abby and Kim collected all their copies, even Abby's hand sketch, and made sure they left nothing behind. James joined them and they headed out to the street.

.....

Michael was watching the morning news on one screen while working his way through his email on the computer. He was frequently shifting his eyes over to the screen showing the vehicle tracking device to verify it had not moved. The news show went to a commercial and he looked over at the monitoring screen yet again. Michael felt startled when he recognized that the vehicle was now moving. He watched as the car began driving north out of Athens. He glanced down at the purse tracking device, but was surprised to see that it was not moving. *Time to wake up Terry.*

"Terry," he called out. "Our subjects are moving, or at least some of them."

He heard a grunt and went back to focusing his attention on the tracking devices. Within a few minutes, the car was eastbound on the highway leading towards South Carolina. The purse tracking device, however, was still sitting at the motel. Terry came out of the sleeping area and joined Michael in watching the screens.

"The car is moving but the purse isn't?" Terry questioned.

"Yes," Michael replied. "If the purse unit had died would the tracking unit continue to show the purse at the last reported position?"

"No, the location would disappear completely."

They watched for a moment and then Terry turned and started heading back to the rear of the trailer. "They're moving fast. They may have split up, and we may just be seeing the professor sitting with the girl in his SUV," he called as he headed into the bathroom. "But something tells me they've found the purse device and have no idea there is a device on one of their vehicles. I bet they are trying to give us the slip."

Terry had reached the bathroom and called out, "What happened while I was sleeping?"

Michael summarized the night's activities while Terry freshened up. Terry then came charging out of the bedroom area.

"I'm going to head over to the hotel and see if the SUV is there, or if they have figured things out."

"Got it brother," Michael replied.

"I'm betting they've figured out something and are now headed somewhere else. If I find out that they did, indeed, find the purse device, then we have to assume that they were trying to trick us all night."

Terry paused and looked at his brother. "That means we cannot be sure of anything."

He turned and headed out the door. "Talk to you soon, brother," he called from over his shoulder.

Abbeville, South Carolina

Sean was fast asleep in the passenger seat for most of their drive east. They had quickly conferred while walking back to the motel and had decided to head to Abbeville. Abby, of course, had thought they were joking until Kim showed her that indeed there was an 'Abbeville' on the map.

Sean had explained that they had a chance to lose their followers. They had stuck the tracking device in a flower bed in the parking lot and then taken off from the motel. Kim drove the sedan, following James and Abby in the SUV. After trying to see if he could spot a tail for a little while, Sean had given up, leaned against the window and fallen fast asleep. A few hours later, he awoke as they turned off the main highway to take the road into Abbeville.

The road shortly crossed the Savannah River, which looked more like a lake.

Sean looked at Kim. "Are you thinking what I'm thinking?"

Kim nodded. "Yes. What if the cave is now underwater?"

Sean frowned. "It certainly won't make things easier."

They sat in silence for a little while, each stewing in their own thoughts. Kim finally spoke.

"Sean, thank you."

Sean looked over at Kim questioningly.

"I mean, you have spent weeks of your life trying to unravel a mystery that really did not concern you." Kim looked over at him as she steered her way through the South Carolina countryside. "You didn't have to do it. God knows where we would be without you. I admit, I have sometimes wondered why you were so interested and willing to step into this. I wondered if you were part of the conspiracy you talked so much about. Now, I think I really understand."

"You do, do you?" Sean said, teasing slightly.

"Yes, I do," Kim said emphatically. "You did all of this because it's the right thing to do."

Sean was silent for a moment. Then he spoke softly. "Thanks for those thoughts. Maybe you're right. I honestly cannot tell you why I jumped into this and then kept jumping in ever deeper. I don't know whether it was the right thing to do or not, but I just knew it was what I should do and, in the long run, what I wanted to do."

Sean looked out the window. "We've been really lucky so far, especially with Abby. Now, I think, the key is simply to move as fast as we can. We definitely need to get ahead of our pursuers and stay ahead of them."

"Do you think we have shaken them?"

"I'm not sure," Sean admitted. "Something tells me they have more resources than we could ever keep track of."

He gestured at the farm setting they were driving through. "If this is typical of this whole area, though, then we have gained an advantage. The roads are quiet and homes are few and far between. Anybody trying to watch us, find us or tail us, will stick out like a sore thumb."

......

A few minutes later, they pulled into the town square of Abbeville and parked. As they got out and stretched, Abby appeared excited.

"This is my town," she said. "They named it after me."

Kim looked around at the square and its massive trees. "This is so quaint, and it really is square." She gestured at the four roads that framed a plaza with some grassy areas. "This place feels old."

James spoke up. "In a way this place is older than its age. It's had to bear a heavy burden."

They all looked at him and he continued. "You are in the town where the Civil War began and ended. The vote to secede occurred on a famous hill in this town and Jefferson Davis signed the cease hostility order here as well. Old Abbeville represents so much of what went wrong in the war and how it ended badly. Somehow, though, I sense that the town has moved on, but kept much of what makes it so authentic."

They were silent for a moment. Then Sean spoke.

"I hate to be the damper on such a positive moment, but we need to move onto business. First, let's get a bite to eat and then find out about local accommodations. The more we stand around in public places, the more likely it is that our pursuers will find us."

Kim spoke up. "I'll go find the Chamber of Commerce or whatever it's called and get hotel information. Order me a ..." She paused, thinking for a moment. "Oh, I don't care, something southern."

She headed into the building in front of their parking space, the City Hall.

Sean looked at Abby. "Okay Abby, tell us where we're eating in YOUR town."

.....

Terry had stopped a few miles outside of town and parked his car. After seeing his prey stop in what appeared to be the heart of Abbeville, he decided that going any closer risked detection. He called Michael and waited patiently for him to answer.

"Hello," the familiar voice called.

"They've stopped in downtown Abbeville. I think this may be their new headquarters."

"Got it," Michael replied. "Where should I go?"

"I passed a campground just before crossing the Savannah River. It's a good location. I'd pull in there. Wait for me to confirm that they are staying here tonight."

"Okay," Michael replied. "How confident are you that they're not digging for treasure right now?"

"It's the wrong setting. They should be out in a rural area. They're probably trying to learn more about the area to help them with their search."

"Well, even I'm running out of patience, brother. I think they need to be on a short leash. If they move again, I think we need to take them and learn what they know."

"I understand," Terry replied. "Let's see what happens." He hung up and then reached his hand down to his side. He felt the butt of the gun he was wearing in a holster under his armpit. The weapon felt comforting.

.....

"This is not working," Sean said. "This is not matching up to the map at all." He was sitting in the passenger seat of the professor's SUV. Kim and Abby were in the back. "Worse, we have a tail."

When he said those words everyone froze.

"A tail?" Kim asked.

"Yes, a black SUV has been behind us for several hours," Sean explained. "They're not very professional though, so I don't think they're the same group that we've been dealing with up until now."

"Somebody else?" Kim asked, sounding exasperated. After finding a small bed and breakfast in Abbeville, they headed out in one vehicle to start their search. They had been driving along country roads for hours. They kept getting confused about where the river was and kept having to backtrack. She was tired and shared Sean's sentiment.

"I think so," Sean said. "Who else could know we're here and what we're doing?"

"Uh," James said. "I might have an idea."

Sean turned to look at James. Kim spoke first.

"Okay spill it!"

"Last Saturday morning in Richmond, I went into the archive after your call. After researching most of the war records, I started digging into the treasure aspect. I called a treasure hunter to learn more about the Atlanta Treasure stories." Still thinking, James paused. "I didn't directly tell him where I was headed, but he was a bit too curious."

There was silence. Then James continued to speak.

"But for him to have found us seems unlikely. They would have needed to follow me here…" James let his voice trail off as he considered that he might have been tailed from his house. "Okay, so maybe it's them."

"Easy enough to find out," Sean said. "Pull over into that clearing. Get as close as you can to the trees."

James did as he was told and they sat there for a little while before a black SUV came around the turn and passed them by. Sean could see two men in the vehicle. They both noticed the professor's SUV and tried to look away immediately.

"Okay, now pullout and follow them. Get right up there close behind them." Sean ordered.

James pressed hard on the accelerator, causing gravel to kick up. Soon, he had caught up with the black SUV. They accelerated at first and James did likewise. Then they slowed down, pulled off the road, and came to a stop.

"Pull up next to them," Sean said, lowering his window. "What's the treasure hunter's name?"

"Kurt Cathey."

James pulled their SUV up next to the black SUV. Sean leaned out the window.

"Be careful, Sean," Kim said quietly.

"Kurt?" Sean called.

The two men in the SUV had been trying to avoid looking at them. However, when Sean called out, the driver reluctantly turned and looked. He then lowered his window.

"Kurt?" Sean repeated himself.

The driver responded in a deep, grouchy tone, "What do you want?"

Sean smiled. "I was just wondering why in the world we kept seeing you so much on these lonely country roads. What a coincidence! You talking with the professor here and then happening to run into him in South Carolina."

The driver said nothing and began to look extremely uncomfortable.

Sean's tone suddenly shifted and became much more serious, "I wanted you to know that we knew you were here. If you're going to tail someone, you really ought to learn more about the skill."

Sean leaned back in the SUV and raised the window. "Let's go back to our rooms!"

James nodded and did a quick turn around in the gravel They then drove off leaving the treasure hunters behind looking startled.

.....

"That was delicious," James said, finishing his ice cream cone. He bunched the napkin up in his hand as they walked in the town square. Looking about, he searched for a garbage can.

Kim and Sean were on one side of him and Abby was walking in front of all three of them. It was a beautiful evening and despite the tension they all felt, the good hearty meal they had just consumed had helped create a brief interlude of tranquility.

"I think I really love this town," Kim said, holding onto Sean's arm. "The people are friendly and so authentic."

"You could always move your garden shop here," Sean said. "You could call it 'Abby's Garden Shop.' Everyone would stop in just to tell you that they don't call their town 'Abby' for short."

Abby looked over her shoulder at Sean and laughed. "They don't call it Abigail either."

"No, they don't," Sean admitted. "In any case, I'm hoping we can make some sense out of what we're doing here and see if we can finish this off." He looked about the town square for a moment, completing his routine surveillance.

"Following the river is really difficult. I'm also worried that the white cliffs are now buried in the lakes that now make up these rivers."

Kim stopped dead in her tracks causing herself to tug on Sean's arm. He turned to look at her.

"You okay?" he asked, his senses going on alert. She appeared to be staring at something in front of her. Sean turned to try and see what had caught her attention.

"Oh, yes, I'm fine," Kim replied absentmindedly. "It's just something you said…" She let her voice dwindle off and then spoke up with enthusiasm.

"What we need to do is use the lake system to our advantage. Don't you think we could rent a boat?"

"Well sure, I would think so. The lakes all have resorts. There's got to be plenty of boat rental options."

"Okay," Kim said. "Let's split up tomorrow. Two of us in a boat while two others use the car to find the locations that we can see from the boat."

Sean thought for a moment. "I like it. We can cover way more ground that way and we would get good sight lines of the cliffs along the river. Abby and I can man a boat while you and the professor work it from the land side."

"Fine with me," James offered.

"Fine with me, too," Abby said.

"Then I make four, so let's do it," Kim said.

They had reached the end of the square where their SUV was parked. Sean pulled a map out of his back pocket and opened it up on the hood of the vehicle. They gathered around him. There was just enough light to see the map decently.

"The Savannah River mostly leads to this one big lake, Strom Thurmond. We can tackle that tomorrow. I'm not sure we can knock out more than one lake at a time, but above it is this lake, Richard B. Russell." Sean's finger tapped on the lakes as he named them.

James had now pulled his copy of Captain Greene's map out. He laid it on the hood next to the lakes. "We think the lower portion of Strom Thurmond is the best fit to match this map. But, we drove as many of the roads as we could find in this area and never saw anything remotely close to what we're looking for, white cliffs."

"Well, that's the idea about trying to see things from a different perspective," Sean replied. "Maybe we'll spot them from the lake. I also really like the idea, because we can cover the river so much more quickly using a boat."

Sean looked at the map again. "There is a resort right here, by the highway we drove in on. Abby and I can head down there at first light tomorrow morning and see about renting a boat. Why don't you two head into Greenwood and see if you can find something that floats in the air, like some big balloons. We can use those to help guide you to spot where we are. While you're at it, I can think of some more things we need."

"Perfect," Kim replied. "We'll take the professor's car." Kim patted her hand on the hood.

"So, my packing was not good enough?" James pretended his feelings were hurt. "You had everything you needed to go grave robbing."

"So we did," Sean said. He glanced around again. "Let's head back to the bed and breakfast. We can discuss our 'competition' while we drive."

They loaded into the SUV, with Abby and James in the front and Kim and Sean in the back. James started the vehicle up.

"I still have a hard time believing that we have shed the Sheriden Corporation folks, but it's clear we at least have these two treasure hunters trying to tail us. They're not as sophisticated, but I think they could be dangerous as well. Perhaps not as willing to hurt us to get the treasure, but probably willing to do so nonetheless."

"Kurt Cathey has quite the ego," James said. "You should see his website. He was a Navy diver like you Sean."

"I was a Seal, not that it's important, but if he was a Navy diver, that makes him smart and strong. My read of him is that he's capable of handling himself in a fight."

"So what do we do?" Kim asked. "We cannot expect to hide from him can we?"

"No," Sean admitted. "And I don't think we can assume that the Sheriden guys are not lurking around either. But, we don't need to hide from them. We just need to trick them, like when we knew we were being tracked in Athens yesterday."

"We need to stop on a random basis and pay close attention to things around us. When we actually see something of interest, we should try not to linger on it too long. Pretend or assume that you are being watched at all times, even when you are certain that you're not."

"If we actually find the spot or think we've found it, we can set up a distraction again. We can even try to sneak there at night."

They had reached their bed and breakfast. James turned onto the gravel driveway. It was on the main road leading north out of downtown. Grand colonial homes and tall shady trees lined the road on each side. Several of the homes along the road had been converted to bed and breakfasts. Sean had chosen this one because they could park in the back. He had also liked the fact that a dog lived there. Abby had pointed out that it was an old, lazy dog, but Sean was not deterred. The lady running the bed and breakfast had three rooms available which allowed Abby to have her own room. They had paid for three nights in advance, using cash and had also given false last names.

They got out of the SUV and stretched. It was now late evening and the back porch light beckoned to them.

Sean looked at all of them. "Let's remember not to talk about what we're doing when we get inside. Anything else to talk about?"

They all shook their heads no and headed inside.

Chapter Thirty-Two

Wednesday, May 13
Lake J. Strom Thurmond, South Carolina and Georgia

They were all up before sunrise and had come down for breakfast at dawn. After munching down a quick meal, they had headed outside and firmed up their plans.

"Okay, Abby and I will head to the lake. We'll hear from you in a few hours."

"Good," James said. "We'll be shopping."

Kim hugged Abby who seemed a bit embarrassed.

"Be careful Abby and do what Sean says," Kim said looking worried.

"Mom! I'm fifteen. I will be careful and I will do what he says. In fact, we will both be careful." She hooked her arm around Sean and smiled.

Sean laughed in agreement, "Yes, we will."

They got into the car and drove out from behind the house and towards the road. The old dog that Sean had been happy to see was lying in the gravel, blocking their exit. Sean tapped the horn and the dog lifted its head to look at them. It slowly lifted itself up and sauntered off the driveway.

"Some guard dog," Abby said.

Sean just smiled and started the car forward again.

.....

"They're moving," Michael said. "The car is moving." He was speaking into his headset attached to his radio. The radio sat on the work surface in front of the monitor screens. The trailer was parked at a campsite in the lake resort on the Georgia side of the Savannah River. Across the river, in Abbeville, Terry was sitting in his car with an identical headset and radio.

"Got it," he answered back. "They're moving pretty early. I'll do a drive by and see if the SUV is out as well."

"They're turning west. Looks like they're headed over to the river."

"Roger," Terry confirmed.

He started up his car and pulled it up onto the road. He had parked in front of an old rundown gas station about a half mile outside town and it took him about ten minutes to reach the bed and breakfast where everyone was staying. He had driven by the night before and realized that he could spot their vehicles behind the house for only a moment as he approached. Then the cars would disappear behind the trees and finally the house itself. He slowed as he approached the house. Both cars were gone.

"Looks like they took both cars out," Terry reported. "Perhaps they are dividing up again."

"We have no reason to think they have detected us though, right?" Michael asked.

"No, none at all. But Sean is a suspicious and careful man. Where is the car headed?"

"It turned south by the river and headed down towards the highway that we're on."

"Let's see where they go and decide from there."

"Roger," Michael replied. He found it a bit silly to use old terms like roger on the radios, but Terry enjoyed it. Michael could go along with such things if it kept his brother entertained. He was growing irritable, though, and developing less tolerance for his brother's idiosyncrasies. Jessica was getting more insistent that he return his focus to his coming campaign. He had refused to tell her exactly where he was, and she was beginning to grow concerned.

He was pulled out of his reverie by the car's movement. It had turned on the highway and was now headed right at the bridge that he could see if he went outside. It was headed right toward him and the resort.

"They've turned west on the highway, headed right at the river and the resort."

"Really?"

Michael said nothing in response, but instead just watched the screen. After another minute, the vehicle went past the final road that showed on the computer map before the river.

"Looks like they are heading over the river, right towards us," Michael called out, ignoring the fact that Terry was not actually there.

Terry decided to head over to the river to get closer, just in case something were to happen. He was not certain that his brother would handle things well.

"Whatever you do, do not get out of the trailer. You can look out its windows, but don't move the curtains aside."

"Okay," Michael replied.

There was a period of silence. Then Michael reported that the car had pulled off the highway and was now headed down the road towards the resort. He continued to update Terry on the progress. The car appeared to stop at the main office. He was able to locate it in the parking lot. Sean and the girl got out and went inside the office.

"Did you see the SUV?" Terry asked.

"No and I've looked around using other windows. Looks like its just the car and the two of them."

"Hmm, let's just sit tight and see what happens."

A little while later, Sean and Abby emerged from the office and went back to the car. They pulled two bags out of the trunk and headed over to the docks.

"I believe they are headed out on the lake. Yes! They're talking to a kid and getting into a boat now."

Michael continued to report as the kid walked Sean through the operation of the boat. Then, Sean started up the boat's engine as the kid stepped off. He cast off the lines and Sean began steering the boat out into the lake.

Michael and Terry discussed what they had seen. They concluded that the duo must be searching for something.

"I'd like to know where they went yesterday, but they used that SUV and so I only got a glimpse of them a few times. They were mostly on the east side of the river. I think they're looking for something on the river."

"That makes sense." Michael agreed.

"Listen, we need to rent a boat and have it ready in case we need to get on the lake in a hurry. Do that and then hang out watching for their return. I'm going to head over to the west side of the river. There are some high bluffs along the lake over there and I think I can get a good view of them from there. I'll keep an eye on their movements and keep you posted."

Michael acknowledged and got up to head over to the resort office.

.....

Sean steered the boat back and forth, trying to get a feel for its maneuverability. He had actually not driven a boat since some training days early in his career as a Seal. He had been a passenger in a few boats near the end of his tour of duty, but even those had been assault zodiac-style boats that were all engine and bounciness. This was a ski boat and even the kid who had checked them out on it could tell they were not going to water ski. First, it was early in the morning. Second, they were wearing pants and sweaters. Sean did not really care at this point, however. All of his senses told him that it was just about time for this quest to end. He just wasn't certain how it would end.

The ski boat felt like it had decent power and it maneuvered quite well. At least it was adequate to meet their needs. He glanced back over his shoulder. Abby was relaxed, sitting at the back of the boat with her arms draped up over the side and her head draped back. She had a wide grin on her face as she enjoyed the morning sunlight. Sean smiled back at her.

"Hold on," he called out.

He turned back to scan the horizon and then pushed the accelerator handle all the way down. The boat lifted up out of the water and quickly picked up speed until it was chopping across the water at about forty-five knots. The cool morning air was hitting him hard in the face and it felt incredibly refreshing. Sean felt out the boat's control at that speed for a moment and then slowly pulled the accelerator handle all the way back to an idle. The bow of the boat sank back towards the water as it began slowing. Once it had stopped, Sean turned around and sat on the gunwale.

"How do you like our boat?" he asked.

"Just fine," Abby answered back, still grinning.

"Well, we did come here to do work, you remember?"

"Of course."

"I figure we have until noon for your mom and James to get back from Greenwood. We're going to focus on the east shore here, but I thought we could take some of the morning to check the west branch out. We've been assuming that the map depicted a location on the eastern side of the eastern branch, but it's possible that we're just plain wrong. Since we'll be concentrating on the east shore with your mom and James, I think we should check out the other side right now. What'd you think?"

"That sounds good to me," Abby replied.

"Okay, so what we know is that Captain Greene hid the materials in a cave on a white cliff above a river, the east side of the river to be exact. When Captain Greene came through here, this of course, was not a lake. Now it is, so we should assume that the cave, or whatever is left of it, is close to water level. We hope it's not underwater. But either way, we're looking for white cliffs."

Sean hopped back up. The boat had been drifting idly and had gradually turned itself all the way around while he had been talking.

"So hold on, while we zip over to the west branch," he called to her as he pulled back on the handle.

.....

Terry lowered his binoculars as the boat accelerated. He could see that Sean had been talking to the girl and had gestured at the shoreline a few times. *They're searching all right. They must have found something back in Athens giving them explicit instructions."* Terry watched as the boat headed west. He was on a ridge on the southwestern end of the lake and realized he was about to enter into a cat and mouse game with Sean. *Only he has no idea he is a mouse or even that a cat is stalking him.* Terry smiled and began trotting down to his car to move to another location.

.....

"Sean, are you out there?" Kim asked. She released the send button and waited for a response on the radio.

"Yep, I'm here," Sean radioed back. "Where are you guys?"

"We're parked on the old dirt road before the north bridge."

"How was the shopping?" Sean asked.

"It went great. No sign of the treasure hunters."

"Well, don't expect them to have turned tail and run. You can be sure they're around somewhere."

Sean and Kim talked some more and refined their plan. He would drive up to the north bridge and then begin slowly working his way south along the shore. He would stop anywhere that looked promising and see if Kim could find him. She explained that she had gotten some balloons and a rental helium tank. They decided to test the balloon idea at the north bridge over the lake.

A little while later, Sean had reached the north bridge.

"Okay, we're about fifty yards south of the bridge," he radioed.

There was a pause and then Kim replied.

"Okay, James is going to release a balloon."

Sean and Abby patiently watched the sky above the trees while Sean kept the boat generally pointed north, parallel to the bank. After about thirty seconds, Abby called out, "There it is" and pointed. Sean looked over and saw a pink balloon floating up and off to the north.

"We see it," he radioed. "But it looks like it has already moved about eighty yards north of the bridge."

"Okay," Kim radioed back.

Sean then explained they would use the balloon release method as a way to tell Kim and James how far north or south of he and Abby that they were. By doing this, he explained, they could identify from the land, exact points along the shore that looked promising. They could put a discrete mark, like a little pile of rocks, along the road for promising spots.

"When we drove the boat up here, Abby and I saw several areas with white rocks. This morning we cruised up and down the western branch of the lake, but saw nothing. So, my guess is that we are in the right spot."

"Okay then, let's get moving," Kim radioed back.

"Roger."

.....

Terry could see Sean, but the distance was so great he could not tell what he was doing. Sean had taken the boat to the north and he could only follow along the western side up until the point that the western branch began. So he was perched near the beginning of the western branch, straining to hold his binoculars steady, and patiently watching Sean's boat. It appeared to be dead in the water and he thought he could see both of them standing in the boat. They were near the bridge that went over the lake at that point. *They must be talking to the two on land*, he thought. *But what are they talking about? That's what I need to know.*

For hours he had been following Sean's movements on the lake. At one point they had stopped a half mile away from him. There they had pointed and gestured at the side of the lake for several minutes. That had helped Terry confirm that they must be looking for a hiding place along the eastern side of the Savannah River. That made sense and gave Terry some excitement that they were close.

"Brother," he radioed.

"Go ahead," Michael said matter-of-factly. *Far too casual*, Terry thought. *He relaxes and drops his guard way too much.*

"I believe that our searchers are very close to the hiding place. Let's plan on taking them tonight if at all possible."

"Amen brother! I cannot stay out here much longer," Michael replied. "Do we need the help of our Columbian team?"

"Negative, but let's order them to be ready all night, just in case."

"Roger, I'll see to it."

"We're almost done, brother."

.....

"Do you think there really is a treasure waiting for us?" Kim asked.

James considered the question for a moment before answering. "Yes, or at least I believe there really was one, but it could be gone by now. The stories themselves were not very convincing to me, but we now have first hand accounts that match up to the stories. That's good enough for me."

Kim and James were sitting in the SUV. They were parked on the side of a road that ran close to the river, about half way down to the south bridge. Behind them, in the rear seat, ten inflated balloons bounced against the ceiling. When they were driving, they would occasionally drift up into the front area and James would knock them back. Kim and James were waiting for a call from Sean. The radio had been silent for a good fifteen minutes.

"The treasure could have been found, moved, and all we may find is a place where it once was," James continued.

"How big of a treasure are we talking about?"

"That depends. There was so much gold and money not accounted for during the war it's hard to tell. It could certainly be pretty huge. If it was a hundred thousand dollars in gold coins back then, for instance, then we're talking millions of dollars today."

"Wow!" Kim said. "What are we going to do if we find it?"

"Well, I think first we need to find whatever it was that Captain Greene added to the treasure. I suspect it's some form of proof of the land taken by officers of Sherman's army. We need to ensure that this information, whatever it may be, gets into the public eye. That's our protection." James paused thoughtfully.

"I don't know where we go or who we call first. If we cannot trust the government, I assume the media. However, if we're also sitting on a huge treasure, we're going to need the government to protect us. It's a catch twenty-two."

"I guess we need to worry about finding it first." She sighed. "This whole quest has been so bizarre. It's also been costly."

"Yes, it has," James said sadly. She knew that he was thinking about his sister

"But, at least we will be telling the world the truth," Kim said. "That's all that matters, right?"

"I guess so," he replied. "But nothing will bring Mary back into this world. I want to see her killers brought to justice."

"Hopefully they will be," Kim finished.

.....

"You're right Abby. That does look really promising," Sean said.

Abby had pointed out a cliff area where the land had risen up along the side of the lake. Sean tried to imagine it when the water level had been down at river level. "It must have been a huge cliff for this area."

He slowed the boat and studied it some more.

"See the streaks of white? Looks like veins of quartz," Sean pointed at several sections of white that ran diagonally across the face of the cliff. The cliff was about eighty feet above the water at its highest point, but it was all rock and essentially vertical or close to it. *Not much erosion here.*

"Sean, there's a weird spot just below the top. Right there," Abby said pointing. "Do you see it?"

Sean followed her hand to the spot where her finger was pointing. It looked like someone had carved a notch in the cliff that ran down about twenty feet. It ended in a sloped pile of rocks. The notch was maybe eight feet wide. As he studied it some more, however, he realized that it was actually more of a pock mark, carved out of the cliff, and that it would probably not be visible from the top of the cliff.

"You may have something, Abby," he said slowly as he digested his observations. "Let's radio your mom."

"Okay," Abby replied, as she picked up the radio.

"Mom?"

After about ten seconds, Kim responded.

"Yes honey?"

"Sean says to release a balloon. We have found a promising location."

"Okay, hold on." After about five seconds she spoke again.

"Okay, one blue balloon on its way."

Sean had picked up the binoculars while Abby was talking with her mom. He was now struggling to survey the cliff while the boat bobbed up and down. He suddenly put the viewing instrument down.

"I'll be damned," he muttered quietly. "I'll be damned!"

"What, what is it?" Abby demanded.

Sean put the binoculars down. "I'll tell you in a minute. Let's watch for that balloon."

They spotted it, but it took longer than their test balloon had earlier.

"Tell her they are about a half mile north of the spot. Tell her it's a big hill that ends as a cliff along the lake."

Sean pulled the accelerator handle back and steered the boat to the south as it lifted out of the water. "Tell her we need to mark another location. It'll be a good mile south of our current one."

Abby was confused, but thought she knew what Sean was up to and relayed the information.

.....

Terry had watched the scene unfold. They had come south down the lake and now he could see them perfectly. The balloon had surprised him, but he quickly figured out what they were doing. *Marking. They're marking locations.* He felt excitement as he watched the boat moving south again. It had accelerated slightly, but had now slowed down continuing its patrol of the eastern side of the lake. Terry watched as they slowed to a stop once again. He saw the two in the boat pointing and gesturing. He could now make out that the girl was talking into a radio.

They sat there for several minutes, the boat doing slow circles. Then a balloon rose above the trees and the girl pointed it out. She then lifted the radio and spoke into it. Then, Sean fired up the boat again.

Terry watched as the pattern repeated itself for a third time. They had passed to the south of Terry and were now closer to the main bridge and the resort than Terry was. It was getting near the end of the day, Terry knew, and that meant they could not stay out on the lake much longer.

"Brother," he called into the radio.

"Go ahead."

"They have marked several locations along the east side of the lake, but they cannot stay out much longer. I'm going to continue watching them as they come in, but I think its safe to say that they have zeroed in on the hiding place."

"So, do we continue to let them go after it?"

"Negative. Let's take over the operation tonight. We'll capture and interrogate them. Then, we'll finish the search ourselves."

"Tell me what to do," Michael replied. His voice had taken on a steely edge that pleased Terry.

"Just be ready for anything."

.....

Sean let Abby take over steering the boat so he could talk with Kim. He gave up on the radio and called Kim on her cell phone, so he could have an easier conversation.

"The first location you marked is it," he said simply.

There was a long pause, and then Kim's voice answered back.

"You mean it's THE spot?"

"Yes."

"How do you know?" Kim demanded, excitement cutting into her voice.

"It fits perfectly. White streaks of quartz run diagonally across what must have been a huge cliff before the lake was here. It's still pretty high."

"But there must be more than one cliff out there," Kim protested.

"Yes, but this one has something else."

"What?" Sean could tell that Kim's patience was running thin.

"Blast marks. The rocks were fractured by explosives."

There was another long pause before Kim responded. "Say that again?"

"There's a hole, kind of, cut out of the cliff. The rocks show signs of having been blasted. There is a pile of rocks that fill the bottom of the cut, like a cave entrance was buried." Sean expected Kim to ask him how he could tell explosives were used, but she didn't.

"Okay. The other spots were red herrings?"

"Yes, exactly," Sean confirmed.

"What's next?"

"I think we need to go after it tonight. We would be too visible during the day anyway, and I'm worried that our friends are watching our every move. Going out on the lake worked, but it also made us visible for miles."

"Which friends?" Kim asked.

"All of them," Sean said seriously.

"Well then, the professor and I are game to do it tonight," Kim replied, sounding just as serious.

"Good, then here is my idea. You guys head into town, but drive right on through. Go south out of town and come up along the river. Find a low spot in the brush, a break in the trees, anything that will allow you to drive into the area at the foot of the hill." Sean paused and looked around. The boat was finally getting close to the marina and Sean knew he needed to take back control soon.

"Did you notice any homes in the area?" he asked Kim while gesturing to Abby to slow the boat down to a crawl.

"No. It's all pretty rugged out there. Mostly overgrown forest."

"Good. So, get the SUV pulled back into the trees as far as you can. Leave a rock the size of a fist on the road's edge where you turned off. Just wait for us. I'll have my cell phone on vibrate if you need me."

"Okay."

"Abby and I will hang out at the marina for a little while, letting you two get firmly in place before we get there. Assume we'll get there around ten o'clock. Okay?"

"Okay," Kim replied again. "Sean, do you think this is really it?"

"It certainly looks perfect. But, it's going to be tough to get at the cave if there really is one there."

They hung up and Sean stepped up to take over control of the boat from Abby. She sat down and Sean eased it into the slip in the growing darkness. A different kid was waiting for them than the one who had checked them out in the morning.

"I was getting worried about you," he said with a strong southern drawl. "It's pretty late."

"Sorry," Sean said sheepishly. "We were just farther up the lake than I thought we were."

"No problem," the kid replied. "Just so long as you're safe."

They tied up the boat and Sean and Abby stepped off onto the dock. There were no lights on the dock and they had to walk carefully down to the shore where they then headed into the office to settle the bill for the boat rental.

......

"They're headed into the office," Michael reported. "I couldn't see what they did after pulling up to the dock. It's too dark."

Terry was sitting in his car listening to his brother's report. He had pulled off the road about a half mile before the resort. He wasn't willing to risk alerting Sean in such a public place. But, he was feeling impatient. He realized he should have headed back to the trailer and gotten inside before Sean had gotten back to the resort.

"I'm staying up here until they leave. I don't want them to get too much of a head start on us, though. So, when I get down there, let's make a quick turn around and head out. We'll need the nine millimeter pistols with two clips each. Also toss a few tarps into a duffel bag with some towels, rope and twine."

"Got it," Michael replied.

"I'll change when I get there. We need to be dressed appropriately."

"Okay, I'll change now."

"Oh, and I'm famished. Can you toss one of those frozen pizzas in the oven?"

"Will do," Michael replied. "Uh oh. Looks like they're sitting on the deck by the office, at that little shop that's here."

"Damn! What are they doing?"

"I think they're eating," Michael replied.

Chapter Thirty-Three

Along Lake J. Strom Thurmond, South Carolina

It was pitch black and Sean could barely see the tree branches in front of his face. He and Abby were working their way toward the end of an old, overgrown lane where he was pretty sure James and Kim were waiting. He had only one red lens flashlight and it was hard to move very quickly without running into a branch or tripping on a tree root. Branches overhung the lane entirely, shutting out any light that might have come from the stars or even the moon. Sean had noticed some dark clouds forming at sunset and was expecting it to be a cloudy, dark night. *Maybe even some rain showers. A perfect night,* he thought sarcastically.

After a few minutes he could hear familiar whispers, so he called out to Kim. She replied, and he and Abby reached them half a minute later. Kim and James had pulled all sorts of gear out of the SUV and had it spread out on the ground. The SUV itself was tucked behind a block of trees making it hard to notice even from the old lane. Kim explained that the cliff was about fifty yards through the forest and that there was virtually no trail to it, as near as they could tell. Sean decided to post James as a sentry with a radio while the three of them would begin hauling gear to the cliff.

"Here," Kim whispered, handing him something.

He took it and looked it over. It was a headlamp with a red lens.

"Thanks," Sean replied. "This is perfect."

"We've got a dozen of 'em and lots of batteries too," Kim whispered back. "Nothing like a good old Army and Navy Surplus store for outfitting a treasure hunting expedition."

Sean quickly assessed the gear on the ground, and then assigned some tools to Abby and Kim. He also chose his first load that consisted of a bag of ropes and an armful of shovels and implements. They headed off towards the river. Kim had her radio on, so she would hear an alert from James if anyone came along.

It took a good half an hour to walk to the cliff and back. This time Sean left Kim at the cliff to act as the sentry there. They went back, and Sean decided that by using James, they could get the rest of the stuff in one trip. They loaded up and headed back to the lake.

Fifteen minutes later, they were at the river and Sean was looking over the edge. There was a pile of large rocks right before the cliff and a tree about fifteen feet back. He could see a few faint lights in the distance and assumed they were either from the resort or were from homes on the Georgia side. The sky was indeed clouded over. To Sean, it felt like rain was on its way.

"Let's tie a rope to that tree," he said pointing.

Abby, James and Kim stood back for the most part, though, and simply let Sean work. He used his red headlamp to see what he was doing and occasionally asked Kim to shine her headlamp in a particular spot. He tied a rope around the tree and attached a metal ring to it. Then he threaded two ropes through the ring and tied one around himself. He tied the other rope to the pickaxe.

"Have any of you ever learned any rock climbing techniques?" he asked his onlookers. They all had their red headlamps on, so when they shook their heads, they looked like a Christmas light display of wavering red lights. Sean smiled.

"Okay, well then James, I am going to need you to lower me down the cliff. Let me show you how it works."

James stepped forward and Sean quickly explained to him how to lower and retrieve, how to hold the rope, and all the basic communication signals in five minutes time.

"The cliff has a decent amount of jagged surfaces for me to hold onto, so you should not have much of my weight unless I slip. But if

I do, and you're not holding onto the rope correctly, it will go ripping through your hand. And of course, I'll go tumbling."

"Have no fear, the professor is here," James joked. "I may be getting old, but I'm still plenty strong."

"I know you are, but strength is not as important as technique. Abby could probably handle me if she did it right. The rough surface will also cause the rope to drag against it, especially if I move laterally. So, occasionally I may have to hold onto the cliff while you shift the rope over so it's vertical again."

"Okay," James said. He was sitting next to a big boulder with his back toward the cliff's edge. The rope ran out from around his waist, through the ring, and then back towards him, where it terminated in its looping around Sean.

"Okay then, let's go." He went over to the cliff's edge and turned his back towards it, lowered himself down to his belly, and began sliding off backwards. Kim and Abby had come over to the edge and were nervously looking at him.

"Sean, please be careful," Kim said.

He smiled at her. "Don't worry, I will."

He then let himself slide down until his hands and feet were holding him on the cliff. He began working his way towards the bottom. Rather than go straight at the notch, he was using an alternate route on one side where it looked less steep and was covered with more handholds and footholds. As he climbed, James paid out rope to keep a gentle tension. James had flipped his headlamp so it shown mostly downward allowing him to easily see the rope in his hands.

Gradually, Sean worked his way down the cliff. After about twenty feet, Kim and Abby could only see the red of his lamp and his general shape. He eventually stopped.

"Okay, I think I'm at the right level, he called up. I'm going to go sideways now so have James hold me at this height, regardless of any tension he feels."

Kim repeated the instructions to James who then acknowledged them.

"James is ready," Kim called down. She had wanted to whisper, but there was a strong breeze blowing in her face which would have drowned out a whisper. The wind seemed to work in reverse though, and she could hear Sean's grunts and breathing quite easily.

Sean began working his way sideways into the crease. He knew this was the trickiest point, where the rock was smooth and the most vertical. His fingers and toes began getting tired as they clung to the small edges he was finding to position them in. After about ten minutes of careful work, though, he made it around the point.

"Tell James I'm going to go down about six feet," he called up. His voice was strained, showing the level of exertion he was expending.

"Okay," Kim replied and again relayed the instruction to James. Sean then began working his way down, and James went back to releasing the rope, maintaining only a gentle tension. Then the rope went slack, and James felt a moment of panic.

"I'm there," Sean called. James heard that and relaxed.

Kim could see that Sean was now crawling around. "What do you see?" she called.

"There's lots of loose rock. Some of it has been fractured like from explosives. It's mounded about ten feet high. It really looks like there was an explosion here a long time ago and then erosion has added more to the pile."

Sean paused and thought for a moment.

"I'll need the pickaxe and that heavy pry bar."

"Okay," Kim acknowledged. They lowered the pickaxe down on the rope it was already tied to. Sean had untied himself from his rope and they used that to tie to the pry bar.

"I'm afraid the pry bar could slide out. So, we need to lower it carefully," Kim called.

Sean acknowledged her and she and James lowered it safely down the slope.

"Okay, I'm getting to work," Sean called up. "You'll hear rocks sliding and probably splashing into the lake."

"Got it!" Kim called.

The three of them settled in above on the big boulders and rocks at the cliff edge and began watching Sean dig. They switched off their headlamps to better see Sean who was marked by his red light. He looked to be about thirty feet down and they could just barely see him.

The wind had gotten colder, and Kim wondered if it was going to start raining.

Sean set to work. They could hear crunches, as he swung the pickaxe, and groans and grunts, as he pried rocks loose. Every minute or so, a few rocks would slide off the ledge and tumble down into the water as Sean had predicted. This went on for an hour, with Sean occasionally taking a break. He was breathing hard and Kim could only imagine how dirty and sweaty he was from his hard labor.

On his fourth break she asked him how he was doing. As she did so, she felt the first raindrop hit her hand.

"I think I'm close," Sean said between breaths. "There was definitely some type of opening here that was filled in with rock."

"Good, because I think it's starting to rain."

"Gee that's great!" Sean called up in his most sarcastic voice.

He went back to work and Kim got up to look for one of the tarps they had brought with them. She found it and was tearing the plastic off it when a cold voice caused her to freeze with terror.

"Hello Ms. Poole," it said in a southerly accent.

A bright light hit her in the face. She could sense another light off to her side flick on, illuminating her daughter and the professor, who were both now laying at the cliff's edge looking down.

"Turn around and walk back to your companions!" the man ordered.

She did as she was told. As she turned, she saw the other man shining a flashlight down on James and Abby. Her heart fluttered as she then saw that the man at the cliff's edge was holding a gun in his other hand. She felt a hard jolt in her back and realized that the man behind her also held a gun and had just jabbed her with it. She moved quickly and then laid down next to Abby after being told to do so.

"You guys have been tremendously annoying," Kim's captor said. "But you have also been useful."

"We need to search them," the other man finally spoke. He sounded nervous to Kim.

"Yes brother, we do," the first man replied. "Leave your gun here with me and do it. Have them turn over so you can check their front as well."

A moment later, Kim felt hands roughly patting down her back side.

They reached her feet and stopped.

"Turn over!" the man commanded. He sounded less nervous now and more authoritative. As panicked as Kim felt, though, she suspected that the man was merely trying to act confident. She did as she was told and the man searched her front pockets. He found her cell phone and pulled it out of her jacket pocket. He then had her turn back over and repeated this process on the other two.

"Let's handcuff them," the second, nervous man suggested.

"Actually, I have a better idea." Kim's captor whispered something to the second man and then a faint conversation began between them. She only heard a few pieces of it. She heard the word "treasure" once and was certain she heard one of the men say, "it's easier if it looks like an accident." Kim heard enough to know that the two men were most likely going to kill all three of them. She thought about Sean below and began trying to think of a way to alert him.

.....

Sean had finally pushed the pry bar through the rocks, into an open cavity. Excited, he began pulling rocks out until he had an opening large enough to shine a light through. He did so, but could only see a ceiling of rock that extended back some ways.

He pulled his head back out and called, "I'm through!" up to the top of the cliff, before going at it in a frenzy. He pried, tugged and kept pulling rocks back until the hole was twice the diameter of his body. He shined his light in again, nearly dropping it in surprise.

"Damn," was all he could manage to mutter.

.....

Up above, the debate had ended.

"Call Sean," the first man said, shining his light on Kim's back. "Ask him if he's close."

Kim pushed herself up onto her knees, as her mind raced with what was happening. *I could try to use the code word, but 'Mary' will sound so weird, they'll know something is amiss.* Suddenly, an idea came to her.

"Sean, did you find the Mary mark? How close are you?"

There was a long pause, then he answered her. Kim thought he had raised his voice a few notches.

"No, not yet. It's supposed to be here, though. I'm going to keep looking."

Bless him, Kim thought. *He understood.*

"Get back up!" the man ordered her. She was just about to obey his command when a third voice rang out.

"No, lay back down now! And the two of you put your guns on the ground and raise your hands."

Kim felt a rush of confusion. *Someone else is here?* Sensing a loss of control with the situation by everyone, she sat down instead of laying down and she turned. As she did so, she could now see what was going on behind her. The rain was falling strong enough now, though, that even the lights did little to show her much of the surroundings. She could see her two captors exchanging glances. Their faces were mostly in the shadows. Only one had a light on and it was pointed at his feet.

"You will both do as I say, or I will drop you here and now. I've got a riot gun aimed right at your bellies." The voice came from behind the two men and Kim strained to see through the windy rain and darkness. His voice sounded faintly familiar and she desperately tried to recall who it reminded her of. Then she realized that if the man did as he had warned and shot at the two men, she would be right in the line of fire. That made her freeze, despite the fact that she knew she should lay down. She lowered her head to keep her voice from being heard.

"Abby," she whispered to her daughter who was laying next to her. "Be ready to jump and run when I tell you to. Tell James."

"Okay," Abby replied in a scared whisper.

Kim could hear Abby whispering to the professor. She looked back up to see one of the two original men glaring at her as he called out over his shoulder to the unknown man.

"If I put my gun down, I'm a dead man," he said in a friendly voice. "Why don't you come out and talk to us? We might be on the same side."

"Somehow I doubt that, but if you put your guns down, I'll consider all options. How about that?"

The other man, who Kim could now tell was the nervous one, spoke. "Terry, do as he says. We're dead otherwise."

"Be calm brother," Terry replied.

"No, you listen brother! We don't need the treasure. We can trade it for our lives." The man was now pleading and Kim had an ugly sense that this man knew that Terry was very likely to try and shoot his way out of the situation. Kim decided she had to speak.

"Listen," she called out. "We're just innocent victims here. Before you guys start shooting at each other we're just going to get up and move out of the way." She was mainly speaking to the man hidden in the shadows, but she was looking straight at Terry as she spoke. She had decided that he was the man that was going to decide how the confrontation would be resolved.

"Be ready," she whispered a bit louder to Abby and James, ignoring the fact that Terry could plainly hear her. Her clothes were getting soaked from the rain, but she was so tense she did not feel the slightest bit of a chill.

"No, stay right where you are!" the voice ordered, sounding irritated.

Terry sensed an opportunity. "You see, you need us. Let's talk." He started to turn when a white flash of light exploded behind him. Terry was shoved towards Kim. She felt something hit her side as the sound of the gunshot pounded in her ears.

"NOW!" she screamed at Abby. "RUN!" She shoved Abby away from her towards James, as she, herself, rose to go the other way. She thought again of Sean down below and wondered where he was and if he understood what was happening. A second gunshot echoed. Suddenly, there was a series of them too close together for Kim to differentiate. She could see James and Abby scrambling north, along the rim, as she turned to go south. Before she could get three steps away though, the unknown voice called out.

"Freeze Ms. Poole!" it commanded. With those words, she finally recognized who the man was behind the voice and froze. She felt another rush of confusion as she slowly turned around. Rainwater was flowing through her hair and across her face. A man was stepping closer. A small, but bright, white light danced back and forth at the man's eye level. It shone first at Kim, and then over to Terry and his brother. Terry was on the rocks, blood pooling around him and mixing with the rain water. The other man, the brother, was holding his hands straight up in the air. The light flicked back to Kim and she realized that the beam was mounted on the side of his head so it moved with him. She could now see his face clearly enough to confirm his identity. It was Alan Nazimi, the FBI agent.

"Come back here!" Alan ordered her. "Call to your friends or you're dead!" He had been walking forward, but now had stopped.

"No," Kim said simply as she put her hands up. "You can go to hell! Until I know what's going on, I'm not telling them anything." She did walk towards the other man holding his hands up, though, praying that Alan would not shoot her. He was holding what seemed to be a shotgun with a pistol grip and a short barrel. She remembered he had called it a "riot" gun. She shuddered at the thought of what that meant.

Alan had to keep turning his head from the other man, still standing with his arms high, to Kim. As he looked away from her, Kim quickly looked for Abby and James, but they were nowhere in sight. *Thank God!* The light came back to shine in her face but the rain diffused it enough that it really did not bother her. She had gotten closer, so that now she was about ten feet from both Alan and the other man.

"You, who are you?" Alan asked of the brother, still shifting his light back and forth.

"Georgia Senator, Michael Sheriden, sir. And who may I ask are you?" The man was still scared, but Kim could sense that he was hoping his words would help him.

Sheriden! Kim suddenly thought. *He is the brother of the other man. They're both Sheridens, the company following us!*

The light had flicked back to the Senator when he said those words and Kim could tell that Alan was shocked. *Didn't expect that, did you Mr. FBI man?* Kim hadn't either, though. But suddenly it all made sense to her. *A Sheriden. Not just someone from Sheriden Corporation, but a Sheriden himself. And a Senator! It was their dirty family secret they were trying to protect.* She then thought of the brother, Terry, laying behind her, on the ground bleeding to death. She started to feel concern for him, but remembered he had been the cold one, the ruthless one. She turned her thoughts back to the FBI agent. *What's he doing here? What's his interest in this?*

Kim never got a chance to answer her own questions though, as a yell from Alan brought her back to the present.

"I asked you where Sean Johnson is!" Alan was yelling at her.

"I don't know." she answered. "Am I under arrest?"

"You're going to be dead on a count of three if you don't start doing what I tell you to do," Alan snarled. Kim could tell that he was losing control of the situation and did not like it. She was ready to start answering when a loud noise behind Alan caused all three of them to jump. Alan spun around, while ducking down. Kim now knew this was her best chance to escape, and bolted south again. The rain caused her to slip several times, but she franticly scrambled to reach the protection of the forest. As she was doing that, Alan's gun exploded twice. His light never shined her way and the explosion sounded as if it was directed towards the woods behind Alan and away from Kim. She reached the trees and ducked into them, rolling to the ground.

.....

"I'm going to be fine," James hissed. His right hand was squeezing his left side and blood was oozing out through his shirt. The rain diluted it though, so essentially it felt like lukewarm water in his fingers.

"No, you're bleeding," Abby whispered back at him. "I know first aid and I need to see the wound."

"Not this instant you don't. You need to get to the road and go for help."

"Help from whom," Abby protested in a hiss. "There's no one within a mile of this place!"

Just then, more loud explosive gun shots rang out. They stopped talking and tried to listen through the noise of the rain, but they heard nothing.

"Okay, Abby. Here's another idea." James said. "I'm just as likely to go into shock as I am to bleed to death, but we have nothing to bind my wound anyway. So, I am going to sit here until you come back. You need to sneak back to the cliff and see what is going on over there."

Abby started to protest, but James cut her off.

"No." James said emphatically. " It's all we can do other than cower here in the rain. And that won't get us anywhere, will it?"

Abby protested lightly but then gave in to him. After taking her sweatshirt off and draping it over the professor, she began working her way back towards where she believed the cliff to be.

.....

Alan was fighting the urge to panic. He knew there was someone on the fringe of the woods. He now realized a rock was thrown to distract him. They had not expected his quick maneuvering, he suspected, and he had got a glimpse of them as he fired. He had been stupid, though, and fired the fourth and fifth rounds from his gun. He had turned off his headlight and rolled over to a different location. Now, he was trying to chamber another five shells into the riot gun. Unfortunately, the gun was directly in the rain and he had little confidence that it would fire correctly. After getting the last shell pushed up into the loading slot, he racked one up into the chamber and rolled over onto his stomach, looking towards the woods. He could not see anything. If he turned on his headlight, he knew, it would be the equivalent of putting a target on his forehead. So, instead, he forced himself to take a few deep breaths so he could think.

Then a voice called out.

"We've got your man. We're coming in."

My man? What are they talking about? Alan was bewildered for a moment and then he thought he knew what was happening. *They've got the senator. They think he's with me!*

Alan kept scanning the horizon, but saw nothing. Then, a light appeared. It was shining on the senator. Someone was walking next to him pointing the light at him. The senator's hands were on his head. He looked absolutely miserable.

Alan popped up and hit the button on his waist to activate his headlight. It turned on and illuminated a rough wiry man with a red beard holding a flashlight. His other hand held a handgun which was pointed at the senator. Alan was confused for a moment. He had no idea who this was. He had mostly been expecting to see Sean Johnson. Then the man smiled, and Alan knew he had screwed up again. He had just been set up.

An explosion erupted from the other side of the senator along with a slight flash. Alan felt tearing and punching in his chest and stomach.

He was thrown backwards, but not before he managed to squeeze the trigger on his riot gun. It fired into the red bearded man, who screamed and dropped his flashlight.

.....

Kim felt herself ducking as the guns fired, even though she knew nothing was pointed at her. Alan Nazimi had fallen backwards and now his headlight was shining upwards at the rain and not moving. The man who had been leading the senator had dropped his flashlight. The senator, the other Sheriden man, had fallen. The renewed gunfire had raised Kim's terror to the point she was ready to run, but thoughts of Abby, the professor and Sean kept her rooted to the ground, peering cautiously over a log.

As Kim continued to watch, another man appeared in the area of chaos. He was holding a gun in one hand and a flashlight, which he had just turned on. He was whipping the flashlight from side to side quickly scanning the ground around him. The light fell upon Terry and stopped there for a moment. Terry was no longer moving at all. He appeared to be dead. The light then left Terry and began scanning the edge of the cliff.

Kim saw some movement in the darkness and suspected it was the senator. The flashlight, that had been held by the red bearded man, was still on. Its light allowed Kim to make out somebody scrambling for the woods. The man with the other flashlight and gun must have seen this as well, because he whirled around and began shooting. As he spun, the light flashed right across Kim's hiding place and she dropped down to the earth, certain she had been seen. As each gunshot erupted, she flinched in terror, but nothing came her way. After what seemed like a hundred shots, the firing ended. Kim stayed down, terrified to even look.

Just then, though, she heard a scream and then a dull thud. Afterwards, there was dead silence except for the sound of the rain hitting the ground. She laid there, scared to stay, but even more scared to move. After what seemed like an eternity, she heard a voice much like Sean's. She listened some more and heard Sean tell someone, "Stay right like you are!"

Kim lifted her head up and saw what she was sure had to be Sean shining a light down on the senator. She got up and called to him.

"Sean?"

"Hey, it's me," Sean replied. Kim had never heard such sweet sounding words in her life.

"I came up over the cliff to the north and snuck back," he called. "I've got one guy here, I think everyone else is either dead or seriously wounded." There was a pause and then a frantic question.

"Where's Abby?"

Before Kim could answer, Abby answered, calling from the other side of the clearing.

"I'm here, but the professor is back in the woods. He's bleeding badly."

"Kim, can you get me some rope?" Sean called.

Kim informed him that she could. From that point on, Kim would later explain, it was like her normal life emerged from a fog. She stood there for a moment and then jumped and ran around until she found her headlamp. She put it on, found some rope and brought it to Sean. Sean, in the meantime, had been checking the red bearded man while holding a flashlight and somebody's gun on the senator. Kim reached him with the rope and Sean traded her for the flashlight he was holding.

Shortly, he had Senator Michael Sheriden tied up. The senator had been shot in his leg and had protested some until Sean had very curtly told the senator to "Shut up!" Sean also ignored the leg wound for the time being, concluding that it was not life threatening. The red bearded man was still alive, but now unconscious. Terry was dead and so was the other mystery man, who Kim later found out was Kurt Cathey, the treasure hunter, they had briefly encountered the day before. The red bearded man had been Kurt's companion in the passenger seat.

Sean sent Kim and Abby into the woods with some cloth and tape to help the professor. In the meantime, he got on his cell phone to call the police.

......

It was now dawn. There were police and investigators all over the cliff area. Sean, Kim and Abby were standing near the edge with blankets wrapped around them. The rain had given way to a partly cloudy dawn, but the three of them were still soaked to the skin. The blankets helped, but they were all really looking forward to a hot shower. The professor had long since been whisked away to the hospital and his condition was also on their minds.

The lead investigator from the state police, Lieutenant Kilpatrick, came over to them.

"Okay, your story has checked out with your buddy in Saint Louis and with your editor in Seattle. I'm happy to tell you that your companion, James Enloe, is at Greenwood General and doing quite well. It's not a life threatening injury."

He paused and looked them over. "Sorry for having to hold you here, but with three dead men, a state senator from Georgia shot and headed to jail, and two other men shot, this is quite the crime scene. I'd like to take you guys down to the jail and get your statements and ask a few more questions."

Sean answered for the three of them. "Lieutenant, we can do that soon, but we need to do a few other things first."

The Lieutenant looked at Sean curiously, "Like what?"

"Well first, I need to show you what's in the cave beneath us. Second, we need to set up security for it. And third, we need to eat something."

The Lieutenant laughed. "Okay, for starters, tell me about the cave. Is this the treasure you mentioned?" He spoke as if he was not treating the treasure concept seriously.

"Yes, lieutenant," Sean replied deadpan. "Beneath us about thirty feet is a small cavern. In 1864, a Union Captain hid a Confederate treasure in that cave. If I understood his note correctly, he actually encountered a group of confederates trying to hide the treasure and, after killing them, hid the treasure by blasting its entrance. We believe it's the lost Atlanta Treasure."

"What kind of stuff are we talking about?" the lieutenant asked showing more interest.

"Oh, I'd say there are five wooden boxes of gold coins to start. There's silver in there, too. There's a full room of stuff down there and it's worth more than we'll ever make in our lifetimes combined. It's worth even more for it's place in history. And there's some type of very old log book down there that, I think we will find, will show us how a group of Union Officers in Sherman's Army stole land from the southerners as they occupied Atlanta and marched through the South. We found this cave from lost letters written by Abraham Lincoln. The Sheridens, I think, were one of the families that benefited from the land taking. The senator knew about the log book and the letters, as well. He was trying to stop us from revealing this to the world."

The lieutenant stood there for a few moments with a blank expression on his face. He seemed to be trying to decide whether they were crazy or not. He must have decided that they were not insane because when he finally spoke, he was full of cooperation.

"Really? Oh, well, you're right! We need to secure the area! We uh, need…"

"A historian?" Kim asked.

"Well, yes that too," the lieutenant laughed. "Wow, a real treasure! Okay, let me make some calls." He walked away talking into his radio.

Sean looked at Kim and Abby.

"I'm really hungry, but after all of this, I don't think I'm willing to take my eyes off this cliff until we know it's truly safe."

"I know exactly what you mean," Kim replied.

"I'm not going anywhere yet either," Abby announced. "Except maybe to see the professor."